BANZAI!

LECTOR HOUSE PUBLIC DOMAIN WORKS

This book is a result of an effort made by Lector House towards making a contribution to the preservation and repair of original classic literature. The original text is in the public domain in the United States of America, and possibly other countries depending upon their specific copyright laws.

In an attempt to preserve, improve and recreate the original content, certain conventional norms with regard to typographical mistakes, hyphenations, punctuations and/or other related subject matters, have been corrected upon our consideration. However, few such imperfections might not have been rectified as they were inherited and preserved from the original content to maintain the authenticity and construct, relevant to the work. The work might contain a few prior copyright references as well as page references which have been retained, wherever considered relevant to the part of the construct. We believe that this work holds historical, cultural and/or intellectual importance in the literary works community, therefore despite the oddities, we accounted the work for print as a part of our continuing effort towards preservation of literary work and our contribution towards the development of the society as a whole, driven by our beliefs.

We are grateful to our readers for putting their faith in us and accepting our imperfections with regard to preservation of the historical content. We shall strive hard to meet up to the expectations to improve further to provide an enriching reading experience.

Though, we conduct extensive research in ascertaining the status of copyright before redeveloping a version of the content, in rare cases, a classic work might be incorrectly marked as not-in-copyright. In such cases, if you are the copyright holder, then kindly contact us or write to us, and we shall get back to you with an immediate course of action.

HAPPY READING!

BANZAI!

FERDINAND HEINRICH GRAUTOFF (PARABELLUM)

ISBN: 978-93-90198-58-0

Published: 1909

LECTOR HOUSE LLP
E-MAIL: lectorpublishing@gmail.com

"THAT'S THE JAPANESE SATSUMA, TOGO'S SATSUMA!"

BANZAI!

BY

PARABELLUM

1909

FOREWORD

Every American familiar with the modern international political horizon must have experienced a feeling of solid satisfaction at the news that a formidable American fleet was to be dispatched to the waters of the Pacific, and the cruise of our warships has been followed with intense interest by every loyal citizen of our Republic. The reasons that rendered the long and dramatic voyage of our fleet most opportune are identical with the motives that actuated the publication of this translation from the German of a work which exhibits a remarkable grasp of facts coupled with a marvelously vivid power of description. It is no secret that our ships were sent to the Pacific to minimize the danger of a conflict with our great commercial rival in the Far East, if not to avert it altogether, and *Banzai!* it seems to me, should perform a similar mission. The graphic recital, I take it, is not intended to incite a feeling of animosity between two nations which have every reason to maintain friendly relations, but rather to call the attention of the American people to the present woeful lack of preparedness, and at the same time to assist in developing a spirit of sound patriotism that prefers silent action to blatant braggadocio. That the Pacific Ocean may become, in truth, the Peaceful Ocean, and never resound to the clash of American arms, is the devout wish of one who believes—implicitly—with Moltke in the old proverb, *Si vis pacem, para bellum*—If you wish for Peace, prepare for War.

P.

CONTENTS

INTRODUCTION

As usual, it had begun quite harmlessly and inconspicuously. It is not my business to tell how it all came to pass, how the way was prepared. That may be left to the spinners of yarns and to those on the trail of the sources of history. I shall leave it to them to ascertain when the idea that there must be a conflict, and that the fruit must be plucked before it had time to ripen, first took root in the minds of the Japanese people.

We Americans realize now that we had been living for years like one who has a presentiment that something dreadful is hanging over him which will suddenly descend upon his head, and who carries this feeling of dread about with him with an uneasy conscience, trying to drown it in the tumult and restlessness of daily life. We realize the situation now, because we know where we should have fixed our gaze and understand the task to the accomplishment of which we should have bent our energies, but we went about like sleep-walkers and refused to see what thousands of others knew, what thousands saw in astonishment and concern at our heedlessness.

We might easily have peeped through the curtain that hid the future from us, for it had plenty of holes, but we passed them by unnoticed. And, nevertheless, there were many who did peep through. Some, while reading their paper, let it fall into their lap and stared into space, letting their thoughts wander far away to a spot whence the subdued clash of arms and tumult of war reached their soul like the mysterious roll and roar of the breakers. Others were struck by a chance word overheard in the rush of the street, which they would remember until it was driven out by the strenuous struggle that each day brought with it. But the word itself had not died; it continued to live in the foundation of the consciousness where our burning thoughts cannot enter, and sometimes in the night it would be born afresh in the shape of wild squadrons of cavalry galloping across the short grass of the prairie with noiseless hoofs. The thunder of cannon could be heard in the air long before the guns were loaded.

I saw no more than others, and when the grim horrors of the future first breathed coldly upon me I, too, soon forgot it. It happened at San Francisco in the spring of 1907. We were standing before a bar, and from outside came the sounds of an uproar in the street. Two men were being thrown out of a Japanese restaurant across the way, and the Japanese proprietor, who was standing in the doorway, kicked the hat of one of them across the pavement so that it rolled over the street like a football.

"Well, what do you think of that," cried my friend, Arthur Wilcox, "the Jap is attacking the white men."

I held him back by the arm, for a tall Irish policeman had already seized the Jap, who protested loudly and would not submit to arrest. The policeman took good hold of him, but before he knew it he lay like a log on the pavement, the Japanese dwarf apparently having thrown him without the least trouble. A wild brawl followed. Half an hour later only a few policemen, taking notes, were walking about in the Japanese restaurant, which had been completely demolished by a frenzied mob. We remained at the bar for some time afterwards engaged in earnest conversation.

"Our grandchildren," said Arthur, "will have to answer for that little affair and fight it out some day or other."

"Not our grandchildren, but we ourselves," I answered, not knowing in the least why I said it.

"We ourselves?" said Wilcox, laughing at me, "not much; look at me, look at yourself, look at our people, and then look at those dwarfs."

"The Russians said the same thing: Look at the dwarfs."

They all laughed at me and presently I joined in the laugh, but I could not forget the Irishman as he lay in the grip of the Jap. And quite suddenly I remembered something which I had almost forgotten. It happened at Heidelberg, during my student days in Germany; a professor was telling us how, after the inglorious retreat of the Prussian army from Valmy, the officers, with young Goethe in their midst, were sitting round the camp fires discussing the reasons for the defeat. When they asked Goethe what he thought about it, he answered, as though gifted with second sight: "At this spot and at this moment a new epoch in the world's history will begin, and you will all be able to say that you were present." And in imagination I could see the red glow of the bivouac fires and the officers of Frederick the Great's famous army, who could not understand how anyone could have fled before the ragged recruits of the Revolution. And near them I saw a man of higher caliber standing on tiptoe to look through the dark curtain into the future.

At the time I soon forgot all these things; I forgot the apparently insignificant street affray and the icy breath of premonition which swept over me then, and not until the disaster had occurred did it again enter my mind. But then when the swords were clashing I realized, for the first time, that all the incidents we had observed on the dusty highway of History, and passed by with indifference, had been sure signs of the coming catastrophe.

Parabellum

BANZAI!

CHAPTER I

IN MANILA

"For God's sake, do leave me in peace with your damned yellow monkeys!" cried Colonel Webster, banging his fist on the table so hard that the whisky and soda glasses jumped up in a fright, then came down again irritably and wagged their heads disapprovingly, so that the amber-colored fluid spilled over the edge and lay on the table in little pearly puddles.

"As you like, colonel. I shall give up arguing with you," returned Lieutenant Commander Harryman curtly. "You won't allow yourself to be warned."

"Warned—that's not the question. But this desire of yours to scent Japanese intrigues everywhere, to figure out all politics by the Japanese common denominator, and to see a Japanese spy in every coolie is becoming a positive mania. No, I can't agree with you there," added Webster, who seemed to regret the passionate outburst into which his temperament had betrayed him.

"Really not?" asked Harryman, turning in his comfortable wicker chair toward Webster and looking at him half encouragingly with twinkling eyes.

Such discussions were not at all unusual in the Club at Manila, for they presented the only antidote to the leaden, soul-killing tedium of the dull monotony of garrison duty. Since the new insurrection on Mindanao and in the whole southern portion of the archipelago, the question as to the actual causes of the uprising, or rather the secret authors thereof, continually gave rise to heated discussions. And when both parties, of which one ascribed everything to Japanese intrigue and the other found an explanation in elementary causes, began to liven up, the debate was apt to wax pretty warm. If these discussions did nothing else, they at least produced a sort of mental excitement after the heat of the day which wore out body and mind alike, not even cooling down toward evening.

The Chinese boy, passing quickly and quietly between the chairs, removed the traces of the Webster thunderbolt and placed fresh bottles of soda water on the table, whereupon the officers carefully prepared new drinks.

"He's a spy, too, I suppose?" asked Webster of Harryman, pointing with his thumb over his shoulder at the disappearing boy.

"Of course. Did you ever imagine him to be anything else?"

Webster shrugged his shoulders. A dull silence ensued, during which they tried to recover the lost threads of their thoughts in the drowsy twilight. Harryman irritably chewed the ends of his mustache. The smoke from two dozen shag pipes settled like streaks of mist in the sultry air of the tropical night, which came in at the open windows. Lazily and with long pauses, conversation was kept up at the separate tables. The silence was only broken by the creaking of the wicker chairs and the gurgling and splashing of the soda water, when one of the officers, after having put it off as long as possible, at last found sufficient energy to refill his glass. Motionless as seals on the sandhills in the heat of midday, the officers lolled in their chairs, waiting for the moment when they could turn in with some show of decency.

"It's awful!" groaned Colonel McCabe. "This damned hole is enough to make one childish. I shall go crazy soon." And then he cracked his standing joke of the evening: "My daily morning prayer is: 'Let it soon be evening, O God; the morrow will come of itself.'" The jest was greeted with a dutiful grunt of approval from the occupants of the various chairs.

Lieutenant Parrington, officer in command of the little gunboat *Mindoro*, which had been captured from the Spaniards some years ago and since the departure of the cruiser squadron for Mindanao been put in commission as substitute guardship in the harbor of Manila, entered the room and dropped into a chair near Harryman; whereupon the Chinese boy, almost inaudible in his broad felt shoes, suddenly appeared beside him and set down the bottle with the pain expeller of the tropics before him.

"Any cable news, Parrington?" asked Colonel McCabe from the other table.

"Not a word," yawned Parrington; "everything is still smashed. We might just as well be sitting under the receiver of an air pump."

Harryman noticed that the boy stared at Parrington for a moment as if startled; but he instantly resumed his Mongolian expression of absolute innocence, and with his customary grin slipped sinuously through the door.

Harryman experienced an unpleasant feeling of momentary discomfort, but, not being able to locate his ideas clearly, he irritably gave up the attempt to arrive at a solution of this instinctive sensation, mumbling to himself: "This tropical hell is enough to set one crazy."

"No news of the fleet, either?" began Colonel McCabe again.

"Positively nothing, either by wire or wireless. It seems as though the rest of the world had sunk into a bottomless pit. Not a single word has reached us from the outer world for six days."

"Do you believe in the seaquake?" struck in Harryman mockingly.

"Why not?" returned the colonel.

Harryman jumped up, walked over to the window with long strides, threw out the end of his cigarette and lighted a new one. In the bright light of the flaming match one could see the commander's features twitching ironically; he was on the warpath again.

"All the same, it's a queer state of affairs. Our home cable snaps between Guam and here, the Hong-Kong cable won't work, and even our island wire has been put out of commission; it must have been a pretty violent catastrophe—" came from another table.

"—All the more violent considering the fact that we noticed nothing of it on land," said Harryman, thoughtfully blowing out a cloud of smoke and swinging himself up backward on the window-sill.

"Exactly," rang out a voice; "but how do you account for that?"

"Account for it!" cried Colonel Webster, in a thundering voice. "Our comrade of the illustrious navy of the United States of America has only one explanation for everything: his Japanese logarithms, by means of which he figures out everything. Now we shall hear that this seaquake can be traced to Japanese villainy, probably brought about by Japanese divers, or even submarine boats." And the colonel began to laugh heartily.

Harryman ignored this attempt to resume their recent dispute, and with head thrown back continued to blow clouds of smoke nervously into the air.

"But seriously, Harryman," began the colonel again, "can you give any explanation?"

"No," answered Harryman curtly; "but perhaps you will remember who was the first to furnish an explanation of the breakdown of the cable. It was the captain of the Japanese *Kanga Maru*, which has been anchored since Tuesday beside the *Monadnock*, which I have the honor to command."

"But, my good Harryman, you have hallucinations," interrupted the colonel. "The Japanese captain gave the latest Hong-Kong papers to the Harbor Bureau, and was quite astonished to hear that our cable did not work——"

"When he was going to send a cablegram to Hong-Kong," added Harryman sharply.

"To announce his arrival at Manila," remarked Colonel Webster dryly.

"And the Hong-Kong papers had already published descriptions of the destruction caused by the seaquake, of the tidal waves, and the accidents to ships," came from another quarter.

"The news being of especial interest to this archipelago, where we have the misfortune to be and where we noticed nothing of the whole affair," returned Harryman.

"You don't mean to imply," broke in the colonel, "that the news of this catastrophe is a pure invention—an invention of the English papers in Hong-Kong?"

"Don't know, I'm sure," said Harryman. "Hong-Kong papers are no criterion for me." And then he added quietly: "Yes, man is great, and the newspaper is his prophet."

"But you can't dispute the fact that a seaquake may have taken place, when you consider the striking results as shown by the cable interruptions which we have been experiencing for the last six days," began Webster again.

"Have we really?" said Harryman. "Are you quite sure of it? So far the only authority we have for this supposed seaquake is a Japanese captain—whom, by the way, I am having sharply watched—and a bundle of worthless Hong-Kong newspapers. And as for the rest of my hallucinations"—he jumped down from the window-sill and, going up to Webster, held out a sheet of paper toward him—"I'm in the habit of using other sources of information than the English-Japanese fingerposts."

Webster glanced at the paper and then looked at Harryman questioningly.

"What is it? Do you understand it?"

"Yes," snapped Harryman. "These little pictures portray our war of extermination against the red man. They are terribly exaggerated and distorted, which was not at all necessary, by the way, for the events of that war do not add to the fame of our nation. Up here," explained Harryman, while several officers, among them the colonel, stepped up to the table, "you see the story of the infected blankets from the fever hospitals which were sent to the Indians; here the butchery of an Indian tribe; here, for comparison, the fight on the summit of the volcano of Ilo-Ilo, where the Tagala were finally driven into the open crater; and here, at the end, the practical application for the Tagala: 'As the Americans have destroyed the red man, so will you slowly perish under the American rule. They have hurled your countrymen into the chasm of the volcano. This crater will devour you all if you do not turn those weapons which were once broken by Spanish bondage against your deliverers of 1898, who have since become your oppressors.'"

"Where did you get the scrawl?" asked the colonel excitedly.

"Do you want me to procure hundreds, thousands like it for you?" returned Harryman coolly.

The colonel pressed down the ashes in his pipe with his thumb, and asked indifferently: "You understand Japanese?"

"Tagala also," supplemented Harryman simply.

"And you mean to say that thousands——?"

"Millions of these pictures, with Japanese and Malayan text, are being circulated in the Philippines," said Harryman positively.

"Under our eyes?" asked a lieutenant naïvely.

"Under our eyes," replied Harryman, smiling, "our eyes which carelessly overlook such things."

Colonel Webster rose and offered Harryman his hand. "I have misjudged you," he said heartily. "I belong to your party from now on."

"It isn't a question of party," answered Harryman warmly, "or rather there will soon be only the one party."

"Do you think," asked Colonel McCabe, "that the supposed Japanese plan of attack on the Philippines, published at the beginning of the year in the *North China Daily News*, was authentic?"

"That question cannot be answered unless you know who gave the document to the Shanghai paper, and what object he had in doing so," replied Harryman.

"How do you mean?"

"Well," continued Harryman, "only two possibilities can exist: the document was either genuine or false. If genuine, then it was an indiscretion on the part of a Japanese who betrayed his country to an English paper—an English paper which no sooner gets possession of this important document than it immediately proceeds to publish its contents, thereby getting its ally into a nice pickle. You will at once observe here three improbabilities: treason, indiscretion, and, finally, England in the act of tripping her ally. These actions would be incompatible, in the first place, with the almost hysterical sense of patriotism of the Japanese; in the second, with their absolute silence and secrecy, and, in the third place, with the behavior of our English cousin since his marriage to Madame Chrysanthemum——"

"The document was therefore not genuine?" asked the colonel.

"Think it over. What was it that the supposed plan of attack set forth? A Japanese invasion of Manila with the fleet and a landing force of eighty thousand men, and then, following the example of Cuba, an insurrection of the natives, which would gradually exhaust our troops, while the Japanese would calmly settle matters at sea, Roschestwenski's tracks being regarded as a sufficient scare for our admirals."

"That would no doubt be the best course to pursue in an endeavor to pocket the Philippines," answered the colonel thoughtfully; "and the plan would be aided by the widespread and growing opposition at home to keeping the archipelago and putting more and more millions into the Asiatic branch business."

"Quite so," continued Harryman quickly, "if Japan wanted nothing else but the Philippines."

"What on earth does she want in addition?" asked Webster.

"The *mastery of the Pacific*," said Harryman in a decided voice.

"Commercial mastery?" asked Parrington, "or——"

"No; political, too, and with solid foundations," answered Harryman.

Colonel McCabe had sat down again, and was studying the pamphlet, Parrington picked at the label on his whisky bottle, and the others remained silent, but buried in thought. In the next room a clock struck ten with a hurried, tinkling sound which seemed to break up the uneasy silence into so many small pieces.

"And if it was not genuine?" began Colonel McCabe again, hoarsely. He cleared his throat and repeated the question in a low tone of voice: "And if it was not genuine?"

Harryman shrugged his shoulders.

"Then it would be a trap for us to have us secure our information from the wrong quarter," said the colonel, answering his own question.

"A trap into which we are rushing at full speed," continued Webster, laying stress on each word, though his thoughts seemed to be far in advance of what he was saying.

Harryman nodded and twisted his mustache.

"What did you say?" asked Parrington, jumping up and looking from Webster to Harryman, neither of whom, however, volunteered a reply. "We are stumbling into a trap?"

"Two regiments," said Webster, more to himself than to the others. And then, turning to Harryman, he asked briskly: "When are the transports expected to arrive?"

"The steamers with two regiments on board left 'Frisco on April 10th, therefore—he counted the days on his fingers—they should be here by now."

"No, they were to go straight to Mindanao," said Parrington.

"Straight to Mindanao?" Colonel McCabe meditated silently. Then, as though waking up suddenly, he went on: "And the cable has not been working for six days——"

"Exactly," interrupted Parrington, "we have known nothing, either of the fleet or of anything else, for the last six days."

"Harryman," said Colonel McCabe seriously, "do you think there is danger? If it is all a trap, it would be the most stupid thing that we could do to send our transports unprotected— But that's all nonsense! This heat positively dries up your thoughts. No, no, it's impossible; they're hallucinations bred by the fermented vapors of this God-forsaken country!" He pressed the electric button, and the boy appeared at the door behind him. "Some soda, Pailung!"

"Parrington, are you coming? I ordered my boat for ten o'clock," said Harryman.

"As early as this, Harryman?" remonstrated Webster. "You'll be on board your boat quite soon enough, or do you want to keep a night watch also on your Japanese of the— What sort of a Maru was it?" he broke off, because Colonel McCabe pointed angrily at the approaching boy.

"Oh, nonsense!" growled Webster ill-humoredly. "A creature like that doesn't see or hear a thing."

The colonel glared at Webster, and then noisily mixed his drink.

Harryman and Parrington walked along the quay in silence, their steps resounding loudly in the stillness of the night. On the other side of the street fleeting shadows showed at the lighted windows of several harbor dens, over the entrance to which hung murky lamps and from which loud voices issued, proving that all was still in full swing there. There were only a few more steps to the spot where the yellow circle of light from the lanterns rendered the white uniforms of the sailors in the two boats visible. Parrington stood still. "Harryman," he said, repeating his former question, "do you believe there is danger——"

"I don't know, I really don't know," said Harryman nervously. Then, seizing Parrington's hands, he continued hurriedly, but in a low voice: "For days I have been living as if in a trance. It is as if I were lying in the delirium of fever; my head burns and my thoughts always return to the same spot, boring and burrowing; I feel as though a horrible eye were fixed on me from whose glance I cannot escape. I feel that I may at any moment awake from the trance, and that the awakening will be still more dreadful."

"You're feverish, Harryman; you're ill, and you'll infect others. You must take some quinine." With these words Parrington climbed into his gig, the sailors gave way with the oars, and the boat rushed through the water and disappeared into the darkness, where the bow oarsman was silhouetted against the pale yellow light of the boat's lantern like a strange phantom.

Harryman looked musingly after the boat of the *Mindoro* for a few minutes, and murmured: "He certainly has no fever which quinine will not cure." Then he got into his own boat, which also soon disappeared into the sultry summer night, while the dark water splashed and gurgled against the planks. The high quay wall, with its row of yellow and white lights, remained behind, and gradually sank down to the water line. They rowed past the side of a huge English steamer, which sent back the splash of the oars in a strange hollow echo, and then across to the *Monadnock*.

Harryman could not sleep, and joined the officer on duty on the bridge, where the slight breeze which came from the mountains afforded a little coolness.

On board the *Mindoro* Parrington had found orders to take the relief guard for the wireless telegraph station to Mariveles the next morning. At six o'clock the little gunboat had taken the men on board, and was now steering across the blue Bay of Manila toward the little rocky island of Corregidor, which had recently been strongly fortified, and which lies like a block of stone between gigantic mountain wings in the very middle of the entrance to the Bay of Manila. Under a gray sail, which served as a slight protection from the sun, the soldiers squatted sullenly on their kits. Some were asleep, others stared over the railing into the blue, transparent water that rippled away in long waves before the bow of the little vessel. From the open skylight of the engine room sounded the sharp beat of the engine, and the smell of hot oil spread over the deck, making the burning heat even more unbearable. Parrington stood on the bridge and through his glass examined the steep cliffs at the entrance to the bay, and the bizarre forms of the little volcanic islands.

Except for a few fishing boats with their brown sails, not a ship was to be seen on the whole expanse of the water. The gunboat now turned into the northern entrance, and the long, glistening guns in the fortifications of Corregidor became visible. Up above, on the batteries hewn in the rocks, not a living soul could be seen, but below, on the little platform where the signal-post stood near the northern battery, an armed sentry marched up and down. Parrington called out to the signalman near him: "Send this signal across to Corregidor: 'We are going to relieve the wireless telegraph detachment at Mariveles, and shall call at Corregidor on our way back.'" The Corregidor battery answered the signal, and informed Parrington that Colonel Prettyman expected him for lunch later on. Slowly the *Mindoro* crept along the coast to the rocky Bay of Mariveles, where, before the few neglected houses of the place, the guard of the wireless telegraph station, which stood on the heights of Sierra de Mariveles, was awaiting the arrival of the gunboat.

The *Mindoro* was made fast to the pier. The exchange of men took place quickly, and the relief guard piled their kits on two mule-carts, in which they were to be carried up the steep hillside to the top, where a few flat, white houses showed the position of the wireless station, the high post of which, with its numerous wires, stood out alone against the blue sky. The relieved men, who plainly showed their delight at getting away from this God-forsaken, tedious outpost, made themselves comfortable in the shade afforded by the sail, and began to chat with the crew of the *Mindoro* about the commonplaces of military service. A shrill screech from the whistle of the *Mindoro* resounded from the mountain side as a farewell greeting to the little troop that was climbing slowly upward, followed by the baggage-carts. The *Mindoro* cast off from the pier, and, having rounded the neck of land on which Mariveles stood, was just on the point of starting in the direction of Corregidor, when the signalman on the bridge called Parrington's attention to a black steamer which was apparently steaming at full speed from the sea toward the entrance to the Bay of Manila.

"A ship at last," said Parrington. "Let's wait and see what sort of a craft it is."

While the *Mindoro* reduced her speed noticeably, Parrington looked across at the strange vessel through his glasses. The ship had also attracted the attention of the crew, who began to conjecture excitedly as to the nationality of the visitor, for during the past week a strange vessel had become a rather unusual sight in Manila. The wireless detachment said that they had seen the steamer two hours ago from the hill.

Parrington put down his glass and said: "About four thousand tons, but she has no flag. We can soon remedy that." And turning to the signalman he added: "Ask her to show her colors." At the same time he pulled the rope of the whistle in order to attract the stranger's attention.

In a few seconds the German colors appeared at the stern of the approaching steamer, and the signal flag, which at the same time was quickly hoisted at the foretopmast, proclaimed the ship to be the German steamer *Danzig*, hailing from Hong-Kong. Immediately afterwards a boat was lowered from the *Danzig* and the steamer stopped; then the white cutter put to sea and headed straight for the *Mindoro*.

"It is certainly kind of them to send us a boat," said Parrington. "I wonder what they want, anyhow." He gave orders to stop the boat and to clear the gangway, and then, watching the German cutter with interest, awaited its arrival. Ten minutes later the commander of the *Danzig* stepped on the bridge of the *Mindoro*, introduced himself to her commander, and asked for a pilot to take him through the mines in the roads.

Parrington regarded him with astonishment. "Mines, my dear sir, mines?

There are no mines here."

The German stared at Parrington unbelievingly. "You have no mines?"

"No," said Parrington. "It is not our custom to blockade our harbors with mines except in time of war."

"In time of war?" said the German, who did not appear to comprehend Parrington's answer. "But you are at war."

"We, at war?" returned Parrington, utterly disconcerted. "And with whom, if I may be allowed to ask?"

"It seems to me that the matter is too serious to be a subject for jesting," answered the German sharply.

At this moment loud voices were heard from the after-deck of the *Mindoro*, the crew of which were swearing with great gusto. Parrington hurried to the railing and looked over angrily. A hot dispute was going on between the crew of the German cutter and the American sailors, but only the oft-repeated words "damned Japs" could be distinguished. He turned again to the German officer, and looked at him hesitatingly. The latter, apparently in a bad temper, looked out to sea, whistling softly to himself.

Parrington walked toward him and, seizing his hand, said: "It's clear that we don't understand each other. What's up?"

"I am here to inform you," answered the German sharply and decisively, "that the steamer *Danzig* ran the blockade last night, and that its captain politely requests you to give him a pilot through the mines, in order that we may reach the harbor of Manila."

"You have run the blockade?" shouted Parrington, in a state of the greatest excitement. "You have run the blockade, man? What the deuce do you mean?"

"I mean," answered the German coolly, "that the Government of the United States of America—a fact, by the way, of which you, as commander of one of her war vessels, ought to be aware—has been at war with Japan for the last week, and that a steamer which has succeeded in running the enemy's blockade and which carries contraband goods for Manila surely has the right to ask to be guided through the mines."

Parrington felt for the railing behind him and leaned against it for support. His face became ashen pale, and he seemed so utterly nonplussed at the German officer's statement that the latter, gradually beginning to comprehend the extraordinary situation, continued his explanation.

"Yes," he repeated, "for six days your country has been at war with Japan, and it was only natural we should suppose that you, as one of those most nearly concerned, would be aware of this fact."

Parrington, regaining his self-control, said: "Then the cable disturbances—" He stopped, then continued disjointedly: "But this is terrible; this is a surprise such as we— I beg your pardon," he went on in a firm voice to the German, "I am sure I need not assure you that your communication has taken me completely by surprise. Not a soul in Manila has any idea of all this. The cable disturbances of the last six days were explained to us by a Japanese steamer as being the result of a volcanic outbreak, and since then, through the interruption of all connections, we have been completely shut off from the outside world. If Japan, in defiance of all international law, has declared war, we here in Manila have noticed nothing of it, except, perhaps, for the entire absence, during the last few days, of the regular steamers and, indeed, of all trading ships, a circumstance that appeared to some of us rather suspicious. But excuse me, we must act at once. Please remain on board."

The *Mindoro's* whistle emitted three shrill screeches, while the gunboat steamed at full speed toward Corregidor.

Parrington went into his cabin, opened his desk, and searched through it with nervous haste. "At last!" He seized the war-signal code and ran upstairs to the bridge, shouting to the signalman: "Signal to Corregidor: 'War-signal code, important communication.'" Then he himself, hastily turning over the leaves of the book, called out the signals and had them hoisted. Then he shouted to the man at the helm: "Tell them not to spare the engines."

Parrington stood in feverish expectation on the bridge, his hands clinched round the hot iron bars of the breastwork and his eyes measuring the rapidly diminishing distance between the *Mindoro* and the landing place of Corregidor. As the *Mindoro* turned into the northern passage between Corregidor and the mainland, the chain of mountains, looking like banks of clouds, which surrounded Manila, became visible in the far distance across the blue, apparently boundless surface of the Bay, while the town itself, wrapped in the white mist that veiled the horizon, remained invisible. At this moment Parrington observed a dark cloud of smoke in the direction of the harbor of Manila suddenly detaching itself from below and sailing upward like a fumarole above the summit of a volcano, where it dispersed in bizarre shapes resembling ragged balls of cotton. Almost immediately a dull report like a distant thunderclap boomed across the water.

"Can that be another of their devilish tricks?" asked Parrington of the German, drawing his attention to the rising cloud, the edges of which glistened white as snow in the bright sunshine.

"Possibly," was the laconic answer.

The wharf of Corregidor was in a state of confused hubbub. The artillerymen stood shoulder to shoulder, awaiting the arrival of the *Mindoro*. Suddenly an officer forced his way through the crowd, and, standing on the very edge of the wharf, called out to the rapidly approaching *Mindoro*: "Parrington, what's all this about?"

"It's true, every word of it," roared the latter through the megaphone. "The Japanese are attacking us, and the German steamer over there is the first to bring us news of it. War broke out six days ago."

The *Mindoro* stopped and threw a line, which was caught by many willing hands and made fast to the landing place.

"Here's my witness," shouted Parrington across to Colonel Prettyman, "the commander of the German steamer *Danzig*."

"I'll join you on board," answered Prettyman. "I've just despatched the news to Manila by wireless. Of course they won't believe it there."

"Then you've done a very stupid thing," cried Parrington, horrified. "Look there," he added, pointing to the cloud above the harbor of Manila; "that has most certainly cost our friend Harryman, of the *Monadnock*, his life. His presentiments did not deceive him after all!"

"Cost Harryman, on board the *Monadnock*, his life?" asked Prettyman in astonishment.

"I'm afraid so," answered Parrington. "The Japanese steamer which brought us the news of the famous seaquake has been anchored beside him for four days. When you sent your wireless message to Manila, the Japanese must have intercepted it, for they have a wireless apparatus on board—I noticed it only this morning."

The *Mindoro* now lay fast beside the wharf, and Colonel Prettyman hurried across the gangway to the gunboat and went straight to Parrington's cabin, where the two shut themselves up with the German officer.

A few minutes later an excited orderly rushed on board and demanded to see the colonel at once; he was let into the cabin, and it was found that he had brought a confirmation of Parrington's suspicions, for a wireless message from Manila informed them that the *Monadnock* had been destroyed in the roads of Manila through some inexplicable explosion.

Parrington sprang from his chair and cried to the colonel: "Won't you at least pay those cursed Japs back by sending the message, 'We suspect that the Japanese steamer anchored beside the *Monadnock* has blown her up by means of a torpedo?' Otherwise it is just possible that they will be naïve enough in Manila to let the scoundrel get out of the harbor. No, no," he shouted, interrupting himself, "we can't wait for that; we must get to work ourselves at once. Colonel, you go ashore, and I'll steam toward Manila and cut off the rogue's escape. And you"—turning to the German—"you can return to your ship and enter the bay; there are no"—here his voice broke—"no mines here."

Then he rushed up on the bridge again. The hawsers were cast off in feverish haste, and the *Mindoro* once more steamed out into the bay at the fastest speed of which the old craft was capable. Parrington had regained his self-command in face of the new task that the events just described, which followed so rapidly upon one another's heels, laid out for him. An expression of fierce joy came over his features when, looking through his glass an hour later, he discovered the *Kanga Maru* holding a straight course for Corregidor.

As calmly as if it were only a question of everyday maneuvers, Parrington gave his orders. The artillerymen stood on either side of the small guns, and everything was made ready for action.

The distance between the two ships slowly diminished.

"Yes, it is the Japanese steamer," said Parrington to himself. "And now to avenge Harryman! There'll be no sentimentality; we'll shoot them down like pirates! No signal, no warning—nothing, nothing!" he murmured.

"Stand by with the forward gun," he called down from the bridge to the men standing at the little 12 pounder on the foredeck of the *Mindoro*. The *Mindoro* turned a little to starboard, so as to get at the broadside of the Japanese, and thus be able to fire on him with both the forward and after guns.

"Five hundred yards! Aim at the engine room! Number one gun, fire!" The shot boomed across the sunny, blue expanse of water, driving a white puff of smoke before it. The shell disappeared in the waves about one hundred yards ahead of the Japanese steamer. The next shot struck the ship, leaving in her side a black hole with jagged edges just above the waterline.

"Splendid!" cried Parrington. "Keep that up and we'll have the villain in ten shots."

Quickly the 12 pounder was reloaded; the gunners stood quietly beside their gun, and shot after shot was fired at the Japanese ship, of which five or six hit her right at the waterline. The stern gun of the *Mindoro* devoted itself in the meantime to destroying things on the enemy's deck. Gaping holes appeared everywhere in the ship's side, and the funnels received several enormous rents, out of which brown smoke poured forth. In a quarter of an hour the deck resembled the primeval chaos, being covered with bent and broken iron rods, iron plates riddled with shot, and woodwork torn to splinters. Suddenly clouds of white steam burst out from all the holes in the ship's sides, from the skylights, and from the remnants of the funnels; the deck in the middle of the steamer rose slowly, and the exploding boilers tossed broken bits of engines and deck apparatus high up into the air. The *Kanga Maru* listed to port and disappeared in the waves, over which a few straggling American shots swept.

"Cease firing!" commanded Parrington. Then the *Mindoro* came about and again steered straight for Manila. The act of retribution had been accomplished; the treacherous murder of the crew of the *Monadnock* had been avenged.

When the *Mindoro* arrived at the harbor of Manila, the town was in a tremendous state of excitement. The drums were beating the alarm in the streets. The spot where only that morning the *Monadnock* had lain in idle calm was empty.

The explosion of the *Monadnock* had at first been regarded as an accident. In spite of its being the dinner hour, a number of boats appeared in the roads, all making toward the scene of the accident, where a broad, thick veil of smoke crept slowly over the surface of the water. As no one knew what new horrors might be hidden in this cloud, none of the boats dared go nearer. Only two white naval cutters belonging to the gunboats lying in the harbor glided into the mist, driven forward by strong arms; and they actually succeeded in saving a few of the crew.

One of the rescued men told the following story: About two minutes after the *Monadnock* had received a wireless message, which, however, was never deciphered, a dull concussion was felt throughout the ship, followed almost immediately by another one. On the starboard side of the *Monadnock* two white, bubbling, hissing columns of water had shot up, which completely flooded the low deck; then a third explosion, possibly caused by a mine striking the ammunition room and setting it off, practically tore the ship asunder. There could be no doubt that these torpedoes came from the Japanese steamer anchored beside the *Monadnock*, for the *Kanga Maru* had suddenly slipped her anchor and hurried off as fast as she could. It was now remembered that the Japanese ship had had steam up constantly for the last few days, ostensibly because they were daily expecting their cargo in lighters, from which they intended to load without delay. It was therefore pretty certain that the *Kanga Maru* had entered the harbor merely for the purpose of destroying the *Monadnock*, the only monitor in Manila. Torpedo tubes had probably been built in the Japanese merchant steamer under water, and this made it possible to blow up the *Monadnock* the moment there was the least suspicion that the Americans in Manila were aware of the fact that war had broken out. Thus the wireless message from Corregidor had indeed sealed the fate of the *Monadnock*. The *Kanga Maru* had launched her torpedoes, and then tried to escape. The meeting with the *Mindoro* the Japanese had not reckoned with, for they had counted on getting away during the confusion which the destruction of the *Monadnock* would naturally cause in Manila.

As a result of these occurrences the few ships in the roads of Manila soon stopped loading and discharging; most of the steamers weighed anchor, and, as soon as they could get up steam, went farther out into the roads, for a rumor had spread that the *Kanga Maru* had laid mines. The report turned out to be entirely unfounded, but it succeeded in causing a regular panic on some of the ships. From the town came the noise of the beating of drums and the shrill call to arms to alarm the garrison; one could see the quays being cleared by detachments of soldiers, and sentries were posted before all the public buildings.

American troops hurried on the double-quick through the streets of the European quarter, and the sight of the soldiers furnished the first element of reassurance to the white population, whose excitement had been tremendous ever since the alarm of the garrison. The old Spanish batteries, or rather what was still left of them, were occupied by artillerymen, while one battalion went on sentry duty on the ramparts of the section of the town called *Intra muros*, and five other battalions left the town at once in order to help garrison the redoubts and forts in the line of defense on the land side.

The town of Manila and the arsenal at Cavite, where measures for defense were also taken, thus gave no cause for apprehension; but, on the other hand, it was noticeable that the natives showed signs of insubordination toward the American military authorities, and that they did not attempt to conceal the fact that they had been better informed as to the political situation than the Americans. These were the first indications as to how the land lay, and gradually it began to be remembered that similar observations had been made within the last few days: for example, a number of revolutionary flags had had to be removed in the town.

The Americans were in a very precarious position, and at the council of war held by the governor in the afternoon it was decided that should the Filipinos show the slightest signs of insurrection, the whole military strength would be concentrated to defend Manila, Cavite, and the single railway running north, while all the other garrisons were to be withdrawn and the rest of the archipelago left to its own devices. In this way the Americans might at least hope, with some chance of success, to remain masters of Manila and vicinity. The island was, of course, proclaimed to be in a state of siege, and a strong military patrol was put in charge of the night watch.

A serious encounter took place in the afternoon before the Government building. As soon as it became known that proclamation of martial law had been made the population streamed in great crowds toward the Government buildings; and when the American flag was suddenly hauled down—it has never been ascertained by whom—and the Catipunàn flag, formerly the standard of the rebels—the tri-color with the sun in a triangular field—appeared in its place, a moment of wild enthusiasm ensued, so wild that it required an American company with fixed bayonets to clear the square of the fanatics. The sudden appearance of this huge Catipunàn flag seemed mysterious enough, but the next few days were to demonstrate clearly how carefully the rebellion among the natives had been prepared.

When the officers of the garrison assembled at the customary place on the evening of the same day, they were depressed and uneasy, as men who find themselves confronted by an invisible enemy. There was no longer any difference of opinion as to the danger that threatened from the Mongolians, and those officers who had been exonerated from the charge of being too suspicious by the rapid developments of the last few hours were considerate enough not to make their less far-sighted comrades feel that they had undervalued their adversaries. No one had expected a catastrophe to occur quite so suddenly, and the uncertainty as to what was going on elsewhere had a paralyzing effect on all decisions. What one could do in the way of defense had been or was being done, but there were absolutely no indications as to the side from which the enemy might be expected.

The chief cause for anxiety at the moment was furnished by the question whether the squadron which had started for Mindanao was already aware of the outbreak of war. In any case, it was necessary to warn both it and the transports expected from San Francisco before they arrived at Mindanao. The only ships available for this purpose were the few little gunboats taken from the Spaniards in 1898; these had been made fit for service in all haste to be used in the harbor when the cruiser squadron left. Although they left much to be desired in the way of speed—a handicap of six days could, however, hardly have been made up even by the swiftest turbine—there was nevertheless a fair chance that these insignificant-looking little vessels, which could hardly be distinguished from the merchant type, might be able to slip past the Japanese blockading ships, which were probably cruising outside of Manila. This, however, would only be possible in case the Japanese had thus far ignored the squadron near Mindanao as they had Manila, for the purpose of concentrating their strength somewhere else. But where? At any rate, it was worth while taking even such a faint chance of being able to warn the squadron, for the destruction of the *Monadnock* could have had no other reason than to prevent communications between Manila and the squadron. The enemy had evidently not given a thought to the rickety little gunboats. Or could it be that all was already at an end out at Mindanao? At all events, the attempt had to be made.

Two gunboats coaled and slipped out of the harbor the same evening, heading in a southeasterly direction among the little islands straight through the archipelago in order to reach the eastern coast of Mindanao and there intercept the transport steamers, and eventually accompany them to Manila. Neither of these vessels was ever heard from again; it is supposed that they went down after bravely defending themselves against a Japanese cruiser. Their mission had meanwhile been rendered useless, for the five mail-steamers had encountered the Japanese torpedo-boats east of Mindanao three days before, and upon their indignant refusal to haul down their flags and surrender, had been sunk by several torpedoes. Only a few members of the crew had been fished up by the Japanese.

As a reward for his decisive action in destroying the *Kanga Maru*, the commander of the *Mindoro* was ordered to try, with the assistance of three other gunboats, to locate the commander of the cruiser squadron somewhere in the neighborhood of Mindanao, probably to the southwest of that island, in order to notify him of the outbreak of the war and to hand him the order to return to Manila.

The gunboats started on their voyage at dawn. In order to conceal the real reason for the expedition from the natives, it was openly declared that they were only going to do sentry duty at the entrance to the Bay of Manila. Each of the four vessels had been provided with a wireless apparatus, which, however, was not to be installed until the ships were under way, so that the four commanders might always be in touch with one another, and with the cruiser squadron as well, even should the latter be some distance away.

The next morning the gunboats found themselves in the Strait of Mindoro. They must have passed the enemy's line of blockade unnoticed, under the cover of darkness. At all events, they had seen nothing of the Japanese, and concluded that the blockade before Manila must be pretty slack. On leaving the Strait of Mindoro, the gunboats, proceeding abreast at small distances from one another, sighted a steamer—apparently an Englishman—crossing their course. They tried to signal to it, but no sooner did the English vessel observe this, than she began to increase her speed. It became clear at once that she was faster than the gunboats, and unless, therefore, the latter wished to engage in a useless chase, the hope of receiving news from the English captain had to be abandoned. So the gunboats continued on their course—the only ships to be seen on the wide expanse of inland sea.

In the afternoon a white steamer, going in the opposite direction, was sighted. Opinions clashed as to whether it was a warship or a merchant-vessel. In order to make certain the commander of the *Mindoro* ordered a turn to starboard, whereupon it was discovered that the strange ship was an ocean-steamer of about three thousand tons, whose nationality could not be distinguished at that distance. Still it might be an auxiliary cruiser from the Japanese merchant service. The commander of the *Mindoro* therefore ordered his vessels to clear for action.

The actions of the strange steamer were followed with eager attention, and it was seen that she continued her direct northward course. When she was about five hundred yards to port of the *Mindoro*, the latter requested the stranger to show her flag, whereupon the English flag appeared at the stern. Eager for battle, the Americans had hoped she would turn out to be a Japanese ship, for which, being four against one, they would have been more than a match; the English colors therefore produced universal disappointment. Suddenly one of the officers of the *Mindoro* drew Parrington's attention to the fact that the whole build of the strange steamer characterized her as one of the ships of the "Nippon Yusen Kaisha" with which he had become acquainted during his service at Shanghai; he begged Parrington not to be deceived by the English flag. The latter at once ordered a blank shot to be fired for the purpose of stopping the strange vessel, but when the latter calmly continued on her course, a ball was sent after her from the bow of the *Mindoro*, the shell splashing into the water just ahead of the steamer. The stranger now appeared to stop, but it was only to make a sharp turn to starboard, whereupon he tried to escape at full speed. At the same time the English flag disappeared from the stern, and was replaced by the red sun banner of Nippon.

Parrington at once opened fire on the hostile ship, and in a few minutes the latter had to pay heavily for her carelessness. Her commander had evidently reckoned upon the fact that the Americans were not yet aware of the outbreak of war, and had hoped to pass the gunboats under cover of a neutral flag. It also seemed unlikely that four little gunboats should have run the blockade before Manila; it was far more natural to suppose that these ships, still ignorant of the true state of affairs, were bound on some expedition in connection with the rising of the natives. The firing had scarcely lasted ten minutes before the Japanese auxiliary cruiser, which had answered with a few shots from two light guns cleverly concealed behind the deck-house near the stern of the boat, sank stern first. It was at any rate a slight victory which greatly raised the spirits of the crews of the gunboats.

Within the next few hours the Americans caught up with a few Malayan sailing ships, to which they paid no attention; later on a little black freight steamer, apparently on the way from Borneo to Manila, came in sight. The little vessel worked its way heavily through the water, tossed about by the ever increasing swell. About three o'clock the strange ship was near enough for its flag—that of Holland—to be recognized. Signals were made asking her to bring to, whereupon an officer from the *Mindoro* was pulled over to her in a gig. Half an hour later he left the *Rotterdam*, and the latter turned and steamed away in the direction from which she had come. The American officer had informed the captain of the *Rotterdam* of the blockade of Manila, and the latter had at once abandoned the idea of touching at that port.

The news which he had to impart gave cause for considerable anxiety. The *Rotterdam* came from the harbor of Labuan, where pretty definite news had been received concerning a battle between some Japanese ships and the American cruiser squadron stationed at Mindanao. It was reported that the battle had taken place about five days ago, immediately after war had been declared, that the American ships had fallen a prey to the superior forces of the enemy, and that the entire American squadron had been destroyed.

At all events, it was quite clear that the squadron no longer needed to be informed of the outbreak of hostilities, so Parrington decided to carry out his orders and return to Manila with his four ships. As the flotilla toward evening, just before sunset, was again passing through the Strait of Mindoro, the last gunboat reported that a big white ship, apparently a war vessel, had been sighted coming from the southeast, and that it was heading for the flotilla at full speed. It was soon possible to distinguish a white steamer, standing high out of the water, whose fighting tops left no room for doubt as to its warlike character. It was soon ascertained that the steamer was making about fifteen knots, and that escape was therefore impossible.

Parrington ordered his gunboats to form in a line and to get up full steam, as it was just possible that they might be able to elude the enemy under cover of darkness, although there was still a whole hour to that time.

Slowly the hull of the hostile ship rose above the horizon, and when she was still at a distance of about four thousand yards there was a flash at her bows, and the thunder of a shot boomed across the waters, echoed faintly from the mountains of Mindoro.

"They're too far away," said Parrington, as the enemy's shell splashed into the waves far ahead of the line of gunboats. A second shot followed a few minutes later, and whizzed between the *Mindoro* and her neighbor, throwing up white sprays of water whose drops, in the rays of the setting sun, fell back into the sea like golden mist. And now came shot after shot, while the Americans were unable to answer with their small guns at that great distance.

Suddenly a shell swept the whole length of the *Mindoro's* deck, on the port side, tearing up the planks of the foredeck as it burst. Things were getting serious! Slowly the sun sank in the west, turning the sky into one huge red flame, streaked with yellow lights and deep green patches. The clouds, which looked like spots of black velvet floating above the semicircle of the sun, had jagged edges of gleaming white and unearthly ruby red. Fiery red, yellow, and green reflections played tremblingly over the water, while in the east the deep blue shadows of night slowly overspread the sky.

The whole formed a picture of rare coloring: the four little American ships, pushing forward with all the strength of their puffing engines and throwing up a white line of foam before them with their sharp bows; on the bridges the weather-beaten forms of their commanders, and beside the dull-brown gun muzzles the gun crews, waiting impatiently for the moment when the decreasing distance would at last allow them to use their weapons; far away in the blue shadows of the departing day, like a spirit of the sea, the white steamer, from whose sides poured unceasingly the yellow flashes from the mouths of the cannon. Several shots had caused a good deal of damage among the rigging of the gunboats. The *Callao* had only half a funnel left, from which gray-brown smoke and red sparks poured forth.

Suddenly there was a loud explosion, and the *Callao* listed to port. A six-inch shell had hit her squarely in the stern, passing through the middle of the ship, and exploded in the upper part of the engine-room. The little gunboat was eliminated from the contest before it could fire a single shot, and now it lay broadside to the enemy, and utterly at the latter's mercy. In a few minutes the *Callao* sank, her flags waving. Almost directly afterwards another boat shared her fate. The other two gunboats continued on their course, the quickly descending darkness making them a more difficult target for the enemy. Suddenly a lantern signal informed the commander of the *Mindoro* that the third ship had become disabled through some damage to the engines. Parrington at once ordered the gunboat to be run ashore on the island of Mindoro and blown up during the night. Then he was compelled to leave the last of his comrades to its fate. His wireless apparatus had felt disturbances, evidently caused by the enemy's warning to the ships blockading Manila, so that his chances of entering the harbor unmolested appeared exceedingly slim.

The Japanese cruiser ceased firing as it grew darker, but curiously enough had made no use whatever of her searchlights. Only the flying sparks from her funnel enabled the *Mindoro* to follow the course of the hostile vessel, which soon passed the gunboat. Either the enemy thought that all four American ships had been destroyed or else they didn't think it worth while to worry about a disabled little gunboat. At all events, this carelessness or mistake on the part of the enemy proved the salvation of the *Mindoro*. During the night she struck a northwesterly course, so as to try to gain an entrance to the Bay of Manila from the north at daybreak, depending on the batteries of Corregidor to assist her in the attempt. Once during the night the *Mindoro* almost collided with one of the enemy's blockading ships, which was traveling with shaded lights, but she passed by unnoticed and gained an entrance at the north of the bay at dawn, while the batteries on the high, rocky terraces of Corregidor, with their long-range guns, kept the enemy at a distance. It was now ascertained that the Japanese blockading fleet consisted only of ships belonging to the merchant service, armed with a few guns, and of the old, unprotected cruiser *Takatshio*, which had had the encounter with the gunboats. The bold expedition of the latter had cleared up the situation in so far that it was now pretty certain that the entire American cruiser squadron had been destroyed or disabled, and that Manila was therefore entirely cut off from the sea.

The batteries at Corregidor now expected an attack from the enemy's ships, but none came. The Japanese contented themselves with an extraordinarily slack blockade—so much so that at times one could scarcely distinguish the outlines of the ships on the horizon. As all commerce had stopped and only a few gunboats comprised the entire naval strength of Manila, Japan could well afford to regard this mockery of a blockade as perfectly sufficient. Day by day the Americans stood at their guns, day by day they expected the appearance of a hostile ship; but the horizon remained undisturbed and an uncanny silence lay over the town and harbor. Of what use were the best of guns, and what was the good of possessing heroic courage and a burning desire for battle, if the enemy did not put in an appearance? And he never did.

When Parrington appeared at the Club on the evening after his scouting expedition he was hailed as a hero, and the officers stayed together a long time discussing the naval engagement. In the early hours of the morning he accompanied his friend, Colonel Hawkins of the Twelfth Infantry Regiment, through the quiet streets of the northern suburbs of Manila to the latter's barracks. As they reached the gate they saw, standing before it in the pale light of dawn, a mule cart, on which lay an enormous barrel. The colonel called the sentry, and learned that the cart had been standing before the gate since the preceding evening. The colonel went into the guard-room while Parrington remained in the street. He was suddenly struck by a label affixed to the cask, which contained the words, "From Colonel Pemberton to his friend Colonel Hawkins." Parrington followed the colonel into the guard-room and drew his attention to the scrap of paper. Hawkins ordered some soldiers to take the barrel down from the car and break open one end of it. The colonel had strong nerves, and was apt to boast of them to the novices in the colonial service, but what he saw now was too much even for such an old veteran. He stepped back and seized the wall for support, while his eyes grew moist.

In the cask lay the corpse of his friend Colonel Pemberton, formerly commander of the military station of San José, with his skull smashed in. The Filipinos had surprised the station of San José and slaughtered the whole garrison after a short battle. Pemberton's corpse—his love for whisky was well known—they had put into a cask and driven to the infantry barracks at Manila. Parrington, deeply touched, pressed his comrade's hand. The insurrection of the Filipinos! In Manila the bells of the Dominican church of *Intra muros* rang out their monotonous call to early mass.

CHAPTER II
ON THE HIGH SEAS

The *Tacoma* was expected to arrive at Yokohama early the next morning; the gong had already sounded, calling the passengers to the farewell meal in the dining-saloon, which looked quite festive with its colored flags and lanterns.

There was a deafening noise of voices in the handsome room, which was beginning to be overpoweringly hot in spite of the ever-revolving electric fans. As the sea was quite smooth, there was scarcely an empty place at the tables. A spirit of parting and farewell pervaded the conversation; the passengers were assembled for the last time, for on the morrow the merry party, which chance had brought together for two weeks, would be scattered to the four winds. Naturally the conversation turned upon the country whose celebrated wonders they were to behold on the following day. The old globe-trotters and several merchants who had settled in East Asia were besieged with questions, occasionally very naïve ones, about Japan and the best way for foreigners to get along there. With calm superiority they paraded their knowledge, and eager ladies made note on the backs of their menus of all the hotels, temples, and mountains recommended to them. Some groups were making arrangements for joint excursions in the Island Kingdom of Tenno; others discussed questions of finance and commerce, each one trying to impress his companions by a display of superior knowledge.

Here and there politics formed the subject of conversation; one lady in particular, the wife of a Baltimore merchant, sitting opposite the secretary of a small European legation who was on his way to Pekin to take up his duties there, plied him with questions and did her level best to get at the secrets of international politics. The secretary, who had no wonderful secrets to disclose, had recourse to the ordinary political topics of the day, and entertained his fair listener with a discussion of the problems that would arise in case of hostilities between America and Japan. "Of course," he declared, vaunting his diplomatic knowledge, "in case of war the Japanese would first surprise Manila and try to effect a landing, and in this they would very likely be successful. It is true that Manila with her strong defenses is pretty well protected against a sudden raid, and the Japanese gunners would have no easy task in an encounter with the American coast batteries. Even though Manila may not turn out to be a second Port Arthur, the Americans should experience no difficulty in repelling all Japanese attacks for at least six months; meanwhile America could send reinforcements to Manila under the protection of her fleet, and then there would probably be a decisive battle somewhere in the Malayan archipelago between the Japanese and American fleets, the results of which——"

"I thought," interrupted a wealthy young lady from Chicago, "I thought we had some ships in the Philippines." The diplomat waved his hand deprecatingly, and smiled knowingly at this interruption. He was master of the situation and well qualified to cast the horoscope of the future—and so he was left in possession of the field.

The lady opposite him was, however, not yet satisfied; with the new wisdom just obtained she now besieged the German major sitting beside her, who was on his way to Kiao-chau via San Francisco. He had not been paying much attention to the conversation, but the subject broached to him for discussion was such a familiar one, that he was at once posted when his neighbor asked him his opinion as to the outcome of such a war.

Nevertheless it was an awkward question, and the German, out of consideration for his environment on board the American steamer, did not allow himself to be drawn out of his usual reserve. He simply inquired what basis they had for the supposition that, in case of war, Japan would occupy herself exclusively with the Philippines.

The secretary of legation had gradually descended from the clouds of diplomatic self-conceit to the level of the ordinary mortal and, overhearing the major's question through the confusion of voices and clatter of plates, shook his head disapprovingly and asked the major: "Don't you think it's likely that Japan will try first of all to get possession of the prize she has been longing for ever since the Peace of Paris?"

"I know as little as anyone else not in diplomatic circles what the plans and hopes of the Japanese Government are, but I do think there is not the slightest prospect of an outbreak of hostilities in the near future; there is, accordingly, not much sense in trying to imagine what might happen in case of a war," answered the German coolly.

"There are only two possibilities," said the English merchant from Shanghai, one of the chief stockholders of the line, who sat next to the captain. "According to my experience"—and here he paused in order to draw the attention of his listeners to this experience—"according to my experience," he repeated, "there are only two possibilities. Japan is overpeopled and is compelled to send her surplus population out of the country. The Manchuria experiment turned cut to be a failure, for the teeming Chinese population leaves no room now for more Japanese emigrants and small tradesmen than there were before the war with Russia; besides, there was no capital at hand for large enterprises. Japan requires a strong foothold for her emigrants where"—and here he threw an encouraging glance at the captain—"she can keep her people together economically and politically, as in Hawaii. The emigration to the States has for years been severely restricted by law."

"And at the same time they are pouring into our country in droves by way of the Mexican frontier," mumbled the American colonel, who was on his way back to his post, from his seat beside the captain.

"That leaves only the islands of the Pacific, the Philippines, and perhaps Australia," continued the Shanghai merchant undisturbed. "In any such endeavors

Japan would of course have to reckon with the States and with England. The other possibility, that of providing employment and support for the ever-increasing population within the borders of their own country, would be to organize large Japanese manufacturing interests. Many efforts have already been made in this direction, but, owing to the enormous sums swallowed up by the army and navy, the requisite capital seems to be lacking."

"In my opinion," interposed the captain at this juncture, "there is a third possibility—namely, to render additional land available for the cultivation of crops. As you are all no doubt aware, not more than one third of Japan is under cultivation; the second third, consisting of stone deserts among the mountains, must of necessity be excluded, but the remaining third, properly cultivated, would provide a livelihood for millions of Japanese peasants. But right here we encounter a peculiar Japanese trait; they are dead set on the growth of rice, and where, in the higher districts, no rice will grow, they refuse to engage in agriculture altogether and prefer to leave the land idle. If they would grow wheat, corn, and grass in such sections, Japan would not only become independent of other countries with respect to her importation of provisions, but, as I said before, it would also provide for the settlement of millions of Japanese peasants; and, furthermore, we should then get some decent bread to eat in Japan."

This conception of the Japanese problem seemed to open new vistas to the secretary of legation. He listened attentively to the captain's words and threw inquiring glances toward the Shanghai merchant. The latter, however, was completely absorbed in the dissection of a fish, whose numerous bones continually presented fresh anatomical riddles. In his stead the thread of the conversation was taken up by Dr. Morris, of Brighton, an unusually cadaverous-looking individual, who sometimes maintained absolute silence for days at a time, and who was supposed to possess Japanese bronzes of untold value and to be on his way to Hokkaido to complete his collection.

"You must not believe everything you see in the papers," he said. "If the Japanese were only better farmers, nobody in Japan need go hungry; there is no question of her being overpeopled, and this mania for emigration is nothing but a disease, a fashion, of which the government at Tokio, to be sure, makes very good use for political purposes. Whoever speaks in all seriousness of Japan's being overpeopled is merely quoting newspaper editorials, and is not acquainted with the conditions of the country."

Dr. Morris had scarcely said as much as this during the whole of his two weeks' stay on board the *Tacoma*. It is true that he had got to know Japan very thoroughly during his many years' sojourn in the interior in search of old bronzes, and he knew what he was talking about. His views, however, were not in accord with those current at the moment, and consequently, although his words were listened to attentively, they did not produce much effect.

The conversation continued along the same lines, and the possibility of a war again came up for discussion. The German officer was the only one to whom they could put military questions, and it was no light task for him to find satisfactory answers. He could only repeat again and again that such a war would offer such endless possibilities of attack and defense, that it was absolutely impossible to forecast the probable course of events. The Shanghai merchant conversed with the captain in a low tone of voice about the system of Japanese spies in America, and related a few anecdotes of his experiences in China in this connection.

"But one can distinguish between a Jap and a Chinaman at a glance," interrupted the son of a New York multi-millionaire sitting opposite him. "I could never understand why the Japanese spies are so overrated."

"If you can tell one from the other, you are more observant than the ordinary mortal," remarked the Englishman dryly. "I can't for one, and if you'll look me up in Shanghai, I'll give myself the pleasure of putting you to the test. I'll invite a party of Chinamen and ask you to pick out from among them a Japanese naval officer who has been in Shanghai for a year and a half on a secret, I had better say, a perfectly open mission."

"You'll lose your bet," said the captain to the New Yorker, "for I've lost a similar wager under the same circumstances."

"But the Japanese don't wear pigtails," said the New Yorker, somewhat abashed.

"Those Japanese do wear pigtails," said the Englishman with a grin.

"What's up?" said the captain, looking involuntarily towards the entrance to the dining-saloon. "What's up? We're only going at half speed."

The dull throbbing of the engine had indeed stopped, and any one who noticed the vibration of the ship could tell that the propeller was revolving only slightly.

The captain got up quietly to go on deck, but as he was making his way out between the long rows of chairs, he met one of the crew, who whispered to him that the first mate begged him to come on the bridge.

"We're not moving," said some one near the center of the table. "We can't have arrived this soon."

"Perhaps we have met a disabled ship," said a young French girl; "that would be awfully interesting."

The captain remained away, while the dinner continued to be served. Suddenly all conversation was stopped by the dull howl of the steam whistle, and when two more calls followed the first, an old globe trotter thought he had discovered the reason for the ship's slowing down, and declared with certainty: "This is the third time on my way to Japan that we have run into a fog just before entering the harbor; the last time it made us a day and a half late. I tell you it was no joke to sit in that gray mist with nothing to do but wait for the fog to lift— —" and then he narrated a few anecdotes about that particular voyage, which at once introduced the subject of fog at his table, a subject that was greedily pounced upon by all. London fog and other fogs were discussed, and no one noticed that the ship had come to a full stop and was gradually beginning to pitch heavily, a motion that soon had the effect of causing several of the ladies to abandon the conversation and play nervously with their coffee-spoons, as the nightmare of seasickness forced itself every moment more disagreeably on their memories.

A few of the men got up and went on deck. A merchant from San Francisco came down and told his wife that a strange ship not far from the *Tacoma* had its searchlights turned on her. No reason for this extraordinary proceeding could be given, as the officers seemed to know as little about it as the passengers.

The fourth officer, whose place was at the head of one of the long tables, now appeared in the dining-saloon, and was at once besieged with questions from all sides. In a loud voice he announced that the captain wished him to say that there was no cause for alarm. A strange ship had its searchlights turned on the *Tacoma*, probably a man-of-war that had some communication to make. The captain begged the passengers not to allow themselves to be disturbed in their dinner. The next course was served immediately afterwards, the reason for the interruption was soon forgotten, and conversation continued as before.

"But we're not moving yet," said a young woman about ten minutes later to her husband, with whom she was taking a honeymoon trip round the world, "we're not moving yet."

The fourth officer gave an evasive answer in order to reassure his neighbor, but, as a matter of fact, the ship had not yet got under way again. To complicate the situation, another member of the crew came in at this moment and whispered something to the officer, who at once hurried on deck.

It was a positive relief to him to escape from the smell of food and the loud voices into the fresh air. It seemed like another world on deck. The stars twinkled in the silent sky, and the soft night air refreshed the nerves that had been exhausted by the heat of the day. The fourth officer mounted quickly to the bridge and reported to the captain.

The latter gave him the following brief order: "Mr. Warren, I shall ask you to see that the passengers are not unnecessarily alarmed; let the band play a few pieces, and see that the dinner proceeds quietly. Make a short speech in my stead, tell the passengers what a pleasant time we have all had on this voyage, and say a few words of farewell to them for me. We've been signaled by a Japanese warship," he continued, "and asked to stop and wait for a Japanese boat. I haven't the slightest idea what the fellows want, but we must obey orders; the matter will no doubt be settled in a few minutes as soon as the boat has arrived."

The officer disappeared, and the captain, standing by the port yardarm on the bridge, waited anxiously for the cutter which was approaching at full speed. The gangway had already been lowered. The cutter, after describing a sharp curve, came alongside, and two marines armed with rifles immediately jumped on the gangway.

"Halloo," said the captain, "a double guard! I wonder what that means?"

The Japanese officer got out of the cutter and came up the gangway, followed by four more soldiers, two of whom were posted at the upper entrance to the gangway. The other two followed the officer to the bridge. A seventh man got out of the boat and carried a square box on the bridge, while finally two soldiers brought a long heavy object up the gangway and set it down against the wall of the cabin in the stern.

The Japanese officer ordered the two marines to take up their stand at the foot of the steps leading to the bridge, and with a wave of his hand ordered the third to station himself with his square box at the port railing. At the same time he gave him an order in Japanese, and the rattling noise which followed made it clear that the apparatus was a lantern which was signaling across to the man-of-war.

"This is carrying the joke a little too far. What does it all mean?" cried the captain of the *Tacoma*, starting to pull the man with the lantern back from the railing. But the Japanese officer laid his hand firmly on his right arm and said in a decisive tone: "Captain, in the name of the Japanese Government I declare the American steamer *Tacoma* a lawful prize and her whole crew prisoners of war."

The captain shook off the grasp of the Japanese, and stepping back a pace shouted: "You must be crazy; we have nothing to do with the Japanese naval maneuvers, and I shall have to ask you not to carry your maneuver game too far. If you must have naval maneuvers, please practice on your own merchant vessels and leave neutral ships alone."

The Japanese saluted and said: "I am very sorry, captain, to have to correct your impression that this is part of our maneuvers. Japan is at war with the United States of America, and every merchantman flying the American flag is from now on a lawful prize."

The captain, a strapping fellow, seized the little Japanese, and pushed him toward the railing, evidently with the intention of throwing the impertinent fellow overboard. But in the same instant he noticed two Japanese rifles pointed at him, whereupon he let his arms drop with an oath and stared at the two Japanese marines in utter astonishment. The lantern signal continued to rattle behind him, and suddenly the pale blue searchlight from the man-of-war was thrown on the bridge of the *Tacoma*, lighting up the strange scene as if by moonlight. At the same time the shot from a gun boomed across the quiet surface of the water. Things really seemed to be getting serious.

From below, through the open skylights of the dining-saloon came the cheers of the passengers for the captain at the close of the fourth officer's speech, and the band at once struck up the "Star Spangled Banner." Everybody seemed to be cheerful and happy in the dining-saloon, and one and all seemed to have forgotten that the *Tacoma* was not moving.

And while from below the inspiring strains of the "Star Spangled Banner" passed out into the night, twenty Japanese marines came alongside in a second cutter and, climbing up the gangway, occupied all the entrances leading from below to the deck—a double guard with loaded guns being stationed at each door.

"I must ask you," said the Japanese officer to the captain, "to continue to direct the ship's course under my supervision. You will take the *Tacoma*, according to your original plans, into the harbor of Yokohama; there the passengers will leave the ship, without any explanations being offered, and you and the crew will be prisoners of the Japanese Government. The prize-court will decide what is to be done with your cargo. The baggage of the passengers, the captain, and the crew will, of course, remain in their possession. There are now twenty of our marines on board the *Tacoma*, but in case you should imagine that they would be unable to command the situation in the event of any resistance being offered by you or your crew, I consider it advisable to inform you that for the last ten minutes there has been a powerful bomb in the stern of the *Tacoma*, guarded by two men, who have orders to turn on the current and blow up your ship at the first signs of serious resistance. It is entirely to the advantage of the passengers in your care to bow to the inevitable and avoid all insubordination—*à la guerre comme à la guerre*."

The Japanese saluted and continued: "You will remain in command on the bridge for the next four hours, when you will be relieved by the first mate. Meanwhile the latter can acquaint the passengers with the altered circumstances." And, waving his hand toward the first mate, who had listened in silent rage, he added: "Please, sir!"

The officer addressed looked inquiringly across to the captain, who hesitated a moment and then said in suppressed emotion: "Hardy, go down and tell the passengers that the *Tacoma*, through an unheard-of, treacherous surprise, has fallen into the hands of a Japanese cruiser, but that the passengers, on whose account we are obliged to submit to this treatment, need not be startled, for they and all their possessions will be landed safely at Yokohama to-morrow morning."

Hardy's soles seemed positively to stick to the steps as he went down, and he was almost overcome by the warm air at the entrance to the dining-saloon, where the noise of boisterous laughter and lively conversation greeted him.

"Halloo, when are we going on?" he was asked from all sides.

Mr. Hardy shook his head silently and went to the captain's place.

"We must drink your health," called several, holding their glasses towards him. "Where's the captain?"

Hardy was silent, but remained standing and the words seemed to choke him.

"Be quiet! Listen! Mr. Hardy is going to speak——"

"It's high time we heard something from the captain," called out a stout German brewer from Milwaukee over the heads of the others. "Three cheers for Mr. Hardy!" came from one corner of the room. "Three cheers for Mr. Hardy!" shouted the passengers on the other side, and all joined in the chorus: "For he is a jolly good fellow." "Do let Mr. Hardy speak," said the Secretary of Legation, turning to the passengers reprovingly.

"Silence!" came from the other side. The hum of voices ceased gradually and silence ensued.

"First give Mr. Hardy something to drink!" said some one, while another passenger laughed out loud.

Hardy wiped the perspiration from his brow with the captain's napkin, which the latter had left on his plate.

"Shocking!" said an English lady quite distinctly; "seamen haven't any manners."

Hardy had not yet found words, but finally began in a low, stammering voice: "The captain wishes me to tell you that the *Tacoma* has just been captured by a Japanese cruiser. The United States of America are said to be at war with Japan. There is a Japanese guard on board, which has occupied all the companionways. The captain requests the passengers to submit quietly to the inevitable. You will all be landed safely at Yokohama early to-morrow and—" Hardy tried to continue, but the words would not come and he sank back exhausted into his chair.

"Three cheers for the captain!" came the ringing shout from one of the end tables, to be repeated in different parts of the room. The German brewer shook with laughter and exclaimed: "That's a splendid joke of the captain's; he ought to have a medal for it."

"Stop your nonsense," said some one to the brewer.

"No, but really, that's a famous joke," persisted the latter. "I've never enjoyed myself so much on a trip before."

"Be quiet, man; it's a serious matter."

"Ha! ha! You've been taken in, too, have you?" was the answer, accompanied by a roar of laughter.

An American jumped up, crying: "I'm going to get my revolver; I guess we can handle those chaps," and several others joined in with "Yes, yes, we'll get our revolvers and chuck the yellow monkeys overboard!"

At this point the German major jumped up from his seat and called out to the excited company in a sharp tone of command: "Really, gentlemen, the affair is serious; it's not a joke, as some of you gentlemen seem to think; you may take my word for it that it is no laughing matter."

Hardy still sat silent in his chair. The Englishman from Shanghai overwhelmed him with questions and even the Secretary of Legation emerged from his diplomatic reserve.

The six men who had gone to get their revolvers now returned to the dining-saloon with their spirits considerably damped, and one of them called out: "It's not a joke at all; the Japanese are stationed up there with loaded rifles."

Some of the ladies screamed hysterically and asked complete strangers to take them to their cabins. All of the passengers had jumped up from their chairs, and a number were busily engaged looking after those ladies who had shown sufficient discretion to withdraw at once from the general excitement by the simple expedient of fainting. In the meantime Hardy had regained control of himself and of the situation, and standing behind his chair as though he were on the captain's bridge declared simply and decisively: "On the captain's behalf I must beg the passengers not to attempt any resistance. Your life and safety are guaranteed by the word of the captain and the bearing of our crew, who have also been forced to submit to the inevitable. I beg you all to remain here and to await the further orders of the captain. There is no danger so long as no resistance is offered; we are in the hands of the Japanese navy, and must accustom ourselves to the altered circumstances."

It was long after midnight before all grew quiet on board the *Tacoma*; the passengers were busy packing their trunks, and it was quite late before the cabin lights were extinguished on both sides of the ship, which continued her voyage quietly and majestically in the direction of Yokohama. The deck, generally a scene of cheerful life and gaiety until a late hour, was empty, and only the subdued steps of the Japanese marines echoed through the still night.

Twice more the searchlights were thrown on the *Tacoma*, but a clattering answer from the signal lantern at once conveyed the information that all was in order, whereupon the glaring ball of light disappeared silently, and there was nothing on the whole expanse of dark water to indicate that invisible eyes were on the lookout for every ship whose keel was ploughing the deep.

The *Tacoma* arrived at Yokohama the next morning, the passengers were sent ashore, and the steamer herself was added as an auxiliary cruiser to the Japanese fleet.

CHAPTER III

HOW IT BEGAN

Ding-ding-ding-ding—Ding-ding-ding-ding—went the bell of the railway telegraph—Ding-ding-ding-ding——

Tom Gardner looked up from his work and leaned his ax against the wall of the low tin-roofed shanty which represented both his home and the station Swallowtown on the Oregon Railway. "Nine o'clock already," he mumbled, and refilling his pipe from a greasy paper-bag, he lighted it and puffed out clouds of bluish smoke into the clear air of the hot May morning. Then he looked at the position of the sun and verified the fact that his nickel watch had stopped again. The shaky little house hung like a chance knot in an endless wire in the middle of the glittering double row of rails that stretched from east to west across the flowery prairie. It looked like a ridiculous freak in the midst of the wide desert, for nowhere, so far as the eye could reach, was it possible to discover a plausible excuse for the washed-out inscription "Swallowtown" on the old box-lid which was nailed up over the door. Only a broad band of golden-yellow flowers crossing the tracks not far from the shanty and disappearing in the distance in both directions showed where heavy cart-wheels and horses' hoofs had torn up the ground.

By following this curious yellow track, which testified to the existence of human intercourse even in the great lonely prairie, in a southerly direction, one could notice about a mile from the station a slight rising of the ground covered with low shrubs and a tangled mass of thistles and creepers: This was Swallowtown No. 1, the spot where once upon a time a dozen people or more, thrown together by chance, had founded a homestead, but whose traces had been utterly obliterated since. The little waves of the great national migration to this virgin soil had after a few years washed everything away and had carried the inhabitants of the huts with them on their backs several miles farther south, where by another mere chance they had located on the banks of the river. The only permanent sign of this ebb and flow was the tin-roofed shanty near the tracks of the Oregon Railway, and the proud name of Swallowtown, fast disappearing under the ravages of storm and rain, on the box-lid over Tom Gardner's door.

Tom Gardner regarded his morning's work complacently. With the aid of his ax he had transformed the tree-stump that had lain behind the station for years into a hitching-post, which he was going to set up for the farmers, so that they could tie their horses to it when they came to the station. Tom had had enough of fastening the iron ring into the outer wall of his shanty, for it had been torn out four times by the shying of the wild horses harnessed to the vehicles sent from Swallowtown to meet passengers. And the day before yesterday Bob Cratchit's horses had added insult to injury by running off with a board out of the back wall. Tom was sick and tired of it; the day before he had temporarily stopped up the hole with a tin advertisement, which notified the inhabitants of Swallowtown who wanted to take the train that Millner's pills were the best remedy for indigestion. Tom decided to set up his post at midday.

He stopped work for the present in order to be ready for station-duty when the express from Pendleton passed through in half an hour. From force of habit and half unconsciously, he glanced along the yellow road running south, wondering whether in spite of its being Sunday there might not be some traveler from Swallowtown coming to catch the local train which stopped at the station an hour later. He shaded his eyes with his right hand and after a careful search did discover a cart with two persons in it approaching slowly over the waving expanse of the flower-bedecked prairie. Tom muttered something to himself and traipsed through the station house, being joined as usual by his dog, who had been sleeping outside in the sun. Then he walked a little way along the tracks and finally turned back to his dwelling, the trampled-down flowers and grass before the entrance being the only signs that the foot of man ever disturbed its solitary peace. The dog now seemed suddenly to become aware of the rapidly approaching cart and barked in that direction. Tom sent him into the house and shut the door behind him, whereupon the dog grew frantic. The cart approached almost noiselessly over the flowery carpet, but soon the creaking and squeaking of the leather harness and the snorting of the horses became clearly audible.

"Halloo, Tom!" called out one of the men.

"Halloo, Winston!" was the answer; "where are you off to?"

"Going over to Pendleton."

"You're early; the express hasn't passed yet," answered Tom.

Winston jumped down from the cart, swung a sack over his shoulder, and stepped toward the shanty.

"Who's that with you?" asked Tom, pointing with his thumb over his right shoulder.

"Nelly's brother-in-law, Bill Parker," said the other shortly.

Nelly's brother-in-law was in the act of turning the cart round to drive back to Swallowtown when Tom, making a megaphone of his hands, shouted across: "Won't the gentleman do me the honor of having a drink on me?"

"All right," rang out the answer, and Nelly's brother-in-law drove the horses to the rear of the station.

"Yes, the ring's gone," said Tom. "Bob Cratchit's horses walked off with it yesterday. You can hunt for it out there somewhere if you want to."

Bill jumped down and fastened the horses with a rope which he tied to Tom's old tree-stump.

"Come on, fellows!" said Tom, going toward the house. Scarcely had he opened the door when his dog rushed madly past him out into the open, barking with all his might at something about a hundred yards behind the station.

"I guess he's found a gopher," said Tom, and then the three entered the hut, and Tom, taking a half-empty whisky bottle out of a cupboard, poured some into a cup without a handle, a shaving-cup, and an old tin cup.

"The express ought to pass in about ten minutes," said Tom, and then began the usual chat about the commonplaces of farm life, about the crops, and the price of cattle, while hunting anecdotes followed. Now and then Tom listened through the open door for sounds of the express, which was long overdue, till suddenly the back door was slammed shut by the wind.

It was Bill Parker's turn to treat, and he then told of how he had sold his foals at a good profit, and Bob launched out into all sorts of vague hints as to a big deal that he expected to pull off at Pendleton the next day. Bill kept an eye on his two horses, which he could just see through the window in the rear wall of the shanty.

"Don't let them run away from you," warned Tom; "horses as fresh as those generally skip off when the express passes by."

"Nothing like that!" said Bill Parker, glancing again through the open window, "but they are unusually restless just the same."

... "He was willing to give twenty dollars, was he?" asked Tom, resuming the former conversation.

But Bill gave no answer and continued to stare out of the window.

"Here's how, gentlemen!" cried Tom encouragingly, touching Bill's tin cup with his shaving-cup.

"Excuse me a minute," answered the latter; "I want to look after my—" He had got up and was moving toward the door, but stopped halfway, staring fixedly at the open window with a glassy expression in his eyes. The other two regarded him with unfeigned astonishment, but when they followed the direction of his glance, they also started with fright as they looked through the window.

Yes, it was the same window as before, and beyond it stood the same team of stamping, snorting horses before the same cart; but on the ledge of the window there rested two objects like black, bristling hedgehogs, and under their prickly skins glistened two pairs of hostile eyes, and slowly and cautiously two gun-barrels were pushed over the ledge of the window into the room. At the same moment the door-knob moved, the door was pushed open, and in the blinding sunlight which suddenly poured into the room appeared two more men in khaki clothes and also armed with guns. "Hands up, gentlemen!" cried one of them threateningly.

The three obeyed the order mechanically, Tom unconsciously holding up his shaving-cup as well, so that the good whisky flowed down his arm into his coat. He looked utterly foolish. Bill was the first to recover, and inquired with apparent nonchalance: "What are you gentlemen after?" In the meantime he had noticed that the two men at the door wore soldiers' caps with broad peaks, and he construed this as a new holdup trick.

The men outside were conversing in an unintelligible lingo, and their leader, who was armed only with a Browning pistol, looked into the hut and asked: "Which of you gentlemen is the station-master?" Tom lowered his shaving-cup and took a step forward, whereupon he was at once halted by the sharp command: "Hands up!"

But this one step toward the door had enabled Tom to see that there were at least a dozen of these brown fellows standing behind the wall of his shanty. At the same time he saw his dog slinking about outside with his tail between his legs and choking over something. He called the dog, and the poor creature crept along the ground toward him, evidently making vain attempts to bark.

"The damned gang," growled Tom to himself; "they have evidently given the poor beast something to eat which prevents his barking."

The man with the Browning pistol now turned to Tom and said: "Has the express passed yet?"

"No."

"No? I thought it was due at 9.30." The highwayman looked at his watch. "Past ten already," he said to himself. "And when is the local train from Umatilla expected?"

"It ought to be here at 10.30."

"The express goes through without stopping, doesn't it?" began the other again. "Good! Now you go out as if nothing had happened and let the express pass! The other two will remain here in the meantime and my men will see that they don't stir. One move and you can arrange your funeral for to-morrow."

The two bristly-headed chaps at the window remained motionless, and followed the proceedings with a broad grin. The two men from Swallowtown were compelled to stand with uplifted hands against the wall opposite the window, so that the gun-barrels on the window-sill were pointing straight at them. Winston had had sufficient time to study the two highwaymen at the window and it gradually dawned upon him what sort of robbers they were; in a low tone of voice he said to Tom: "They're Japs."

The man with the Browning overheard the remark; he turned around quickly and repeated in a determined voice: "If you move you'll die on the spot."

Then he allowed Tom to leave the station, and showed him how two of his men opened the shutters of the windows that looked out on the tracks and cut two oblong holes in them down on the side, through which they stuck the barrels of their guns. Then Bill's cart was pushed forward, so that only the horses were hidden by the station. One of the men held the horses to prevent their running away when the train came, and two armed men climbed into the cart and kneeled ready to shoot, concealing themselves from the railroad side behind two large bags of corn. Thereupon the leader told Tom once more that he was to stand in front of the station as usual when the train approached. If he attempted to make any sign which might cause the train to stop, or if he merely opened his mouth, not only he, but also the occupants of the train, would have to pay for it with their lives.

Ding—ding—ding—ding went the railway telegraph, ding—ding—ding—ding. The man with the Browning consulted his note-book and asked Tom: "What signal is that? Where is the express now?"

Tom did not answer.

"Go out on the platform!" commanded the other. With a hasty glance along the tracks, Tom assured himself that the spot back there, where the two tracks, which glittered like silver in the sun, crossed, was still empty. So there was still a little more time to think. Then he began to stroll slowly up and down. Fifteen steps forward, fifteen back, eighteen forward, twenty back. Suppose he ran to meet the train— —

"Halloo! Where are you going?" shouted the leader to him. "Don't you dare go five steps beyond the station house!"

Fifteen steps forward, fifteen back. And suppose now that he did jump across and run along the tracks? What would it matter—he, one among millions, without wife or child? Yes, he would warn the engineer; and if they shot at him, perhaps the people on the train also had revolvers. The express must come soon—it must be nearly half past ten. Mechanically, he read the name Swallowtown on the old box-lid.

Not a sound from the interior of the station. Would they hit him or miss him when the train came? He examined the rickety old shutters. Yes, there was a white incision in the wood near the bottom, and above it the tin was bent back almost imperceptibly, while below it there was a small, blackish-brown ring. On the other side there was another little hole, and here the tin was bent back rather more, showing a second small, blackish-brown ring. And suppose he did call out as the train rushed by? He would call out!—A burst of flame from the two blackish-brown rings—If he could only first explain everything to the engineer—then they could shoot all they wanted to.

Horrid to be wounded in the back! Long ago at school there had often been talk about wounds in the back and in the chest—the former were disgraceful, because they were a sign of running away. But this was not running away—this was an effort to save others.

Were the rails vibrating? Four steps more, then a quiet turn, one look into the air, one far away over the prairie. He knew that the eyes behind the dark-brown rings were following his every movement. Now along the tracks—is there anything coming way back there? No, not yet. He walked past the station, then along the tracks again, and looked to the left across the prairie.

Now his glance rested on the cart. It stood perfectly still. Sure enough, there, between the sacks, was another one of those bristly heads! Where on earth had the fellows come from, and what in the world did they want? Winston had said they were Japs.

Could this be war? Nonsense! How could the fellows have come so far across country? A short time ago some one had said that a troop of Japs had been seen far away, down in Nevada, but that they had all disappeared in the mountains. That was two months ago. Could these be the same?

But it couldn't be a war. War begins at the borders of a country, not right in the middle. It is true that the Japanese immigrants were all said to be drilled soldiers. Had they brought arms along? These certainly had!

Now the turn again. Ah! there was the train at last. Far away along the tracks a black square rose and quite slowly became wider and higher. Good God! if the next ten minutes were only over—if one could only wipe such a span as this out of one's life! Only ten minutes older! If one could only look back on those ten minutes from the other side! But no; one must go through the horror, second by second, taste every moment of it. What would happen to the two inside? This didn't matter much after all—they couldn't, in any case, overpower the others without weapons. A thousand yards more perhaps and then the train would be there! And then a thousand yards more, and he would either be nothing but an unconscious mass of flesh and bones, or——

Now the rails were reverberating—from far away he heard the rumble of the approaching mass of iron and steel. And now, very low but distinct, the ringing of the bell could be distinguished—gang, gang, gang, gang, gang, gang— He threw a hasty glance at the two blackish-brown rings; four steps further and he could again see the cart. The next time——

"Stand straight in front of the station and let the train pass!" sounded close behind him. He obeyed mechanically.

"Nearer to the house—right against the wall!" He obeyed.

All his muscles tightened. If he could now take a leap forward and manage to get hold of something—a railing or something—as the train rushed by, then they could shoot as much as they liked. A rumbling and roaring noise reached his ears, and he could hear the increasing thunder of the wheels on the rails, the noise of the bell—gang, gang, gang—growing more and more distinct. The engine, with its long row of clattering cars behind, assumed gigantic dimensions before his wide-open eyes.

Not a sound came from the house; now the rails trembled; now he heard the hissing of the steam and the rattle of the rods; he saw the little curls of steam playing above the dome of the boiler. Like a black wall, the express came nearer, rushing, rumbling, hammering along the tracks. Yes, he would jump now—now that the engine was almost in front of him! The rush of air almost took his breath away. Now!

The engineer popped his head out of the little cab-window. Now! Tom bent double, and, with one tremendous leap he was across the narrow platform in front of his shanty, and flew like a ball against the line of rushing cars, of railings and steps and wheels. He felt his hand touching something—nothing but flat, smooth surfaces. At last! He had caught hold of something! With a tremendous swing,

Tom's body was torn to the left, and his back banged against something. Something in his body seemed to give way. As in a dream, he heard two shots ring out above the fearful noise of the roaring train.

Too late! Tom was clinging to a railing between two cars and being dragged relentlessly along. He was almost unconscious, but could hear the wheels squeaking under the pressure of the brakes as he was hurled to and fro. But his hand held fast as in a vise. The wheels scraped, squeaked, and groaned. The train began to slow down! He had won! The train stood still.

Tom's body fell on the rail between two cars, almost lifeless; he heard a lot of steps all about him; people spoke to him and asked him questions. But his jaws were shut as if paralyzed; he couldn't speak a word. He felt the neck of a bottle being pushed between his lips, and the liquid running down his throat. It was something strong and invigorating, and he drank greedily. And then he suddenly shouted out loud, so that all the people stepped back horrified: "The station has been attacked by Japs."

Excited questions poured in from all sides. "Where from? What for?" Tom only cried: "Save the two others; they're shut up in the station!" More people collected round him. "Quick, quick!" he cried. "Run the train back and try to save them!"

Tom was lifted into a car and stretched out on a soft end-seat. Some of the passengers stood round him with their revolvers: "Tell us where it is! Tell us where they are!" Slowly the train moved back, slowly the telegraph poles slipped past the windows in the opposite direction.

Now they were there, and Tom heard wild cries on the platform. Then a door was pulled open and some one asked: "Where are the robbers?" Tom was lifted out, for his right shin-bone had been smashed and he couldn't stand. A stretcher was improvised, and he was carried out. Dozens of people were standing round the station. The wagon was gone, and so were the horses. Where to? The wide, deserted prairie gave no answer. A great many footprints in the sand showed at least that Tom had spoken the truth. He pointed out the holes made in the shutters by the bandits, and told the whole story a dozen times, until at last he fainted away again. When he came to half an hour later it all seemed like a horrible dream—like a scene from a robber's tale. He found himself in a comfortable Pullman car on the way to Umatilla, where he had to tell his story all over again, in order that the fairly hopeless pursuit of the highwaymen might be begun from there.

CHAPTER IV

ECHOES IN NEW YORK

Walla Walla, May 7.

"This morning, at ten o'clock, the station Swallowtown, on the Oregon line, was surprised by bandits. They captured the station in order to hold up the express train to Umatilla. The plot was frustrated by the decisive action of the station official, who jumped on the passing train and warned the passengers. Unfortunately, the robbers succeeded in escaping, but the Umatilla police have started in pursuit. The majority of the bandits are said to have been Japanese."

In these words the attack on Swallowtown was wired to New York, and when John Halifax went to the office of the *New York Daily Telegraph* at midnight, to work up the telegrams which had come in during Sunday for the morning paper, his chief drew his attention in particular to the remark at the end of the message, and asked him to make some reference in his article to the dangers of the Japanese immigration, which seemed to be going on unhindered over the Mexican and Canadian frontiers. John Halifax would have preferred to comment editorially on the necessity of night rest for newspaper men, but settled down in smothered wrath to write up the highwaymen who had committed the double crime of desecrating the Sabbath and robbing the train.

But scarcely had he begun his article under the large headlines "Japanese Bandits—A Danger no longer Confined to the Frontier, but Stalking about in the Heart of the Country,"—he was just on the point of setting off Tom's brave deed against the rascality of the bandits, when another package of telegrams was laid on the table. He was going to push them irritably aside when his glance fell on the top telegram, which began with the words, "This morning at ten o'clock the station at Connell, Wash., was attacked by robbers, who——"

"Hm!" said John Halifax, "there seems to be some connection here, for they probably meant to hold up the express at Connell, too." He turned over a few more telegrams; the next message began: "This morning at eleven o'clock—" and the two following ones: "This morning at twelve o'clock—" They all reported the holding up of trains, which had in almost every instance been successful. John Halifax got up, and with the bundle of telegrams went over to the map hanging on the wall and marked with a pencil the places where the various attacks had taken place. The result was an irregular line through the State of Washington running from north to south, along which the train robbers, apparently working in unison, had begun their operations at the same time. Nowhere had it been possible to capture them.

John Halifax threw his article into the waste basket and began again with the headlines, "A Gang of Train-Robbers at Work in Washington," and then gave a list of the places where the gang had held up the trains. He wrote a spirited article, which closed with a warning to the police in Washington and Oregon to put an end to this state of affairs as soon as possible, and if necessary to call upon the militia for aid in catching the bandits. While Halifax was writing, the news was communicated from the electric bulletin-board to the people hurrying through the streets at that late hour.

John Halifax read the whole story through once more with considerable satisfaction, and was pleased to think that the *New York Daily Telegraph* would treat its readers Monday morning to a thoroughly sensational bit of news. When he had finished, it struck him that all these attacks had been directed against trains running from west to east, and that the train held up at Swallowtown was the only one going in the opposite direction. He intended in conclusion to add a suggestive remark about this fact, but it slipped out of his mind somehow, and, yawning loudly, he threw his article as it was into the box near his writing table, touched a button, and saw the result of his labors swallowed noiselessly by a small lift. Then the author yawned again, and, going over to his chief, reported that he had finished, wished him a gruff "good morning," and started on his way home.

As he left the newspaper offices he observed the same sight that had met his eyes night after night for many years—a crowd of people standing on the opposite side of the street, with their heads thrown back, staring up at the white board upon which, in enormous letters, appeared the story of how Tom, with his bold leap, had saved the train. The last sentence, explaining that the robbers had been recognized as Japanese, elicited vigorous curses against the "damned Japs."

High up in the air the apparatus noiselessly and untiringly flashed forth one message after the other in big, black letters on the white ground—telling of one train attack after another. But of that living machine in the far West, working with clocklike regularity and slowly adding one link after the other to the chain, that machine which at this very moment had already separated three of the States by an impenetrable wall from the others and had thus blotted out three of the stars on the blue field of the Union flag—of that uncanny machine neither John Halifax nor the people loitering opposite the newspaper building in order to take a last sensation home with them, had the remotest idea. Not till the next morning was the meaning of these first flaming signs to be made clear.

At ten o'clock the telephone bell rang noisily beside John Halifax's bed. He seized the receiver and swore under his breath on learning that important telegrams required his presence at the office. "There isn't any reason why Harry Springley shouldn't go on with those old train-robbers," he grumbled; "I don't see what they want of me, but I suppose the stupid fellow doesn't know what to do, as usual."

An hour later, when he entered the editorial rooms of the *New York Daily Telegraph*, he found his colleagues in a great state of excitement. Judging by the loud talk going on in the conference room, he concluded at once that something out of the common must have happened. The editor-in-chief quickly explained to him that an hour ago the news, already disseminated through an "extra," had arrived, that not only were all messages from the Pacific coast, especially from San Francisco, held up, but the Canadian wire had furnished the news that a foreign strange squadron had been observed on Sunday at Port Townsend, and that it had continued its voyage through Puget Sound toward Seattle. In addition the news came from Walla Walla that since Sunday noon all telegraphic communication between Seattle, Tacoma, and Portland had been broken off. Attempts to reach Seattle and Tacoma over the Canadian wire had also proved vain while, on the other hand, the report came from Ogden that no trains from the west, from the direction of San Francisco, had arrived since Sunday noon, and that the noon express had been attacked this side of Reno by bandits, some of whom had been distinctly recognized as Japanese.

John Halifax recalled the first message of the evening before, in which there was a mention of the Japanese. He quickly put the separate news items together, and, after having glanced hurriedly at the messages in the extra, turned to the managing editor and in a low voice, which sounded strange and hard even to himself, said: "I believe this means war!"

The latter slapped him on the back in his brusque fashion, crying: "John Halifax, we're not making war on Japan."

"But they're making war on us," answered Halifax.

"Do you mean to imply that the Japanese are surprising us?" asked the editor, staring at Halifax.

"Exactly, and it makes no difference whether you believe it or not," was the reply.

"The Japanese fleet is lying off the Pacific coast, there's no doubt about that," remarked a reporter.

"And, what's more, they're right in our country," said Halifax, looking up.

"Who? The fleet?" inquired Harry Springley in a lame effort to be funny.

"No, the enemy," answered Halifax coldly; "the so-called bandits," he added sarcastically.

"But if you really mean it," began the editor again, "then it must be a gigantic plot. If you think that the bandits—the Japanese——" he said, correcting himself.

"The Japanese outposts," interposed Halifax.

"Well, yes, the Japanese outposts, if you wish; if they have succeeded in destroying all railway connections with the West, then the enemy is no longer off our coast, but——"

A stenographer now rushed into the room with a new message. The editor glanced over it and then handed it to Halifax, who took the paper in both hands, and, while all listened attentively, read aloud the following telegram from Denver:

"According to uncertain dispatches, Sunday's attacks on trains were not made by gangs of robbers, but by detachments of Japanese troops, who have suddenly and in the most incomprehensible manner sprung up all over the country. Not only have single stations on the Union Pacific line been seized, but whole towns have been occupied by hostile regiments, the inhabitants having been taken so completely by surprise, that no resistance could be offered. The rumor of a battle between the Japanese ships and the coast defences at San Francisco has gained considerable currency. The concerted attacks on the various trans-continental lines have cut off the western States entirely from telegraphic communication and in addition interrupted all railway traffic."

The telegram shook in John Halifax's hands; he ran his fingers through his hair and looked at the editor, who could only repeat the words spoken by Halifax a few minutes before: "Gentlemen, I fear this means war."

Halifax collected the telegrams and went silently into his room, where he dropped into the chair before his desk, and sat staring in front of him with his head, full of confused thoughts, resting on his hands. "This means war," he repeated softly. Mechanically he took up his pen with the intention of putting his thoughts on paper, but not a line, not a word could he produce under the stress of these whirling sensations. Unable to construct a single sentence, he drew circles and meaningless figures on the white paper, scribbled insignificant words, only to cross them out immediately afterwards, and repeated again and again: "This means war."

Outside in the halls people hurried past; some one seized the door-knob, so he got up and locked himself in. Then he sat down again. The fresh, mild air blew in through the wide open windows, and the dull roar of the immense crowds in the street, now swelling and now retreating, floated up to him. His thoughts flew to the far West, and everywhere he could see the eager, industrious Asiatics pouring like a yellow flood over his country. He saw Togo's gray ships, with the sun-banner of Nippon, ploughing the waves of the Pacific; he saw the tremendous many-hued picture of a great international struggle; he saw regiments rush upon each other and clash on the vast prairies; he saw bayonets flashing in the sun; and he saw glittering troops of cavalry galloping over the bleak plains. High up in the air, over the two great opposing hosts, he saw the white smoke of bursting shells. He saw this gigantic drama of a racial war, which caused the very axis of the earth to quiver, unraveled before his eyes, and with ardent enthusiasm he seized his pen, at last master of himself once more.

Suddenly his mood of exaltation vanished; it seemed as though the sun had been extinguished, and cold, dark shadows fell across the brilliant picture of his imagination, subduing its colors with an ashy light. He began slowly to realize that this did not only mean war, but that it was his war, his country's war—a bitter struggle for which they were but poorly prepared. At this thought he shivered, and the man who had weathered many a storm laid his head down on both arms and cried bitterly. The mental shock had been too great, and it was in vain that they knocked at and shook his door. It was some time before John Halifax recovered his self-possession. Then he lifted his head bravely and proudly, and going to the door with a firm step, gave directions to the staff with the calmness of a veteran general.

CHAPTER V

FATHER AND SON

Mr. Horace Hanbury paced restlessly up and down his study, and presently stopped before a huge map on the wall and carefully traced the long lines of the trans-continental railroads across the Rocky Mountains. "Will Harriman sell? No, he'll buy, of course he'll buy; he'd be an idiot if he didn't. Of course he'll buy, and Gould and Stillman will buy, too. Well, there'll be a fine tussle in Wall Street to-day." Thus he soliloquized, puffing thoughtfully at his short pipe. Then he picked up the heap of narrow tape on his desk containing the latest news from the West, and read the reports once more as the paper slipped through his fingers.

"This fiendish plot of the yellow curs seems to be a pretty clever one," he murmured; "they've simply cut off all railway connections. I can't help admiring the fellows—they've learned a lot since 1904." He threw himself into his comfortable Morris chair, and after having carefully studied the Stock Exchange quotations of Saturday, went once more to the map on the wall, and marked several spots with a blue pencil; these he connected by means of a long line which cut off the Pacific States of Washington, Oregon, and California, and large districts of Nevada and Arizona from all communication with points to the East. He then looked at his watch and pressed one of the electric buttons on his desk.

The door opened noiselessly, and an East Indian, dressed in the bright costume of his native country, entered, and, crossing his arms, made a deep bow. "When Mr. Gerald Hanbury returns, tell him I want to see him immediately." The Indian disappeared, and Mr. Hanbury sat down on his desk, folded his hands under his knees, and swung his feet to and fro, puffing out the smoke of his pipe from between his teeth. "If only the boy won't spoil everything with his ridiculous altruistic ideas— Ah, Gerald, there you are!"

"Did you send for me, father?"

"Sit down, my boy," said the old gentleman, pointing to a chair; but he himself remained sitting on the desk.

The son was the very image of his father—the same slender, muscular figure, the same piercing eyes, the same energetic mouth. "Well, father, what do you think of it?"

"Think of it? What do *you* think of it?"

"Isn't it awful, this sudden attack on our country? Isn't it awful the way we have been taken by surprise? Think of it, three of our States in the enemy's hands!"

"We'll soon get them back, don't worry about that," said the old gentleman calmly.

"Have you read the orders for mobilization?"

"I haven't read them, and don't intend to."

"Colonel Smiles told me just now that it will not be possible to dispatch our troops to the West in less than three weeks. Fortunately there are about a dozen ships of the Pacific fleet off the west coast, and they will be able to attack the Japanese in the rear."

"If there's still time," supplemented his father. "Anyhow, we can leave these matters to others. It's none of our business; they can attend to all that at Washington. War is purely and simply a question of finances so far as the United States is concerned, and it's as plain as day that we can hold out ten times longer than those yellow monkeys. That the money will be forthcoming goes without saying; Congress will do all that is needed in that direction, and the subscriptions for the war-loan will show that we are fully prepared along that line. So let us drop that subject. The question is, what shall we do? What do you propose doing with our factory during the war?"

"Go on working, of course, father."

"Go on working—that is to say, produce surplus stock. If we go on working we shall have goods on our hands which no one will buy, and be compelled to store them. Ironclads, cannon, powder, uniforms, guns, these are the things for which there is a demand now; whisky, too, will be bought and bread will be baked, and the meat trust will make money hand over fist; but do you suppose the United States Government is going to buy our pianos to play tunes to the soldiers?"

"But what about our workmen?" interposed Gerald.

"Yes, our workmen," said the old gentleman, jumping energetically off the desk and standing before his son with his legs wide apart and his hands in his pockets: "Our workmen—that brings us to your favorite subject, to which you devote your entire time and interest!" He transferred his pipe into the right-hand corner of his mouth and continued: "I intend to dismiss our workmen, my boy, and shut up shop; we couldn't earn a cent more even if we kept the machines going. Besides, our Government needs soldiers now, not workmen. Let your dear workmen shoulder their guns and march to the West. When I was your age, and starting in with one hundred and fifty dollars in my pocket, no one offered me pensions for sickness and old age or insurance against non-employment or whatever this new-fangled nonsense is called. We ought to increase the energy of the people, instead of stuffing pillows for them. A man who has anything in him will make his way even in these times."

"Father!" The young man jumped up from his chair and faced his father with all the idealistic enthusiasm of youth.

"Keep your seat, my boy, subjects of this nature can be better discussed sitting."

"No, father, I can't keep still. This question concerns four thousand workmen and their families."

"Three thousand of whom I shall dismiss at noon to-day," interrupted the old gentleman decisively.

"What! You don't mean to say you'll send three thousand workmen, quiet, industrious, faithful, reliable workmen, begging to-day? Why, father! That would be perfectly barbarous, that would be a crime against humanity! The people have stuck by us in days of prosperity, and now when our sales may perhaps," he emphasized the last word, "may perhaps be diminished, you will stop the wheels and shut down the factory?"

"Look here, my son, I'm not a socialists' meeting. Such sentiments may sound very nice from the platform, but there's no need of your trying your speeches on me. The question at issue is, shall we suffer the consequences or shall they, and I don't mind telling you that I prefer the latter. Do you suppose that I've worked hard all my life and worn myself out for the express purpose of turning our factory into a workingmen's home? No, my boy, I can't support you in your little hobby."

"But, father, capital and labor——"

"O, cut out those silly phrases," interrupted the old gentleman irritably, "Karl Marx and Henry George and all your other stand-bys may be all right in your library, and help to decorate your bookshelves, but I prefer to settle our practical problems on the basis of my experience and not of your books. As manager and proprietor of our plant I want to tell you that when the whistle blows at noon to-day I shall notify our workingmen that in consequence of the totally unforeseen breaking out of hostilities—here I shall insert a few words about the sacred duty of patriotism and of defending one's country—we are unwillingly forced to dismiss three thousand of our workmen. We'll pay wages for, let's say, a fortnight longer, but then good-by to the men; we'll shut up shop, and the thousand men that are left can finish the standing orders and any new ones that may come in. And if no new ones turn up, then the remaining workingmen will be dismissed at once. In the meantime I'll subscribe one hundred thousand dollars to the war-loan, and then engage passage on a Lloyd steamer, the most expensive cabins with every possible luxury, for your mother, your two sisters, myself, and I hope for you, too, and we'll be off to old Europe. Shall we make it the Riviera? We've been there before, and, besides, it's a little too hot there now—let's say Norway or Switzerland. In my humble opinion we had better watch developments from a distance, and, as I said, I earnestly hope that my only son and heir will join our party, unless he should prefer to remain here and become a lieutenant in our glorious army and draw his sword against the enemy? This is my final decision and the last word I have to say on the subject, unless you think that some friend of ours in the financial world may have a better suggestion to offer."

"I should never have thought, father, that you could be so hard-hearted and unfeeling, that you could be capable of ruining the lives of thousands with one stroke of your pen. Your attitude towards the relations between employer and employee is absolutely incomprehensible to me; the socialistic conscience——"

"Listen, my boy," said the old gentleman, going over to his son and laying his hand gently on his shoulder: "I've always allowed you an absolutely free hand in your schemes, and you know we've always tried to meet our employees more than half way in all their wishes, but now it's a question of who's to suffer—we or they? In times of peace there may be some excuse for these nice socialistic ideas: they give a man a certain standing and bring him into the public eye. There's a good man, they say; he understands the demands of the times. But there's a limit to everything. One man rides one hobby, and some one else another. One keeps a racing-stable, another sports a steam-yacht, and still another swears by polo or cricket, but these things must not be carried to excess. The minute the owner of the racing-stable turns jockey, he ceases to be a business man, and the same is true of the man who keeps a racing-yacht and spends all of his time at the start, and, after all is said and done, it's our business we want to live on. You've selected the workingman as your favorite sport, and that also has its limits. If we squander our hard-earned millions on socialistic improvements now, we'll have to begin over again in about two years' time. I doubt whether I should have sufficient genius left to discover a new piano-hammer, and I entertain still more serious doubts as to your ability to invent a panacea that will render the whole world happy and make you richer instead of poorer. *Ergo*, we'll shut up shop. In Hoboken we'll sing Yankee Doodle and as we pass the Statue of Liberty The Star Spangled Banner, in token of farewell, and then off we go! If things turn out better than we anticipate, we can come back, but this is my last word for the present: At noon the following notice will be posted at all the entrances and in all the rooms of our factory: 'Three thousand workmen are herewith dismissed; wages will be paid for a fortnight longer, when the factory will be closed indefinitely.' By the way, are you going to the Stock Exchange to-day?"

"I'm not in a mood for the Stock Exchange, father. If that is your last word, then my last word is: I am your partner— —"

"So much the worse," said the father.

"—and therefore have a right to dispose as I please of my interest in the business. I therefore demand the immediate payment of so much of my inheritance as will be required to pay the wages of the workmen you've dismissed for at least another year, with the exception of the single men who enter the army."

"No, my boy, we won't do anything of the sort. Don't forget that I'm running this business. According to the contract made when you came of age, you may demand a million dollars upon severing your connection with the firm. This sum will be at your disposal at the bank to-day at noon, but not a cent more. What you do with it is a matter of complete indifference to me, but let me remind you that ordinarily when a man throws money out of the window, he at least likes to hear it drop."

"That surely cannot be your last word, father, otherwise we must part."

"All right, my boy, let's part till dinner-time. I hope to find you in a more sensible frame of mind when the family assembles this evening. I've told you what will be done in the factory in the meantime, and as for our trip, we'll discuss that to-night with your mother. Now leave me, I must get ready for Wall Street."

The door closed noiselessly after Mr. Hanbury, Junior. "The scamp," said the father to himself, "I can't help admiring him. Thirty years ago I entertained just such ideas, but what has become of them!" He thought a moment, passed his hand over his forehead, then jumped up quickly and exclaimed: "Now to work!" He pressed a button on the desk, his secretary entered, and the conversation that ensued dealt exclusively with coming events in Wall Street.

CHAPTER VI
A NIGHT IN NEW YORK

The *New York Daily Telegraph* had already issued several regular editions and a number of extras, without really having conveyed much definite information, for the dispatches consisted for the most part of rumors that arose like distant lightning on the western horizon, and it was quite impossible to ascertain just where. A dark bank of clouds lay over the Pacific States, completely shutting in the territory that had been cut off from all communication, both by wire and rail. The natural supposition was, that the Japanese outposts were stationed at the points just beyond which to the east telegraphic communication had not yet been interrupted, but the messages that were constantly pouring in from places along this border-line revealed clearly that these outposts were continually pushing further eastwards. A serious battle didn't seem to have occurred anywhere. The utter surprise caused by the sudden appearance of the Japanese troops, who seemed to spring up out of the ground, had from the very beginning destroyed every chance of successful resistance.

Shortly after the first vague rumors of battles said to have been fought at San Francisco, Port Townsend, and Seattle, had arisen, even these sources of information ran dry. The question from where all the hostile troops had come, remained as much of a riddle as ever. That was a matter of indifference after all; the chief consideration was to adopt measures of defense as speedily as possible.

But the War Department worked slowly, and the news received from headquarters at Washington consisted only of the declaration that the regulars were going to be sent to the West immediately, that the President had already called out the reserves, and that Congress would meet on May eleventh to discuss means for placing the militia on a war-footing and for creating an army of volunteers. The regular army! Three States with their regiments and their coast-defenses had to be deducted at the very start. What had become of them? Had they been able to hold their own between the enemy and the coast? What had happened to the Philippines and to Hawaii? Where was the fleet? None of these questions could be answered, simply because all telegraphic connection was cut off. The strength of the enemy was an absolutely unknown quantity, unless one cared to rely on the figures found in the ordinary military statistics, which had probably been doctored by the Japanese. Was this the Japanese army at all? Was it an invading force? Could such a force have pushed so far to the East in such a short space of time after landing? The press could find no satisfactory answer to these questions, and therefore contented itself with estimating the number of American soldiers available after subtracting the three coast States. The newspapers also indulged in rather awkward calculations as to when and how the troops could best be dispatched to the invaded territory. But this optimism did not last long and it convinced nobody.

Another serious question was, how would the masses behave upon the breaking-out of this sudden danger, and what attitude would be assumed by the foreign elements of the population. It was most important to have some inkling as to how the Germans, the Irish, the Scandinavians, the Italians and the various people of Slavonic nationality would act when called upon to defend their new country. It was of course absolutely certain that the two great political parties—the Republicans and the Democrats—would work together harmoniously under the stress of a common danger.

Francis Robertson, the well-known reporter of the *New York Daily Telegraph*—called the Flying Fish on account of his streaming coat-tails—had been on the go all day. He had scarcely finished dictating the shorthand notes made on his last tour of inspection, to the typewriter, when he received orders—it was at seven o'clock in the evening—to make another trip through the streets and to visit the headquarters of the various national and political societies. First he went to a restaurant a few doors away, and in five minutes succeeded in making way with a steak that had apparently been manufactured out of the hide of a hippopotamus. Then he jumped into a taxicab and directed the chauffeur at the corner of Twenty-ninth Street to drive as quickly as possible through the crowd down Broadway. But it was impossible for the chauffeur on account of the mob to move at more than a snail's pace, and the cab finally came to a dead stop at Madison Square, which was packed with excited people. Robertson left the cab and hurled himself boldly into the seething mass of humanity, but soon discovered that if he wished to make any progress at all he would have to allow himself to be carried forward by the slowly moving crowd. At the corner of Twenty-second Street he managed to disentangle himself and hurried through the block, only to find a new crowd on Fourth Avenue.

He intended to cross Fourth Avenue and then push on to Third Avenue, in order to reach Tammany Hall by that route, but he was doomed to disappointment, for the human stream simply carried him down Fourth Avenue as far as Union Square, where it ceased moving for a time. Presently it got under way again, proceeding even more slowly than before, and Robertson soon found himself in the middle of the square, being suddenly pushed against the basin of the fountain upon which he climbed for the double purpose of regaining his breath and of looking around to see if it were possible to make his way through to Tammany Hall. In vain! His eyes were greeted by an interminable sea of heads and hats, which did not offer the slightest chance of his being able to slip through. The trees, the statues and the fountain in the square appeared to be buried to a height of two yards in a black flood. He looked longingly across Sixteenth Street over to Third Avenue, but nowhere could he find an opening.

He felt like a ship-wrecked mariner cast ashore on a desert island. The sullen roar of the crowd echoed against the buildings enclosing the square like the dull boom of the surf. Over on Third Avenue the yellow lights of the elevated cars crossed the dark opening of Sixteenth Street at regular intervals, and recalled to Robertson a piece of scenery at a fair, where a lighted train ran continually between the mouths of two tunnels in the mountains. He pulled out his note-book and by the light of the electric arc-lamp made a note of the observation.

Then he jumped down from the ledge where he had taken refuge and once more joined the human stream. The latter, as if animated by a common purpose, was moving downtown, and if Robertson's neighbors were properly posted, it was headed for the Chinese quarter. It was evident that they intended to vent their fury for the present on these allies of the Japanese. This longing for revenge, this elementary hatred of the yellow race kept the crowd in Union Square in motion and shoved everyone without discrimination towards Broadway and Fourth Avenue. The square resembled a huge machine, which by means of some hidden automatic power forced tens of thousands of unresisting bodies into the narrow channels. The crowd rolled on unceasingly. Here and there a hat flew off into the air, came down again, bobbed up and down once or twice, and then continued its journey somewhere else on the surface. It was fortunate that those who had become insensible from the dreadful noise and the foul, dusty air were unable to fall down; they were simply held up by the close pressure of their neighbors and were carried along until a few blocks farther on they regained consciousness. Nevertheless a few fell and disappeared in the stream without leaving a trace behind them. No pen could describe their terrible fate; they must have been relentlessly ground to pieces like stones on the rocky bed of a glacier.

Above this roaring stream of human beings there swept unceasingly, in short blasts like a tearing whirlwind, the hoarse cry of a people's passion: "Down with the yellow race! Down with the Japanese! Three cheers for the Stars and Stripes!" The passionate cry of a crowd thirsting for revenge rose again and again, as if from a giant's lungs, until the cheers and yells of "down" turned into a wild, deafening, inarticulate howl which was echoed and re-echoed a thousand times by the tall buildings on both sides of the avenue. Now and then an electric street-car, to which clung hundreds of people, towered like a stranded vessel above the waving mass of heads and hats.

Robertson decided to give up the idea of reaching Tammany Hall and to drift with the crowd to the Chinese quarter. At Astor Place a branch of the human stream carried him to the Bowery, where he found himself on the edge of the crowd and was scraped roughly along the fronts of several houses. He stood this for another block, but determined to escape at the next corner into a side street. Before he could reach it, however, he was crushed violently against the wall of a house and turned round three or four times by the advancing throng; during this maneuver his right coat-tail got caught on something and before he knew it, he had left the coat-tail behind. At last he reached the corner and clung tightly to a railing with his right hand, but the next moment he flew like a cork from a champagne-bottle into the quiet darkness of Fifth Street, bumping violently against several men who had been similarly ejected from the current and who pushed him roughly aside.

Robertson was bursting with rage, for just before he had been propelled into Fifth Street, he had caught a glimpse of the grinning face of Bob Traddles, of the

Tribune, his worst competitor, only a few feet away. The latter showed clearly how delighted he was at this involuntary discomfiture of his rival in the mad race for the latest sensational news. Robertson attempted for a while to get back into the current, but all of his efforts proved futile. Then he tried at least to find out what the people intended to do, and in spite of the contradictory information he received, he was pretty well convinced that they were really going to make an attack on the inhabitants of the Chinese quarter. Although hopelessly separated from Tammany Hall by the countercurrent of the human stream, he at last succeeded in reaching the Eighth Street station of the Second Avenue Elevated, where he took an uptown train to Forty-second Street. Then he walked over to Third Avenue and took a downtown train, which was crowded to suffocation, as far as Grand Street, for the purpose of reaching the Chinese quarter from the uptown side. The trip had consumed fully two hours. At the crossing of Grand and Mott Streets he found the entrance to the latter barred by a line of policemen standing three deep. He showed his badge to a sergeant and received permission to pass.

The dead silence of Mott Street seemed almost uncanny after the noisy roar of the mob, the echoes of which still rang in his ears. The basements of the houses were all barricaded with shutters or boards, the doors were locked, and there was scarcely a light to be seen in the windows of the upper stories. A person paying his first visit to this busy, bustling ant-hill of yore would, if he had not been reminded by the peculiar penetrating smell of the yellow race of their proximity, scarcely have believed that he was really in the notorious Chinese quarter of New York.

The policeman who acted as Robertson's guide told him that they had known all about the movements and intentions of the mob long before it had reached the police headquarters, by way of the Bowery and Elm Street, and begun to force its way from the Bowery through some of the side streets into the Chinese quarter. Fearing that the latter would be set on fire, the chief of police had given orders to protect it from the irresponsible mob by barricading the streets with all the available members of the force. In this attempt, however, they had been only partially successful. It was out of the question for six hundred men to hold out against tens of thousands; the enormous pressure from the rear had hurled the front rows like driftwood against the thin chain of policemen, which, after a stubborn resistance, had simply been broken through at several spots.

A hand-to-hand fight had ensued and shots were soon fired on both sides, so that the police had to content themselves with an effort to check the worst excesses. Then, too, the spirit of patriotism was just as rampant in the breasts of the police as it was in the breasts of those who urged on the mob. As it was impossible to catch hold of the treacherous invaders themselves, their natural allies should at least not escape unscathed. The Chinese were of course prepared for such an attack. The howling, raging mob found barricaded doors and windows wherever they went, and even when they did succeed, after considerable labor, in breaking these down, it was usually only to find that the birds had flown, that the occupants had made their escape in time. Wherever resistance had been offered by the Chinese, the mob had gone beyond all bounds in its frenzy.

"Several hundred Chinamen must have been killed," said the policeman, "and it would be best for the papers to hush up what went on inside the houses." Robertson and his companion stopped near a lamp-post, and the former hurriedly made some shorthand notes of all the information he had received.

"Look," said the policeman, "Judge Lynch has done his work well," and he pointed with his club to a lamp-post on the other side of the street from which two dark bodies were hanging. "Simply hanged 'em," he added laconically.

As the policeman would not allow him to enter any of the houses because, as he said, it meant certain death, Robertson decided to go to the nearest telephone pay-station in order to 'phone his story to the paper. The policeman went with him as far as the police-station. By the uncertain light of the street-lamps they stumbled along the pavement, which was often almost entirely hidden by heaps of rubbish and regular mountains of refuse. They saw several more bodies suspended from lamp-posts, and the blood on the pavement before many of the mutilated houses testified eloquently to the manner in which the mob had wreaked its vengeance on the sons of the Celestial Kingdom. Ambulance officers were carrying away the wounded and dead on stretchers, and after Robertson had stayed a little while at the police-station and received information as to the number of people killed thus far, he walked in the direction of Broadway, having found the entrance to the Subway closed.

At Broadway he again came upon a chain of police, and learned that the troops had been called out and that a battalion was marching up Broadway.

Robertson plunged once more into the seething human whirlpool, but made little progress. For about fifteen minutes he stood, unable to move, near a highly excited individual, who, with a bloody handkerchief tied around his head and with wild gesticulations was reciting his experiences during the storming of a Chinese house. This was his man. A momentary lull in the roar around him gave him a chance of getting closer to him and screaming into his ear: "I'll give you two dollars if you'll step into the nearest hallway with me and tell me that story!"

The man stared at him in astonishment but when Robertson added, "It's for the *New York Daily Telegraph*," he was posted at once. They made their way with considerable difficulty to the edge of the crowd and managed to squeeze into a wide doorway full of people, whose attention, however, was not directed to the doings on Broadway, but rather to a meeting that was being held in a large rear room. Robertson managed to find an unoccupied chair in a neighboring room, which was packed to the door, and sitting astride it, proceeded to use the back of the chair as a rest for his note-book. The story turned out to be somewhat disjointed, for every time a push from the crowd sent the man flying against the hard wall, he uttered a long series of oaths.

"For Heaven's sake," said Robertson, "quit your swearing! Make a hole in the wall behind you and hustle with your story!"

"This'll mean at least a column in the *Telegraph*," mused Robertson as the story neared its end. But he was already listening with one ear to what was going on in the big room, whence the sharp, clear tones of a speaker could be heard through the suffocating tobacco fumes. Over the heads of the attentive crowd hung a few gas-lamps, the globes of which looked like large oranges. Robertson gave his Mott Street hero the promised two dollar bill and then made his way to the rear room. Standing in the doorway, he could clearly distinguish the words of the speaker, who was apparently protesting in the name of some workmen against a large manufacturer who had at noon dismissed three thousand of them.

The orator, who was standing on a table in the rear of the room, looked like a swaying shadow through the smoke, but his loud appeal completely filled the room, and the soul-stirring pictures he drew of the misery of the workmen, who had been turned out on the streets at the word of the millionaire manufacturer, caused his hearers' cheeks to burn with excitement.

"—and therefore," concluded the speaker, "we will not submit to the absolutely selfish action of Mr. Hanbury. As leader of our Union I ask you all to return to work at the factory to-morrow at the usual hour, and we will then assert our right to employment by simply continuing our work and ignoring our dismissal. Of course the simplest and most convenient thing for Mr. Hanbury is to shut down his plant and skip with his millions to the other side. But we demand that the factory be kept running, and if our wages aren't paid, we'll find means for getting them. Our country cannot fight the enemy even with a thousand millionaires. When the American people take the field to fight for the maintenance of American society and the American state, they have a right to demand that the families they are compelled to leave at home shall at least be suitably cared for. Again I say: We'll keep Mr. Hanbury's factory open."

The air shook with thunderous applause, and a firm determination lighted up hundreds of faces, wrinkled and scarred from work and worry. And who would have dared oppose these men when animated by a single thought and a common purpose? Again and again enthusiastic shouts filled the room, and the speaker was assured that not a man present would fail to be on hand the next morning.

Leaning against the door-post, Robertson made notes of this occurrence also and then looked round in a vain endeavor to find a means of escape from the suffocating atmosphere. While doing so his glance fell on the spot where only a few moments before he had observed the swaying shadow of the speaker. The latter's place had been taken by another, who was making a frantic but vain effort to secure quiet and attention. With his arms waving in the air he looked through the murky atmosphere for all the world like a quickly turning wind-mill.

Gradually the applause ceased, while everybody in the room, Robertson included, was startled by the announcement of the chairman that Mr. Hanbury was most anxious to address the assemblage. A moment of astonished silence and then Bedlam broke loose. "What, Mr. Hanbury wants to speak?" "Not the old one, the young one!" "He must be mad. What does he want here?" "Three cheers for Mr. Hanbury!" "Down with him! We don't want him here, we can manage our own affairs!" "Let him speak!" "Three cheers for Mr. Hanbury!" "Be quiet, damn you, why don't you shut up?" These and other similarly emphatic shouts reached Robertson's ears. He hunted for his last pencil in his vest-pocket, and when he looked up again, he saw through the cloud of smoke a tall, refined person standing on the table.

"We don't want to be discharged! Don't let our wives starve!" the voices began again, and it was some time before it became possible for the speaker to make himself heard.

"Is that really Mr. Hanbury?" Robertson asked one of his neighbors.

"Yes, the son."

"It seems incredible! He's taking his life in his hands."

Gerald Hanbury's first words were lost in the uproar, but gradually the crowd began to listen. He spoke only a few sentences, and these Robertson took down in shorthand:

"—The demand just made by your speaker, and supported by all present, that my father's factory should not be shut down in these turbulent times, was made by myself this very morning, the moment I heard the news of the base attack on our country. I don't want any credit for having presented the matter to my father in most vigorous fashion, and I regret to say I have accomplished nothing thus far. But the same reasons which you have just heard from the lips of Mr. Bright have guided me. I, too, should consider it a crime against the free American people, if we manufacturers were to desert them in this hour of national danger. I am not going to make a long speech; I have come here simply to tell you that I shall go straight to my father from here and offer him the whole of my fortune from which to pay you your wages so long as the war lasts, and not only those employed in the factory, but also the families of those who may enter the army to defend their homes and their country."

Such an outburst of passionate enthusiasm, such wild expressions of joy as greeted this speech Robertson had never witnessed. The crowd screamed and yelled itself hoarse, hats were thrown into the air, and pandemonium reigned supreme. Mr. Hanbury was seized by dozens of strong arms as he jumped down from the table and was carried through the room over the heads of the crowd. After he had made the rounds of the hall several times and shaken hundreds of rough hands, the group of workmen surrounding the foreman on whose shoulders young Hanbury was enthroned marched to the entrance, while the whole assembly joined in a marching song.

By pure chance Robertson found himself near this group as they came to a halt before the door, just in time to save Mr. Hanbury from having his skull smashed against the top. So they let him slide down to the ground, and then the whole crowd made a rush for the Broadway entrance. Such a jam ensued here, that another meeting was held on the spot, which, however, consisted chiefly in cheers for Mr. Hanbury.

Suddenly some one shouted: "We'll go with Mr. Hanbury to his father!" Inch by inch they moved towards Broadway, whence a terrific roar and wild shouts greeted the ears of the closely packed mass at the entrance.

Robertson was standing close to Mr. Hanbury, whose face shone with happy excitement. Just as they reached the entrance to the street, the crowd outside suddenly started to run north in mad haste.

"This is the proudest day of my life as an American citizen!" said Robertson to Hanbury. Hardly had he finished the sentence, when a crashing sound like thunder rent the air and resounded down the whole length of Broadway, as if the latter were a cañon surrounded by precipitous walls of rock.

"They're firing on the people," burst from thousands of lips in the wildest indignation.

Some one shouted: "Pull out your revolvers!" and in response red sparks flashed here and there in the crowd and the rattle of shots greeted the troops marching up Broadway. The mob seemed to be made up largely of Russians.

Just in front of Robertson and Gerald Hanbury a young woman, who had been wounded by a stray shot, lay on the pavement screaming with pain and tossing her arms wildly about.

"Three cheers for Mr. Hanbury!" came the loud cry once more from the entrance. At this instant a big workman, apparently drunk, and dressed only in shirt and trousers, stepped in front of the door, and swinging the spoke of a large wheel in his right hand shouted: "Where's Mr. Hanbury?" And some one shouted as in reply: "The blackguard has turned three thousand workmen out on the streets today so that he can go traveling with his millions." The workman yelled once more: "Where is Mr. Hanbury?" Gerald moved forward a step and, looking the questioner straight in the eye, said: "I'm Mr. Hanbury, what do you want?"

The workman glared at him with wild, bloodshot eyes and cried in a fierce rage: "That's what I want," and quick as a flash the heavy spoke descended on Hanbury's head. The terrific blow felled Gerald to the ground, and he sank without uttering a sound beside the body of the wounded woman lying at his feet.

Robertson flew at the drunken brute as he prepared for a second blow, but some of the other laborers had already torn his weapon out of his hand, and, as if in answer to this base murder, the troops discharged a fresh volley only a hundred yards away, which was again received with shots from dozens of revolvers.

Robertson felt a stinging pain in his left arm and, in a sudden access of weakness, he leaned for support against the doorway. His senses left him for a moment, and when he came to, he saw a company of soldiers passing the spot where he stood. The next instant the butt-end of a musket pushed him backwards into the doorway.

"This is madness!" he cried. "You're firing on the people."

"Because the people are murdering and plundering downtown!" answered an officer. Gradually the tumult calmed down. Another company passed by Robertson, who had sat down on the step before the door. He examined his arm and found that he was uninjured; a stone splinter must have struck his left elbow, for the violent pain soon disappeared. The mob was quickly lost to view up Broadway, while some ambulance surgeons appeared on the other side of the street. Robertson called over to them and told them Mr. Hanbury had been murdered, whereupon they crossed the street at once.

Gerald Hanbury's corpse was lifted on a stretcher.

"How terrible, they've broken in his skull," said one of the surgeons, and taking a gray shawl from the shoulders of the charwoman who was writhing with agony, he threw it over the upper part of Gerald's body.

"Where shall we take it?" asked one of the surgeons.

"To Mr. Hanbury's house, two blocks north," directed Robertson, and going up to one of the surgeons he added: "I'll take your place at the stretcher, for you can make yourself useful elsewhere."

"How about her?" asked one of the ambulance attendants, pointing to the woman on the ground.

"I'm afraid we can't do much for her," replied one of the surgeons, "she seems to be near death's door."

Then the men lifted their burden and slowly the sad procession walked up Broadway, which was now almost deserted.

A few shots could still be heard from the direction of Union Square; to the left the sky was fiery red while clouds of smoke traveled over the high buildings on Broadway, shutting out the light of the stars. Robertson looked back. The street lay dark and still. Suddenly far away in the middle of the street two glaring white lights appeared and above them flared and waved the smoky flames of the petroleum torches, while gongs and sirens announced the approach of the fire-engines. And now they thundered past, the glaring lights from the acetylene lamps in front of the fire-engines lighting up the whole pavement. Streams of light and rushing black shadows played up and down the walls of the buildings. Next came the rattling hook and ladder wagons and the hosecarts, the light from the torches dancing in red and yellow stripes on the helmets of the firemen. And then another puffing, snorting engine, with hundreds of sparks and thick smoke pouring out of its wide funnel, hiding the vehicle behind it in dark clouds. They're here one moment, and gone the next, only to make way for another hook and ladder, which sways and rattles past. The clanging of the gongs and the yells of the sirens grow fainter and fainter, and finally, through the clouds of sparks and smoke the whole weird cavalcade was seen to disappear into a side-street. Little bits of smoldering wood and pieces of red-hot coal remained lying on the street and burned with quivering, quick little flames.

As they walked on the man next to Robertson told him why the troops had been compelled to interfere. The excited mob which had tasted blood, as it were, in the Chinese quarter and become more and more frantic, had continued plundering in some of the downtown streets without any discrimination—simply yielding to an uncontrollable desire for destruction. As a result a regular battle ensued between this mob, which consisted chiefly of Russian and Italian rabble, on one hand, and Irish workingmen who were defending their homes, on the other. The Russian contingent seemed to consist largely of the riff-raff which had found such a ready refuge in New York during the Russian Revolution, and some of these undesirable citizens now had recourse to dynamite. Some of the bombs caused great loss of life among the Irish people living in that part of town, and several policemen had also been killed in the performance of their duty. It was at this point that the authorities deemed it advisable to call out the troops, with whose arrival affairs immediately began to take on a different turn.

The soldiers did not hesitate to use their bayonets against the rabble. At several corners they encountered barricades, but they hesitated resorting to their firearms until several bombs were thrown among the troops while they were storming a barricade defended by Russian Terrorists. That was the last straw. With several volleys the soldiers drove the gang of foreign looters up Broadway, where a volley discharged near the spot where Gerald Hanbury had been murdered, dispersed the last compact mass of plunderers.

In the meantime the men had reached Mr. Hanbury's house and Robertson rang the bell. Not until they had rung loudly several times did the butler appear, and then only to announce gruffly that there was no one at home. A policeman ordered him to open the door at once, so that Mr. Hanbury's dead body might be brought in.

"But Mr. Hanbury is at home, you can't possibly have his dead body there!"

"Tell Mr. Hanbury right away!" interrupted the policeman. "It's young Mr. Hanbury, and he's been murdered. Open the door, do you hear!"

Silently the heavy bronze door turned on its hinges and, with the policeman in the lead, the men were ushered into the high marble entrance-hall of the Hanbury palace. They carried the stretcher on which lay the murdered body of the son of the house up the broad staircase, the thick carpets deadening the sound of their steps. At the top of the stairs they lowered their burden and waited in silence. Doors opened and shut in the distance; from one of them a bright stream of light fell on the shining onyx pillars and on the gilt frames of the paintings, which in the light from strange swinging lamps looked like huge black patches. Then the light from the door disappeared, a bell rang somewhere and figures hurried to and fro. A fantastically dressed East Indian next appeared and made signs to the ambulance-men to carry the stretcher into a room which, in its fabulous, Oriental splendor represented one of the most beautiful of the Indian mosques. The men carried their burden carefully into the middle of the room and then set it down and looked at one another in embarrassment. The policeman assumed a dignified posture and cleared his throat. Suddenly the heavy gold-embroidered curtain before one of the doors was pushed aside by a brown hand and fell back in heavy folds; an old white-haired man stood for a moment in the doorway and then advanced towards the officer with a firm step.

The latter cleared his throat again and then began in a dry and business-like tone to give his report of Gerald Hanbury's murder, ending with the words "— and these gentlemen picked him up and brought him here."

"I thank you, gentlemen," said the old man, and taking out his pocket-book he handed each of them, including Robertson, a twenty-dollar bill. Then he sat down wearily on the edge of the stretcher and rested his head in his hands. He seemed to be oblivious of his surroundings. The men stood round for a few moments not knowing what to do, until finally the policeman led the ambulance-men and Robertson to the door, which opened automatically.

As the Indian closed the door behind them the officer said to Robertson: "This is like the last act in a Third Avenue melodrama."

"Life has a liking for such plays," answered Robertson. As they left the Hanbury mansion the clock of Grace Church struck midnight. Robertson glanced down Broadway once more and saw that the long thoroughfare was almost deserted; only here and there the bluish-white light from the electric lamps shone on the bayonets of the sentinels patrolling up and down at long intervals. Then he repaired to the *Daily Telegraph* offices to dictate his notes, so that the huge rolls of printed paper might announce to the world to-morrow that the first victims of the terrible war had fallen on the streets of New York.

The factory of Horace Hanbury & Son was not shut down.

CHAPTER VII
THE RED SUN OVER THE GOLDEN GATE

Too-oo-ot, bellowed the whistle of a big steamer that was proceeding gingerly through the fog which enveloped the broad Bay of San Francisco early on the morning of May seventh. The soft, white mist crept through the Golden Gate among the masts and funnels of the ships made fast to the docks, enveloped the yellow flame of the lanterns on the foremast in a misty veil, descended from the rigging again, and threatened to extinguish the long series of lights along the endless row of docks. The glistening bands of light on the Oakland shore tried their best to pierce the fog, but became fainter and fainter in the damp, penetrating, constantly moving masses of mist. Even the bright eye on Angel Island was shut out at last. Too-oo-ot, again sounded the sullen cry of warning from the steamer in the Golden Gate—Too-oo-ot. And then from Tiburon opposite the shrill whistle of the ferry-boat was heard announcing its departure to the passengers on the early train from San Rafael. The flickering misty atmosphere seemed like a boundless aquarium, an aquarium in which gigantic prehistoric, fabulous creatures stretched their limbs and glared at one another with fiery eyes. Trembling beams of light hovered between the dancing lights on and between the ships, rising and falling like transparent bars when the shivering sentries on deck moved their lanterns, and threw into relief now some dripping bits of rigging, and again the black outline of a deck-house as the sailor hurried below for a drink to refresh his torpid spirits.

The cold wind blew the damp fog into Market Street, forced it uphill and then let it roll down again, filling every street with its gray substance.

Too-oo-ot, came the whistle from the Golden Gate again and further off still another whistle could be heard. Over in Tiburon the ferry-boat had calmed down, as it found itself unable to budge in the fog. One after the other, the tower-clocks struck half-past four, the strokes sounding loud and unnatural in the fog. From Telegraph Hill at the northern end of San Francisco a splendid view could be obtained of this undulating sea of mist. A few of the isolated houses situated in the higher parts of the town looked like islands floating on the ever-moving glossy gray billows, while the top stories of several sky-scrapers rose up here and there like solemn black cliffs. A faint light in the east heralded the approach of day. Too-oo-ot, sounded the whistle of the approaching steamer once again; then its voice broke and died out in a discordant sob, which was drowned in the nervous gang, gang, gang of the ship's bell. The steamer had been obliged to anchor on account of the fog. Too-oo-ot, came from the other steamer further out. Then life in the bay came to a stand-still: nothing could be done till the sun rose and brought warmth in its train.

"This damned fog," said Tom Hallock, a telegraph boy, to his colleague, Johnny Kirkby, as he jumped off his bicycle in front of the Post Office, "this damned fog is enough to make one choke."

Johnny muttered some unintelligible words, for he was still half asleep; the effect of last night's eighteen drinks had not yet quite worn off. "You can't see the nearest lamp-post," he blurted out after a while. "I nearly ran into a company of infantry just now that suddenly popped up in front of me out of the fog. What's going on this morning, anyhow? What are they marching out to Golden Gate for?"

"Oh, you jay," said Tom, "naval maneuvers, of course! Are you blind? Haven't you read the *Evening Standard*? There are to be naval maneuvers this morning, and Admiral Perry is going to attack San Francisco."

"This war-game is a crazy scheme," grumbled Johnny. They both left their bicycles downstairs in a room in the Post Office and then went up to their quarters on the first story.

"Naval maneuvers?" began Johnny again. "I really don't know anything about them. It was in last night's *Evening Standard*. It said that the orders had been changed quite unexpectedly, and that the maneuvers would take place outside the bay to-day."

"It looks as though we'd have a long wait before daylight appears," said Tom impatiently, pointing out of the windows, while Johnny tackled the dilapidated tea-kettle in an effort to make himself an early morning drink. Tom stamped up and down the room to warm himself, remarking: "Thank the Lord it's Sunday and there isn't much going on, otherwise we'd all get sick chasing around with telegrams in this beastly fog."

Boom! The roar of a distant cannon suddenly made the windows rattle; boom again! It sounded as though it came from the Fort. "There you are," said Tom, "there's your naval maneuvers. Perry won't stand any nonsense. He's not afraid of the fog; in fact, it gives him a fine chance for an attack."

Johnny didn't answer, for he had meanwhile dozed off. As soon as he had with considerable trouble got his tea-kettle into working order, he had fallen fast asleep, and now began to snore with his nose pressed flat on the table, as if he meant to saw it through before his tea was ready.

Tom shrugged his shoulders in disgust, and said: "Those blamed drinks."

Another boom! from outside. The door opened behind Tom and a telegraph official looked in. "One, two," he counted, "two are there," and then he closed the door again.

Downstairs in the street a motor-cycle hurried past puffing and rattling, the rider's figure looking like a gigantic elusive shadow through the fog.

Tom started to walk up and down again as the clock in the hall struck a quarter to five. A bell rung in the next room. Steps were heard coming up the stairs and a colleague of the other two came in, swearing at the fog. He passed Johnny, poured out some of the latter's tea for himself and drank it, meanwhile looking at the sleeper inquiringly.

"It's the drinks," said Tom, grinning.

"H'm," growled the other. Another motor-cycle went by on the street below, and then another.

Later on a group of ten motor-cycles rode past.

"Did you see that, Harry?" asked Tom, who was standing at the window.

"What?"

"Didn't they have guns?"

"They probably have something to do with the naval maneuvers."

At this moment another group of ten men passed, and there was no doubt of the fact that they carried guns.

"I guess it is the naval maneuvers," asserted Tom.

Boom! came the sound of another shot.

"That's queer," said Tom. "What do you suppose it is?" He opened the window and listened. "Do you hear it?" he asked Harry, who admitted that he could also hear a rattling, scraping noise as though drums were being beaten far away or as though a handful of peas had been thrown against a pane of glass.

Tom leaned further out of the window in time to see a bicycle rider stop in front of the Post Office, take a big sheet of paper, moisten it with a large brush, and stick it on the wall near the entrance; then he rode off. Tom shut the window, for the fog seemed to be getting thicker and thicker, and now, in the pale light of approaching dawn, it was almost impossible to recognize the yellow spots of light on the lamp-posts. By this time Johnny had awakened and they all had some tea together.

They were interrupted by a fourth messenger boy, who entered the room at this moment and exclaimed:

"That's a great scheme of Admiral Perry's, and the fog seems to have helped him a lot. What do you think? He has surprised San Francisco. There's a notice posted downstairs stating that the Japanese have taken possession of San Francisco and that the Japanese military governor of San Francisco asks the citizens to remain quiet or the city will be bombarded from the harbor by the Japanese fleet."

"Perry is a great fellow, there's no use trying to fool with him," said Tom. "San Francisco surprised by the Japs—that's a mighty fine scheme."

Outside some one was tearing up the stairs two at a time, doors banged noisily, and several bells rang. "Somebody's in a h—- of a hurry," said Harry; "we'll have something to do in a minute."

A telegraph operator hurriedly opened the door and with great beads of perspiration rolling down his face, shouted at the top of his lungs: "Boys, the Japanese have surprised San Francisco."

A roar of laughter greeted this piece of information.

"Stung!" cried Harry. "Stung! Perry is the Jap."

"Perry?" inquired the newcomer, staring at the other four. "Who's Perry?"

"Don't you know, Mr. Allen, that there are naval maneuvers going on to-day and that Admiral Perry is to surprise San Francisco with the fleet?"

"But there are notices at all the street-corners saying that the Japanese governor of San Francisco begs the citizens— —"

"Yes, that's where the joke comes in. Perry is going to attack the town as a Jap—that's his scheme."

"You haven't had enough sleep," cried Tom. "If all the Japs looked like Admiral Perry, then— —"

Tom broke off short and dropped his tea-cup on the floor, staring blankly at the door as if he saw a ghost. Just behind Mr. Allen stood a Jap, with a friendly grin on his face, but a Jap all the same, most certainly and without the slightest doubt a Jap. He looked around the bare office and said in fluent English: "I must ask you to remain in this room for the present." With these words he raised his revolver and kept a sharp eye on the five occupants.

Johnny jumped up and felt instinctively for the revolver in his hip pocket, but in a flash the muzzle of the Jap's gun was pointed straight at him and mechanically he obeyed the order "Hands up!"

"Hand that thing over here," said the Jap; "you might take it into your head to use it," and he took Johnny's revolver and put it in his pocket. Several Japanese soldiers passed by outside. Mr. Allen sank down on a chair; not one of them could make head or tail of the situation.

They were kept waiting for half an hour. Down below in the street, where the wagons were beginning to rattle over the pavement, could be heard the steady march of bodies of soldiers, frequently interrupted by the noise of motor-cycles. There could no longer be any doubt—the affair was getting serious.

The lamps were extinguished and the gray light of dawn filled the rooms as the head Postmaster made his rounds, guarded by a Japanese officer.

The official was perspiring profusely from sheer nervousness. He begged the employees to keep calm, and assured them that it was no joke, but that San Francisco was really in the hands of the Japanese. It was the duty of the employees and the citizens, he said, to refrain from all resistance, so that a worse misfortune—a bombardment, he added in a whisper—might not befall the city.

The men were obliged to give up any weapons they had in their possession, and these were collected by the Japanese. At seven o'clock, when these details had been attended to, and the few telegraph instruments which were kept in commission were being used by Japanese operators—all the others had been rendered useless by the removal of some parts of the mechanism—one of the regular operators asked to be allowed to speak to the Postmaster. Permission having been granted by the Japanese guard, he told his chief, in a low voice, that the moment the Japanese soldiers had taken possession of the telegraph room he had hurriedly dispatched a message to Sacramento, telling them that San Francisco had been surprised by the Japanese fleet and that the whole city was occupied by Japanese troops.

"I thank you in the name of our poor country," said the Postmaster, shaking the operator's hand, "I thank you with all my heart; you have done a brave deed."

Just at the time when the operator sent off his telegram to Sacramento, a little, yellow, narrow-eyed fellow, lying in a ditch many miles inland, far to the east of San Francisco, connected his Morse apparatus with the San Francisco-Sacramento telegraph-wire, and intercepted the following message: "Chief of Police, Sacramento.—San Francisco attacked by Japanese fleet this morning; whole city in hands of Japanese army. Resistance impossible, as attack took place in thick fog before dawn. Help imperative."

The little yellow man smiled contentedly, tore off the strip, and handed it to the officer standing near him. The latter drew a deep breath and said: "Thank Heaven, that's settled."

At the time of the occupation of the Post Office building, the Japanese outposts had already spun their fine, almost invisible silver threads around all the telegraph-wires far inland and thus cut off all telegraphic communication with the east. The telegram just quoted therefore served only to tell the Japanese outposts of the overwhelming success of the Japanese arms at the Golden Gate.

But how had all this been accomplished? The enemy could not possibly have depended on the fog from the outset. Nevertheless an unusual barometrical depression had brought in its train several days of disagreeable, stormy weather. The Japanese had been fully prepared for a battle with the San Francisco forts and with the few warships stationed in the harbor. The fact that they found such a strong ally in the fog was beyond all their hopes and strategical calculations.

When the sun sank in the waves of the Pacific on the sixth of May, every Japanese had his orders for the next few hours, and the five thousand men whose part it was to attend to the work to be accomplished in San Francisco on the morning of the seventh, disappeared silently into the subterranean caves and cellars of the Chinese quarter, to fetch their weapons and be ready for action soon after midnight.

CHAPTER VIII

IN THE BOWELS OF THE EARTH

It was thought that the earthquake had done away forever with the underground labyrinth of the Chinese quarter—those thousands of pens inhabited by creatures that shunned the light of day, those mole-holes which served as headquarters for a subterranean agitation, the mysterious methods of which have never been revealed to the eye of the white man. When had the old Chinatown been laid out; when had those hidden warehouses, those opium dens and hiding-places of the Mongolian proletariat been erected, those dens in which all manner of criminals celebrated their indescribable orgies and which silently hid all these evil-doers from the far-reaching arm of the police? When had the new Chinatown sprung up? When had the new quarter been provided with an endless network of subterranean passages, so that soon all was just as it had been before the earthquake? No one had paid any attention to these things. The Mongolian secret societies never paused for a moment in their invisible conspiracy against the ruling whites, and succeeded in creating a new underground world, over which the street traffic rolled on obliviously.

A narrow cellar entrance and greasy, slippery steps led into Hung Wapu's store, behind which there was a chop-house, which in turn led into an opium-den. The rooms behind the latter, from which daylight was forever excluded, were reserved for still worse things. No policeman would ever have succeeded in raiding these dens of iniquity; he would have found nothing but empty rooms or bunks filled with snoring Chinese; the abominable stench would soon have driven him out again, but if, by any chance, he had attempted to penetrate further and to explore the walls for the purpose of discovering hidden openings, the only result would have been a story in the next day's papers about a "missing" policeman.

Hung Wapu, whose plump face, with its enormous spectacles, resembled that of an old fat boarding-house keeper, was standing at the entrance to his cellar-shop late on the evening of May sixth. A disgusting odor and the murmur of many voices reached the street from the cellar. The policeman had just made his rounds, and Hung Wapu looked after him with a cunning grin as his heavy steps died away in the distance.

The coast was clear for two hours. Hung Wapu went in and locked the door, above which a green paper-lantern swung gently to and fro in the soft night wind. Hung Wapu passed through the store to the chop-house, where several dozen Chinese were squatting on the ground dining on unmentionable Chinese delicacies, which consisted of anything and everything soft enough to be chewed. No one watching the vacant expression of these people would have dreamed for a moment that anything was wrong; no one observing these chattering, shouting sons of the Celestial Kingdom would have guessed that anything out of the ordinary was on foot. They kept on eating, and did not even look up when several Japs stole, one by one, through their midst and disappeared through a door at the back. The Japs apparently attracted no attention whatsoever, but a keen observer would have noticed that Hung Wapu placed a little saki-bowl on a low table for every Japanese visitor that had entered his shop.

The Japs all went through a side-door of the opium-den into a large room, where they took off their outer clothing and put on uniforms instead. Then they lay down to sleep either on the mats on the floor or on the bundles of clothing which were stacked on the floor along the walls of the room.

Hung Wapu now accompanied one of his Chinese guests up the cellar-steps to the street, and sitting down on the top step began to chat in a low voice with his apparently half-intoxicated countryman. At the same time he polished about two dozen little saki-bowls with an old rag, afterwards arranging them in long rows on the pavement.

The animated traffic in the narrow alley gradually died down. One by one most of the gas-lamps closed their tired eyes, and only the green paper-lantern above Hung Wapu's door continued to swing to and fro in the night-wind, while similar spots of colored light were visible in front of a few of the neighboring houses. Far away a clock struck the hour of midnight, and somewhere else, high up in the air, a bell rang out twelve strokes with a metallic sound. A cool current of air coming from the harbor swept through the hot, ill-smelling alley.

Hung Wapu went on whispering with his companion, and all the time he continued to polish his little saki-bowls. After a while the visitor fell asleep against the door-post and snored with all his might. Misty shadows began to fall slowly and the lights of the street lamps took on a red glow. Suddenly the figure of a drunken man appeared a little distance away; he was carefully feeling his way along the houses, but as soon as he came in sight of Hung Wapu's cellar, he suddenly seemed to sober up for a minute and made directly for it. "Saki!" he stammered, planting himself in front of Hung Wapu, whereupon the latter made a sign. The drunken man, a Japanese, whose face looked ghastly pale in the green light from the lantern, stared stupidly at the saki-bowls, which Hung Wapu was trying to shield from the tottering wretch with his arm.

"Twenty-eight bowls," he stammered to himself, "twenty-eight sa-ki-bowls ——"

At this moment the sleeping Chinaman awoke and looked at the drunken man with a silly laugh.

"Yes, twenty-eight saki-bowls; it's all right—twenty-eight saki-bowls," repeated the drunken Jap, and reeled on along the houses.

Hung Wapu seemed to have ended his day's work with the polishing of the twenty-eight saki-bowls; he piled them up in a heap and disappeared with them into his cellar, followed with extraordinary agility by the Chinese sleeper. He hurried through the chop-house, the occupants of which were all fast asleep on their straw mats, passed through the opium-den, and then, in the third room, divested himself of his Chinese coat. The silk-cap with the pigtail attached was flung into a corner, and then, dressed in a khaki uniform, he seated himself at a table and studied a map of the city of San Francisco, making notes in a small book by the light of a smoky oil lamp.

The drunken Jap, who had apparently had doubts about entering Hung Wapu's chop-house, tottered on down the quiet street and made for another paper-lantern, which hung above another cellar door about ten houses farther on.

Here too, curiously enough, he found the Chinese landlord sitting on the top step. He wanted to push him aside and stumble down the steps, but the Chinaman stopped him.

"How much?" stuttered the drunken man.

"How much?" answered the Chinaman. "How much money will the great stranger pay for a meal for his illustrious stomach in Si Wafang's miserable hut? Forty kasch, forty kasch the noble son of the Rising Sun must pay for a shabby meal in Si Wafang's wretched hut."

"Forty kasch? I'll bring the forty kasch, most noble Si Wafang. 'I won't go home till morning, till daylight does appear,'" bawled the tipsy man, and staggered on down the street, whereupon this landlord also disappeared in his cellar, after extinguishing the paper lantern over the doorway.

A death-like stillness reigned in the street, and no one imagined that the rats were assembling, that the underground passages were full of them, and that it only needed a sign to bring the swarming masses to the surface.

A cold breeze from the sea swept through the deserted streets and a misty veil enveloped the yellow light of the gas-lamps. The lanterns hanging in front of the Chinese cellars were extinguished one by one, and everyone apparently turned in. The fog became thicker and thicker, and covered the pavement with moisture.

Suddenly the door of Hung Wapu's cellar squeaked; it was opened cautiously and a low clatter came up from below. Thirty dark forms crept slowly up the steps, one after the other, and without a word they began their march. Ten houses farther on a similar detachment poured out of the other Chinese cellar and joined their ranks.

The gas-lamps shed a dull, yellowish-red light on the gun-barrels of the Japanese company, which was marching down to the docks.

Two thousand steps farther on it had become a battalion, which marched rapidly in the direction of the barracks of the Fifth Regiment of regulars in the old Presidio. At the next corner the leader of the battalion unobtrusively saluted a man in uniform who stepped suddenly out of a doorway. A few Japanese words were exchanged in a low tone.

"This is an unexpected ally," said the Japanese colonel, holding out his hand in the dense fog.

Four o'clock struck from the tower of the Union Ferry Depot, and out from the sea, from the Golden Gate, came the bellowing voice of a steamer's whistle. The two officers looked at each other and smiled, and the troops continued their march.

"Halloo!" shouted a roundsman to a policeman who had been leaning against a lamp-post half asleep. "Halloo, Tom, wake up! Who are those fellows over there; where the deuce are they going?"

Tom opened his eyes, and up on the hill, a few blocks away, he could faintly distinguish through the thick fog the outline of a group of rapidly moving soldiers. "I guess they are some of our boys taking part in the naval maneuver. You know, Perry's going to attack us to-day."

"Well, I didn't know that," replied the roundsman. "They're great boys, all right; up and about at four in the morning." Just then the angry bellow from a steamer's whistle came across the water and abruptly ended this early morning conversation.

"I suppose that's Perry now," said Tom. "Well, he can't do much in this beastly fog, anyway."

"So long, Tom," answered the roundsman curtly as he slowly proceeded to resume his interrupted rounds.

An advance guard of a few men had been sent ahead. They found the sentry at the barrack-gates fast asleep. When he awoke it was to discover himself surrounded by a dozen men. He stared at them, still heavy with sleep, and then reached mechanically for his gun; it was gone. He tried to pull himself together, felt something cold pressed against his right temple, and saw the barrel of a Browning pistol in the hand of the man in front of him.

"Hands up!" came the command in a low tone, and a few seconds later he was bound and gagged. As he lay on the ground, he saw a whole battalion of foreign soldiers half in the court-yard before the barracks, and vague thoughts of naval maneuvers and surprises, of Admiral Perry and the Japs went through his mind, till all at once the notion "Japs" caused him to sit up mentally—weren't these men real Japanese? And if so, what did it all mean?

In the meantime double guards had occupied all the men's quarters, in which Uncle Sam's soldiers began gradually to wake up. The guns and ammunition had long ago passed into the hands of the Japs, and when at last the reveille from a Japanese bugle woke up the garrison completely, there was nothing to be done but to grind their teeth with rage and submit to the inevitable. They had to form in line in the court-yard at eight o'clock, and then, disarmed and escorted by Japanese troops, they had to board the ferry-boats and cross over to Angel Island, while the cannon on Fort Point (Winfield Scott) thundered out the last notes of American resistance in San Francisco.

When, shortly after midnight, the guard had been relieved for the last time, and only a few sleepy soldiers remained in the sentry-boxes of the coast batteries of San Francisco, the enemy lay in ambush behind the coast-line, ready, to the last man, to rise at a given signal and render the unsuspecting American troops *hors de combat* in their sleep. And thus, before the sentinels had any idea what was going on, they were disarmed and gagged. Not a single cry or shot was heard to warn the sleeping soldiers. They awoke to find themselves confronted by Japanese bayonets and gun-barrels, and resistance was utterly useless, for the enemy, who seemed to be remarkably well posted, had already taken possession of the ammunition and arms.

And where, all this time, was Admiral Perry with his fleet? Nowhere. The Japanese had made no mistake in relying on the traditional love of sensation of the American press. The telegram sent on May sixth from Los Angeles to the San Francisco *Evening Standard* was nothing but a Japanese trick. It notified the *Standard* that Admiral Perry intended during the naval maneuvers (which were actually to take place within the next fortnight) to gain an entrance through the Golden Gate, and the Japanese felt certain that the editor would not make inquiries at the last moment as to the veracity of this report, which was not at all in accord with previous arrangements, but would print it as it was, more especially as it was signed by their usual correspondent.

Thus the Japanese had reason to hope that no immediate suspicions would be aroused by the appearance of warships in the Bay of San Francisco. And so it turned out. The five Japanese armored cruisers and the torpedo flotilla, which were to surprise and destroy the naval station and the docks, were able to cross the entire bay under cover of the fog without being recognized and to occupy the docks and the arsenal. Four mortar-boats threatened Point Bonita and Lime Point, till they both surrendered.

What could the two cruisers *New York* and *Brooklyn*, lying in dock for repairs, do without a single ball-cartridge on board? What was the good of the deck guards using up their cartridges before the red flag of Nippon was hoisted above the Stars and Stripes?

It is true there was a fight at one spot—out at Winfield Scott. Although the fog proved of great assistance to the Japanese in a hundred cases, the stipulated signal for attack, that is, the whistle of the Japanese auxiliary cruiser *Pelung Maru*, for example, being taken for a fog-signal, nevertheless an annoying surprise awaited the enemy elsewhere.

A steamer headed towards the Golden Gate in the wake of the *Pelung Maru* heard the roar of the sealions, and as this showed how near they were to the cliffs, the vessel dropped anchor and instead of blowing its whistle ordered the ship's bell to be rung. This was heard by the *Pelung Maru* a short distance ahead and interpreted as a sign that something had occurred to disturb the plan of attack. A steamlaunch was therefore sent out to look for the anchored ship.

The latter was the German steamer *Siegismund*, whose captain, standing on the bridge, suddenly saw a dripping little launch approaching with its flag trailing behind it in the water. And just as in every cleverly arranged plan one stupid oversight is apt to occur so it happened now. The launch carried the Japanese flag and the lieutenant at the helm called to the *Siegismund* in Japanese. As they were directly before the guns of the American batteries, the German captain didn't know what to make of it. He couldn't imagine what the launch from a Japanese warship could be doing here at dawn before the Golden Gate fortifications, and thinking that the fact would be likely to be of interest to the commander of the fort, he sent him the following wireless message: "Have just met launch of a Japanese warship off Seal-Rocks; what does it mean?"

This information alarmed the garrison at Winfield Scott, and the men at once received orders to man the guns. Then they waited breathlessly to see what would happen next.

An inquiry sent by wireless to the other stations remained unanswered, because these were already in the hands of the Japanese, whose operators were not quick-witted enough to send back a reassuring answer. As the commander of the fort received no answer, he became suspicious, and these suspicions were soon justified when a number of soldiers were discovered trying to force their way into the narrow land entrance of the fort. A few shots fired during the first bayonet assault and the bullets landing within the fort showed that it was a serious matter. Besides, a puff of wind dispersed the fog for a few seconds just then, and the shadowy silhouettes of several large ships became visible. Without a moment's hesitation the commander of Winfield Scott ordered the men to open fire on them from the heavy guns. These were the shots that had been heard at the San Francisco Post Office and Tom was quite right in thinking that he heard the rattle of musketry directly afterwards.

But with the small stock of ammunition doled out to the coast defenses in times of peace—there were plenty of blank cartridges for salutes—it was impossible to hold Winfield Scott. The fort sent out a few dozen shells into the fog pretty blindly, and, as a matter of fact, they hit nothing. Then began the hopeless battle between the garrison and the Japanese machine-guns, and although the shots from the latter were powerless to affect the walls and the armor-plating, still they worked havoc among the men. And the ammunition of the Americans disappeared even more quickly than their men, so that when at ten o'clock two Japanese regiments undertook to capture the fort by storm, the last defender fell with practically the last cartridge. Then the Rising Sun of Dai Nippon was substituted on the flagstaff of Winfield Scott for the Stars and Stripes.

In the city itself small Japanese guards were posted at the railway station, the Post Office and the telegraph offices, at the City Hall and at most of the public buildings, and as early as this, on the morning of May seventh, troops for the march eastward were being landed at the pier at Oakland. A standing garrison of only five thousand men was left in San Francisco, and these at once occupied the coast-batteries and prepared them for defense. The same thing was of course done with the docks and the naval station, with Oakland and all the other towns situated on the bay.

The sudden appearance of the enemy had in every case had a positively paralyzing effect. Among the inhabitants of the coast the terrible feeling prevailed everywhere that this was the end, that nothing could be done against an enemy whose soldiers crept out of every hole and cranny, and even when a few courageous men did unite for the purpose of defending their homes, they found no followers. It is a pity that others did not show the resolute courage of a Mexican fisherman's wife, who reached the harbor of San Francisco with a good catch early on Monday morning and made fast to the pier close to a Japanese destroyer. Almost immediately a Japanese petty officer came on board and demanded the catch for the use of the Japanese army. The woman, a coarse beauty with a fine mustache, planted herself in front of the Jap and shouted: "What, you shrimp, you want our fish, do you?" and seizing a good-sized silver fish lying on the deck, she boxed the astonished warrior's ears right and left till he fell over backwards into the water and swam quickly back to the destroyer, snorting like a seal, amidst the laughter of the bystanders.

The question naturally suggests itself at this point: Why didn't a people as determined as the Americans rise like one man and, arming themselves with revolvers and pistols and if it came to the worst with such primitive weapons as knives and spokes, attack the various small Japanese garrisons and free their country from this flood of swarming yellow ants? The white handbills posted up at every street corner furnished the answer to the question.

The municipal authorities were made responsible to the Japanese military governor, who was clever enough to leave the entire American municipal administration unaltered, even down to the smallest detail. Even the local police remained in office. The whole civil life went on as before, and only the machine-guns in front of the Japanese guard-houses situated at the various centers of traffic showed who was now ruler in the land. All the officials and the whole city administration were bound by a marvelously clever and effective system.

In the proclamations issued by the Japanese military governor the city was threatened, should the slightest sign of resistance occur, with acts of vengeance that positively took one's breath away. Three Japanese cruisers, with their guns constantly loaded and manned and aimed directly at the two cities, lay between Oakland and San Francisco. They had orders to show no mercy and to commence a bombardment at the first sign of trouble. It did not seem to have occurred to any one that although the bombardment of a town like San Francisco by a few dozen guns might indeed have a bad moral effect, it would nevertheless be impossible to do much harm. But the Japanese had other trump cards up their sleeves. The military governor declared that the moment they were compelled to use the guns, he would cut off all the available supply of water and light, by which means all resistance would be broken down within twenty-four hours. For this reason all the gas-works and electric plants were transformed into little forts and protected by cannon and machine-guns. Tens of thousands might try, in vain, to take them by storm; the city would remain wrapped in darkness, except, as the Japanese general remarked with a polite smile to the Mayor of San Francisco, for the bright light of bursting shells.

In the same way the municipal waterworks in San Francisco and all the other towns occupied by the Japanese were insured against attack. Not one drop of water would the town receive, and what that meant could be best explained to the Mayor by his wife. And thus, in spite of their often ridiculously small numbers, the Japanese troops were safe from surprise, for the awful punishment meted out to the town of Stockton, where a bold and quickly organized band of citizens destroyed the Japanese garrison, consisting only of a single company, was not likely to be disregarded. The entire population of the Pacific Coast was forced to submit quietly, though boiling with rage, while at the same time all listened eagerly for the report of cannon from the American army in the east. But was there such a thing as an American army? Was there any sense in hoping when months must pass before an American army could take the field?

The deception of the *Evening Standard* by means of the fatal telegram was preceded by an instructive episode. Indeed, it might well be asked whether anything that happened in this terrible time could not be traced back pretty far. In order that the news of the naval maneuvers in the *Evening Standard* should receive sufficient attention on the critical day, this paper and consequently the inhabitants of San Francisco had for some months past been taught to expect over the signature "Our Naval Correspondent," amazingly correct accounts of the movements of the American fleet and all matters pertaining to the navy.

Mr. Alfred Stephenson had hard work to keep his head above water as editor of the *Los Angeles Advertiser* at Los Angeles. The struggle for existence gave him considerable cause for worry, and this was due to the fact that Mrs. Olinda Stephenson wished to cut a figure in society, a figure that was not at all compatible with her husband's income. Mr. Stephenson was therefore often called upon to battle with temptation, but for a long time he successfully withstood all offers the acceptance of which would have lowered him in his own estimation. The consequence was that financial discussion had become chronic in the Stephenson household, and, like a Minister of Finance, he was compelled to develop considerable energy in order to diminish the financial demands of the opposition or render them void by having recourse to passive resistance. This constant worry gradually exhausted Mr. Stephenson, however, and the check-book, which, to save his face, he always carried with him, was nothing more than a piece of useless bluff.

He could therefore scarcely be blamed for eagerly seizing the opportunity offered him one evening at a bar in Los Angeles, when a stranger agreed to furnish him regularly with news from the Navy Department for the *Evening Standard*. The affair had, of course, to be conducted with the greatest secrecy. The stranger told Stephenson that a clerk in the Navy Department was willing to send him such news for two hundred dollars per annum. The result was astonishing. The articles signed "Our Naval Correspondent" soon attracted wide attention, and the large fees received from San Francisco quite covered the deficits in the Stephenson household. Mrs. Olinda was soon rolling in money and the tiresome financial discussions came to a speedy end. From that time on Stephenson regularly received secret communications, which were mailed at Pasadena, and as to the origin of which he himself remained in complete ignorance. But these same messages enabled the *Evening Standard* in a brief space of time to establish a national reputation for its naval news, which was at no time officially contradicted.

The matter did not, of course, pass unnoticed in Washington, for it soon became evident that secret dispatches were being misappropriated. Vigorous efforts were made to discover the guilty person in the Navy Department, but they all proved vain for the following reason: Among the wireless stations used for maintaining constant communication between the Navy Department at Washington and the various naval ports and naval stations, and the fleet itself when at sea, was the large station on Wilson's Peak near the observatory, whose shining tin-roof can be seen plainly from Los Angeles when the sun strikes it. All messages arriving there for transmission to San Diego and Mare Island could be readily intercepted by the wireless apparatus attached inconspicuously to the huge wind-wheel on an orange plantation between Pasadena and Los Angeles. The uninitiated would have concluded that the wires had something to do with a lightning-rod. The Japanese proprietor of the plantation had simply to read the messages from the Morse key of his apparatus and forward what he considered advisable to Mr. Stephenson by mail. A few hours later the *Evening Standard* was in a position to make a scoop with the dispatches of its infallible naval correspondent.

Thus Stephenson, without having the slightest suspicion of it, formed a wheel in the great chain which prepared the way for the enemy, and since the *Evening Standard* had earned a reputation for publishing absolutely reliable news in this field, no one for a moment doubted the announcement of Admiral Perry's attack, although this was the first spurious message which Stephenson had furnished to his paper.

CHAPTER IX
A FORTY-EIGHT-HOUR BALANCE

A steamer is lying at the pier taking in cargo. Long-legged cranes are taking hold of bales and barrels and boxes and lowering them through the ship's hatches with a rattle of chains. Wooden cases bound with steel ropes and containing heavy machinery are being hoisted slowly from the lorries on the railway tracks; the swaying burden is turning round and round in the air, knocking against the railing with a groaning noise, and tearing off large splinters of wood. The overseer is swearing at the men at the windlass and comparing his papers with the slips of the customs officer, the one making a blue check on the bill of lading and the other taking note of each article on his long list. Suddenly a small box comes to light, which has been waiting patiently since yesterday under the sheltering tarpaulin. "A box of optical instruments," says the customs officer, making a blue check. "A box of optical instruments," repeats the overseer, making a mark with his moistened pencil-stump: "Careful!" he adds, as a workman is on the point of tipping the heavy box over. Then the hook of the crane seizes the loop in the steel rope and with a stuttering rattling sound the wheels of the windlass set to work, the steel wire grips the side of the box tightly, the barrel beside it is pushed aside, and a wooden case enclosing a piece of cast-iron machinery is scraped angrily over the slippery cobble-stones. Heave ho, heave ho, chant the men, pushing with all their might. To the accompaniment of splashing drops of oily water, puffs of steam, groans of the windlass and the yells and curses of the stevedores, the whole load, including the box of optical instruments, at last disappears in the hold of the ship. It is placed securely between rolls of cardboard next to some nice white boxes filled with shining steel goods. But when the noise up above has died down, when with the approach of darkness the rattling of the chains and the groaning of the windlasses has ceased, when only the slow step of the deck-watch finds an echo—then it can be heard. Inside the box you can hear a gentle but steady tick, tick, tick. The clock-work is wound up and set to the exact second. Tick, tick, tick it goes. When the ship is far out at sea and the passengers are asleep and the watch calls out: "Lights are burning. All's well!" then the works will have run down, the spring will stop and loosen a little hammer. Ten kilograms of dynamite suffice. A quarter of an hour later there'll be nothing left of the proud steamer but a few boats loaded down with people and threatening every moment to be engulfed in the waves.

Tick, tick, tick, it goes down in the hold; the clock is set. Tick, tick, tick, it goes on unceasingly, till the unknown hour arrives. No one suspects the true nature of a piece of the cargo which certainly looked innocent enough. Yet the hour is bound to come sooner or later, but no one knows just when.

Nor had the country at large recognized that the hour was at hand. In the time that it took the short hand of the clock to complete its round four times, our country had completely changed its complexion, and the balance drawn by the press on Tuesday morning after an interval of forty-eight hours, had a perfectly crushing effect. Of course the appearance of the enemy in the West at once produced a financial panic in New York. On Monday morning the Wall Street stock-quotations of the trans-continental railroads fell to the lowest possible figure, rendering the shares about as valuable as the paper upon which they were printed. Apparently enormous numbers of shares had been thrown on the market in the first wild panic, but an hour after the opening of the Stock Exchange, after billions had changed hands in mad haste, a slight rise set in as a result of wholesale purchases by a single individual. Yet even before this fact had been clearly recognized, the railway magnates of the West had bought up all the floating stock without exception. They could afford to wait for the millions they would pocket until the American army had driven the enemy from the country.

At the same time selling orders came pouring in from the other side by way of London. The Old World lost no time in trying to get rid of its American stocks, and the United States were made to realize that in the hour of a political catastrophe every nation has to stand on its own feet, and that all the diplomatic notes and the harmless sentimentalities of foreign states will avail nothing. So it was after the terrible night of Port Arthur and so it was now.

It was of course as yet impossible to figure out in detail how the Japanese had managed to take possession of the Pacific States within twenty-four hours. But from the dispatches received from all parts of the country during the next few days and weeks the following picture could be drawn. The number of Japanese on American soil was in round numbers one hundred thousand. The Japanese had not only established themselves as small tradesmen and shopkeepers in the towns, but had also settled everywhere as farmers and fruit-growers; Japanese coolies and Mongolian workmen were to be found wherever new buildings were going up as well as on all the railways. The yellow flood was threatening to destroy the very foundations of our domestic economy by forcing down all wage-values. The yellow immigrant who wrested spade and shovel, ax and saw, from the American workman, who pushed his way into the factory and the workshop and acted as a heartless strike breaker, was not only found in the Pacific States but had pushed his way across the Rockies into the very heart of the eastern section. And scarcely had he settled anywhere, before, with the typical Tsushima grin, he demanded his political rights. The individual Jap excited no suspicion and did not become troublesome, but the Mongolians always managed to distribute their outposts on American soil in such a way that the Japanese element never attracted undue attention in any one particular spot. Nevertheless they were to be found everywhere.

We had often been told that every Japanese who landed on the Pacific Coast or crossed the Mexican or Canadian borders was a trained soldier. But we had always regarded this fact more as a political curiosity or a Japanese peculiarity than as a warning. We never for a moment realized that this whole immigration scheme was regulated by a perfect system, and that every Japanese immigrant had received his military orders and was in constant touch with the secret military centers at San Francisco, who at stated periods sent out Japanese traders and agents—in reality they were officers of the general staff, who at the same time made important topographical notes for use in case of war—to control their movements. Both the lumber companies in the State of Washington, which brought hundreds of Japanese over from Canada, and the railways which employed Japanese workmen were equally ignorant of the fact that they had taken a Japanese regiment into their employ.

Thus preparations for the coming war were conducted on a large scale during the year 1907, until the ever-increasing flow of Japanese immigrants finally led to those conflicts with which we are familiar. At the time we regarded it as a triumph of American diplomacy when Japan, in the face of California's threatening attitude, apparently gave in after a little diplomatic bickering and issued the well-known proclamation concerning emigration to Hawaii and the Pacific States, at the same time dissolving several emigration companies at home.

As a matter of fact Japan had already completed her military preparations in our country in times of absolute peace, the sole difficulty experienced being in connection with the concentration of the remaining coolie importations. The Japanese invasion, which our politicians dismissed as possible only in the dim and distant future, was actually completed at the beginning of the year 1908. A Japanese army stood prepared and fully armed right in our midst, merely waiting until the military and financial conditions at home rendered the attack feasible.

When we glance to-day through the newspapers of that period, we cannot help but smile at allowing ourselves to be persuaded that the Japanese danger had been removed by the diplomatic retreat in Tokio and the prohibition of emigration to North America. Our papers stated at the time that Japan had recognized that she had drawn the bow too tight and that she had yielded because Admiral Evans's fleet had demonstrated conclusively that we were prepared. That only goes to show how little we knew of the Mongolian character!

We had become so accustomed to the large Japanese element in the population of our Western States, that we entirely neglected to control the harmless looking individuals. To be sure there wasn't a great deal to be seen on the surface, but it would have been interesting to examine some of the goods smuggled so regularly across the Mexican and Canadian borders. Why were we content to allow the smuggling to continue without interference, simply because we felt it couldn't be stamped out anyhow? The Japanese did not resort to the hackneyed piano-cases and farming machinery; they knew better than to employ such clumsy methods. The goods they sent over the line consisted of neat little boxes full of guns and other weapons which had been taken apart. And when a Japanese farmer ordered a hay-cart from Canada, it was no pure chance that the remarkably strong wheels of this cart exactly fitted a field-gun. The barrel was brought over by a neighbor, who ordered iron columns for his new house, inside of which the separate parts of the barrel were soldered. It was in this way that, in the course of several years, the entire equipment for the Japanese army came quietly and inconspicuously across our borders.

And then the Japanese are so clever, clever in putting together and mounting their guns, clever in disguising them. Did it ever enter anyone's head that the amiable landlord who cracked so many jokes at the Japanese inn not far from the railroad station at Reno commanded a battalion? Did anyone suppose that the casks of California wine in his cellar in reality enclosed six machine-guns, and that in the yard behind the house there was sufficient material to equip an entire company of artillery inside of two hours, and that plenty of ammunition was stored away in the attic in boxes and trunks ostensibly left by travelers to be held until called for? As long as there's sufficient time at disposal, all these things can be imported into the country bit by bit, and without ever coming into conflict with the government.

Things began to stir about the end of April. A great many Japs were traveling about the country, but there was no reason why this circumstance should have attracted special notice in a country like ours where so much traveling is constantly done. The enemy were assembling. The people arrived at the various stations and at once disappeared in the country, bound for the different headquarters in the solitudes of the mountains. There each one found his ammunition, his gun and his uniform exactly as it was described in Japanese characters on the paper which he had received on landing, and which had more than once been officially revised or supplemented as the result of information received from chance acquaintances who had paid him a visit.

Everything worked like a charm; there wasn't a hitch anywhere. No one had paid any particular attention to the fact, for example, in connection with the fair to be held in the small town of Irvington on May eighth, that numerous carts with Japanese farmers had arrived on the Saturday before and that they had brought several dozen horses with them. And who could object to their putting up at the Japanese inn which, with its big stables, was specially suited to their purpose. At first the Japanese owner had been laughed at, but later on he was admired for his business ability in keeping the horse trade of Irvington entirely in his own hands.

When on the following day during church hours—the Japanese being heathens—the streets lay deserted in their Sunday calm, the few people who happened to be on Main Street and saw a field battery consisting of six guns and six ammunition wagons turn out of the gate next to the Japanese inn thought they had seen an apparition. The battery started off at once at a sharp trot and left the town to take up a position out in a field in the suburbs, where a dozen men were already busily at work with spades and pick-axes digging a trench.

The police of Irvington were at once notified, a sleepy official at the Post Office was roused out of his slumbers, and a telegram was directed to the nearest military post, but the latter proceeding was useless and no answer was received, since the copper wires were long ago in the control of the enemy. Even if it had got through, the telegraphic warning would have come too late, for the military post in question, of which half of the troops were, as usual, on leave, had been attacked and captured by the Japanese at nine o'clock in the morning.

A hundred thousand Japanese had established the line of an eastern advance-guard long before the Pacific States had any idea of what was up. During Sunday, after the capture of San Francisco, the occupation of Seattle, San Diego and the other fortified towns on the coast, the landing of the second detachment of the Japanese army began, and by Monday evening the Pacific States were in the grip of no less than one hundred and seventy thousand men.

When, on Sunday morning, the Japanese had cut off the railway connections, they adopted the plan of allowing all trains going from east to west to pass unmolested, so that there was soon quite a collection of engines and cars to be found within the zone bounded by the Japanese outposts. On the other hand, all the trains running eastward were held up, some being sent back and others being used for conveying the Japanese troops to advance posts or for bringing the various lines of communication into touch with one another. In some cases these trains were also used for pushing boldly much farther east, the enemy thus surprising and overpowering a number of military posts and arsenals in which the guns and ammunition for the militia were stored.

Only in a very few instances did this gigantic mechanism fail. One of these accidents occurred at Swallowtown, where the mistake was made of attacking the express-train to Umatilla instead of the local train to Pendleton. The lateness of the former and the occupation of the station too long before the expected arrival of the latter, and coupled to this the heroic deed of the station-master, interfered unexpectedly with the execution of the plan. The reader will remember that when the express returned to Swallowtown, Tom's shanty was empty. The enemy had disappeared and had taken the two captive farmers with them. The mounted police, who had been summoned immediately from Walla Walla, found the two men during the afternoon in their wagon, bound hand and foot, in a hollow a few miles to the west of the station. They also discovered a time-table of the Oregon Railway in the wagon, with a note in Japanese characters beside the time for the arrival of the local train from Umatilla. This time-table had evidently been lost by the leader of the party on his flight. Soon after the police had returned to the Swallowtown station that same evening, a Japanese military train passed through, going in the direction of Pendleton. The train was moving slowly and those within opened fire on the policeman, who lost no time in replying. But the odds were too great, and it was all over in a few minutes.

By Monday evening the enemy had secured an immense quantity of railway material, which had simply poured into their arms automatically, and which was more than sufficient for their needs.

The information received from Victoria (British Columbia) that a fleet had been sighted in the Straits of San Juan de Fuca, whence it was said to have proceeded to Port Townsend and Puget Sound, was quite correct. A cruiser squadron had indeed passed Esquimault and Victoria at dawn on Sunday, and a few hours later firing had been heard coming from the direction of Port Townsend. The British harbor officials had suddenly become extremely timid and had not allowed the regular steamer to leave for Seattle. When, therefore, on Monday morning telegraphic inquiries came from the American side concerning the foreign warships, which, by the way, had carried no flag, ambiguous answers could be made without arousing suspicion. Considerable excitement prevailed in Victoria on account of the innumerable vague rumors of the outbreak of war; the naval station, however, remained perfectly quiet. On Monday morning a cruiser started out in the direction of Port Townsend, and after exchanging numerous signals with Esquimault, continued on her course towards Cape Flattery and the open sea. It will be seen, therefore, that no particular zeal was shown in endeavoring to get at the bottom of the matter.

A battle between the Japanese ships and the forts of Port Townsend had actually taken place. Part of the hostile fleet had escorted the transport steamers to Puget Sound and had there found the naval depots and the fortifications, the arsenal and the docks in the hands of their countrymen, who had also destroyed the second-class battleship *Texas* lying off Port Orchard by firing at her from the coast forts previously stormed and captured by them. They had surprised Seattle at dawn much in the same way as San Francisco had been surprised, and they at once began to land troops and unload their war materials. On the other hand, an attempt to surprise Port Townsend with an insufficient force had failed. The Americans had had enough sense to prohibit the Japanese from coming too near to the newly armed coast defenses, and the better watch which the little town had been able to keep over the Asiatics had made it difficult for them to assemble a sufficiently large fighting contingent. The work here had to be attended to by the guns, and the enemy had included this factor in their calculations from the beginning.

How thoroughly informed the Japanese were as to every detail of our coast defenses and how well acquainted they were with each separate battery, with its guns as well as with its ammunition, was clearly demonstrated by the new weapon brought into the field in connection with the real attack on the fortifications. Of course Japanese laborers had been employed in erecting the works—they worked for such ridiculously low wages, those Japanese engineers disguised as coolies. With the eight million two hundred thousand dollars squeezed out of Congress in the spring of 1908—in face of the unholy fear on the part of the nation's representatives of a deficit, it had been impossible to get more—two new mortar batteries had been built on the rocky heights of Port Townsend. These batteries, themselves inaccessible to all ships' guns, were in a position to pour down a perpendicular fire on hostile decks and could thus make short work of every armored vessel.

Now the Japanese had already had a very unpleasant experience with the strong coast fortifications of Port Arthur. In the first place, bombarding of this nature was very injurious to the bores of the ships' guns, and secondly, the results on land were for the most part nominal. Not without reason had Togo tried to get at the shore batteries of Port Arthur by indirect fire from Pigeon Bay. But even that, in spite of careful observations taken from the water, had little effect. And even the strongest man-of-war was helpless against the perpendicular fire of the Port Townsend mortar batteries, because it was simply impossible for its guns, with their slight angle of elevation, to reach the forts situated so high above them. And if the road to Seattle, that important base of operations in the North, was not to be perpetually menaced, then Port Townsend must be put out of commission.

But for every weapon a counter-weapon is usually invented, and every new discovery is apt to be counterbalanced by another. The world has never yet been overturned by a new triumph of skill in military technics, because it is at once paralyzed by another equally ingenious. And now, at Port Townsend, very much the same thing happened as on March ninth, 1862. In much the same way that the appearance of the *Merrimac* had brought destruction to the wooden fleet until she was herself forced to flee before Ericsson's *Monitor* at Hampton Roads, so now at Port Townsend on May seventh a new weapon was made to stand the crucial test. Only this time we were not the pathfinders of the new era.

While the Japanese cruisers, keeping carefully beyond the line of fire from the forts, sailed on to Seattle, four ships were brought into action against the mortar batteries of Port Townsend which appeared to set at defiance all known rules of ship-building, and which, indestructible as they were, threatened to annihilate all existing systems. They were low vessels which floated on the water like huge tortoises. These mortar-boats, which were destined to astound not only the Americans but the whole world, had been constructed in Japanese shipyards, to which no stranger had ever been admitted. In place of the ordinary level-firing guns found on a modern warship, these uncanny gray things carried 17.7-inch howitzers, a kind of mortar of Japanese construction. There was nothing to be seen above the low deck but a short heavily protected funnel and four little armored domes which contained the sighting telescopes for the guns, the mouths of which lay in the arch of the whaleback deck. Four such vessels had also been constructed for use at San Francisco, but the quick capture of the forts had rendered the mortar-boats unnecessary.

We were constantly being attacked in places where no thought had been given to the defense, and the fortifications we did possess were never shot at from the direction they faced. Our coast defenses were everywhere splendidly protected against level-firing guns, which the Japanese, however, unfortunately refrained from using. With their mortar-boats they attacked our forts in their most vulnerable spot, that is, from above. With the exception of Winfield Scott, the batteries at Port Townsend were the only ones on our western coast which at once construed the appearance of suspicious-looking ships on May seventh as signs of a Japanese attack, and they immediately opened fire on the four Japanese cruisers and on the transport steamers. But before this fire had any effect, the hostile fleet changed its course to the North and the four mortar-boats began their attack. They approached to within two nautical miles and opened fire at once.

What was the use of our gunners aiming at the flat, gray arches of these uncanny ocean-tortoises? The heavy shells splashed into the water all around them, and when one did succeed in hitting one of the boats, it was simply dashed to pieces against the armor-plate, which was several feet thick, or else it glanced off harmlessly like hail dancing off the domed roof of a pavilion. The only targets were the flames which shot incessantly out of the mouths of the hostile guns like out of a funnel-shaped crater.

By noon all the armored domes of the Port Townsend batteries had been destroyed and one gun after another had ceased firing. The horizontal armor-plates, too, which protected the disappearing gun-carriages belonging to the huge guns of the other forts, had not been able to withstand the masses of steel which came down almost perpendicularly from above them. One single well-aimed shot had usually sufficed to cripple the complicated mechanism and once that was injured, it was impossible to bring the gun back into position for firing. The concrete roofs of the ammunition rooms and barracks were shot to pieces and the traverses were reduced to rubbish heaps by the bursting of the numerous shells of the enemy. And all that was finally left round the tattered Stars and Stripes was a little group of heavily wounded gunners, performing their duty to the bitter end, and these heroes were honored by the enemy by being permitted to keep their arms. They were sent by steamer from Seattle to the Canadian Naval Station at Esquimault on the seventh of May, and their arrival inspired the populace to stormy demonstrations against the Japanese, this being the first outward expression of Canadian sympathy for the United States. The Canadians felt that the time had come for all white men to join hands against the common danger, and the policy of the Court of St. James soon became intensely unpopular throughout Canada. What did Canada care about what was considered the proper policy in London, when here at their very door necessity pressed hard on their heels, and the noise of war from across the border sounded a shrill Mene Tekel in the white man's ear?

There were therefore no less than one hundred and seventy thousand Japanese soldiers on American soil on Tuesday morning, May ninth. In the north, the line of outposts ran along the eastern border of the States of Washington and Oregon and continued through the southern portion of Idaho, always keeping several miles to the east of the tracks of the Oregon Short Line, which thus formed an excellent line of communication behind the enemy's front. At Granger, the junction of the Oregon Short Line and the Union Pacific, the Japanese reached their easternmost bastion, and here they dug trenches, which were soon fortified by means of heavy artillery. From here their line ran southward along the Wasatch Mountains, crossed the great Colorado plateau and then continued along the high section of Arizona, reaching the Mexican boundary by way of Fort Bowie.

Only in the south and in the extreme north did railroads in any respectable number lead up to the Japanese front. In the center, however, the roads by way of which an American assault could be made, namely the Union Pacific at Granger, the Denver and Rio Grande at Grand Junction, and further south the Atcheson, Topeka & Santa Fé, approached the Japanese positions at right angles, and at these points captive balloons and several air-ships kept constant watch toward the east, so that there was no possibility of an American surprise. In the north strong field fortifications along the border-line of Washington and Idaho furnished sufficient protection, and in the south the sunbaked sandy deserts of New Mexico served the same purpose. Then, too, the almost unbroken railway connection between the north and the south allowed the enemy to transport his reserves at a moment's notice to any point of danger, and the Japs were clever enough not to leave their unique position to push further eastward. Any advance of large bodies of troops would have weakened all the manifold advantages of this position, and besides the Japanese numbers were not considerable enough to warrant an unnecessary division of forces.

And what had we in the way of troops to oppose this hostile invasion? Our regular army consisted, on paper, of sixty thousand men. Fifteen thousand of these had been stationed in the Pacific States, composed principally of the garrisons of the coast forts; all of these without exception were, by Monday morning, in the hands of the Japanese. This at once reduced the strength of our regular army to forty-five thousand men. Of this number eighteen thousand were in the Philippines and, although they were not aware of it, they had to all intents and purposes been placed *hors de combat,* both at Mindanao and in the fortifications of Manila. Besides these the two regiments on the way from San Francisco to Manila and the garrison of Pearl Harbor in the Hawaiian Islands, could be similarly deducted. It will be seen, therefore, that, only twenty-five thousand men of our regular army were available, and these were scattered over the entire country: some were in the numerous prairie-forts, others on the Atlantic coast, still others in Cuba and in Porto Rico. Thus twenty-five thousand men were pitted against a force not only seven times as large, but one that was augmented hourly by hundreds of newcomers. On Monday the President had called out the organized militia and on the following day he sent a special message to Congress recommending the formation of a volunteer army. The calls to arms were posted in the form of huge placards at all the street-corners and at the entrances to the speedily organized recruiting-offices. In this way it was possible, to be sure, within a few months to raise an army equal to that of the enemy so far as mere numbers were concerned, and the American citizen could be relied upon. But where were the leaders, where was the entire organization of the transport, of the commissariat, of the ambulance corps—we possessed no military train-corps at all—and most important of all, where were the arms to come from?

The arsenals and ammunition-depots in the Pacific States were in the hands of the enemy, the cannon of our far western field-artillery depots had aided in forming Japanese batteries, and the Japanese flag was waving above our heavy coast guns. The terrible truth that we were for the present absolutely helpless before the enemy had a thoroughly disheartening effect on all classes of the population as soon as it was clearly recognized. In impotent rage at this condition of utter helplessness and in their eagerness to be revenged on the all-powerful enemy, men hurried to the recruiting-offices in large numbers, and the lists for the volunteer regiments were soon covered with signatures. The citizens of the country dropped the plow, stood their tools in the corner and laid their pens away; the clattering typewriters became silent, and in the offices of the sky-scrapers business came to a stand-still. Only in the factories where war materials were manufactured did great activity reign.

For the present there was at least one dim hope left, namely the fleet. But where was the fleet? After our battle-fleet had crossed the Pacific to Australia and Eastern Asia, it returned to the Atlantic, while a squadron of twelve battleships and four armored cruisers was sent under Admiral Perry to the west coast and stationed there, with headquarters at San Francisco. To these ships must be added the regular Pacific squadron and Philippine squadron. The remaining ships of our fleet were in Atlantic waters.

That was the fatal mistake committed in the year of our Lord 1909. In vain, all in vain, had been the oft-repeated warning that in face of the menacing Japanese danger the United States navy should be kept together, either in the west or in the east. Only when concentrated, only in the condition in which it was taken through the Straits of Magellan by Admiral Evans, was our fleet absolutely superior to the Japanese. Every dispersal, every separation of single divisions was bound to prove fatal. Article upon article and pamphlet upon pamphlet were written anent the splitting-up of our navy! And yet what a multitude of entirely different and mutually exclusive tasks were set her at one and the same time! Manila was to be protected, Pearl Harbor was to have a naval station, the Pacific coast was to be protected, and there was to be a reserve fleet off the eastern coast.

And yet it was perfectly clear that any part of the fleet which happened to be stationed at Manila or Hawaii would be lost to the Americans immediately on the outbreak of hostilities. But we deluded ourselves with the idea that Japan would not dare send her ships across the Pacific in the face of our little Philippine squadron, whereas not even a large squadron stationed at Manila would have hindered the Japanese from attacking us. Even such a squadron they could easily have destroyed with a detachment of equal strength, without in any way hindering their advance against our western shores, while the idea of attempting to protect an isolated colony with a few ships against a great sea-power was perfectly ridiculous. The strong coast fortifications and a division of submarines—the two stationed there at the time, however, were really not fit for use—would have sufficed for the defense of Manila, and anything beyond that simply meant an unnecessary sacrifice of forces which might be far more useful elsewhere.

After our fleet had been divided between the east and the west, both the Pacific fleet and the reserve Atlantic fleet were individually far inferior to the Japanese fleet. The maintenance of a fleet in the Pacific as well as of one in the Atlantic was a fatal luxury. It was superfluous to keep on tap a whole division of ships in our Atlantic harbors merely posing as maritime ornaments before the eyes of Europe or at the most coming in handy for an imposing demonstration against a refractory South-American Republic. All this could have been done just as well with a few cruisers. English money and Japanese intrigues, it is true, succeeded in always keeping the Venezuelan wound open, so that we were constantly obliged to steal furtive glances at that corner of the world, one that had caused us so much political vexation. Matters had indeed reached a sorry pass if our political prestige was so shaky, that it was made to depend on Mr. Castro's valuation of the forces at the disposal of the United States!

In consideration of the many unforeseen delays that had occurred in the work of digging the Panama Canal, there was only one policy for us to adopt until its completion, and that was to keep our fleet together and either to concentrate it in the Pacific and thus deter the enemy from attacking our coasts, regardless of what might be thought of our action in Tokio, or to keep only a few cruisers in the Pacific, as formerly, and to concentrate the fleet in the Atlantic, so as to be able to attack the enemy from the rear with the full force of our naval power. But these amateur commissioners of the public safety who wished to have an imposing squadron on view wherever our flag floated—as if the Stars and Stripes were a signal of distress instead of a token of strength—condemned our fleet to utter helplessness. In 1908, when there was no mistaking the danger, we, the American people, one of the richest and most energetic nations of the world, nevertheless allowed ourselves in the course of the debate on the naval appropriations to be frightened by Senator Maine's threat of a deficit of a few dollars in our budget, should the sums that were absolutely needed in case our fleet was to fulfill the most immediate national tasks be voted. This was the short-sighted policy of a narrow-minded politician who, when a country's fate is hanging in the balance, complains only of the costs. It was most assuredly a short-sighted policy, and we were compelled to pay dearly for it.

The voyage of our fleet around South America had shown the world that the value of a navy is not impaired because a few drunken sailors occasionally forget to return to their ship when in port: on the contrary, foreign critics had been obliged to admit that our navy in point of equipment and of crews was second to none. And lo and behold, this remarkable exhibition of power—the only sensible idea evolved by our navy department in years—is followed by the insane dispersal of our ships to so many different stations.

How foolish had it been, furthermore, to boast as we did about having kept up communication with Washington by wireless during the whole of our journey around South America. Had not the experience at Trinidad, where a wireless message intercepted by an English steamer had warned the coal-boats that our fleet would arrive a day sooner, taught us a lesson? And had not the way in which the Japanese steamer, also provided with a wireless apparatus, stuck to us so persistently between Valparaiso and Callao shown us plainly that every new technical discovery has its shady side?

No, we had learned nothing. In Washington they insisted on sending all orders from the Navy Department to the different harbors and naval stations by wireless, yet each of the stations along the whole distance from east to west provided possibilities of indiscretion and treachery and of unofficial interception. Why had we not made wireless telegraphy a government monopoly, instead of giving each inhabitant of the United States the right to erect an apparatus of his own if he so wished? Did it never occur to anybody in Washington that long before the orders of the Navy Department had reached Mare Island, Puget Sound and San Diego they had been read with the greatest ease by hundreds of strangers? It required the success of the enemy to make all this clear to us, when we might just as well have listened to those who drew conclusions from obvious facts and recommended caution.

In spite of all this, the press on Tuesday morning still adhered to the hope that Admiral Perry would attack the enemy from the rear with his twelve battleships of the Pacific squadron, and that, meeting the Japanese at their base of operations, he would cut off all threads of communication between San Francisco and Tokio. It was no longer possible to warn Perry of his danger, since the wireless stations beyond the Rockies were already in the enemy's hands. The American people could therefore only trust to luck; but blind chance has never yet saved a country in its hour of direst need. It can only be saved by the energy, the steady eye and the strong hand of men. All hope centered in Admiral Perry, in his energy and his courage, but the people became uneasy when no answer was received to the oft-repeated question: "Where is the Pacific fleet?" Yes, where was Admiral Perry?

CHAPTER X

ADMIRAL PERRY'S FATE

The wireless apparatus on board Admiral Perry's flag-ship, the *Connecticut*, rattled and crackled and on the strip of white paper slowly ejected by the Morse machine appeared the words: "Magdalen Bay to Commander-in-chief of Squadron, May 7, 8h. 25. A cruiser and two torpedo-boats sighted four miles N.W. with course set towards Magdalen Bay; uncertain whether friend or foe. Captain Pancoast."

The man at the instrument tore off the duplicate of the strip and pasted it on the bulletin, touched the button of an electric bell and handed the message to the signalman who answered the ring. The telephone bell rang directly afterwards and from the bridge came the order: "Magdalen Bay to establish immediate connection by wireless with cruiser and torpedoes; ascertain whether they belong to blue or yellow party."

The officer ticked off the message at great speed.

"This looks like bad weather," he said to himself, while waiting for the answer. The increased rocking of the ship showed that the sea was getting rougher. A black pencil, which had been lying in the corner between the wall and the edge of the table, suddenly came to life and began rolling aimlessly about. The officer picked it up and drew a map of the location of Magdalen Bay as far as he could remember it. "Four miles," he murmured, "they ought to be able to identify the ships at that distance with the aid of a glass."

Suddenly the instrument began to buzz and rattle and amidst a discharge of little electric sparks the strip of white paper began to move out slowly from beneath the letter roller.

> "Magdalen Bay to Commander-in-chief of Squadron, May 7,
> 8 h. 53: Approaching cruiser, probably yellow armored cruiser
> *New York*; does not answer call. Captain Pancoast."

The officer hadn't had time to get the message ready for the bridge, when the instrument again began to rattle madly:

"Take care of Kxj31mpTwB8d—951SR7—J," warned the strip in its mute language; then nothing further; complete silence reigned. "What does this mean?" said the officer, "this can't be all."

He knocked on the coherer, then put in a new one: not a sign. He took a third, a fourth, he knocked and shook the instrument, but it remained dumb. With his

Morse-key he asked back:

"Magdalen Bay, repeat message!"

No answer.

Then he asked: "Did you understand question?"

No answer.

The signalman was standing beside him, and he handed him the message with the order to take it at once to the bridge; then he went to the telephone and took off the receiver. "This is Sergeant Medlow. I've just received from Magdalen Bay the message now on the way to the bridge: 'Take care of—' then the connection was cut off.... All right, sir."

Two minutes later an excited lieutenant rushed in crying: "What's the matter with the apparatus?"

"It won't work, sir; it stopped in the middle of a sentence."

"Take a new coherer!"

"I've tried four."

They both tapped the coherer, but nothing happened. All questions remained unanswered, and they seemed to be telegraphing into space.

"Probably a breakdown," said the lieutenant naïvely.

"Yes, sir, probably a breakdown," repeated Medlow; and then he was alone once more.

The officer on duty on the bridge of the *Connecticut* had informed Captain Farlow, commander of the ship, of the latest messages from Magdalen Bay, and when he now appeared on the bridge in company with Admiral Perry, the officer held out the two bulletins. The admiral studied them thoughtfully and murmured: "*New York*, it's true she belongs to the yellow fleet, but what brings her to Magdalen Bay? Admiral Crane cannot possibly be so far to the southeast with his squadron, for the latest news from our outposts led us to believe that he intended to attack us from the west."

"But he may be going to surprise Magdalen Bay, Admiral," said Captain Farlow.

"Perhaps," replied the Admiral, rather sharply, "but will you tell me what for? There are only two torpedo-boats at Magdalen Bay, and to destroy a wireless station from which there are no messages to be sent would be a rather silly thing for an overzealous commander of the yellow fleet to do. And besides we have special orders from Washington to draw Magdalen Bay as little as possible into the maneuvers, so as to avoid all unpleasantness with Mexico and not to attract the attention of foreigners to the importance which the bay would assume in case of war."

A lieutenant stepped up to Captain Farlow and reported, saluting: "All attempts to establish connection with Magdalen Bay have failed."

"Well, let it go," grumbled Admiral Perry, "Crane seems to have deprived us of Magdalen Bay, but the commander of the *New York* will reap a fine reprimand from Washington for this."

With these words Admiral Perry left the bridge, steadying himself by holding on to the railing on both sides of the steps, as the sea was becoming rougher every minute.

The increasing northeast wind tore through the rigging, whistled in the wires, howled through all the openings, screamed its bad temper down the companion-ways, pulled savagely at the gun-covers and caused the long copper-wires belonging to the wireless apparatus to snap like huge whips. The bluish-gray waves broke with a hollow sound against the sides of the six battleships of the *Connecticut* class, which were running abreast in a northwesterly direction through the dreary watery wastes of the Pacific at the rate of ten knots an hour.

There was a high sea on. A barometric depression that was quite unusual in these sunny latitudes at that particular time of year had brought nasty weather in its train. During the night violent rain-storms had flooded the decks. Now the wind freshened and swept low-hanging clouds before it. The sharp white bow of the *Connecticut* with the pressure of 16,000 tons of steel behind it plowed its way through the water, throwing up a hissing foaming wave on each side. The wind lashed the waves on the starboard-side so that they splashed over the forepart of the cruiser like a shower of rain, enveloping it in a gray mist. The thick, black smoke pouring out of the three long funnels was blown obliquely down to the edge of the water and hung there like a thick cloud which shut off the western horizon and made the passage of the squadron visible a long distance off. The small openings in the casemates of the armored guns had been closed up long before, because the waves had begun to wash over them, and even the turrets on the upper deck had received a few heavy showers which had flooded their interiors. It was indeed nasty weather.

Captain Farlow had taken up his stand on the upper conning-tower of the *Connecticut* the better to examine the horizon with his glass, but a thick curtain of rain rendered it almost invisible.

"Nothing to be seen of our cruisers," he said to the navigating officer of the squadron, "this is disgusting weather for maneuvers."

Then he gave the command to telephone across to the two leading cruisers *California* and *Colorado* and ask if, on account of the thick weather, they required the assistance of two small cruisers in order to be sufficiently protected against the yellow fleet?

The commander of the *California* answered in the affirmative and asked that the three destroyers in the van, which had all they could do to maintain their course in such a heavy sea, and were therefore of little use in their present position, be recalled and replaced by two cruisers.

The admiral recalled the three destroyers by a wireless signal and ordered them to take up their position in the rear beside the other three destroyers and to assist in protecting the rear of the squadron. At the same time he strengthened his front line by sending the cruisers *Galveston* and *Chattanooga*, which had formed the port and starboard flank, respectively, to the van. His advance, consisting now of the two last-named cruisers and the two armored cruisers, proceeded in a flat wedge formation, while the cruiser *Denver* to starboard and the *Cleveland* to port, at a distance of three knots from the squadron, established the connection between the van and the rather dubious rear-guard of destroyers, which could scarcely do much in such weather.

The *Galveston* and *Chattanooga*, both pouring forth clouds of smoke, quickly assumed their positions at the head of the line.

Captain Farlow paced restlessly up and down the bridge in his oilskins. "I suppose this is the last remnant of the spring storms," he said to his navigating officer, "but it's a good-sized one. If we didn't have a fairly good formation the yellow fleet could play us a nasty trick by taking us by surprise in such weather."

"A wireless message from the cruiser *California*," said a lieutenant, handing it to the captain, who read:

"*Chattanooga* and *Galveston* stationed on right and left flanks of advance guard; *Denver* and *Cleveland* establish connection between latter and squadron. No sign of yellow fleet."

Just then an orderly appeared and requested Captain Farlow to report to Admiral Perry.

The squadron continued on its way. The northeast wind increased, driving black scurrying clouds before it which swept across the foaming waves and suddenly enveloped everything in glimmering darkness. The rain poured down on the decks in sheets and everything was swimming in a splashing flood. What with the downpour of the rain and the splashing of the waves, it was often impossible for the lookouts to see a yard ahead. Added to all this was a disagreeable sticky, humid heat. It was surely more comfortable below deck.

"What do you think of this Magdalen Bay affair?" asked the admiral of the captain as the latter entered the admiral's cabin; "it is worrying me considerably."

"In my opinion," was the answer, "it's a piece of crass stupidity on the part of the commander of the *New York*. It is all nonsense to play such tricks with a country where we are not particularly welcome guests at any time, in spite of all the diplomatic courtesies of Porfirio Díaz. The gentlemen over in Tokio have every movement of ours in the bay watched by their many spies, and their diplomatic protests are always ready."

"Certainly," said the admiral, "certainly, but our maneuvers are supposed to reflect actual war, and—between ourselves—there's no doubt but that we should treat Magdalen Bay in time of war just as though it were American soil."

"In time of war, yes," answered the captain eagerly, "but it's foolish to show our hand in a maneuver, in time of peace. Even if we do act as though Magdalen Bay belonged to us, whereas in reality we have only been permitted to use it as a coaling-station and had no right to erect a wireless station as we did, it is nevertheless inexcusable to use that particular spot for maneuver operations. If it once becomes known in Mexico, the diplomats there, who are always dying of ennui, will make trouble at once, and as we don't suffer from a surplus of good friends at any time, we ought to avoid every opportunity of giving them a diplomatic lever through maneuver blunders."

"Then the best plan," said the admiral in a thoughtful tone, "would be to report the circumstances to Washington at once, and suggest to them that it would be advisable to represent the attack on Magdalen Bay as the result of too much zeal on the part of a poorly posted commander and to apologize to Mexico for the mistake."

"That would certainly be the correct thing to do," answered Farlow, adding, "for when we do have our reckoning with the yellow...."

Here the telephone bell in the cabin rang madly and Captain Farlow jumped up to answer it; but in his excitement he had forgotten all about the rolling of the ship, and consequently stumbled and slipped along the floor to the telephone. The admiral could not help smiling, but at once transformed the smile into a frown when the door opened to admit an orderly, who was thus also a witness of Captain Farlow's sliding party. The latter picked himself up with a muttered oath and went to the telephone.

"What," he shouted, "what's that, Higgins? You must be crazy, man! Admiral Crane's fleet, the yellow fleet? It's impossible, we've got our scouts out on all sides!"

Then he turned halfway round to the admiral, saying: "The navigator is seeing ghosts, sir; he reports that Admiral Crane with the yellow fleet has been sighted to windward three knots off!" He hurried towards the door and there ran plumb against the orderly, whom he asked sharply: "What are you doing here?"

"The navigator, Lieutenant Higgins, reports that several ships have been sighted to starboard three miles ahead. Lieutenant Higgins thinks...."

"Lieutenant Higgins thinks, of course, that it is Admiral Crane's yellow fleet," snarled Farlow.

"Yes, sir," answered the orderly, "the yellow fleet," and stared in astonishment at the commander of the *Connecticut*, who, followed by Admiral Perry, rushed up the stairs.

"Oh, my oilskins!..." With this exclamation the commander reached the top of the staircase leading to the bridge deck, where a violent rush of greenish-gray water from a particularly enormous wave drenched him from head to foot.

"Now, then, Mr. Higgins," he called, wiping the water from his eyes and mustache, "where is the yellow fleet?"

The navigator was staring out to sea through his glass trying to penetrate the thick veil of rain. The storm howled and showers of foam burst over the decks of the *Connecticut*, the water washing over everything with a dull roar.

Captain Farlow had no need to inquire further. That was Admiral Crane and his yellow fleet sure enough!

The silhouettes of six large battleships looking like phantom-ships rising from the depths of the boiling ocean could be plainly seen through the rain and waves about six thousand yards to starboard of the *Connecticut*.

"Clear ships for action!" commanded the captain. The navigator and another lieutenant hurried to the telephones and transmitted the order. The flag lieutenant of the squadron rushed to the telephone leading to the wireless room, and ordered a message forwarded to all of the ships of the squadron to proceed at full speed. For safety's sake the order was repeated by means of flag signals.

While from the bridge the officers were watching the gray phantoms of the strange armored fleet, it continued calmly on its course. The leading ship threw up great masses of foam like huge exploding fountains, which covered the bow with showers of gray water.

In a few minutes things began to get lively within the steel body of the *Connecticut*. The sounds of shrill bugle-calls, of the loud ringing of bells, of excited calls and a hurried running to and fro, came up from below.

In the midst of the water pouring over the deck appeared the sailors in their white uniforms. They at once removed the gun-coverings, while peculiarly shrill commands resounded above the roar of the wind and the waves.

Great quantities of thick, black smoke poured from the yellowish brown funnels, to be immediately seized and broken up by the wind. The reserve signalmen for duty on the bridge as well as the fire-control detail took up their positions.

One lieutenant climbed hastily up into the military top of the foremast. Two other officers and a few midshipmen followed him as far as the platform above the conning-tower, where the instruments connected with the fire-control were kept. Orderlies came and went with messages. All this was the work of a few minutes. Captain Farlow was inwardly delighted that everything should have gone off so well before the admiral. Now the other ships reported that they were clear for action. Just as the bright ensigns were being run to the mastheads, the sun broke through the black clouds for a moment. The six monster ships continued on their way in the sunlight like sliding masses of white iron, with their long yellowish brown funnels emitting clouds of smoke and their rigid masts pointing upward into the angry sky. The sunshine made the deck structures sparkle with thousands of glistening drops for a brief moment; then the sun disappeared and the majestic picture was swallowed up once more by the gray clouds.

"Shall we go up to the conning-tower?" inquired the flag lieutenant of the admiral.

"Oh, no, we'll stay here," said the latter, carefully examining the yellow fleet through his glass. "Can you make out which ship the first one is?" he asked.

"I think it's the *Iowa*," said the commander, who was standing near him. But the wind tore the words from his lips.

"What did you say?" screamed back the admiral.

"*Iowa*," repeated Farlow.

"No such thing, the *Iowa* is much smaller and has only one mast. The ship over there also has an additional turret in the center."

"No, it's not the *Iowa*," corroborated the captain, "but two funnels ... what ship can it be...?"

"Those ships are painted gray, too, not white like ours. It's not the yellow fleet at all," interrupted the admiral, "it's, it's—my God, what is it?"

He examined the ships again and saw numerous little flags running up the mast of the leading ship, undoubtedly a signal, then the forward turret with its two enormously long gun-barrels swung slowly over to starboard, the other turrets turned at the same time, and then a tongue of flame shot out of the mouths of both barrels in the forward turret; the wind quickly dispersed the cloud of smoke, and three seconds later a shell burst with a fearful noise on the deck of the *Connecticut* between the base of the bridge and the first gun-turret, throwing the splinters right on the bridge and tearing off the head of the lieutenant who was doing duty at the signal apparatus. The second shell hit the armored plate right above the openings for the two 12-inch guns in the fore-turret, leaving behind a great hole with jagged edges out of which burst sheets of flame and clouds of smoke, which were blown away in long strips by the wind. A heartrending scream from within followed this explosion of the cartridges lying in readiness beside the guns. The forward turret had been put out of action.

For several seconds everyone on the bridge seemed dazed, while thoughts raced through their heads with lightning-like rapidity.

Could it be chance...? Impossible, for in the same moment that the two shots were fired by the leading ship, the whole fleet opened fire on Admiral Perry's squadron with shells of all calibers. The admiral seized Farlow's arm and shook it to and fro in a blind rage.

"Those," he cried, "those ... why, man, those are the Japanese! That's the enemy and he has surprised us right in the midst of peace! Now God give me a clear head, and let us never forget that we are American men!" He scarcely heard the words of the flag lieutenant who called out to him: "That's the Japanese *Satsuma*, Togo's *Satsuma*!"

The admiral reached the telephone-board in one bound and yelled down the artillery connection: "Hostile attack!... Japanese. We've been surprised!"

And it was indeed high time, for scarcely had the admiral reached the conning-tower, stumbling over the dead body of a signalman on the way, when a hail-storm of bullets swept the bridge, killing all who were on it.

As there was no other officer near, Captain Farlow went to the signaling instrument himself to send the admiral's orders to those below deck.

The *Connecticut*, which had been without a helmsman for a moment because the man at the helm had been killed by a bursting shell that had literally forced his body between the spokes of the wheel, was swaying about like a drunken person owing to the heavy blows of the enemy's shells. Now she recovered her course and the commander issued his orders from the bridge in a calm and decisive voice.

We have seen what a paralyzing effect the opening of fire from the Japanese ships had had on the commander and officers of the *Connecticut* on the bridge, and the reader can imagine the effect it must have had on the crew—they were dumfounded with terror. The crashing of the heavy steel projectiles above deck, the explosion in the foreward gun-turret, and several shots which had passed through the unarmored starboard side of the forepart of the ship in rapid succession—they were explosive shells which created fearful havoc and filled all the rooms with the poisonous gases of the Shimose-powder—all this, added to the continual ring of the alarm-signals, had completely robbed the crew below deck of their senses and of all deliberation.

At first it was thought to be an accident, and without waiting for orders from above, the fire-extinguishing apparatus was got ready. But the bells continued to ring on all sides, and the crashing blows that shook the ship continually became worse and worse. On top of this came the perfectly incomprehensible news that, unprepared as they were, they were confronted by the enemy, by a Japanese fleet.

All this happened with lightning-like rapidity—so quickly, indeed, that it was more than human nerves could grasp and at the same time remain calm and collected. The reverberations of the bursting shells and the dull rumbling crashes against the armored sides of the casemates and turrets produced an infernal noise which completely drowned the human voice. Frightful horror was depicted on all faces. It took some time to rally from the oppressive, heartrending sensation caused by the knowledge that a peaceful maneuver voyage had suddenly been transformed into the bloody seriousness of war. It is easy enough to turn a machine from right to left in a few seconds with the aid of a lever, but not so a human being.

The men, to be sure, heard the commands and after a few moments' reflection, grasped the terrible truth, but their limbs failed them. It had all come about too quickly, and it was simply impossible to get control of the situation and translate commands into deeds as quickly as the hostile shots demolished things above deck. Many of the crew stood around as though they were rooted to the spot, staring straight in front of them. Some laughed or cried, others did absolutely senseless things, such as turning the valves of the hot-air pipes or carrying useless things from one place to another, until the energetic efforts of the officers brought them to their senses.

Someone called for the keys of the ammunition chambers, and then began a search for the ordnance officer in the passages filled with the poisonous fumes of the Shimose-powder. But it was all in vain, for he lay on the front bridge torn into an unrecognizable mass by the enemy's shells.

At last a young lieutenant with the blood pouring down his cheek in bright red streaks, rushed into the captain's cabin, broke open the closet beside the desk with a bayonet and seized the keys of the ammunition rooms. Now down the stairs and through the narrow openings in the bulkheads, where the thud of the hostile projectiles sounds more and more hollow, and here, at last, is the door of the shell-chamber containing the shells for the 8-inch guns in the forward starboard turret.

Inside the bells rang and rattled, calling in vain for ammunition; but the guns of the *Connecticut* still remained silent.

The petty officer, hurrying on before his three men, now stood at the telephone.

"Armor-piercing shells, quickly!" came the urgent order from above. And when the electric lever refused to work, the two sailors raised the shell weighing over two hundredweight in their brawny arms and shoved it into the frame of the lift, which began to move automatically.

"Thank God," said the lieutenant in command of the turret, as the first shell appeared at the mouth of the dark tube. Into the breech with it and the two cartridges after it. When the lieutenant had taken his position at the telescope sight in order to determine the direction and distance for firing, orders came down from the commander to fire at the enemy's leading ship, the *Satsuma*. The distance was only 2800 yards, so near had the enemy come. And at this ridiculously short distance, contrary to all the rules of naval warfare, the Americans opened fire.

"2800 yards, to the right beneath the first gun-turret of the *Satsuma*," called the lieutenant to the two gunners. They took the elevation and then waited for the ship that was rolling to port to regain the level after being lifted up by the waves. Detached clouds hurried across the field of the telescope, but suddenly the sun appeared like a bright spot above the horizon and dark brown smoke became visible. The foremast of the *Satsuma* with its multicolored signal-flags appeared in the field of vision.... A final quick correction for elevation ... a slight pressure of the electric trigger. Fire! The gray silhouette of the *Satsuma*, across which quivered the flash from the gun, rose quickly in the round field; then came foaming, plunging waves, and columns of water that rose up as the shells struck the water.

The loud reverberation of the shot—the first one fired on the American side—acted as a nerve-tonic all round, and all felt as though they had been relieved from an intolerable burden.

While the right gun was being reloaded and the stinking gases escaping from the gun filled the narrow chamber with their fumes, the lieutenant looked for traces of the effect of the shot. The wind whistled through the peep-hole and made his eyes smart. The shot did not seem to have touched the *Satsuma* at all. The foam seen in the bow was that produced by the ship's motion.

"Two hundred and fifty yards over," came through the telephone, and on the glass-plate of the distance-register, faintly illuminated by an electric lamp, appeared the number 2550.

"2550 yards!" repeated the lieutenant to the captain of the left gun, giving the angle of direction himself. The *Connecticut* again heaved over to port, and the thunder of cannon rolled over the waves of the Pacific.

"The shell burst at a thousand yards!" called the lieutenant. "What miserable fuses!"

"Bad shot," came down reproachfully through the telephone, "use percussion fuses."

"I am, but they're no good, they won't work," roared back the lieutenant. Then he went down into the turret and examined the new shell on the lift before it was pushed into the breech.

"All right," he said aloud, but added under his breath, suppressing an oath: "We mustn't let the men notice there's anything wrong, for the world!"

Another shot rang out, and again the shell burst a few hundred yards from the *Connecticut*, sending the water flying in every direction.

Again came the reproachful voice from above: "Bad shot, take percussion fuses!"

"That's what these are supposed to be," replied the lieutenant in a terrible state of excitement; "the shells are absolutely useless."

"Fire at the forepart of the *Satsuma* with shrapnel," rang out the command from the wall.

"Shrapnels from below!" ordered the lieutenant, and "shrapnels from below" was repeated by the man at the lift into the 'phone leading to the ammunition chamber.

But the lift continued to bring up the blue armor-piercing shells; five times more and then it stopped.

During a momentary pause in the firing on both sides, the buzzing and whirring of the electric apparatus of the lift could be distinctly heard. Then the lift appeared once more, this time with a red explosive shell.

"Aim at the forepart of the *Satsuma*, 1950 yards!"

The *Connecticut* rolled over heavily to starboard, the water splashed over the railing, rushing like a torrent between the turrets; then the ship heeled over to the other side. The shot rang out.

"At last," cried the lieutenant proudly, pointing through the peep-hole. High up in the side of the *Satsuma*, close to the little 12-cm. quick-firing gun, a piece was seen to be missing when the smoke from the bursting shell had disappeared.

"Good shot," came from above; "go on firing with shrapnel!"

The distance-register silently showed the number 1850. Then came a deafening roar from below and the sharp ring of tearing iron. A hostile shell had passed obliquely below the turret into the forepart of the *Connecticut*, and clouds of thick black smoke completely obscured the view through the peep-hole.

"Four degrees higher!" commanded the lieutenant.

"Not yet correct," he grumbled; "three degrees higher still!" He waited for the *Connecticut* to roll to port.

"What's the matter?"

"Use higher elevation in turrets. The *Connecticut* has a leak and is listing to starboard," said the telephone. "Three degrees higher!" ordered the lieutenant.

A shot from the left barrel.

"Splendid," cried the lieutenant; "that was a fine shot! But lower, lower, we're merely shooting their upper plates to bits," and the gun went on steadily firing.

The turrets on the starboard side were hit again and again, the hostile shells bursting perpetually against their armored sides. As if struck by electric discharges the gunners were continually thrown back from the rumbling walls, and they were almost deaf from the fearful din, so that all commands had to be yelled out at the top of the lungs.

The raging storm and the rough sea prevented the Americans from using a part of their guns. While the explosive shells from the enemy's heavy intermediate battery were able to demolish everything on deck and to pass through the unarmored portions of the sides, working fearful havoc in the interior and among the crew, the light American secondary battery was compelled to keep silence.

An attempt had been made, to be sure, to bring the 7-inch guns into action, but it proved of no avail. The gunners stood ready at their posts to discharge the shells at the enemy, but it was utterly impossible, for no sooner had they taken aim, than they lost it again as the hostile ships disappeared in the foaming glassy-green waves that broke against their sides. The water penetrated with the force of a stream from a nozzle through the cracks in the plates and poured into the casemates till the men were standing up to their knees in water. At last the only thing that could be done was to open the doors behind the guns in order to let the water out; but this arrangement had the disadvantage of allowing a good deal of the water which had run out to return in full force and pile up in one corner the next time the ship rolled over, and on account of this perpetual battle with the waves outside and the rolling water inside, it was impossible for the men to aim properly or to achieve any results with their shots. It was therefore deemed best to stop the firing here, and to have the gunners relieve the men at the turret-guns, who had suffered greatly from the enemy's fire. The men in charge of the completely demolished small guns on the upper deck had already been assigned to similar duty.

We therefore had to depend entirely on our 12-inch and 8-inch guns in the turrets, while the enemy was able to bring into action all his broadside guns on the starboard side, which was only little affected by the storm. And this superiority had been used to such advantage in the first eleven minutes of the battle, before the surprised Americans could reply, that the decks of the latter's ships, especially of the admiral's flag-ship, were a mass of wreckage even before the first American shot had been fired. The decks were strewn with broken bridges, planks, stanchions and torn rigging, and into the midst of this chaos now fell the tall funnels and pieces of the steel masts. In most instances the water continually pouring over the decks put out the fires; but the *Vermont* was nevertheless burning aft and the angry flames could be seen bursting out of the gaping holes made by the shells.

Admiral Perry, in company with the commander and staff-officers, watched the progress of the battle from the conning-tower. The officers on duty at the odometers calmly furnished the distance between their ship and the enemy to the turrets and casemates, and the lieutenant in command of the fire-control on the platform above the conning-tower coolly and laconically reported the results of the shots, at the same time giving the necessary corrections, which were at once transmitted to the various turrets by telephone. The rolling of the ships in the heavy seas made occasional pauses in the firing absolutely necessary.

The report that a series of shells belonging to the 8-inch guns in the front turret had unreliable fuses led to considerable swearing in the conning-tower, but while the officers were still cursing the commission for accepting such useless stuff, a still greater cause for anxiety became apparent.

Even before the Americans had begun their fire, the Japanese shells had made a few enormous holes in the unprotected starboard side of the *Connecticut*, behind the stem and just above the armored belt, and through these the water poured in and flooded all the inner chambers. As the armored gratings above the hatchways leading below had also been destroyed or had not yet been closed, several compartments in the forepart of the ship filled with water. The streams of water continually pouring in through the huge holes rendered it impossible to enter the rooms beneath the armored deck or to close the hatchways. The pumps availed nothing, but fortunately the adjacent bulkheads proved to be watertight. Nevertheless the *Connecticut* buried her nose deep into the sea and thereby offered ever-increasing resistance to the oncoming waves. Captain Farlow therefore ordered some of the watertight compartments aft to be filled with water in order to restore the ship's balance. Similar conditions were reported from other ships.

But scarcely had this damage been thus fairly well adjusted, when a new misfortune was reported. Two Japanese projectiles had struck the ship simultaneously just below her narrow armor-belt as she heaved over to port, the shells entering the unprotected side just in front of the engine-rooms, and as the adjacent bulkheads could not offer sufficient resistance to the pressure of the inpouring water, they were forced in, and as a result the *Connecticut* heeled over badly to starboard, making it necessary to fill some of the port compartments with water, since the guns could not otherwise obtain the required elevation. This caused the ship to sink deeper and deeper, until the armor-belt was entirely below the standard waterline and the water which had rushed in through the many holes had already reached the passageways above the armored deck. The splashing about in these rushing floods, the continual bursting of the enemy's shells, the groans and moans of the wounded, and the vain attempts to get out the collision-mats on the starboard side—precautions that savored of preservation measures while at the same time causing a great loss of life—all this began to impair the crew's powers of resistance.

As the reports from below grew more and more discouraging, Captain Farlow sent Lieutenant Meade down to examine into the state of the chambers above the armored deck. The latter asked his comrade, Curtis, to take his place at the telephone, but receiving no answer, he looked around, and saw poor Curtis with his face torn off by a piece of shell still bending over his telephone between two dead signalmen.... Lieutenant Meade turned away with a shiver, and, calling a midshipman to take his place, he left the conning-tower, which was being struck continually by hissing splinters from bursting shells.

Everywhere below the same picture presented itself—rushing water splashing high up against the walls in all the passages, through which ambulance transports were making their way with difficulty. In a corner not far from the staircase leading to the hospital lay a young midshipman, Malion by name, pressing both hands against a gaping wound in his abdomen, out of which the viscera protruded, and crying to some one to put him out of his misery with a bullet. What an end to a bright young life! Anything but think! One could only press on, for individual lives and human suffering were of small moment here compared with the portentous question whether the steel sides of the ship and the engines would hold out.

"Shoot me; deliver me from my torture!" rang out the cry of the lieutenant's dying friend behind him; and there before him, right against the wall, lay the sailor Ralling, that fine chap from Maryland who was one of the men who had won the gig-race at Newport News; now he stared vacantly into space, his mouth covered with blood and foam. "Shot in the lung!" thought Meade, hurrying on and trying, oh so hard, not to think!

The black water gurgled and splashed around his feet as he rushed on, dashing with a hollow sound against one side of the passage when the ship heeled over, only to be tossed back in a moment with equal force.

What was that?—Lieutenant Meade had reached the officers' mess—was it music or were his ears playing him a trick? Meade opened the door and thought at first he must be dreaming. There sat his friend and comrade, Lieutenant Besser, at the piano, hammering wildly on the keys. That same Johnny Besser who, on account of his theological predilections went by the nickname of "The Reverend," and who could argue until long after midnight over the most profound Biblical problems, that same Johnny Besser, who was perpetually on the water-wagon. There he sat, banging away as hard as he could on the piano! Meade rushed at him angrily and seizing him by the arm cried: "Johnny, what are you doing here? Are you crazy?"

Johnny took no notice of him whatever, but went on playing and began in a strange uncanny voice to sing the old mariner's song:

> "Tom Brown's mother she likes whisky in her tea,
> As we go rolling home.
> Glory, Glory Hallelujah."

Horror seized Meade, and he tried to pull Johnny away from the piano, but the resistance offered by the poor fellow who had become mentally deranged from sheer terror was too great, and he had to give up the struggle.

From the outside came the din of battle. Meade threw the door of the mess shut behind him, shivering with horror. Once more he heard the strains of "Glory, Glory, Hallelujah," and then he hurried upstairs. He kept the condition in which he had found Johnny to himself.

"IT WENT UP IN A SLANTING DIRECTION AND THEN, ... IT STEERED STRAIGHT FOR THE ENEMY'S BALLOON...."

When Lieutenant Meade got back to the conning-tower to make his report, the two fleets had passed each other in a parallel course. The enemy's shells had swept the decks of the *Connecticut* with the force of a hurricane. The gunners from the port side had already been called on to fill up the gaps in the turrets on the starboard side. By this time dead bodies were removed only where they were in the way, and even the wounded were left to lie where they had fallen.

When large pieces of wood from the burning boats began to be thrown on deck by the bursting shells, a fresh danger was created, and the attempt was made to toss them overboard with the aid of the cranes. But this succeeded only on the port side. The starboard crane was smashed to bits by a Japanese explosive shell just as it was raising a launch, the same shot carrying off the third funnel just behind it. When Togo's last ship had left the *Connecticut* behind, only one funnel full of gaping holes and half of the mainmast were left standing on the deck of the admiral's flag-ship, which presented a wild chaos of bent and broken ironwork. Through the ruins of the deck structures rose the flames and thick smoke from the boilers.

The Japanese ships seemed to be invulnerable in their vital parts. It is true that the *Satsuma* had lost a funnel, and that both masts of the *Kashima* were broken off, but except for a few holes above the armor-belt and one or two guns that had been put out of action and the barrels of which pointed helplessly into the air, the enemy showed little sign of damage. Those first eleven minutes, during which the enemy had had things all to himself, had given him an advantage which no amount of bravery or determined energy could counteract. In addition to this, many of the American telescope-sights began to get out of order, as they bent under the blows of the enemy's shells against the turrets. Thus the aim of the Americans, which owing to the heavy seas and to the smoke from the Japanese guns blown into their eyes by the wind was poor enough as it was, became more uncertain still. As the enemy passed, several torpedoes had been cleared by the Americans, but the shining metal-fish could not keep their course against the oncoming waves, and Admiral Perry was forced to notify his ships by wireless to desist from further attempts to use them, in order that his own ships might not be endangered by them.

The enemy, on the contrary, used his torpedoes with better success. A great mass of boiling foam rose suddenly beside the *Kansas*, which was just heeling to port, and this was followed immediately by sheets of flame and black clouds of smoke which burst from every hole and crevice in the sides and the turrets. The *Kansas* listed heavily to starboard and then disappeared immediately in the waves. The torpedo must have exploded in an ammunition chamber. On the burning *Vermont* the steering-gear seemed to be out of order. The battleship sheered sharply to port, thus presenting its stern, which was almost hidden in heavy clouds of smoke, to the enemy, who immediately raked and tore it with shells. The *Minnesota* was drifting in a helpless condition with her starboard-railing deep under water, while thick streams of water poured from her bilge-pumps on the port side. She gradually fell behind, whereupon the last ship of the line, the *New Hampshire*, passed her on the fire side, covering her riddled hull for a moment, but then steamed on to join the only two ships in Admiral Perry's fleet which were still in fairly good condition, namely the *Connecticut* and the *Louisiana*.

When the hostile fleet began to fall slowly back—the battle had been in progress for barely half an hour—Admiral Perry hoped for a moment that by swinging his three ships around to starboard he would be able to get to windward of the enemy and thus succeed in bringing his almost intact port artillery into action. But even before he could issue his commands, he saw the six Japanese ironclads turn to port and steam towards the Americans at full speed, pouring out tremendous clouds of smoke. Misfortunes never come singly; at this moment came the report that the boilers of the *New Hampshire* had been badly damaged. Unless the admiral wished to leave the injured ship to her fate, he was now forced to reduce the speed of the other two ships to six knots. This was the beginning of the end.

It was of no use for Admiral Perry to swing his three ships around to starboard. The enemy, owing to his superior speed, could always keep a parallel course and remain on the starboard side. One turret after the other was put out of action. When the casemate with its three intact 7-inch guns could at last be brought into play on the lee-side, it was too late. At such close quarters the steel-walls of the casemates and the mountings were shot to pieces by the enemy's shells. The fire-control refused to act, the wires and speaking-tubes were destroyed, and each gun had to depend on itself. The electric installation had been put out of commission on the *Louisiana* by a shell bursting through the armored deck and destroying the dynamos. As the gun-turrets could no longer be swung around and the ammunition-lifts had come to a stand-still in consequence, the *Louisiana* was reduced to a helpless wreck. She sank in the waves at 11.15, and shortly afterwards the *New Hampshire*, which was already listing far to starboard because the water had risen above the armored deck, capsized. By 12.30 the *Connecticut* was the sole survivor. She continued firing from the 12-inch guns in the rear turret and from the two 8-inch starboard turrets.

At this point a large piece of shell slipped through the peep-hole of the conning-tower and smashed its heavy armored dome. The next shot might prove fatal. Admiral Perry was compelled to leave the spot he had maintained so bravely; in a hail of splinters he at last managed to reach the steps leading from the bridge; they were wet with the blood of the dead and dying and the last four had been shot away altogether. The other mode of egress, the armored tube inside the turret, was stopped up with the bodies of two dead signalmen. The admiral let himself carefully down by holding on to the bent railing of the steps, and was just in time to catch the blood-covered body of his faithful comrade, Captain Farlow, who had been struck by a shell as he stood on the lowest step. The admiral leaned the body gently against the side of the military-mast, which had been dyed yellow by the deposits of the hostile shells.

Stepping over smoldering ruins and through passages filled with dead and wounded men, over whose bodies the water splashed and gurgled, the admiral at last reached his post below the armored deck.

To this spot were brought the reports from the fire-control stationed at the rear mast and from the last active stations. It was a mournful picture that the admiral received here of the condition of the *Connecticut*. The dull din of battle, the crashing and rumbling of the hostile shells, the suffocating smoke which penetrated even here below, the rhythmic groaning of the engine and the noise of the pumps were united here into an uncanny symphony. The ventilators had to be closed, as they sent down biting smoke from the burning deck instead of fresh air. The nerves of the officers and crews were in a state of fearful tension; they had reached the point where nothing matters and where destruction is looked forward to as a deliverance.

Who was that beside the admiral who said something about the white flag, to him, the head of the squadron, to the man who had been intrusted with the honor of the Stars and Stripes? It was only a severely wounded petty-officer murmuring to himself in the wild delirium of fever. For God's sake, anything but that! The admiral turned around sharply and called into the tube leading to the stern turret: "Watch over the flag; it must not be struck!"

No one answered—dead iron, dead metal, not a human sound could be heard in that steel tomb. And now some of the electric lights suddenly went out. "I won't die here in this smoky steel box," said the admiral to himself; "I won't drown here like a mouse in a trap." There was nothing more to be done down here anyway, for most of the connections had been cut off, and so Admiral Perry turned over the command of the *Connecticut* to a young lieutenant with the words: "Keep them firing as long as you can." Then murmuring softly to himself, "It's of no use anyhow," he crept through a narrow bulkhead-opening to a stairway and groped his way up step by step. Suddenly he touched something soft and warm; it groaned loudly. Heavens! it was a sailor who had dragged his shattered limbs into this corner. "Poor fellow," said the admiral, and climbed up, solitary and alone, to the deck of his lost ship. The din of battle sounded louder and louder, and at last he reached the deck beneath the rear bridge. A badly wounded signalman was leaning against a bit of railing that had remained standing, staring at the admiral with vacant eyes. "Are the signal-halyards still clear?" asked Perry. "Yes," answered the man feebly.

"Then signal at once: Three cheers for the United States!" The little colored flags flew up to the yardarm like lightning, and it grew quiet on the *Connecticut*.

The last shell, the last cartridge was shoved into the breech, one more shot was aimed at the enemy from the heated barrels, and then all was still except for the crash of the hostile projectiles, the crackling of the flames and the howling of the wind. The other side, too, gradually ceased firing. With the *Satsuma* and the *Aki* in the van and the four other ships following, the enemy's squadron advanced, enveloped in a thin veil of smoke.

High up in the stern of the *Connecticut* and at her mastheads waved the tattered Stars and Stripes. The few gunners, who had served the guns to the end, crept out of the turrets and worked their way up over broken steps. There were fifty-seven of them, all that remained of the proud squadron. Three cheers for their country came from the parched throats of these last heroes of the *Connecticut*. "Three cheers for the United States!" Admiral Perry drew his sword, and "Hurrah" it rang once more across the water to the ships sailing under the flag which bore the device of a crimson Rising Sun on a white field. There memories of the old days of the Samurai knighthood were aroused, and a signal appeared on the rear top mast of the *Satsuma*, whereupon all six battleships lowered their flags as a last tribute to a brave enemy.

Then the *Connecticut* listed heavily to starboard, and the next wave could not raise the heavy ship, bleeding from a thousand wounds. It sank and sank, and while Admiral Perry held fast to a bit of railing and waited with moist eyes for the end, the words of the old "Star-Spangled Banner," which had been heard more than once in times of storm and peril, rang out from the deck of the *Connecticut*. Then, with her flag waving to the last, the admiral's flag-ship sank slowly beneath the waves, leaving a bloody glow behind her. That was the end.

CHAPTER XI

CAPTAIN WINSTANLEY

Captain Winstanley slowly opened his eyes and stared at the low ceiling of his cabin on the white oil-paint of which the sunbeams, entering through the porthole, were painting numerous circles and quivering reflections. Slowly he began to collect his thoughts. Could it have been a dream or the raving of delirium? He tried to raise himself on his narrow bed, but fell back as he felt a sharp pain. There was no mistake about the pain—that was certainly real. What on earth had happened? He asked himself this question again and again as he watched the thousands of circles and quivering lines drawn by the light on the ceiling.

Winstanley stared about him and suddenly started violently. Then it was all real, a terrible reality? Yes, for there sat his friend Longstreet of the *Nebraska* with his back against the wall of the cabin, in a dripping wet uniform, fast asleep.

"Longstreet!" he called.

His friend awoke and stared at him in astonishment.

"Longstreet, did it all really happen, or have I been dreaming?"

No answer.

"Longstreet," he began again more urgently, "tell me, is it all over, can it be true?"

Longstreet nodded, incapable of speech.

"Our poor, poor country," whispered Winstanley.

After a long pause Longstreet suddenly broke the silence by remarking: "The *Nebraska* went down at about six o'clock."

"And the *Georgia* a little earlier," said Winstanley; "but where are we? How did I get here?"

"The torpedo boat *Farragut* fished us up after the battle. We are on board the hospital ship *Ontario* with about five hundred other survivors."

"And what has become of the rest of our squadron?" asked Winstanley apprehensively. Longstreet only shrugged his shoulders.

Then they both dozed again and listened to the splashing and gurgling of the water against the ship's side and to the dull, regular thud of the engine which by degrees began to form words in Winstanley's fever-heated imagination—meaningless words which seemed to pierce his brain with painful sharpness: "Oh, won't you come across," rose and fell the oily melody, keeping time with the action of the piston-rods of the engine, "Oh, won't you come across," repeated the walls, and "Oh, won't you come across," clattered the water-bottle over in the wooden rack. Again and again Winstanley said the words to himself in an everlasting, dull repetition.

Longstreet looked at him compassionately, and murmured: "Another attack of fever." Then he got up, and bending over his comrade, looked out of the porthole.

Water everywhere; nothing but sparkling, glistening water, broad, blue, rolling waves to be seen as far as the eye could reach. Not a sign of a ship anywhere.

"Oh, won't you come across," repeated Longstreet, listlessly joining in the rhythm of the engines. Then he stretched himself and sank back on his chair in a somnolent state, thinking over the experiences of the night.

So this was all that was left of the Pacific Fleet — a hospital ship with a few hundred wounded officers and men, all that remained of Admiral Crane's fleet, which had been attacked with torpedo boats by Admiral Kamimura at three o'clock on the night of May eighth, after Togo had destroyed Perry's squadron.

It had been a horrible surprise. The enemy must have intercepted the signals between the squadron and the scouts, but as the Japanese had not employed their wireless telegraph at all, none of the American reconnoitering cruisers had had its suspicions aroused. Then the wireless apparatus had suddenly got out of order and all further intercommunication among the American ships was cut off, while a few minutes later came the first torpedo explosions, followed by fountains of foam, the dazzling light of the searchlights and sparks from the falling shells. The Americans could not reply to the hostile fire until much, much later, and then it was almost over. When the gray light of dawn spread over the surface of the water, it only lighted up a few drifting, sinking wrecks, the irrecognizable ruins of Admiral Crane's proud squadron, which were soon completely destroyed by the enemy's torpedoes.

Kamimura had already disappeared beyond the horizon with his ships, not being interested in his enemy's remains.

"Oh, won't you come across," groaned and wailed the engine quite loudly as a door to the engine-room was opened. Longstreet jumped up with a start, and then climbed wearily and heavily up the stairs. The entire deck had been turned into a hospital, and the few doctors were hurrying from one patient to another.

Longstreet went up to a lieutenant in a torn uniform who was leaning against the railing with his head between his hands, staring across the water. "Where are we going, Harry?" asked Longstreet.

"I don't know; somewhere or other; it doesn't matter much where."

Longstreet left him and climbed up to the bridge. Here he shook hands in silence with a few comrades and then asked the captain of the *Ontario* where they were going.

"If possible, to San Francisco," was the answer. "But I'm afraid the Japanese will be attacking the coast-batteries by this time, and besides that chap over there seems to have his eyes on us," he added, pointing to port.

Longstreet looked in the direction indicated and saw a gray cruiser with three high funnels making straight for the *Ontario*. At this moment a signalman delivered a wireless message to the captain: "The cruiser yonder wants to know our name and destination."

"Signal back: United States hospital ship *Ontario* making for San Francisco," said the captain. This signal was followed by the dull boom of a shot across the water; but the *Ontario* continued on her course.

Then a flash was seen from a forward gun of the cruiser and a shell splashed into the water about one hundred yards in front of the *Ontario*, bursting with a deafening noise.

The captain hesitated a second, then he ordered the engines to stop, turned over the command on the bridge to the first officer and went himself to the signaling apparatus to send the following message: "United States hospital ship *Ontario* with five hundred wounded on board relies on protection of ambulance-flag."

A quarter of an hour later, the Japanese armored cruiser *Idzumo* stopped close to the *Ontario* and lowered a cutter, which took several Japanese officers and two doctors over to the *Ontario*.

While a Japanese officer of high rank was received by the captain in his cabin in order to discuss the best method of providing for the wounded, Longstreet went down to Winstanley.

"Well, old man, how are you?" he asked.

"Pretty miserable, Longstreet; what's going to become of us?"

Longstreet hesitated, but Winstanley insisted: "Tell me, old chap, tell me the truth. Where are we bound to—what's going to become of us?"

"We're going to San Francisco," said Longstreet evasively.

"And the enemy?"

Longstreet remained silent again.

"But the enemy, Longstreet, where's the enemy? We mustn't fall into his hands!"

"Brace up, Winstanley," said Longstreet, "we're in the hands of the Japanese now."

Winstanley started up from his bed, but sank back exhausted by the terrible pain in his right arm which had been badly wounded.

"No, no, anything but that! I'd rather be thrown overboard than fall into the hands of the Japanese! It's all over, there's no use struggling any more!"

"Longstreet," he cried, with eyes burning with fever, "Longstreet, promise me that you'll throw me overboard rather than give me up to the Japanese!"

"No, Winstanley, no; think of our country, remember that it is in sore need of men, of men to restore the honor of the Stars and Stripes, of men to drive the enemy from the field and conquer them in the end."

At this moment the door opened and a Japanese lieutenant entered, carrying a small note-book in his hand.

At sight of him Winstanley shouted: "Longstreet, hand me a weapon of some sort; that fellow — —"

The Jap saluted and said: "Gentlemen, I am sorry for the circumstances which compel me to ask you to give me your names and ships. Rest assured that a wounded enemy may safely rely on Japanese chivalry. If you will follow the example of all the other officers and give your word of honor not to escape, you will receive all possible care and attention in the hospital at San Francisco without any irksome guard. Will you be so good as to give me your names?"

"Lieutenant Longstreet of the *Nebraska.*"

"Thank you."

"Captain Winstanley, commander of the *Georgia,*" added Longstreet for Winstanley.

"Will you give me your word of honor?"

Longstreet gave his, but Winstanley shook his head and said: *"You can do what you like with me; I refuse to give my word of honor."*

The Jap shrugged his shoulders and disappeared.

"Longstreet, nursed in San Francisco, is that what the Jap said? Then San Francisco must be in their hands." At these words the wounded captain of the *Georgia* burst into bitter tears and sobs shook the body of the poor man, who in his ravings fancied himself back on board his ship giving orders for the big guns to fire at the enemy. Longstreet held his friend's hand and stared in silence at the white ceiling upon which the sunbeams painted myriads of quivering lines and circles.

At one o'clock the *Ontario* came in sight of the Golden Gate, where the white banner with its crimson sun was seen to be waving above all the fortifications.

While the Japanese were attacking San Francisco early on the morning of May seventh, their fleet was stationed off San Diego on the lookout for the two American maneuvering fleets. The intercepted orders from the Navy Department had informed the enemy that Admiral Perry, with his blue squadron of six battleships of the *Connecticut* class, intended to attack San Francisco and the other ports and naval-stations on the Pacific, and that the yellow fleet, under command of Admiral Crane, was to carry out the defense. The latter had drawn up his squadron in front of San Francisco on May second, and on May fifth Admiral Perry had left Magdalen Bay. From this time on every report sent by wireless was read by harmless looking Japanese trading-vessels sailing under the English flag.

The first thing to be done on the morning of the seventh was to render Magdalen Bay useless, in order to prevent all communication with distant ships. A trick put the station in the enemy's possession. Here, too, there were several Japanese shopkeepers who did good business with their stores along the Bay. Early on Sunday morning these busy yellow tradesmen were suddenly transformed into a company of troops who soon overpowered the weak garrison in charge of the signal-station. The Japanese cruiser *Yakumo*, approaching from the North, had been painted white like the American cruisers, and this is why she had been taken, as the reader will remember, for the armored cruiser *New York*, which was actually lying off San Francisco assigned to Admiral Crane's yellow fleet. The *Yakumo* was to prevent the two destroyers *Hull* and *Hopkins* from escaping from the Bay, and both boats were literally shot to pieces when they made the attempt. This action hopelessly isolated the maneuvering fleets.

By eight o'clock in the morning Togo's squadron, consisting of the flag-ships *Satsuma*, the *Aki*, *Katou*, *Kashimi*, *Mikasa* and *Akahi*, and forming the backbone of the Japanese battle-fleet, had succeeded in locating Admiral Perry's squadron, thanks to intercepted wireless dispatches. The Japanese refrained from using their wireless apparatus, so as to avoid attracting the attention of the American squadron. The unfinished message sent at nine o'clock from Magdalen Bay told Togo that the surprise there had been successful, and a little later the order to strengthen the American advance, sent in the same way, enabled him to ascertain the exact position of both the main group of cruisers and the scouts and lookout ships. Similarly it was learned that the latter were extremely weak, and accordingly Togo detached four armored cruisers, the huge new 25-knot *Tokio* and *Osaka*, and the *Ibuki* and *Kurama*, to destroy the American van, and this he succeeded in accomplishing after a short engagement which took place at the same time as the attack on Perry's armored ships.

The *Denver* and *Chattanooga* were soon put out of business by a few shells which entered their unprotected hulls, and the five destroyers, which were unable to use their torpedoes in such a heavy sea, were likewise soon done for.

Under cover of a torrent of rain, Togo came in sight of the American ships when the distance between the two squadrons was only 5,500 yards.

At the moment when Admiral Perry's ships emerged out of the rain, Admiral Togo opened the battle by sending the following signal from the *Satsuma*:

"To-day must avenge Kanagawa. As Commodore Perry then knocked with his sword at the gate of Nippon, so will we to-day burst open San Francisco's Golden Gate."[1]

The signal was greeted with enthusiasm and loud cries of "*Banzai!*" on board all the ships. Then the battle began, and by the time the sun had reached its zenith, Admiral Perry's squadron had disappeared in the waves of the Pacific. The first eleven minutes, before the Americans could bring their guns into action, had determined the outcome of the battle. The ultimate outcome of the battle had, of course, been accelerated by the fact that the first shells had created such fearful havoc in the fore-parts of three of the American ships, quantities of water pouring

---

[1] Perry, the American commodore, with a fleet of only eight ships, forced Japan to sign the agreement of Kanagawa, opening the chief harbors in Japan to American trading-vessels, in the year 1854.

in which caused the ships to list and made it necessary to fill the compartments on the opposite side in order to restore the equilibrium.

Admiral Kamimura was less fortunate at first with the second squadron. He was led astray by the wrong interpretation of a wireless signal and did not sight Admiral Crane's fleet till towards evening, and then it was not advisable to begin the attack at once, lest the Americans should escape under cover of darkness. Kamimura, therefore, decided to wait until shortly after midnight, and then to commence operations with his eight destroyers and apply the finishing touches with his heavy guns.

Admiral Crane's squadron consisted of six battleships—the three new battleships *Virginia*, *Nebraska* and *Georgia*, the two older vessels *Kearsage* and *Kentucky*, and, lastly, the *Iowa*. Then there were the two armored cruisers *St. Louis* and *Milwaukee*, and the unprotected cruisers *Tacoma* and *Des Moines*, which, on account of their speed of 16.5 knots and their lack of any armor, were as useless as cruisers as were their sister ships in Admiral Perry's squadron. One single well-aimed shell would suffice to put them out of action.

It was a terrible surprise when the Japanese destroyers began the attack under cover of the night. Not until dawn did the Americans actually catch sight of their enemy, and that was when Kamimura left the field of battle, which was strewn with sinking American ships, with his six practically unharmed battleships headed in a southwesterly direction to join Togo's fleet, who had already been informed of the victory. The work of cleaning up was left to the destroyers, who sank the badly damaged American ships with their torpedoes. The hospital ship *Ontario*, attached to the yellow fleet, and a torpedo boat fished up the survivors of this short battle. Then the *Ontario* started for San Francisco, while the leaking *Farragut* remained behind.

The Americans had been able to distinguish, with a fair degree of certainty, that Kamimura's squadron consisted of the *Shikishima*, the battleships *Iwami* (ex *Orel*), the *Sagami* (ex *Peresvjet*), and *Tumo* (ex *Pobjeda*), all three old Russian ships, and of the two new armored cruisers *Ikoma* and *Tsukuba*. Then there were the two enormous battleships which were not included in the Japanese Navy List at all, and the two huge cruisers *Yokohama* and *Shimonoseki* which, according to Japanese reports, were still building, while in reality they had been finished and added to the fleet long ago.

The circumstances connected with these two battleships were rather peculiar. The report was spread in 1906 that China was going to build a new fleet and that she had ordered two big battleships from the docks at Yokosuka. This rumor was contradicted both at Pekin and at Tokio. The Americans and everybody in Europe wondered who was going to pay for the ships. The trouble is, we ask altogether too many questions, instead of investigating for ourselves. As a matter of fact, the ships were laid down in 1908, though everybody outside the walls of the Japanese shipyard was made to believe that only gunboats were being built. We have probably forgotten how, at the time, a German newspaper called our attention to the fact that not only these two battleships—of the English *Dreadnought* type—but also the two armored cruisers building at Kure ostensibly for China, would probably never sail under the yellow dragon banner, but in case of war, would either be added directly to Japan's fleet or be bought back from China.

And so it turned out. Just before the outbreak of the war, the Sun Banner was hoisted quietly on the two battleships and they were given the names of *Nippon* and *Hokkaido*, respectively; but they were omitted from the official Japanese Navy List and left out of our calculations. How Pekin and Tokio came to terms with regard to these two ships remains one of the many secrets of east Asiatic politics. The generally accepted political belief that China was not financially strong enough to build a new fleet and that Japan, supposedly on the very verge of bankruptcy, could not possibly carry out her *postbellum* programme, was found to have rested on empty phrases employed by the press on both sides of the ocean merely for the sake of running a story. There has never yet been a time in the history of the world when war was prevented by a lack of funds. How could Prussia, absolutely devoid of resources, have carried on the war it did against Napoleon a hundred years ago, unless this were so?

In the redistribution of our war vessels in the Atlantic and the Pacific after the return of the fleet from its journey round the world, the Navy Department had calculated as follows: Japan had fifteen battleships, six large new ones and nine older ones; in addition she had six large new and eight older armored cruisers. We have one armored cruiser and three cruisers in Manila, and these can take care of at least five Japanese armored cruisers. Japan therefore has fifteen battleships and nine armored cruisers left for making an attack. Now if we keep two squadrons, each consisting of six battleships—the *Texas* among them—off the Pacific coast and add to these the coast-batteries, the mines and the submarines, we shall possess a naval force which the enemy will never dare attack.

Japan, on the other hand, figured as follows: We have two squadrons, each consisting of six battleships, among which there are six that are superior to any American fighting ship; these with the nine armored cruisers and the advantage of a complete surprise, give us such a handicap that we have nothing to fear. As a reserve, lying off San Francisco, are the ironclads *Hizen* (ex *Retvisan*), *Tango* (ex *Poltawa*), *Iki* (ex *Nicolai*), and the armored cruisers *Azuma*, *Idzumo*, *Asama*, *Tokiwa*, and *Yakumo*. Besides these there are the two mortar-boat divisions and the cruisers sent to Seattle, while the armored cruiser *Iwate* and two destroyers were sent to Magdalen Bay. All that remained in home waters were the fourth squadron, consisting of former Russian ships, and the cruisers which would soon be relieved at the Philippines.

The enemy had figured correctly and we had not. The two battles of the seventh and eighth of May were decided in the first ten minutes, before we had fired a single shot. And would the Japanese calculation have been correct also if Perry had beaten Togo or Crane Kamimura? Most decidedly so, for not a single naval harbor or coaling-station, or repairing-dock on the Pacific coast would have been ready to receive Perry or Crane with their badly damaged squadrons. On the other hand, the remnants of our fleet would have had all the Japanese battleships, all the armored cruisers and a large collection of torpedo-boats continually on their heels, and would thus have been forced to another battle in which, being entirely without a base of operations, they would without a doubt have suffered a complete defeat.

Our mines in the various arsenals and our three submarines at the Mare Island Wharf in San Francisco fell into the enemy's hands like ripe plums. It was quite superfluous for the Japanese to take their steamer for transporting submarines, which had been built for them in England, to San Francisco.

Nothing remained to us but the glory that not one of our ships had surrendered to the enemy—all had sunk with their flags flying. After all, it was one thing to fight against the demoralized fleet of the Czar and quite another to fight against the Stars and Stripes. Our blue-jackets had saved the honor of the white race in the eyes of the yellow race on the waves of the Pacific, even if they had thus far shown them only how brave American sailors die. But the loss of more than half our officers and trained men was even a more severe blow than the sinking of our ships. These could not be replaced at a moment's notice, but months and months of hard work would be required and new squadrons must be found. But from where were they to come?

Only a single vessel of the Pacific fleet escaped from the battle and the pursuing Japanese cruisers: this was the torpedo-destroyer *Barry*, commanded by Lieutenant-Commander Dayton, who had been in command of the torpedo flotilla attached to Admiral Perry's squadron. He had attempted twice, advancing boldly into the teeth of the gale, to launch a torpedo in the direction of the *Satsuma*, but the sea was too rough and each time took the torpedo out of its course.

The badly damaged destroyer entered the harbor of Buenaventura on the coast of Colombia on May eleventh, followed closely by the Japanese steamer Iwate, which had been lying off the coast of Panama. Grinding his teeth with rage, Dayton had to look on while a Colombian officer in ragged uniform, plentifully supplied with gilt, who was in the habit of commanding his tiny antediluvian gunboat from the door of a harbor saloon, came on board the *Barry* and ordered the breeches of the guns and the engine-valves to be removed, at the same time depriving the crew of their arms. The Japanese waiting outside the harbor had categorically demanded this action of the government in Bogota. This humiliating degradation before all the harbor loafers and criminals, before the crowds of exulting Chinese and Japanese coolies, who were only too delighted to see the white man compelled to submit to a handful of marines the entire batch of whom were not worth one American sailor, was far harder to bear than all the days of battle put together. And even now, when Admiral Dayton's fame reaches beyond the seas and the name of James Dayton is in every sailor's mouth as the savior of his people, yes, even now, he will tell you how at the moment when, outside the Straits of Magellan, he crushed the Japanese cruisers with his cruiser-squadron, thereby once again restoring the Star Spangled Banner to its place of honor, the vision of that grinning row of faces exulting in the degradation of a severely damaged American torpedo-boat appeared before him. It is only such men as he, men who experienced the horrors of our downfall to the bitter end, who could lead us to victory—such men as Dayton and Winstanley.

CHAPTER XII

ARE YOU WINSTANLEY?

The bow of the English freighter *Port Elizabeth* was plowing its way through the broad waves of the Pacific on the evening of the fourteenth of September. The captain and the first mate were keeping a sharp lookout on the bridge, for they were approaching San Francisco. The steamer had taken a cargo of machinery and rails on board at Esquimault for San Francisco, as was duly set forth in the ship's papers. In Esquimault, too, the second mate enlisted, though the captain was not particularly eager to take a man who carried his arm in a sling. Since, however, he could find no one else to take the place of the former second mate, who had gone astray in the harbor saloons of Victoria, the captain engaged the volunteer, who called himself Henry Wilson, and thus far he had had no cause to regret his choice, as Wilson turned out to be a quiet, sober man, thoroughly familiar with the waters along the Pacific coast.

Wilson was in the chart-room, carefully examining the entrance to San Francisco; suddenly he turned and called through the open door to the captain on the bridge: "Captain, we are now eight miles from the Golden Gate; it's a wonder the Japs haven't discovered us yet."

"I should think they would station their cruisers as far out as this," answered the captain.

"After all, why should they?" asked Wilson, "there's nothing more to be done here, and the allies of our illustrious government can scarcely be asked to show much interest in an English steamer with a harmless cargo."

Wilson joined the captain and the first mate on the bridge, and all three leaned against the railing and tried through their glasses to discover the fires of the Golden Gate through the darkness; but not a gleam of light was to be seen.

"I don't believe we'll be allowed to enter the harbor at night," began the first mate again, "more especially as our instructions are to reach the Golden Gate at noon."

"Yes, but if the engines won't work properly, how the devil can they expect us to be punctual!" grumbled the captain.

"Look," cried Wilson, pointing to the blinding flash of a searchlight in front of them, "they've got us at last!" A few minutes later the brilliant bluish white beam of a searchlight was fixed on the *Port Elizabeth*.

"We'll keep right on our course," said the captain rather hurriedly to the man at the helm, "they'll soon let us know what they want. Wilson, you might get the ship's papers ready, we'll have visitors in a minute."

Scarcely had Wilson reached the captain's cabin when a bell rang sharply in the engine-room, and soon after this the engines began to slow down. When he returned to the bridge, the masts and low funnels of a ship and a thick trailing cloud of smoke could be seen crossing the reflection of the searchlight a few hundred yards away from the *Port Elizabeth*. Then a long black torpedo-boat with four low funnels emerged from the darkness, turned, and took the same course as the freighter. A boat was lowered and four sailors, a pilot and an officer stepped on board the *Port Elizabeth*.

The captain welcomed the Japanese lieutenant at the gangway and spoke a few words to him in a low tone, whereupon they both went into the captain's cabin. The Jap must have been satisfied by his examination of the ship's papers, for he returned to the bridge conversing with the captain in a most friendly and animated manner.

"This is my first mate, Hornberg," said the captain.

"An Englishman?" asked the Japanese.

"No, a German."

"A German?" repeated the Jap slowly. "The Germans are friends of Japan, are they not?" he asked, smiling pleasantly at the first mate, who, however, did not appear to have heard the question and turned away to go to the engine-room telephone.

"And this is my second mate, Wilson."

"An Englishman?" asked the Jap again.

"Yes, an Englishman," answered Wilson himself.

The Japanese officer looked at him keenly and said: "I seem to know you."

"It is not impossible," said Wilson, "I have been navigating Japanese waters for several years."

"Indeed?" asked the lieutenant, "may I inquire on which line?"

"On several lines; I know Shanghai, I have been from Hongkong to Yokohama in tramp steamers, and once during the Russian war I got to Nagasaki—also with a cargo of machinery," he added after a pause. "That was a dangerous voyage, for the Russians had just sailed from Vladivostock."

"With a cargo of machinery," repeated the Japanese officer, adding, "and you are familiar with these waters also?"

"Fairly so," said Wilson.

"Have you any relatives in the American Navy?" asked the Jap sharply.

"Not that I know of," answered Wilson, "my family is a large one, and as an Englishman I have relatives in all parts of the world, but none in the American Navy, so far as I know."

"Mr. Wilson, you will please take charge of the ship under the direction of the pilot brought along by the lieutenant. Mr. Hornberg's watch is up," said the captain, and went off with the Jap to his cabin.

Five minutes later the captain sent for the first mate, who returned to the bridge almost directly, saying: "Mr. Wilson, I am to take your place at the helm. The captain would like to see you."

"Certainly," answered Wilson curtly. The captain and the Jap were sitting together in the cabin over a glass of whisky. "The lieutenant," said the captain, "wants to know something about Esquimault; you know the harbor there, don't you?"

"Very slightly," answered Wilson, "I was only there three days."

"Were there any Japanese ships at Esquimault when you were there?"

"Yes, there was a Japanese cruiser in dock."

"What was her name?"

Wilson shrugged his shoulders and answered: "I couldn't say, I don't know the names of the Japanese ships."

"Won't you sit down and join us in a glass of whisky?" said the captain.

"What did you do to your arm?" asked the Japanese.

"I was thrown against the railing in a storm and broke it on the way from Shanghai to Victoria."

A long pause ensued which was at last broken by the Jap, who inquired: "Do you know Lieutenant Longstreet of the American Navy?"

"I know no one of that name in the American Navy."

The Jap scrutinized Wilson's face, but the latter remained perfectly unconcerned.

"You told the captain that you've been in San Francisco often," began the Jap again; "on what line were you?"

"On no line, I was at San Francisco for pleasure."

"When?"

"The last time was two years ago."

"May I see your papers?"

"Certainly," said Wilson, getting up to fetch them from his cabin.

The Japanese studied them closely.

"Curious," he said at last, "I could have sworn that I've seen you before."

Then he glanced again at one of the certificates and looking up at Wilson suddenly, over the edge of the paper, asked sharply: "Why have you two names?"

"I have only one," returned Wilson.

"Winstanley and Wilson," said the Jap with a decided emphasis on both names.

"I'm very sorry," said Wilson, "but I don't know anyone of the name of Winstanley, or whatever you called it. The name cannot very well be in my papers."

"Then I must be mistaken," said the Jap peevishly.

Wilson left the captain's cabin and went up to the bridge, where he drew a deep breath of relief.

The pilot gave directions for the ship's course, and the torpedo-boat steamed along on her port side like a shadow.

"I wonder why we have a wireless apparatus on board?" asked Hornberg.

"It never occurred to me until you mentioned it. I imagine it's merely an experiment of the owners," answered Wilson. Then they both lapsed into silence and only attended to the pilot's directions for the ship's course.

Wilson presently looked at his watch and remarked: "We must be about two miles from the Golden Gate by this time."

"It's possible," said Hornberg, "but as all the ships use shaded lights, it's a difficult thing to determine."

"Can we enter the harbor by night?" he asked of the Japanese pilot.

"Yes, sir, whenever you like, under our pilotage you can enter the harbor by day or night."

"How's that?"

"You'll see directly."

At this moment the torpedo-boat's siren bellowed sharply three times, and immediately the red lights at the masthead and the side of a steamer about half a mile off became visible, and the bright flash of her searchlight was thrown on the *Port Elizabeth*. The pilot sent a short signal across, which was immediately answered by the Japanese guardship.

"Now you'll see the channel," said the pilot to Wilson, "it's really an American invention, but we were the first to put it to practical use. We can't possibly lose our way now."

"Yes, captain, you'll see something wonderful now," said the lieutenant, as he came on the bridge with the captain. "You'll open your eyes when you see us steering through the mines."

Suddenly a bright circle of light appeared on the surface of the water, which was reflected from some source of light about ten yards below the surface. "It's an anchored light-buoy," explained the lieutenant, "which forms the end of the electric light cable, and there to the right is another one. All we have to do now is to keep a straight course between the two rows of lantern-buoys which are connected with the cable, and in that way we'll be able to steer with perfect safety between the mines into the harbor of San Francisco." And indeed, about a hundred yards ahead a second shining circle of light appeared on the water, and further on a whole chain of round disks was seen to make a turn to the left and then disappear in the distance. The same kind of a line appeared on the right. Half an hour later three bright red reflections, looking like transparent floating balls of light filled with ruby-red, bubbling billows, marked a spot where the helm had to be turned to port in order to bring the ship through a gap in the line of mines. Thus the *Port Elizabeth* reached San Francisco early in the morning. She did not make fast at the quay, but at the arsenal on Mare Island, her crew then being given shore leave. When the last man had gone, the *Port Elizabeth*, unloaded her cargo of machinery and rails which, in the hands of the Chinese coolies, was transformed into gun-barrels, ammunition and shells in the most marvelous manner. *"Le pavilion couvre la marchandise*, especially under the Union Jack," said Hornberg sarcastically, as he watched this metamorphosis, but the captain only looked at him angrily.

That was the second time during the war that Captain Winstanley of the United States Navy, and late commander of the battleship *Georgia*, saw San Francisco, whence he had escaped by night from the naval hospital two months before. The Japanese lieutenant was the same who had received the word of honor of the officers on board the hospital ship *Ontario* on May eighth, and to whom Winstanley had refused to give his. Two months after his voyage as second mate on board the *Port Elizabeth*, which enabled him to gather information concerning the Japanese measures for the defense of San Francisco, Winstanley stood on the bridge of the battleship *Delaware* as commander of the second Atlantic squadron. And four months later the name of the victor in the naval battle off the Galapagos Islands went the rounds of the world!

CHAPTER XIII
THE REVENGE FOR PORTSMOUTH

The more one examined the complicated machinery of the Japanese plan of attack, the more one was forced to admire the cleverness and the energy of the Mongolians in preparing for the war, and the more distinctly these were recognized, the clearer became the wide gulf between the Mongolian's and the white man's point of view concerning all these matters.

We might have learned a lesson in 1904, if we had not so carelessly and thoughtlessly looked upon the Russo-Japanese war as a mere episode, instead of regarding it as a war whose roots were firmly embedded in the inner life of a nation that had suddenly come to the surface of a rapid political development. The interference of the European powers in the Peace of Shimonoseki in 1895 robbed Japan of nearly all the fruits of her victory over China. Japan had been forced to vacate the conquered province of Liaotung on the mainland because she was unable to prevail against three European powers, who were for once agreed in maintaining that all Chinese booty belonged to Europe, for they regarded China as a bankrupt estate to be divided among her creditors. When, therefore, after the second Peace of Shimonoseki, Japan was compelled to relinquish all her possessions on the mainland and to console herself for her shattered hopes with a few million taels, every Japanese knew that the lost booty would at some time or other be demanded from Russia at the point of the sword. With the millions paid by China as war indemnity, Japan procured a new military armament, built an armored fleet and slowly but surely taught the nation to prepare for the hour of revenge. Remember Shimonoseki! That was the secret shibboleth, the free-mason's sign, which for nine long years kept the thoughts of the Japanese people continually centered on one object.

"One country, one people, one God!" were words once emphatically pronounced by Kaiser Wilhelm. But with the Japanese such high-sounding words as these are quite unnecessary. In the heart of all, from the Tenno to the lowest rickshaw coolie, there exists a jealous national consciousness, as natural as the beating of the heart itself, which unites the forces of religion, of the political idea and of intellectual culture into one indivisible element, differing in the individual only in intensity and in form of expression. When a citizen of Japan leaves his native land, he nevertheless remains a Japanese from the crown of his head to the soles of his feet, and can no more mix with members of another nation than a drop of oil can mix with water: a drop of oil poured on water will remain on its surface as an alien element, and so does a Japanese among another people.

While the streams of emigrants passing over the boundaries of Europe into other countries soon adapt themselves to new conditions and eventually adopt not only the outward but also the inward symbols of their environment, until finally they think and feel like those round about them, the Japanese remains a Jap for all time. The former sometimes retain a sentimental memory of their former home, but the Mongolian is never sentimental or romantic. He is sober and sensible, with very little imagination, and his whole energy, all his thoughts and endeavors are directed towards the upholding of the national, intellectual and religious unity of Japan. His country is his conscience, his faith, his deity.

Ordinary nations require hundreds and even thousands of years to inspire their people with a national consciousness, but this was not necessary in Japan, for there patriotism is inborn in the people, among whom an act of treason against the fatherland would be impossible because it is looked upon as spiritual suicide. The inner solidarity of the national character, the positive assurance of the fulfillment of all national duties, and the absolute silence of the people towards strangers— these are the weapons with which Japan enters the arena, clothed in a rattling ready-made steel armor, the like of which her opponents have yet to manufacture. The discretion shown by the Japanese press in all questions relating to foreign policy is regarded as the fulfillment of a patriotic duty just as much as the joyous self-sacrifice of the soldier on the field of battle.

From the moment that Marquis Ito had returned from Portsmouth (in 1905) empty-handed and the Japanese had been sorely disappointed in their hopes through President Roosevelt's instrumentality in bringing about peace, every Japanese knew whose turn would come next. The Japanese people were at first exceedingly angry at the way in which they had been deprived of their expected indemnity, but the government only allowed them to let off steam enough to prevent the boilers from bursting. Here and there, where it could do no harm, they let the excited mob have its way, but very soon both government and press began their new work of turning the people's patriotic passions away from the past to prepare for the future control of the Pacific. When in return for the prohibition of Chinese immigration to the United States, China boycotted our goods, and the ensuing panic in Wall Street forced the government in Washington to grant large concessions, Japan did not attempt to make use of this sharp weapon, for one of their most extensive industries, namely the silk industry, depended upon the export to the United States. Japan continued to place orders in America and treated the American importers with special politeness, even when she saw that the beginning of the boycott gave the gentlemen in Washington a terrible scare, prompting them to collect funds to relieve the famine in China and even renouncing all claim to the war indemnity of 1901 to smooth matters over. But Japan apparently took no notice of all this and continued to be deferential and polite, even when the growing heaps of unsold goods in the warehouses at Shanghai made the Americans ready to sacrifice some of their national pride. Since Japan wished to take the enemy by surprise, she had to be very careful not to arouse suspicions beforehand.

"Never speak of it, but think of it always," was the watchword given out by the little Jewish lawyer in the president's chair of France, when the longing for revenge filled the soul of every Frenchman during the slow retreat of the German army after its victorious campaign; "never speak of it, but think of it always," that was the watchword of the Japanese people also, although never expressed in words. It was nine years before the bill of exchange issued at Shimonoseki was presented on that February night in the roads of Port Arthur; for nine years the Japanese had kept silence and thought about it, had drilled and armed their soldiers, built ships and instructed their crews. The world had seen all this going on, but had no idea of the real reason for these warlike preparations on a tremendous scale. It was not Japan who had deceived the world, for everything went on quite openly, it being impossible to hide an army of over a million men under a bushel basket; but the world had deceived itself. When ships are built and cannon cast in other parts of the world, everyone knows for whom they are intended, and should anyone be ignorant, he will soon be enlightened by the after-dinner speeches of diplomats or indiscreet newspaper articles. The military and naval plans of the old world are common property, and this political indiscretion is characteristic of America as well as of Europe. In striking contrast thereto are the cool calculation, the silent observation and the perfect harmony of the peoples of Asia and Africa, all of whom, without exception, are inspired by a deep and undying hatred of the white race.

You may live for years among disciples of Mohammed, know all in your environment, penetrate into their thoughts and feelings, and still be utterly incapable of judging when the little spark that occasionally glows in their eyes in moments of great enthusiasm, will suddenly develop into an immense flame, when a force will make its appearance of the existence of which you have never dreamed, and which will, without a sign of warning, devastate and destroy all around it. But when this does happen and the corpses of the slain encumber the streets, when the quiet, peaceful, apparently indolent Moslem who for years has worked faithfully for you, is transformed in a few hours into a fanatical hero, whom thousands follow like so many sheep, then, at the sight of the burning ruins you will be forced to admit that the white man will forever be excluded from the thoughts and the national sentiment of the followers of Islam.

You walk across a sandy plain in the heat of the midday sun and you return the same way the next morning after a rainy night—what has happened? The ground which yesterday looked so parched and barren is now covered with millions of tiny blades. Where has this sudden life come from? It was there all the time. There is always latent life beneath the surface, but it is invisible. And as soon as a fertilizing rain comes, it springs up, and everyone perceives what has been slumbering beneath the crust.

In the dense jungles from which the sacred Nile receives its waters, there stands a tent and before it a saddled horse. From the tent steps forth a man with large glowing eyes, dressed all in white, who is greeted by his followers with fanatical cries of Allah, Allah! He mounts his steed, the camels rise, and the long caravan swings slowly out of sight and disappears in the bush. Once more dead silence reigns in the African jungle. Whither are they going? You don't know; you see only a rider dressed in a white burnoose, only a few dozen men hailing a prophet, but in the very same moment in which you see only a sheik riding off, millions know that the Caliph, the Blessed of Allah, has started on his journey through the lands whose inhabitants he intends to lead either to victory or to destruction. In the same moment millions of hearts from Mogador to Cape Guardafui, from Tripoli to the burning salt deserts of Kalahari, rejoice in the thought that the hour of deliverance has come for the peoples of Islam. A victorious feeling of buoyant hope arises in the hearts of the Faithful simply because a plain Arabian sheik has started on the road pointed out by Allah. How they happen to know it and all at the same time, will forever remain a mystery to the white man, as much of a mystery as the secret inner life of the yellow races of Asia.

"Never speak of it, but think of it always," had been the watchword, and everything that had transpired, even the apparently inconsistent and senseless things, had been ruled by it. The world could not be deceived about the things that were plainly visible; all the Japanese had to do was to make sure that the world would deceive itself as it had done during the preparations for Port Arthur. A perfectly equipped army could be seen by all on the fields of Nippon, Hokkaido and Kiushiu, and the fleet was surely not hidden from view. It was the world's own fault that it could not interpret what it saw, that it imagined the little yellow monkey would never dare attack the clumsy polar-bear. Because the diplomatic quill-drivers would only see what fitted into their schemes, because they were capable only of moving in a circle about their own ideas, they could not understand the thoughts of others, and the few warning voices died away unheeded. It was not Japan's fault that the roads at Port Arthur roused the world out of its slumber. What business had the world to be asleep?

"Never speak of it, but think of it always" — the adversary must be put to sleep again, he must be lulled into security and his thoughts directed towards the points where there was nothing to be seen, where no preparations were in progress. He must be kept in the dark about the true nature of the preparations, and on the other hand put on as many false scents as possible, so that he might not get the faintest idea of the real plan.

This is the reason why all those things were done, why the quarrel over the admission of Japanese children to the public schools of San Francisco was cooked up, why so much national anger was exhibited, why the Japanese press took up the quarrel like a hungry dog pouncing upon a bone, why so much noise was made about it at public meetings that one would have thought the fate of Japan hung on the result. And then, as soon as Washington began to back down, the dogs were whipped back to their kennels and the "national anger" died out as soon as Japan had "saved her face." The Americans were allowed to doze off again, fully persuaded that the school question was settled once and for all and that there was nothing further to fear in that direction. Then, too, Japan apparently yielded in the vexed question of Japanese immigration to the United States, but instead of sending the immigrants to San Francisco and Seattle, as she had done hitherto, they were simply dispatched across the Mexican frontier, where it was impossible to exercise control over such things, for no one could be expected to patrol the sandy deserts of Arizona and New Mexico merely to watch whether a few Japs slipped across the border now and then. It was therefore impossible to keep track of the number of Japanese who entered the country in this way, more especially as the official emigration figures issued at Tokio were purposely inaccurate, so as to confuse the statistics still more.

"Never speak of it, but think of it always!" That is why a Japanese photographer was sent to San Diego to photograph the walls of Fort Rosecrans. He was to get himself arrested. But of course we had to let the fellow go when he proved that better and more accurate photos than he had taken could be purchased in almost any store in San Diego. The object of this game was the same as that practiced in Manila, where we were induced to arrest a spy who was ostentatiously taking photographs. Both of these little maneuvers were intended to persuade us that Japan was densely ignorant with regard to these forts which as a matter of fact would play no rôle at all in her plan of attack; America was to be led to believe that Japan's system of espionage was in its infancy, while in reality the government at Tokio was in possession of the exact diagram of every fort, was thoroughly familiar with every beam of our warships—thanks to the Japanese stewards who had been employed by the Navy Department up to a few years ago—knew the peculiarities of every one of our commanders and their hobbies in maneuvers, and finally was informed down to the smallest detail of our plans of mobilization, and of the location of our war headquarters and of our armories and ammunition depots.

For the same reason the Japanese press, and the English press in Eastern Asia which was inspired by Japan, continually drew attention to the Philippines, as though that archipelago were to be the first point of attack. For this reason, too, the English-Chinese press published at the beginning of the year the well-known plans for Japan's offensive naval attack and the transport of two of her army corps to the Philippines. And the ruse proved successful. Just as Russia had been taken completely by surprise because she would persist in her theory that Japan would begin by marching upon Manchuria, so now the idea that Japan would first try to capture the Philippines and Hawaii had become an American and an international dogma. The world had allowed itself to be deceived a second time, and, convinced that the first blow would be struck at Manila and Hawaii, they spent their time in figuring out how soon the American fleet would be able to arrive on the scene of action in order to save the situation in the Far East.

"Never speak of it, but think of it always!" While Japan was disseminating these false notions as to the probable course of a war, the actual preparations for it were being conducted in an entirely different place, and the adversary was induced to concentrate his strength at a point where there was no intention of making an attack. The Japanese were overjoyed to observe the strengthening of the Philippine garrison when the insurrection inspired by Japanese agents broke out at Mindanao as well as the concentration of the cruiser squadron off that island, for Manila, the naval base, was thus left unprotected. With the same malignant joy they noticed how the United States stationed half of its fleet off the Pacific coast and, relying on her mobile means of defense, provided insufficient garrisons for the coast-defenses, on the supposition that there would be plenty of time to put the garrisons on a war-footing after the outbreak of hostilities.

Japan's next move came in March and April, when she quietly withdrew all the regular troops from the Manchurian garrisons and replaced them with reserve regiments fully able to repulse for a time any attack on the part of Russia. The meaning of this move was not revealed until weeks later, when it became known that the transport ships from Dalny and Gensan, which were supposed to have returned to Japan, were really on their way to San Francisco and Seattle with the second detachment of the invading army.

After the destruction of the Philippine squadron, the Japanese reduced their blockade of the Bay of Manila to a few old cruisers and armed merchant-steamers, at the same time isolating the American garrisons in the archipelago, whose fate was soon decided. The blockading ships could not of course venture near the heavy guns of the Corregidor batteries, but that was not their task. They had merely to see that Manila had no intercourse with the outside world, and this they did most efficiently. The Japanese ships had at first feared an attack by the two little submarines *Shark* and *Porpoise* stationed at Cavite; they learned from their spies on land, however, that the government shipyards at Cavite had tried in vain to render the little boats seaworthy: they returned from each diving-trial with defective gasoline-engines. And when, weeks later, they at last reached Corregidor, the four Japanese submarines quickly put an end to them. The strongly fortified city of Manila had thus become a naval base without a fleet and was accordingly overpowered from the land side.

As the far too weak garrison of scarcely more than ten thousand men was insufficient to defend the extensive line of forts and barricades, the unfinished works at Olongapo on Subig Bay were blown up with dynamite and vacated, then the railways were abandoned, and finally only Manila and Cavite were retained. But the repeated attacks of the natives under the leadership of Japanese officers soon depleted the little garrison, which was entirely cut off from outside assistance and dependent absolutely on the supplies left in Manila itself. The only article of which they had more than enough was coal; but you can't bake bread with coal, and so finally, on August twenty-fourth, Manila capitulated. Twenty-eight hundred starving soldiers surrendered their arms while the balance lay either in the hospitals or on the field of battle. Thus the Philippines became a Japanese possession with the loss of a single man, Lieutenant Shirawa. All the rest had been accomplished by the Filipinos and by the climate that was so conducive to the propagation of mosquitoes and scorpions.

Hawaii's fate had been decided even more quickly than that of the Philippines. The sixty thousand Japanese inhabitants of the archipelago were more than enough to put an end to American rule. The half-finished works at Pearl Harbor fell at the first assault, while the three destroyers and the little gunboat were surprised by the enemy. Guam, and Pago-Pago on Tutuila, were also captured, quite incidentally. About the middle of May, a Japanese transport fleet returning from San Francisco appeared at Honolulu and took forty thousand inhabitants to Seattle, where they formed the reserve corps of the Northern Japanese Army.

Japan's rising imperialism, the feeling that the sovereignty of the Pacific rightly belonged to the leading power in yellow Asia had, long before the storms of war swept across the plains of Manchuria, come into conflict with the imperialistic policy of the United States, although invisibly at first. Prior to that time the Asiatic races had looked upon the dominion of the white man as a kind of fate, as an irrevocable universal law, but the fall of Port Arthur had shattered this idol once and for all. And after the days of Mukden and Tsushima had destroyed the belief in the invincibility of the European arms, the Japanese agents found fertile soil everywhere for their seeds of secret political agitation. In India, in Siam, and in China also, the people began to prick their ears when it was quite openly declared that after the destruction of the czar's fleet the Pacific and the lands bordering on it could belong only to the Mongolians. The discovery was made that the white man was not invincible. And beside England, only the United States remained to be considered—the United States who were still hard at work on their Philippine inheritance and could not make up their mind to establish their loudly heralded imperialistic policy on a firm footing by providing the necessary armaments.

Then came the Peace of Portsmouth. Absolutely convinced that his country would have to bear the brunt of the next Asiatic thunder-storm, Theodore Roosevelt gained one of the most momentous victories in the history of the world when he removed the payment of a war indemnity from the conditions of peace. And he did this not because he had any particular love for the Russians, but because he wished to prevent the strengthening of Japan's financial position until after the completion of the Panama Canal. America did exactly what Germany, Russia and France had done at the Peace of Shimonoseki, and we had to be prepared for similar results. But how long did it take the American people, who had helped to celebrate the victories of Oyama, Nogi and Togo, to recognize that a day of vengeance for Portsmouth was bound to come. In those days we regarded the Manchurian campaign merely as a spectacle and applauded the victors. We had no idea that it was only the prelude of the great drama of the struggle for the sovereignty of the Pacific. We wanted imperialism, but took no steps to establish it on a firm basis, and it is foolish to dream of imperial dominion when one is afraid to lay the sword in the scales. We might bluff the enemy for the time being by sending our fleet to the Pacific; but we could not keep him deceived long as to the weakness of our equipment on land and at sea, especially on land.

The wholesale immigration of Mongolians to our Pacific States and to the western shores of South America was clearly understood across the sea. But we looked quietly on while the Japanese overran Chili, Peru and Bolivia, all the harbors on the western coast of South America; and while the yellow man penetrated there unhindered and the decisive events of the future were in process of preparation, we continued to look anxiously eastward from the platform of the Monroe Doctrine and to keep a sharp lookout on the modest remnants of the European colonial dominion in the Caribbean Sea, as if danger could threaten us from that corner. We seemed to think that the Monroe Doctrine had an eastern exposure only, and when we were occasionally reminded that it embraced the entire continent, we allowed our thoughts to be distracted by the London press with its talk of the "German danger" in South America, just as though any European state would think for a moment of seizing three Brazilian provinces overnight, as it were.

We have always tumbled through history as though we were deaf and dumb, regarding those who warned us in time against the Japanese danger as backward people whose intellects were too weak to grasp the victorious march of Japanese culture. Any one who would not acknowledge the undeniable advance of Japan to be the greatest event of the present generation was stamped by us an enemy of civilization. We recognized only two categories of people—Japanophobes and Japanophiles. It never entered our heads that we might recognize the weighty significance of Japan's sudden development into a great political power, but at the same time warn our people most urgently against regarding this development merely as a phase of feuilletonistic culture. Right here lies the basis for all our political mistakes of the last few years. The revenge for Portsmouth came as such a terrible surprise, because, misled by common opinion, we believed the enemy to be breaking down under the weight of his armor and therefore incapable of conducting a new war and, in this way undervaluing our adversary, we neglected all necessary preparations. No diplomatic conflict, not the slightest disturbance of our relations with Japan prepared the way for the great surprise. The world was the richer by one experience—that a war need have no prelude on the diplomatic stage provided enough circumstances have led up to it.

CHAPTER XIV
ON THE OTHER SIDE OF THE WHIRLPOOL

On the rear deck of a ferry-boat bound for Hoboken on the morning of May 12th stood Randolph Taney, with his hands in his pockets, gazing intently at the foaming waters of the Hudson plowed up by the screw. It was all over: he had speculated in Wall Street, putting his money on Harriman, and had lost every cent he had. What Harriman could safely do with a million, Randolph Taney could not do with a quarter of a million. That's why he had lost. Fortunately only his own money. The whole bundle of papers wasn't worth any more than the copy of the *Times* tossed about in the swirling water in the wake of the boat.

Randolph Taney kept on thinking. Just why he was going to Hoboken he really didn't know, but it made little difference what he did.

"Halloo, Taney," called out an acquaintance, "where are you going?"

"I don't know."

"You don't know? How's that?"

"I'm done for."

"You're not the only one; Wall Street is a dangerous vortex."

"But I'm absolutely cleaned out."

"How so?"

"Do you know what I'm going to do, James Harrison?" asked Taney, with bitter irony in his voice. "I'll apprentice myself to a paperhanger, and learn to paper my rooms with my worthless railway shares. I imagine I can still learn that much."

"Ah, that's the way the wind blows!" cried the other, whistling softly.

"What did you think?"

"It was pretty bad, I suppose?"

"Bad? It was hell——"

"Were you in Wall Street on Monday?"

"Yes, and on Tuesday, too."

"And now you want to learn paperhanging?"

"Yes."

"Does it have to be that?"

"Can you suggest anything else?"

"Yes."

"Well?"

Hubert pointed to the button-hole in the lapel of his coat and said: "Do you see this?"

"What is it?"

"A volunteer button."

Taney looked with interest at the little white button with the American flag, and then said: "Have I got to that point? The last chance, I suppose?" he added after a pause.

"Not the last, but the first!"

"How so?"

"At any rate it's better than paperhanging. Look here, Taney, you'll only worry yourself to death. It would be far more sensible of you to take the bull by the horns and join our ranks. You can at least try to retrieve your fortunes by that means."

The ferry-boat entered the slip at Hoboken and both men left the boat.

"Now, Taney, which is it to be, paperhanging or—," and James Harrison pointed to the button.

"I'll come with you," said Taney indifferently. They went further along the docks towards the Governor's Island ferry-boat.

"I have a friend over there," said Harrison, "a major in the 8th Regulars; he'll be sure to find room for us, and we may be at the front in a month's time."

Taney stuffed his pipe and answered: "In a month? That suits me; I have no affairs to arrange."

The two men looked across in silence at Manhattan Island, where the buildings were piled up in huge terraces. All the color-tones were accentuated in the bright clear morning air. The sky-scrapers of the Empire City, mighty turreted palaces almost reaching into the clouds, stood out like gigantic silhouettes. The dome of the Singer Building glistened and glittered in the sun, crowning a region in which strenuous work was the order of the day, while directly before them stretched the broad waters of the Hudson with its swarm of hurrying ferry-boats. Further on, between the piers and the low warehouses, could be seen a long row of serious-looking ocean-steamers, whose iron lungs emitted little clouds of steam as the cranes fed their huge bodies with nice little morsels.

The two men had seen this picture hundreds of times, but were impressed once again by its grandeur.

"Taney," said Harrison, "isn't that the most beautiful city in the world? I've been around the world twice, but I've never seen anything to equal it. That's our home, and we are going to protect it by shouldering our guns. Come on, old chap, leave everything else behind and come with me!"

"Yes, I'll come, I certainly shall!" came the quick response. Then they took the boat to Governor's Island and Taney enlisted. They promised to make him a lieutenant when the troops took the field.

When they returned two hours later Randolph Taney also wore the button with the flag in the center: he was a full-fledged volunteer in the United States Army.

On the return trip Taney became communicative, and told the story of the eighth of May, that terrible day in Wall Street when billions melted away like butter, when thousands of persons were tossed about in the whirlpool of the Stock Exchange, when the very foundations of economic life seemed to be slipping away. He described the wild scenes when desperate financiers rushed about like madmen, and told how some of them actually lost their reason during the bitter struggle for existence, when not an inch of ground was vacated without resistance. Men fought for every projecting rock, every piece of wreckage, every straw, as they must have fought in the waves of the Flood, and yet one victim after another was swallowed by the vortex. In the midst of the mad scrimmage on the floor of the Exchange one excited individual, the general manager of a large railroad—with his hair disheveled and the perspiration streaming down his face, one of his sleeves ripped out and his collar torn off—suddenly climbed on a platform and began to preach a confused sermon accompanied by wild gestures; others, whose nerves were utterly unstrung by the terrible strain, joined in vulgar street-songs.

Harrison had read about these things in the papers, but his friend's graphic description brought it all vividly to mind again and caused him to shudder. He seemed to see all the ruined existences, which the maelstrom in Wall Street had dragged down into the depths, staring at him with haggard faces. He thought of his own simple, plain life as compared with the neurasthenic existence of the men on the Stock Exchange, who were now compelled to look on in complete apathy and let things go as they were. The rich man, whom in the bottom of his heart he had often envied, was now poorer than the Italian bootblack standing beside him.

The ferry-boat now turned sharply aside to make room for the giant *Mauretania*, which was steaming out majestically from its pier into the broad Hudson River.

The thrilling notes of the "Star Spangled Banner" had just died away, and a sea of handkerchiefs fluttered over the railings, which were crowded with passengers waving their last farewells to those left behind. Then the ship's band struck up a new tune, and the enormous steamer plowed through the waves towards the open sea.

"There go the rats who have deserted the sinking ship," said Randolph Taney bitterly, "our leading men of finance are said to have offered fabulous prices for the plainest berths."

The flight of the homeless had begun.

CHAPTER XV
A RAY OF LIGHT

Only a small Japanese garrison was left at Seattle after the first transports of troops had turned eastward on the seventh and eighth of May, and the northern army under Marshal Nogi had, after a few insignificant skirmishes with small American detachments, taken up its position in, and to the south of, the Blue Mountains. Then, in the beginning of June, the first transport-ships arrived from Hawaii, bringing the reserve corps for the northern army, with orders to occupy the harbors and coast-towns behind the front and to guard the lines of communication to the East.

Communication by rail had been stopped everywhere. No American was allowed to board a train, and only with the greatest difficulty did a few succeed in securing special permission in very urgent cases. The stations had one and all been turned into little forts, being occupied by Japanese detachments who at the same time attended to the Japanese passenger and freight-service.

In all places occupied by the Japanese the press had been silenced, except for one paper in each town, which was allowed to continue its existence because the Japs needed it for the publication of edicts and proclamations issued to the inhabitants, and for the dissemination of news from the seat of war, the latter point being considered of great importance. This entire absence of news from other than Japanese sources gave rise to thousands of rumors, which seemed to circulate more rapidly by word of mouth than the former telegraphic dispatches had through the newspapers.

On the morning of June eighth the news was spread in Tacoma that the city would that day receive a Japanese garrison, as several transport-steamers had arrived at Seattle. Up to that time only one Japanese company had been stationed at Tacoma, and they had occupied the railroad station and the gas and electric works and intrenched themselves in the new waterworks outside the town. Through some strange trick of fortune the gun-depot for the arming of the national guard which had been removed to Tacoma a year ago and which contained about five thousand 1903 Springfield rifles had escaped the notice of the enemy. The guns had been stored provisionally in the cellars of a large grain elevator and it had been possible to keep them concealed from the eyes of the Japs, but it was feared that their hiding-place might be betrayed any day. This danger would of course be greatly increased the moment Tacoma received a stronger garrison.

Martin Engelmann, a German who had immigrated to the great Northwest some twenty years ago, owned a pretty little home in the suburbs of Tacoma. The family had just sat down to dinner when the youngest son, who was employed in a large mercantile establishment in the city, entered hurriedly and called out excitedly:

"They're coming, father, they're in the harbor."

Then he sat down and began to eat his soup in haste.

"They're coming?" asked old Engelmann in a serious tone of voice, "then I fear it is too late."

The old man got up from the table and going over to the window looked out into the street. Not a living thing was to be seen far and wide except a little white poodle gnawing a bone in the middle of the street. Engelmann stared attentively at the poodle, buried in thought.

"How many of them are there?" he asked after a pause.

"At least a whole battalion, I'm told," answered the son, finishing his soup in short order.

"Then it's all over, of course. Just twenty-four hours too soon," sighed Engelmann softly as he watched the poodle, who at that moment was jumping about on the street playing with the gnawed bone.

Engelmann tried hard to control himself, but he did not dare turn his head, for he could hear low, suppressed sobbing behind him. Martha, the faithful companion of his busy life, sat at the table with her face buried in her hands, the tears rolling uninterruptedly down her cheeks, while her two daughters were trying their best to comfort her.

Old Engelmann opened the window and listened.

"Nothing to be heard yet; but they'll have to pass here to get to the water-works," he said. Then he joined his family, and turning to his wife, said: "Courage, mother! Arthur will do his duty."

"But if anything should happen to him—" sobbed his wife.

"Then it will be for his country, and his death and that of his comrades will give us an example of the sacrifices we must all make until the last of the yellow race has been driven out."

The mother went on crying quietly, her handkerchief up to her eyes: "When was it to be? Tell me!" she cried.

"To-night," said the father, "and they would surely have been successful, for they could easily have overpowered the few men at the station and in the town. Listen, there are the Japs!"

From outside came the regular beat of the drums. Bum—bum—bum, bum, bum they went, and then the shrill squeaking of the fifes could also be heard.

"Yes, there they are, the deuce take 'em," said Engelmann. The sound of the drums became more and more distinct and presently the sound of troops marching in step could be clearly distinguished. Then the steps became firmer, and the window-panes began to rattle as the leader of the battalion appeared on horseback in the middle of the street, followed by the fife and drum corps, and with the little white poodle barking at his heels. It was a Japanese battalion of reserves marching in the direction of the new waterworks outside the town.

"Courage, mother!" comforted the old man. "If they only stay at the waterworks all may yet be well."

"Wouldn't it be possible to warn Arthur?" began the mother again.

"Warn him?" said Engelmann, shrugging his shoulders, "all you have to do is to go to the telegraph office and hand in a telegram to the Japanese official, telling them to remain where they are."

"But couldn't we make it a go after all?" asked the youngest son thoughtfully. "The boxes are all ready, and can be packed in half an hour. We have three hundred men and thirty wagons. The latter were to be loaded at eleven o'clock to-night. And then at them with our revolvers! There aren't more than twenty men at the station," he went on with sparkling eyes. "At eleven o'clock sharp the telegraph-wire to the waterworks will be cut, also the wires to all the stations; then let them telegraph all they like. The minute the train arrives, the engine will be switched to another track and then backed in front of the train. Meanwhile the boxes will be packed in the cars and then we'll be off with the throttle wide open. At each station a car will be dropped, and wagons will be waiting to receive their loads and get away as fast as the horses can pull them. Safe hiding-places have been found for all the boxes, and whatever hasn't been captured by to-morrow morning will certainly never fall into the enemy's hands."

"Where is the telegraph-wire to the waterworks?" asked the father.

"That's my job, to cut the wire just before the arrival of the train," said his son proudly.

"Richard," cried the mother in a horrified voice, "are you in it, too?"

"Yes, mother, you didn't suppose I'd stand and look on while Arthur was risking his life, did you? What would they think of us on the other side if we were to hesitate at such a time as this? 'Germans to the front,' that's our slogan now, and we'll show the people in Washington that the German-Americans treat the duties of their new country seriously."

Old Engelmann laid his hand on his son's shoulder, saying: "Right you are, my boy, and my blessing go with you! So you are to cut the telegraph-wire?"

"Yes, father. We happen to know where it is. The Japs were of course clever enough to lay it underground, but we have discovered it under the paving near Brown & Co.'s store. We dug through to it very carefully from the cellar, and so as to make quite sure in case they should notice anything out of the way at the waterworks, we attached a Morse apparatus to the wire in the cellar. In case they suspect anything at the works and begin to telegraph, I'm to work the keys a little so that they won't know the wire is cut. In addition we laid a wire to the station last night, which will give a loud bell-signal in case any danger threatens."

The young fellow had talked himself into a state of great excitement, and his two sisters, watching him proudly, began to be infected by his enthusiasm.

The shades of night were falling slowly as Richard Engelmann bade a touching farewell to his family and left the house, whistling a lively tune as he walked towards the town.

CHAPTER XVI
THROUGH FIRE AND SMOKE

A train was always kept in readiness at Centralia on the Northern Pacific Railway, which could get up full steam at a moment's notice in case of necessity. Two Japanese, the engineer and the fireman, were squatting on the floor of the tender in front of the glistening black heaps of coal, over which played the red reflections from the furnace. They had just made their tea with hot water from the boiler and eaten their modest supper. Then the engineer pulled out his pipe and stuffing its little metal bowl with a few crumbs of tobacco, took one or two puffs at it and said, "Akoki, it is time," whereupon the stoker seized his shovel, dug into the heap of coals and threw the black lumps with a sure aim into the open door of the furnace. With a hissing sound the draft rushed into the glowing fire, and the engine sent out masses of black smoke which, mixed with hundreds of tiny sparks, was driven like a pillar of fire over the dark row of cars. The engineer climbed down the little iron steps and examined the steel rods of his engine with clinking knocks from his hammer.

Up and down in front of the dark station walked a Japanese sentinel and each time that he passed beyond the ring of light thrown by the two dimly burning lamps he seemed to be swallowed up in the darkness. Only two little windows at one end of the station were lighted up; they belonged to the Japanese guard-room and had been walled up so that they were no wider than loop-holes. The train which inspected this district regularly between eight and nine o'clock each evening had passed by at 8.30 and proceeded in the direction of Portland. With the exception of the non-commissioned officer and the man in charge of the three arc-lamps on the roof that were to light up the surrounding country in case of a night-attack most of the soldiers had gone to sleep, although a few were engaged in a whispered conversation.

Suddenly the sergeant sprang up as a muffled cry was heard from the outside. "The lamps!" he yelled to the man at the electric instrument. The latter pushed the lever, but everything remained pitch dark outside.

The soldiers were up in a second. The sergeant took a few steps towards the door, but before he could reach it, it was torn open from the outside.

A determined looking man with a rifle slung over his shoulder appeared in the doorway, and the next moment a dark object flew through the air and was dashed against the wall. A deafening report followed, and then the guard-room was filled with yellow light caused by the blinding explosion, while thick black smoke forced its way out through the loop-holes. Armed men were running up and down in front of the station, and when the man who had thrown the bomb and who was only slightly injured but bleeding at the nose and ears from the force of the concussion, was picked up by them, they were able to assure him triumphantly that his work had been successful and that the guard-room had become a coffin for the small Japanese detachment.

Stumbling over the dead body of the sentinel lying on the platform, the leader of the attacking party rushed towards the engine, out of the discharge-valves of which clouds of boiling steam poured forth. With one bound he was up in the cab, where he found the Japanese fireman killed by a blow from an ax. Other dark figures climbed up from the opposite side bumping into their comrades.

"Halloo, Dick, I call that a good job!" And then it began to liven up along the row of cars. Wild looking men with rifles over their shoulders and revolvers in their right hands tore open the carriage doors and rushed quickly through the whole train.

"Dick, where's Forster?"

"Here," answered a rough voice.

"Off to the engine! Into the cars, quick! Are you ready? Is anyone missing? Arthur! Where's Arthur?"

"Here, Dick!"

"Good work, Arthur, that's what I call good work," said the leader; "well done, my boys! We're all right so far! Now for the rest of it."

Fighting Dick distributed his men among the different cars and then he and Forster, formerly an engineer on the Northern Pacific, climbed into the cab.

"They've made it easy for us," said Forster, "they've only just put fresh coal on! We can start at once! And if it isn't my old engine at that! I only hope we won't have to give her up! The Japs shan't have her again, anyhow, even if she has to swallow some dynamite and cough a little to prevent it."

"We're off," shouted Fighting Dick, whose fame as a desperado had spread far beyond the borders of the State of Washington. With such men as these we were destined to win back our native land. They were a wild lot, but each of them was a hero: farmers, hunters, workmen from shop and factory, numerous tramps and half-blooded Indian horse-thieves made up the company. Only a few days ago Fighting Dick's band had had a regular battle in the mountains with a troop of Japanese cavalry, and in the woods of Tacoma more than one Japanese patrol had never found its way back to the city. These little encounters were no doubt also responsible for the strengthening of the Japanese garrison at Tacoma.

The thing to do now was to get the five thousand guns and ammunition cases out of Tacoma by surprising the enemy.

Thus far, nothing but the explosion of the bomb at the Centralia station could have betrayed the plot. It is true that the distant mountains had sent the echoes of the detonation far and wide, but a single shot didn't have much significance at a time like this when our country resounded with the thunder of cannon day in day out!

The train rushed through the darkness at full speed. A misplaced switch, a loose rail, might at any moment turn the whole train into a heap of ruins and stop the beating of a hundred brave American hearts. The headlight of Forster's engine lighted up the long rows of shining rails, and in the silent woods on both sides of the track, beneath the branches of the huge trees, lights could be seen here and there in the windows of the houses, where the dwellers were anxiously awaiting the return of the train from Tacoma! And now a hollow roll of thunder came up from below.

"The bridges?" asked Fighting Dick.

"Yes, the bridges," said Forster, nodding.

Then a faint light appeared in the distance. The train was nearing Tacoma.

Houses began to spring up more frequently out of the darkness, now to the right and now to the left; dancing lights popped up and disappeared. Tall, black buildings near the tracks gave out a thundering noise like the crash of hammers and accompanied the roar of the passing train. A beam of light is suddenly thrown across the rails, green and red lanterns slip by with the speed of lightning, and then the brakes squeak and the train runs noisily into the dark station.

A few figures hurry across the platform. Shots ring out from all sides. A mortally-wounded Jap is leaning against a post, breathing heavily.

The wheels groan beneath the pressure of the brakes and then, with a mighty jerk that shakes everybody up, the train comes to a stand-still. Down from the cars! Fighting Dick in the lead, revolver in hand, and the others right on his heels. They entered the station only to find every Jap dead—the men of Tacoma had done their duty.

Now the clatter of hoofs was heard out in the street. The heavy wagons with their heaps of rifles and long tin boxes full of cartridges were driven up at a mad pace. A wild tumult ensued as the boxes were rushed to the train—two men to a box—and the doors slammed to. Then the empty wagons rattled back through the silent streets. Meanwhile Forster ran his engine on the turntable, where it was quickly reversed, and in a few moments it stood, puffing and snorting, at the other end of the train.

All this consumed less than half an hour. Suddenly shots rang out in the neighboring streets, but as no detachment of hostile troops appeared, the Americans concluded that they had been fired by a patrol which was coming from the electric-works to see what the noise at the station was about. Several rockets with their blinding magnesium light appeared in the dark sky and illumined the roofs of the houses. Was it a warning signal?

All at once the electric gongs near the station which were connected with Brown & Co.'s cellar began to ring, a sign that something suspicious had been noticed at the waterworks. Forster was waiting impatiently in his engine for the signal of departure and could not imagine why Fighting Dick was postponing it so long. He was standing in the doorway of the station and now called out: "Where is Arthur Engelmann?"

"Not here," came the answer from the train.

"Where can he be?"

The name was called out several times, but no one answered. The train was ready to start and the men were distributing the boxes carefully inside the cars, so as to be able to unload them without loss of time at their respective destinations. And now, at last, Arthur Engelmann came running into the station.

"Hurry up!" called Fighting Dick.

"No, wait a minute! We'll have to take this fellow along," cried Engelmann, pointing to a wounded man, who was being carried by two comrades.

"Put him down! We'll have to be off! We've got plenty of men, but not enough guns."

"You must take him!"

"No, we're off!"

"You'll wait," said Arthur Engelmann, seizing Dick's arm; "it's my brother."

"I can't help it, you'll have to leave him behind."

"Then I'll stay too!"

"Go ahead, if you want to."

At this moment shrill bugle-calls resounded from one of the nearby streets.

"The Japanese!" roared Fighting Dick; "come on, Arthur!"

But Arthur snatched his wounded brother from the two men who were carrying him and lifted him across his own shoulder, while the others, led by Fighting Dick, rushed past him and jumped on the train.

Bullets were whizzing past and several had entered the walls of the station when Fighting Dick's voice gave the command: "Let her go, Forster! Let her go!"

Puffing and snorting, and with the pistons turning the high wheels, which could not get a hold on the slippery rails, at lightning speed, the engine started just as the Japanese soldiers ran into the station, from the windows of which they commenced to fire blindly at the departing train. The bullets poured into the rear cars like hail-stones, smashing the wooden walls and window-panes.

Fighting Dick, standing beside Forster, looked back and saw the station full of soldiers. The two Germans must have fallen into their hands, he thought.

But they must hustle with the train now, for although the telegraph wires had been cut all along the line, they still had light-signals to fear! And even as this thought occurred to him, a glare appeared in the sky in the direction of the waterworks, then went out and appeared again at regular intervals. Those silent signs certainly had some meaning. Perhaps it was a signal to the nearest watch to pull up the rails in front of the approaching train? With his teeth set and his hand on the throttle, Forster stood in his engine while the fireman kept shoveling coals into the furnace.

"Forster," said Dick suddenly, "what's that in front of us? Heavens, it's burning!"

"The bridges are burning, Fighting Dick!"

"That's just what I thought, the damned yellow monkeys! Never mind, we'll have to go on. Do you think you can get the engine across?"

"The bridges will hold us all right. It would take half a day to burn the wood through and we'll be there in ten minutes."

Now fluttering little flames could be seen running along the rails and licking the blood-red beams of the long wooden bridges, giant monuments of American extravagance in the use of wood. Clouds of smoke crept towards the train, hiding the rails from view, and soon the engine rolled into a veritable sea of flames and smoke. Forster screamed to his companion: "They've poured petroleum over the wood."

"We'll have to get across," answered Fighting Dick, "even if we all burn to death."

Biting smoke and the burning breath of the fiery sea almost suffocated the two men. The air was quivering with heat, and all clearly defined lines disappeared as the angry flames now arose on both sides.

"Press hard against the front," screamed Forster; "that's the only way to get a little air, otherwise we'll suffocate."

The high-pressure steam of the speeding locomotive hissed out of all the valves, shaking the mighty steel frame with all its force; the heat of the flames cracked the windows, and wherever the hand sought support, pieces of skin were left on the red-hot spots. A few shots were fired from the outside.

"One minute more," yelled Forster, "and we'll be over."

Fighting Dick collapsed under the influence of the poisonous gases and fainted away on the floor of the cab. And now the flames grew smaller and smaller and gradually became hidden in clouds of smoke.

"Hurrah!" cried Forster; "there's a clear stretch ahead of us!" Then he leaned out of the cab-window to look at the train behind him and saw that the last two cars were in flames. He blew the whistle as a signal that the last car was to be uncoupled and left where it was, for he had just noticed a man standing near the track, swinging his bicycle lamp high above his head.

"Perhaps they'll be able to unload the car after all," he said to Fighting Dick, who was slowly coming to. But the sound of the explosion of some of the boxes of cartridges in the uncoupled car made it fairly certain that there wouldn't be much left to unload.

Five minutes later, after they had passed a dark station, the same signal was noticed, and another car was uncoupled, and similarly one car after another was left on the track. The guns and ammunition-boxes were unloaded as expeditiously as possible and transferred to the wagons that were waiting to receive them. The moment they were ready, the horses galloped off as fast as they could go and disappeared in the darkness, leaving the burning cars behind as a shining beacon.

When, on the morning of June ninth, a Japanese military train from Portland traveled slowly along the line, it came first upon the ruins of an engine which had been blown up by dynamite, and after that it was as much as the Japanese could do to clear away the remnants of the various ruined cars by the end of the day. The bridge, which had been set on fire by a Japanese detachment with the help of several barrels of petroleum, was completely burned down.

But the plot had been successful and Fighting Dick's fame resounded from one ocean to the other, and proved to the nations across the sea that the old energy of the American people had been revived and that the war of extermination against the yellow race had begun, though as yet only on a small scale. And the Japanese troops, too, began to appreciate that the same irresistible force—a patriotic self-sacrifice that swept everything before it—which had in one generation raised Japan to the heights of political power, was now being directed against the foreign invader.

Half the town had known of the plan for removing the rifles and ammunition from Tacoma, but a strong self-control had taken the place of the thoughtless garrulousness of former times. Not a sign, not a word had betrayed the plot to the enemy; every man controlled his feverish emotion and wore an air of stolid indifference. We had learned a lesson from the enemy.

Fourteen Americans were captured with weapons in hand, and in addition about twenty-eight badly wounded. The Japanese commander of Tacoma issued a proclamation the following evening that all the prisoners, without exception, would be tried by court-martial in the course of the next day and condemned to death—the penalty that had been threatened in case of insurrection. The Japanese court-martial arrived in the city on June ninth with a regiment from Seattle. The Tacoma board of aldermen were invited to send two of their number to be present at the trial, but the offer being promptly refused, the Japanese pronounced judgment on the prisoners alone. As had been expected, they were all condemned to death by hanging, but at the earnest pleading of the mayor of Tacoma, the sentence was afterwards mitigated to death by shooting.

Old Martin Engelmann tried in vain to secure permission to see his sons once more; his request was brusquely refused.

In the light of early dawn on June eleventh the condemned men were led out to the waterworks to be executed, the wounded being conveyed in wagons. Thousands of the inhabitants took part in this funeral procession—in dead silence.

Old Engelmann was standing, drawn up to his full height, at the window of his home, and mutely he caught the farewell glances of his two sons as they passed by, the one marching in the midst of his comrades, the other lying in the first wagon among the wounded. Frau Martha had summoned sufficient courage to stand beside her husband, but the moment the procession had passed, she burst into bitter tears. Her life was bereft of all hope and the future stretched out dark and melancholy before her.

Suddenly a gentle hand was laid on her white head. "Mother," said one of her daughters, "do you hear it? I heard it yesterday. They're singing the song of Fighting Dick and of our dear boys. No one knows who composed it, it seems to have sprung up of itself. They were singing it on the street last night, the song of Arthur Engelmann, who sacrificed his life for his brother."

"Yes," said the father, "it's true, mother, they are singing of our lads; be brave, mother, and remember that those who are taken from us to-day will live forever in the hearts of the American people."

And louder and louder rang out the notes of that proud song of the citizens of Tacoma—the first pæan of victory in those sad days.

CHAPTER XVII
WHAT HAPPENED AT CORPUS CHRISTI

The attitude of the European press left no room for doubt as to the honest indignation of the Old World at the treacherous attack on our country. But what good could this scathing denunciation of the Japanese policy do us? A newspaper article wouldn't hurt a single Japanese soldier, and what good could all the resolutions passed at enthusiastic public meetings in Germany and France do us, or the daily cablegrams giving us the assurance of their sympathy and good-will?

These expressions of public opinion did, however, prove that the Old World realized at last that the yellow danger was of universal interest, that it was not merely forcing a single country to the wall, casually as it were, but that it was of deep and immediate concern to every European nation without exception. They began to look beyond the wisdom of the pulpit orators who preached about the wonderful growth of culture in Japan, and to recognize that if the United States did not succeed in conquering Japan and driving the enemy out of the country, the victorious Japanese would not hesitate a moment to take the next step and knock loudly and peremptorily at Europe's door, and this would put an end once and for all to every single European colonial empire.

But while European authorities on international law were busily parading their paper wisdom, and wondering how a war without a declaration of war and without a diplomatic prelude could fit into the political scheme of the world's history, at least one real item of assistance was at hand.

The American press, it is true, still suffered from the delusion that our militia—consisting of hundreds of thousands of men—and our volunteers would be prepared to take the field in three or four weeks, but the indescribable confusion existing in all the military camps told a different story. What was needed most were capable officers. The sad experiences of the Spanish-American campaign were repeated, only on a greatly magnified scale. We possessed splendid material in the matter of men and plenty of good-will, but we lacked completely the practical experience necessary for adapting the military apparatus of our small force of regular soldiers to the requirements of a great national army. We felt that we could with the aid of money and common-sense transform a large group of able-bodied men accustomed to healthy exercise into a serviceable and even a victorious army, but we made a great mistake. The commissariat and sanitary service and especially the military train-corps would have to be created out of nothing. When in June the governor of one State reported that his infantry regiment was formed and only waiting for rifles, uniforms and the necessary military wagons, and when another declared that his two regiments of cavalry and six batteries were ready to leave for the front as soon as horses, guns, ammunition-carts and harness could be procured, it showed with horrible distinctness how utterly ridiculous our methods of mobilization were.

The London diplomats went around like whipped curs, for all the early enthusiasm for the Japanese alliance disappeared as soon as the English merchants began to have such unpleasant experiences with the unscrupulousness of the Japanese in business matters. As a matter of fact the alliance had fulfilled its object as soon as Japan had fought England's war with Russia for her. But the cabinet of St. James adhered to the treaty, because they feared that if they let go of the hawser, a word from Tokio would incite India to revolt. The soil there had for years been prepared for this very contingency, and London, therefore, turned a deaf ear to the indignation expressed by the rest of the world at Japan's treacherous violation of peace.

At last at the end of July the transportation of troops to the West began. But when the police kept a sharp lookout for Japanese or Chinese spies at the stations where the troops were boarding the trains, they were looking in the wrong place, for the enemy was smart enough not to expose himself unnecessarily or to send spies who, as Mongolians, would at once have fallen victims to the rage of the people if seen anywhere near the camps.

Besides, such a system of espionage was rendered unnecessary by the American press, which, instead of benefiting by past experience, took good care to keep the Japanese well informed concerning the military measures of the government, and even discussed the organization of the army and the possibilities of the strategical advance in a way that seemed particularly reprehensible in the light of the fearful reverses of the last few months. The government warnings were disregarded especially by the large dailies, who seemed to find it absolutely impossible to regard the events of the day in any other light than that of sensational news to be eagerly competed for.

This competition for news from the seat of war and from the camps had first to lead to a real catastrophe, before strict discipline could be enforced in this respect. A few patriotic editors, to be sure, refused to make use of the material offered them; but the cable dispatches sent to Europe, the news forwarded triumphantly as a proof that the Americans were now in a position "to toss the yellow monkeys into the Pacific," quite sufficed to enable the Japanese to adopt preventive measures in time.

While the American Army of the North was advancing on Nogi's forces in the Blue Mountains, the Army of the South was to attack the Japanese position in Arizona by way of Texas. For this purpose the three brigades stationed in the mountains of New Mexico were to be reënforced by the troops from Cuba and Porto Rico and the two Florida regiments. All of these forces were to be transported to Corpus Christi by water, as it was hoped in this way to keep the movement concealed from the enemy, in order that the attack in the South might come as far as possible in the nature of a surprise, and thus prevent the sending of reënforcements to the North where, at the foot of the Blue Mountains, the main battle was to be fought. But unfortunately our plan of attack did not remain secret. Before a single soldier had set foot on the transport ships which had been lying for weeks in the harbors of Havana and Tampa, the Japanese news bureaus in Kingston (Jamaica) and Havana had been fully informed as to where the blow was to fall, partly by West Indian half-breed spies and partly by the obliging American press. One regiment of cavalry had already arrived at Corpus Christi from Tampa on July 30th, and the Cuban troops were expected on the following day.

Two American naval officers were standing on the small gallery of the white light-house situated at the extreme end of the narrow tongue of land lying before the lagoon of Corpus Christi, gazing through their glasses at the boundless expanse of blue water glittering with myriads of spots in the rays of the midday sun. Out in the roads lay seven large freight steamers whose cargoes of horses and baggage, belonging to the 2d Florida Cavalry Regiment, were being transferred to lighters. A small tug, throwing up two glittering streaks of spray with its broad bow, was towing three barges through the narrow opening of the lagoon to Corpus Christi, whose docks showed signs of unusual bustle. Short-winded engines were pulling long freight-trains over the tracks that ran along the docks, ringing their bells uninterruptedly. From the camps outside the town the low murmur of drums and long bugle-calls could be heard through the drowsy noon heat. A long gray snake, spotted with the dull glitter of bright metal, wound its way between the white tents: a detachment of troops marching to the station. Beyond the town one could follow the silver rails through the green plantations for miles, as plainly as on a map, until they finally disappeared on the horizon.

Now the whistle of the tug sounded shrilly, blowing scattered flakes of white steam into the air. The quick, clear tolling of church-bells rang over the roofs of the bright houses of the city. It was twelve o'clock and the sun's rays were scorching hot.

One of the naval officers pulled out his watch to see if it were correct, and then said: "Shall we go down and get something to eat first, Ben?"

"The steamers from Havana ought really to be in sight by this time," answered Ben Wood; "they left on the twenty-sixth."

"Well, yes, on the twenty-sixth. But some of those transport-ships palmed off on us are the limit and can't even make ten knots an hour. Their rickety engines set the pace for the fleet, and unless the *Olympia* wishes to abandon the shaky old hulks to their fate, she must keep step with them."

Lieutenant Gibson Spencer swept the horizon once more with his marine-glass and stopped searchingly at one spot. "If that's not the *Flying Dutchman*, they're ships," he remarked, "probably our ships."

The light-house keeper, a slender Mexican, came on the gallery, saying: "Ships are coming over there, sir," as he pointed in the direction which Spencer had indicated. Lieutenant Ben Wood stepped to the stationary telescope in the light-room below the place for the lamps, and started to adjust the screws, but the heat of the metal, which had become red-hot beneath the burning rays of the sun, made him start: "Hot hole," he swore under his breath.

Lieutenant Spencer conversed a moment with the keeper and then looked again through his glass at Corpus Christi, where the tug was just making fast to the pier. The third barge knocked violently against the piles, so that a whole shower of splinters fell into the water.

"Gibson," cried Lieutenant Wood suddenly from his place in the light-room, his voice sounding muffled on account of the small space, "those are not our ships."

Spencer looked through the telescope and arrived at the same conclusion. "No," he said; "we have no ships like that, but they're coming nearer and we'll soon be able to make out what they are!"

"Those ships certainly don't belong to our fleet," he repeated after another long look at the vessels slowly growing larger on the horizon. They had two enormous funnels and only one mast and even the arched roofs of their turrets could now be clearly distinguished.

"If I didn't know that our English friends owned the only ships of that caliber, and that our own are unhappily still in process of equipment at Newport News, I should say that those were two *Dreadnoughts*."

"I guess you've had a sunstroke," rang out the answer.

"Sunstroke or no sunstroke, those are two *Dreadnoughts*."

"But where can they come from?"

The three men examined the horizon in silence, till Lieutenant Wood suddenly broke it by exclaiming: "There, do you see, to the left, just appearing on the horizon, that's our transport fleet—eight—ten ships; the one in front is probably the *Olympia*."

"Twelve ships," counted the keeper, "and if I may be allowed to say so, the two in front are battleships."

"There they are then," said Ben Wood, "and now we'll get something to eat in a jiffy, for we'll have our work cut out for us in an hour!"

"Where shall we eat?" asked Spencer, "I'll gladly dispense with the grub at Signor Morrosini's to-day."

"I'll tell you what," said the other, "we'll go across to one of the transport-steamers; or, better still, we'll go to the captain of the *Marietta*—we'll be sure to get something decent to eat there."

"Right you are!" said Spencer, peering down over the edge of the railing. "Our cutter is down there," he added.

At the foot of the light-house lay a small, white cutter with its brass appointments glittering in the sunlight. Her crew, consisting of three men, had crept into the little cabin, while the black stoker was resting on a bench near the boiler.

"Ho, Dodge!" shouted Spencer, "get up steam. We're going over to the transport-ships in ten minutes."

The firemen threw several shovels of coal into the furnace, whereupon a cloud of smoke poured out of the funnel straight up along the light-house. Lieutenant Wood telephoned over to Corpus Christi that the transports with the troops on board had been sighted and that they would probably arrive in the roads in about two hours.

"We're going over to one of the transport-ships meanwhile," he added, "and will await the arrival of the squadron out there."

While Lieutenant Spencer was climbing down the narrow staircase, Lieutenant Wood once more examined the horizon and suddenly started. The thunder of a shot boomed across the water. Boom—came the sound of another one!

The lieutenant clapped his marine-glasses to his eyes. Yes, there were two *Dreadnoughts* out there, evidently saluting. But why at such a distance?

"Gibson," he called down the staircase.

"Come on, Ben!" came the impatient answer from below.

"I can't, I wish you'd come up again for a minute, I'm sure something's wrong!"

The gun-shots were booming loudly across the water as Lieutenant Spencer reached the gallery, covered with perspiration.

"I suppose they're saluting," exclaimed Spencer somewhat uncertainly.

Ben Wood said nothing, but with a quick jerk turned the telescope to the right and began examining the transport-ships.

"Heavens," he shouted, "they mean business. I can see shells splashing into the water in front of the *Olympia*—no, there in the middle—away back there, too— One of the transports listed. What can it mean? Can they be Japanese?"

Again the roar of guns rolled across the quiet waters.

"Now the *Olympia* is beginning to shoot," cried Ben Wood. "Oh, that shot struck the turret. Great, that must have done some good work! But what in Heaven's name are we going to do?"

Lieutenant Spencer answered by pushing the light-house keeper, who was in abject fear, aside, and rushing to the telephone. Trembling with excitement, he stamped his foot and swore loudly when no notice was taken of his ring.

"All asleep over there as usual! Ah, at last!"

"Halloo! what's up?"

"This is the light-house. Notify the commander at Corpus Christi at once that the Japanese are in the roads and are attacking the transports."

Over in Corpus Christi people began to collect on the piers, the bells stopped ringing, but the sound of bugles could still be heard coming from the encampments.

Now the light-house telephone rang madly and Spencer seized the receiver.

"They are, I tell you. Can't you hear the shots?" he shouted into the instrument. "There are two large Japanese ships out in the roads shooting at the *Olympia* and the transports. Impossible or not, it's a fact!"

Suddenly a thick column of smoke began to ascend from the funnel of the little American gunboat *Marietta*, which was lying among the transports out in the roads. The whistles and bugle-calls could be heard distinctly, and the crew could be seen on deck busy at the guns. The steam-winch rattled and began to haul up the anchor, while the water whirled at the stern as the vessel made a turn. Even before the anchor appeared at the surface the gunboat had put to sea with her course set towards the ships on the horizon, which were enveloped in clouds of black smoke.

"There's nothing for us to do," said Spencer despairingly, "but stand here helplessly and look on. There isn't a single torpedo-boat, not a single submarine here! For Heaven's sake, Ben, tell us what's happening out there!"

"It's awful!" answered Wood; "two of the transport-ships are in flames, two seem to have been sunk, and some of those further back have listed badly. The *Olympia* is heading straight for the enemy, but she seems to be damaged and is burning aft. There are two more cruisers in the background, but they are hidden by the smoke from the burning steamers; I can't see them any more."

"Where on earth have the Japanese ships come from? I thought their whole fleet was stationed in the Pacific. Not one of their ships has ever come around Cape Horn or through the Straits of Magellan; if they had, our cruisers off the Argentine coast would have seen them. And besides it would be utter madness to send just two battleships to the Atlantic. But where else can they have come from?"

"There's no use asking where they come from," cried Wood excitedly, "the chief point is, they're there!"

He gave up his place at the telescope to his comrade, thought for a moment, and then went to the telephone.

His orders into town were short and decisive: "Send all the tugs out to sea immediately. Have them hoist the ambulance-flag and try to rescue the men of the transports."

"And you, Spencer," he continued, "take the cutter and hurry over to the trans-port-steamers in the roads and have them hoist the Red Cross flag and get to sea as quickly as possible to help in the work of rescue. That's the only thing left for us to do. I'll take command of the *President Cleveland* and you take charge of the Swedish steamer *Olsen*. And now let's get to work! Signor Alvares can play the rôle of idle onlooker better than we can. Our place is out there!"

Both officers rushed down the stairs and jumped into the cutter, which steamed off at full speed and took them to their ships.

Three-quarters of an hour later the tug mentioned in the beginning of the chapter appeared again at the entrance to the lagoon. Several men could be seen in the stern holding a large white sheet upon which a man was painting a large red cross, and when the symbol of human love and assistance was finished, the sheet was hoisted at the flagstaff. Two other tugs followed the example of the first one.

But could the enemy have taken the three little tugs for torpedo-boats? It seemed so, for suddenly a shell, which touched the surface of the water twice, whizzed past and hit the first steamer amidships just below the funnel. And while the little vessel was still enveloped by the black smoke caused by the bursting of the shell, her bow and stern rose high out of the water and she sank immediately, torn in two. The thunder of the shot sounded far over the water and found an echo among the houses at Corpus Christi.

"Now they're even shooting at the ambulance flag," roared Ben Wood, who was rushing about on the deck of the *President Cleveland* and exhorting the crew to hoist the anchor as fast as possible so as to get out to the field of battle. But as the boiler-fires were low, this seemed to take an eternity.

At last, about three o'clock in the afternoon, they succeeded in reaching a spot where a few hundred men were clinging to the floating wreckage. The rest had been attended to by the enemy's shots, the sea and the sharks.

The enemy had wasted only a few shots on the transport-steamers, as a single well-aimed explosive shell was quite sufficient to entirely destroy one of the merchant-vessels, and the battle with the *Olympia* had lasted only a very short time, as the distance had evidently been too great to enable the American shots to reach the enemy. That was the end of the *Olympia*, Admiral Dewey's flag-ship at Cavite! The two smaller cruisers had been shot to pieces just as rapidly.

The results of this unexpected setback were terribly disheartening, since all idea of a flank attack on the Japanese positions in the South had to be abandoned.

But where had the two *Dreadnoughts* come from? They had not been seen by a living soul until they had appeared in the roads of Corpus Christi. They had risen from the sea for a few hours, like an incarnation of the ghostly rumors of flying squadrons of Japanese cruisers, and they had disappeared from the field of action just as suddenly as they had come. If it had not been for the cruel reality of the destruction of the transport fleet, no one would soon have believed in the existence of these phantom ships. But the frenzied fear of the inhabitants of the coast-towns cannot well take the form of iron and steel, and nightmares, no matter how vivid, cannot produce ships whose shells sweep an American squadron off the face of the sea.

It had been known for years that two monster ships of the *Dreadnought* type were being built for Brazil in the English shipyards. No one knew where Brazil was going to get the money to pay for the battleships or what the Brazilian fleet wanted with such huge ships, but they continued to be built. It was generally supposed that England was building them as a sort of reserve for her own fleet; but once again was public opinion mistaken. Only those who years before had raised a warning protest and been ridiculed for seeing ghosts, proved to be right. They had prophesied long ago that these ships were not intended for England, but for her ally, Japan.

The vessels were finished by the end of June and during the last days of the month the Brazilian flag was openly hoisted on board the *San Paulo* and *Minas Ger-aes*, as they were called, the English shipbuilders having indignantly refused to sell them to the United States on the plea of feeling bound to observe strict neutrality. The two armored battleships started on their voyage across the Atlantic with Brazilian crews on board; but when they arrived at a spot in the wide ocean where no spectators were to be feared, they were met by six transport-steamers conveying the Japanese crews for the two warships, no others than the thousand Japs who had been landed at Rio de Janeiro as coolies for the Brazilian coffee plantations in the summer of 1908. They had been followed in November by four hundred more.

We were greatly puzzled at the time over this striking exception to the Japanese political programme of concentrating streams of immigrants on our Pacific coasts. Without a word of warning a thousand Japanese coolies were shipped to Brazil, where they accepted starvation wages greatly to the disgust and indignation of the German and Italian workmen—not to speak of the lazy Brazilians themselves. This isolated advance of the Japs into Brazil struck observers as a dissipation of energy, but the Government in Tokio continued to carry out its plans, undisturbed by our expressions of astonishment. Silently, but no less surely, the diligent hands of the coolies and the industrious spirit of Japanese merchants in Brazil created funds with which the two warships were paid at least in part. The public interpreted it as an act of commendable patriotism when, in June, the one thousand four hundred Japs turned their backs on their new home, in order to defend their country's flag. They left Rio in six transport-steamers.

Brazil thereupon sold her two battleships to a Greek inn-keeper at Santos, named Petrokakos, and he turned them over to the merchant Pietro Alvares Cortes di Mendoza at Bahia. This noble Don was on board one of the transport-steamers with the Japanese "volunteers," and on board this Glasgow steamer, the *Kirkwall*, the bill of sale was signed on July 14th, by the terms of which the "armed steamers" *Kure* and *Sasebo* passed into the possession of Japan. The Brazilian crews and some English engineers went on board the transports and were landed quietly two weeks later at various Brazilian ports.

These one thousand four hundred Japanese plantation-laborers, traders, artisans, and engineers—in reality they were trained men belonging to the naval reserve—at once took over the management of the two mighty ships, and set out immediately in the direction of the West Indies. At Kingston (Jamaica) a friendly steamer supplied them with the latest news of the departure of the American transports from Cuba, and the latter met their fate, as we saw, in the roads of Corpus Christi.

A terrible panic seized all our cities on the Gulf of Mexico and the Atlantic coast, as the Japanese monsters were heard from, now here, now there. For example, several shells exploded suddenly in the middle of the night in the harbor of Galveston when not a warship had been observed in the neighborhood, and again several American merchant-vessels were sent to the bottom by the mysterious ships, which began constantly to assume more gigantic proportions in the reports of the sailors. At last a squadron was dispatched from Newport News to seek and destroy the enemy, whereupon the phantom-ships disappeared as suddenly as they had come. Not until Admiral Dayton ferreted out the Japanese cruisers at the Falkland Islands did our sailors again set eyes on the two battleships.

CHAPTER XVIII
THE BATTLE OF THE BLUE MOUNTAINS

It had been found expedient to send a few militia regiments to the front in May, and these regiments, together with what still remained of our regular army, made a brave stand against the Japanese outposts in the mountains. Insufficiently trained and poorly fed as they were, they nevertheless accomplished some excellent work under the guidance of efficient officers; but the continual engagements with the enemy soon thinned their ranks. These regiments got to know what it means to face a brave, trained enemy of over half a million soldiers with a small force of fifty thousand; they learned what it means to be always in the minority on the field of battle, and thus constant experience on the battle-field soon transformed these men into splendid soldiers. Especially the rough-riders from the prairies and the mountains, from which the cavalry regiments were largely recruited, and the exceedingly useful Indian and half-breed scouts, to whom all the tricks of earlier days seemed to return instinctively, kept the Japanese outposts busy. Their machine-guns, which were conveyed from place to place on the backs of horses, proved a very handy weapon. But their numbers were few, and although this sort of skirmishing might tire the enemy, it could not effectually break up his strong positions.

Ever on the track of the enemy, surprising their sentries and bivouacs, rushing upon the unsuspecting Japs like a whirlwind and then pursuing them across scorching plains and through the dark, rocky defiles of the Rockies, always avoiding large detachments and attacking their commissariat and ammunition columns from the rear, popping up here, there and everywhere on their indefatigable horses and disappearing with the speed of lightning, this is how those weather-beaten rough-riders in their torn uniforms kept up the war and stood faithful guard! Brave fellows they were, ever ready to push on vigorously, even when the blood from their torn feet dyed the rocks a deep red! No matter how weary they were, the sound of the bugle never failed to endow their limbs with renewed energy, and they could be depended on to the last man to do whatever was required of them.

It was on these endless marches, these reckless rides through rocky wastes and silent forests—to the accompaniment of the tramp of horses, the creaking of saddles and the rush and roar of rolling stones on lonely mountain-trails—that those strange, weird rhythms and melodies arose, which lived on long afterwards in the minds and hearts of the people.

By the end of July affairs had reached the stage where it was possible for the

Northern army, commanded by General MacArthur and consisting of one hundred and ten thousand men, to start for the Blue Mountains in the eastern part of Oregon, and the Pacific army of almost equal strength to set out for Granger on the Union Pacific Railway. The troops from Cuba and Florida, together with the three brigades stationed at New Mexico, were to have advanced against the extreme right wing of the Japanese army, but the grievous disaster at Corpus Christi had completely frustrated this plan.

The German and Irish volunteer regiments were formed into special brigades in the Northern and Pacific armies, whereas the other militia and volunteer regiments were attached to the various divisions promiscuously. General MacArthur's corps was composed of three divisions, commanded by Fowler, Longworth and Wood, respectively, each consisting of thirty thousand men. To these must be added one German and one Irish brigade of three regiments each, about sixteen thousand men altogether, so that the Northern army numbered about one hundred and ten thousand men and one hundred and forty guns.

Wood's division left the encampment near Omaha the last week of July. They went by rail to Monida, where the Oregon Short Line crosses the boundary of Montana and Idaho. The same picture of utter confusion was presented at all the stops and all the stations on the way. Soldiers of all arms, exasperated staff-officers, excited station officials, guns waiting for their horses and horses waiting for their guns, cavalry-men whose horses had been sent on the wrong train, freight-cars full of ammunition intended for no one knew whom, wagons loaded with camp equipment where food was wanted and with canned goods where forage was needed, long military trains blocking the line between stations, and engines being switched about aimlessly: perfect chaos reigned, and the shortness of the station platforms only added to the confusion and the waste of precious time. If it had not been for the Americans' strongly developed sense of humor, which served as an antidote for all the anger and worry, this execrably handled army apparatus must have broken down altogether. But as it was, everybody made the best of the situation and thanked the Lord that each revolution of the wheels brought the troops nearer to the enemy. The worst of it was that the trains had to stop at the stations time and time again in order to allow the empty trains returning from the front to pass.

The 28th Regiment of Wisconsin Volunteers, under command of Colonel Katterfeld, had at last, after what seemed to both officers and soldiers an endless journey, reached the foothills of the Rocky Mountains on the twenty-second of July via the Northern Pacific Railway. A warm meal had been prepared for the regiment at a little station; then the roll was called once more and the three long trains transporting the regiment started off again.

Colonel Katterfeld had soon won the affection of his men. He was a thin little man with grizzly hair and beard; a soldier of fortune, who had an eventful life behind him, having seen war on three continents. But he never spoke of his experiences. His commands were short and decisive, and each man felt instinctively that he was facing an able officer. He had given up his practice as a physician in Milwaukee, and when, at the outbreak of the war, he had offered his services to the Governor of Wisconsin, the latter was at once convinced that here was a man upon whom he could rely, and it had not taken Colonel Katterfeld long to establish the correctness of the Governor's judgment. He succeeded in being the first to raise the full complement of men for his regiment in Wisconsin, and was therefore the first to leave for the front. The rush for officers' commissions was tremendous and the staff of officers was therefore excellent. One day an officer, named Walter Lange, presented himself at the recruiting office of the regiment. When the colonel heard the name, he glanced up from his writing, and looking inquiringly at the newcomer, asked in an off-hand fashion: "Will you take command of the Seventh Company as captain?"

"Sir?"

"Yes, I know, you were at Elandslaagte and afterwards at Cronstadt, were you not?"

"Yes, sir."

"We need some officers like you who can keep their men together when under fire. Do you accept or not?"

"Certainly, but — —"

"We'll have no buts."

And so the two became war-comrades for the second time, Captain Lange taking command of the Seventh Company.

In thousands of ways the colonel gave proof of his practical experience; above all else he possessed the knack of putting the right people in the right place, and his just praise and blame aroused the ambition of officers and men to such an extent, that the 28th Militia Regiment soon became conspicuous for its excellence. But no one, not even his comrade from Elandslaagte, succeeded in getting nearer to the colonel's heart. Colonel Katterfeld was a reticent man, whom no one dared bother with questions.

In order to make the best possible use of what little room there was in the cars, the colonel had ordered two-hour watches to be kept. Half the men slept on the seats and on blankets on the floor, while the other half had to stand until the order, Relieve watch! rang out at the end of two hours.

Captain Lange was standing at the window looking out at the moonlit landscape through which the train was rushing. Wide valleys, rugged mountain peaks and steep, rocky bastions flew past. A whistle—a low rumble in the distance—the sound of approaching wheels—a flash of light on the track—and then the hot breath of the speeding engine sweeps across the captain's face, as a long row of black cars belonging to an empty train returning from the mountains tears past on its way to the encampments.

And then on and on, over bridges and viaducts, where the rolling wheels awaken echo after echo, on into the narrow ravine, above the forest-crowned edges of which the quiet light of the stars twinkles and gleams in the purple sky of night.

The captain was thinking of the colonel. He could not remember having met him on any of the South African battle-fields, and he had never heard the name of Katterfeld. And yet he was positive he had seen those penetrating blue eyes beneath their bushy brows before. No one who had once seen it could ever forget that glance. But he racked his brain in vain. He looked at the time and found that the present watch still had a whole hour to run. The soldiers were leaning sleepily against the sides of the car, and loud snores came from the seats and the floor. Suddenly a rifle fell to the ground with a clatter and several men woke up and swore at the noise. On went the train, and the monotonous melody of the rolling wheels gradually lulled the weary thoughts to sleep.

Captain Lange thought of Elandslaagte again and of Colonel Schiel and Dinizulu, the Kafir chief, and of the story the colonel had told, as they bivouacked round the fire, of the latter's royal anointment with castor-oil. They had made the fire with the covers of "Mellin's Food" boxes—Mellin's Food—a fine chap, Mellin—Mellin?— Wasn't that the name of the captain with whom he had once sailed to Baltimore? And Daisy Wilford had been on board with her two cats— cats— My, how he used to chase cats when he was a boy—it was a regular hunt— No, it hadn't been his fault, but Walter Wells'— But he had been caught and shut up in the attic, where his father gave him a chance to recollect that it is cruel to torment animals—but it really had been Walter's fault, only he wasn't going to tell on him—and then, after he had been alone, he had knocked his head against the wall in his rage at the injustice of the world—always—knocked—his—head— against—the—wall—always—knocked——

Bang! went the captain's head against the window-frame and he woke up with a start and put his hand up to his aching forehead. Where under the sun was he? Ah, of course—there were the soldiers snoring all around him and tossing about in their sleep. He felt dead tired. Had he been asleep? He looked at the time again—still fifty-five minutes to the next watch.

The roaring and clattering of the wheels came to his ears on the fresh night air as he again looked out of the window. The train had just rounded a curve, and the other two trains could be seen coming on behind. Now they were passing through a gorge between bright rocky banks, which gleamed like snow in the moonlight. Whirling, foaming waters rushed down the mountain-side to join the dark river far below. Then on into a dark snowshed where the hurrying beat of the revolving wheels resounded shrilly and produced a meaningless rhythm in his thoughts. Kat—ter—feld, Kat—ter—feld, Kat—ter—feld, came the echo from the black beams of the shed. Katter—feld, Kat—ter—feld, Kat—ter—feld, came the reply from the other side. Then the rattling noise spreads over a wider area. There is a final echo and the beams of the shed disappear in the distance, and on they go in the silent night until the sergeant on duty pulls out his watch and awakens the sleepers with the unwelcome call, Relieve the guard!

Two days later the regiment arrived at Monida, where they had to leave the train. The line running from there to Baker City was only to be used for the transportation of baggage, while the troops had to march the rest of the way—about two hundred and fifty miles. While the field-kitchen wagons were being used for the first time near Monida, the men received new boots, for the two pairs of shoes which each had received in camp had turned out such marvels of American manufacture, that they were absolutely worn out in less than no time. It was thought wiser, in consideration of the long marches before the soldiers, to do away with shoes altogether and to provide strong boots in their stead. The hard leather of which the latter were made gave the soldiers no end of trouble, and the strange foot-gear caused a good deal of grumbling and discomfort.

It was here that the experience of the old troopers was of value. The old devices of former campaigns were revived. An old, gray-bearded sergeant, who had been in the Manchurian campaign against the Japanese, advised his comrades to burn a piece of paper in their boots, as the hot air would enable them to slip the boots on much more easily. Captain Lange employed a more drastic method. He made his company march through a brook until the leather had become wet and soft, and as a result his men suffered least from sore feet on the march.

During the ten days' march to Baker City, officers and men became thoroughly acquainted with one another, and the many obstacles they had had to overcome in common cemented the regiments into real living organisms. And when, on the tenth of August, the different columns reached Baker City, the Northern Army had firmly established its marching ability. The transport-service, too, had got over its first difficulties. From the front, where small detachments were continually skirmishing with the enemy, came the news that the Japanese had retreated from Baker City after pulling up the rails. On the evening of the eleventh of August the 28th Militia Regiment was bivouacking a few miles east of Baker City. The outposts towards the enemy on the other side of the town were composed of a battalion of Regulars.

Every stone still burned with the glowing heat of the day, which spread over the warm ground in trembling waves. The dust raised by the marching columns filled the air like brown smoke.

The last glimmer of the August day died down on the western horizon in a crimson glow, and a pale gleam of light surrounded the dark silhouettes of the mountains, throwing bluish gray shadows on their sides. Then all the colors died out and only the stars twinkled in the dark blue heavens. Far away in the mountains the white flashes of signal-lanterns could occasionally be seen, telling of the nearness of the enemy. Colonel Katterfeld had ordered the officers of his regiment to come to his quarters in a farm-house lying near the road, and a captain of Regulars was asked to report on the number of skirmishes which had taken place in the last few days and on the enemy's position. It was learned that Marshal Nogi had retreated from Baker City and had withdrawn his troops to the Blue Mountains, taking up his central position at the point of the pass crossed by the railroad. It had not been possible to ascertain how far the wings of the Japanese army extended to the North or South. It was certain that the enemy maintained strong lines of communication in both directions, but it was difficult to determine just how far their lines penetrated into the wooded slopes and valleys.

When the guard was relieved at 5 o'clock in the morning, one of the non-commissioned officers was struck by a curiously-shaped bright cloud the size of a hand, which hung like a ball over the mountains in the west in the early morning light.

"It must be an air-ship!" said some one.

"It evidently is; it's moving!" said the sergeant, and he at once gave orders to awaken Captain Lange.

The captain, who had gone to sleep with the telephone beside him, jumped up and could not at first make out where the voice came from: "A Japanese air-ship has been sighted over the mountains." He was up in a second and looking through his glasses! Sure enough! It was an air-ship!

Its light-colored body hovered above the mountains in the pale-blue sky like a small silver-gray tube.

"Spread the report at once!" called the captain to the telephone operator; and bustle ensued on all sides.

"What shall we do?" asked a lieutenant. "There's no use in shooting at it; by the time it gets within range we should shoot our own men."

The air-ship came slowly nearer, and at last it was directly over the American line of outposts.

"They can see our whole position!" said Captain Lange, "they can see all our arrangements from up there."

Boom! came the sound of a shot from the right.

"That probably won't do much good."

A few hundred yards below the air-ship a little flame burst out. The smoke from a shrapnel hung in the air for a moment like a ball of cotton, and then that, too, disappeared. Boom! it went again.

"We shall never reach it with shrapnel," said the lieutenant, "there's no use trying to beat it except on its own ground."

"We have some newly constructed shrapnel," answered the captain, "the bullets of which are connected with spiral wires that tear the envelope of the balloon."

Now two shots went off at the same time.

"Those seem to be the balloon-guns," said the lieutenant.

Far below the air-ship hovered the clouds of two shrapnel shots.

"They're getting our air-ship ready over there," cried the captain; "that's the only sensible thing to do." He pointed to a spot far off where a large, yellow motor-balloon could be seen hanging in the air like a large bubble.

It went up in a slanting direction, and then, after describing several uncertain curves, steered straight for the enemy's balloon, which also began to rise at once.

Hundreds of thousands of eyes were following the course of those two little yellow dots up in the clear, early morning air, as the mountain edges began to be tipped with pink. The Japanese air-ship had reached a position a little to one side of that occupied by the 28th Regiment, when a tiny black speck was seen to leave it and to gain in size as it fell with increasing velocity. When it reached the ground a vivid red flame shot up. Tremendous clouds of smoke followed, mixed with dark objects, and the distant mountains resounded with loud peals of thunder which died away amid the angry rumblings in the gorges.

"That was a big bomb," said the captain, "and it seems to have done considerable mischief."

Now a little puff of white smoke issued from the American air-ship and ten seconds later an explosive body of some sort burst against a wall of rock.

"If they keep on like that they'll only hit our own men," said the lieutenant.

"The Jap is ascending," cried some one, and again all the field-glasses were directed towards the two ships.

Now both were seen to rise.

"The Japs are throwing down everything they've got in the way of explosives," cried the captain. A whole row of black spots came rushing down and again came the thunder caused by the bursting of several bombs one after the other.

The Jap went up rapidly and then crossed the path of the American balloon about two hundred yards above it.

Suddenly the yellow envelope of the American air-ship burst into flames, lost its shape and shrunk together, and the ship fell rapidly among the valleys to the left, looking like the skeleton of an umbrella that has been out in a gale of wind.

"All over," said the lieutenant with a sigh. "What a shame! We might just as well have done that ourselves."

High up in the blue ether hovered the Japanese air-ship; then it described a curve to the left, went straight ahead and then seemed suddenly to be swallowed up in the morning light. But soon it appeared again as a gray speck against the clear blue sky, and turning to the right once more, got bigger and bigger, came nearer, and finally steered back straight for the Blue Mountains. And then the thunder of cannon was heard from the right.

The assault on Hilgard, the center of the Japanese position in the broad valley of the Blue Mountains, had failed; two regiments had bled to death on the wire barricades outside the little town, and then all was over. It would be necessary to break up the enemy's position by flank movements from both sides before another attack on their center could be attempted. For two long days the artillery contest waged; then Longworth's division on our right wing gained a little ground, and when the sun sank to rest behind the Blue Mountains on August 14th, we had reason to be satisfied with our day's work, for we had succeeded, at a great sacrifice, it is true, in wresting from the enemy several important positions on the sides of the mountains.

Towards evening six fresh batteries were sent forward to the captured positions, whence they were to push on towards the left wing of the Japanese center the next morning. Telephone messages to headquarters from the front reported the mountain-pass leading to Walla Walla free from the enemy, so that a transport of ammunition could be sent that way in the evening to replenish the sadly diminished store for the decisive battle to be fought the next day.

While the newspapers all over the East were spreading the news of this first victory of the American arms, Lieutenant Esher was commanded by General Longworth to carry the orders for the next day to the officer in charge of the Tenth Brigade, which had taken up its position before the mountain-pass on the right wing. For safety's sake General Longworth had decided to send his orders by word of mouth, only giving instructions that the receipt of each message should be reported to headquarters by each detachment either by field-telegraph or telephone.

Lieutenant Esher, on his motor-cycle, passed an endless chain of ammunition wagons on his way. For a long time he could make only slow progress on account of the numerous ambulances and other vehicles which the temporary field-hospitals were beginning to send back from the front; but after a time the road gradually became clear.

The motor rattled on loudly through the silent night, which was disturbed only now and then by the echo of a shot. Here and there along the road a sentry challenged the solitary traveler, who gave the password and puffed on.

He had been informed that the quickest way to reach General Lawrence would be by way of the narrow mountain-path that turned off to the left of the road, which had now become absolutely impassable again on account of innumerable transports. It was a dangerous ride, for any moment the bicycle might smash into some unseen obstacle and topple over into the abyss on the right, into which stones and loose earth were continually falling as the cycle pushed them to one side.

Lieutenant Esher therefore got off his wheel and pushed it along. At the edge of a wood he stopped for a moment to study his map by the light of an electric pocket-lamp, when he heard a sharp call just above him. He could not quite make it out, but gave the password, and two shots rang out simultaneously close to him. — When Lieutenant Esher came to, he found a Japanese army doctor bending over him.

He had an uncertain feeling of having been carried over a rocky desert, and when he at last succeeded in collecting his thoughts, he came to the conclusion that he must have strayed from the path and run straight into the enemy's arms.

He tried to raise his head to see where he was, but a violent pain in his shoulder forced him to lie still. The noises all around made it clear to him, however, that he was among Japanese outposts. The doctor exchanged a few words with an officer who had just come up, but they spoke Japanese and Esher could not understand a word they said.

"Am I wounded?" he asked of the ambulance soldier beside him. The latter pointed to the doctor, who said, "You will soon be all right again."

"Where am I wounded?"

"In the right thigh," answered the doctor, sitting down on a stone near Esher. The doctor didn't seem to have much work to do.

The stinging pain in his right shoulder robbed Esher of his senses for a moment, but he soon came to again and remembered his orders to Lawrence's brigade. Thank God he had no written message on his person. As it was, the enemy had succeeded in capturing only a broken motor-cycle and a wounded, unimportant officer. The division staff would soon discover by telephoning that General Lawrence had not received his orders and then repeat the message.

Esher managed to turn his head, and watched the Japanese officer copying an order by the light of a bicycle lamp. The order had just been delivered by a mounted messenger, who sat immovable as a statue on his exhausted and panting steed.

Suddenly the Japanese cavalryman seemed to grow enormous bats' wings, which spread out until they obscured the whole sky. The ghostly figure resembled a wild creature of fable, born of the weird fancy of a Doré, or an avenging angel of the Apocalypse. Then the rider shrank together again and seemed to be bouncing up and down on the back of his horse like a little grinning monkey.

The wounded man rubbed his eyes. What was that? Was he awake or had he been dreaming?

He asked the ambulance soldier for a drink, and the latter at once handed him some water in a tin cup. Now a real Japanese cavalryman was once more sitting up there on his horse, while the officer was still writing. Then the officer's arm began to grow longer and longer, until at last he was writing on the sky with a fiery pencil:

"In case there is no Japanese attack on August 15th, the Tenth Brigade under General Lawrence is to retain its present positions until the attack of our center——"

Good Lord, what was that? Yes, those were the very words of the message he was to have delivered to the Tenth Brigade, and not only were the words identical, but the hand-writing was the same, for the flaming letters had burnt themselves into his memory stroke for stroke and word for word and line for line.

He tried to get up, but could not. The lieutenant kept on writing, while the horseman stood beside him. The horse was brushing off the flies with his tail.

Then the awful, maddening thought came to him: This must be the beginning of wound-fever. If it kept up and he began to get delirious, he might betray his orders for Lawrence's brigade to the enemy.

And he saw hundreds of Japanese standing around him, all stretching their necks to catch his words, and more and more came from over the mountain ridges like a swarm of ants, and they all wanted to hear the secrets that he was trying to keep in his aching head, while the officer waved his note-book over him like a fluttering flag. Then the doctor seized him, and arm in arm they hopped to and fro—to and fro—to and fro.

Yes, he was certainly delirious. Lieutenant Esher thought of his home. He saw his little house on 148th Street. He came home from business, he walked through the garden, hung up his coat on the rack, opened the door, his young wife welcomed him, she nodded to him—Eveline—groaned the lieutenant, and then his thoughts turned to God.

Then the writing officer again, the rider on his horse, and the dark night-sky, in which the stars were dancing like silver gnats. Collecting his whole willpower, he succeeded in getting into a sitting posture, and the Japanese soldier attending him awoke out of a doze only to find his revolver in the American's hands. But it was too late, for a shot resounded at the same moment. Lieutenant Esher had brought his weary brain to rest; his head toppled over and landed hard on the rocky ground.

Thus died a real hero, and those were hard times when men of stout heart and iron courage were sorely needed.

Opposite Hilgard, the center of the enemy's position in the Blue Mountains, trenches had been thrown up, and the 28th Militia Regiment had occupied them in the night of August 13th-14th. The Japanese were apparently not aware of their presence, as the regiment had taken no part in the fighting on the fourteenth. On the evening of the same day, the 32d Regiment was pushed forward to the same position, while the searchlights were playing over the plain and on the mountain sides, and dazzling the eyes of the sentries who were keeping a sharp lookout for the enemy from various ambushes. And whenever the beam of light landed on dark shadows, which jumped quickly aside, flames shot out on the opposite side and flashes of fire from bursting shrapnel drew trembling streaks across the sky and lighted up the immediate neighborhood.

The wires which connected the headquarters with all the sentries and outposts vibrated perpetually with the thoughts and commands of a single individual, who managed this whole apparatus from a little schoolroom in Baker City far behind the front, allowing himself scarcely a moment for much-needed night-rest.

The 28th Regiment had thrown up trenches the height of a man in the hard ground opposite the little town of Hilgard on the night of August 13th-14th. Now a company of pioneers was busy widening them and building stands for the troops where they would be safe from splinters, for it was highly probable that the assault on Hilgard would be undertaken from here on the following evening. The covering for these stands was made of thick boards and planks taken from a sawmill near by, and over these the dug up earth was spread. The enemy's attention seemed to be directed elsewhere, for the reflections from the searchlights were continually crossing one another over to the right. In this direction music could be distinctly heard coming from Longworth's Division—a lively march waking the echoes of the night with its clear full tones.

Music? Those who were swearing at the stupidity of allowing the band to play in the very face of the enemy, did not know that the troops over there on their way to quarters had marched over forty miles that day, and that only the inspiring power of music could help the stumbling men to gather their remaining strength and press forward.

The cheerful melody of the old Scotch song,

> "Gin a body, meet a body,
> Comin' thro' the rye,"

rang out in common time across the silent battle-field, fifes squeaking and drums rolling, while the silent searchlights continued flashing in the dark sky.

> "Gin a body, meet a body,
> Comin' thro' the rye."

Meanwhile the picks and spades were kept going in the trenches of the 28th Regiment. The earth and stones flew with a rattle over the top of the breastworks, making them stronger and stronger, pioneers and infantry working side by side in the dark, hollow space. The battalion on guard kept strict watch in the direction of the enemy, continually expecting to see creeping figures suddenly pop up out of the darkness.

"Didn't you hear something, captain?" asked one of the men on watch.

"No, where?"

A curious purring sound like the whizzing of a small dynamo became audible.

Some one gave a low whistle, and the pioneers stopped work, and leaned on their spades. All the men listened intently, but no one could make out whence the strange sound came.

Suddenly some one spoke quite loudly and another voice replied. Up in the air—that's where it was! A black shadow swept across the sky. "An air-ship!" cried one of the men in the trench, and sure enough the whirring of the screw of a motor balloon could be distinctly heard. Bang—bang—bang, went a few shots into the air.

"Stop the fire!" called a commanding voice from above.

"Stop! It is our own balloon!"

"No, it's a Japanese one!"

Bang—bang, it went again. From the rear came the deep bass of a big gun and close by sounded the sharp bang—bang—bang of a little balloon-gun in the second trench. There was a burst of flame up in the air, followed by a hail of metal splinters. "Cut that out. You're shooting at us!" roared Captain Lange across to the battery.

"Stop firing!" came a quick order from there. A few cannon shots were heard coming from the rear.

Suddenly a bright light appeared up in the air and a white magnesium cluster descended slowly, lighting up all the trenches in a sudden blaze which made the pioneers look like ghosts peering over the black brink of the pits. Then the light went out, and the eyes trying in vain to pierce the darkness saw nothing but glittering fiery red circles. The Japanese batteries on the other side opened fire. The air-ship had entirely disappeared, and no one knew whether the uncanny night-bird had been friend or foe.

The assault on Hilgard was to be begun by the 28th and 32d Volunteers: General MacArthur had originally planned to have the attempt made at dawn on August 15th; but as one brigade of Wood's Division had not yet arrived, he postponed the attack for twenty-four hours, to the sixteenth of August, while the fifteenth was to be taken up with heavy firing on the enemy's position, which seemed to have been somewhat weakened. As soon, therefore, as day broke, the Americans opened fire, and all the time that almost sixty American guns were bombarding Hilgard and sending shell after shell over the town, and the white flakes of cotton from the bursting shrapnels hovered over the houses and almost obscured the view of the mountains and the shells tore up the ground, sowing iron seed in the furrows, the 28th and 32d Volunteers lay in the trenches without firing a single shot.

The commander of the 16th Brigade, to which the two regiments belonged, was in the first trench during the morning, and, in company with Colonel Katterfeld, inspected the results of the bombardment through his telescope, which had been set up in the trench. A shrapnel had just destroyed the top of the copper church tower, which the Japanese were using as a lookout.

Although the American shells had already created a great deal of havoc in Hilgard, the walls of the houses offered considerable resistance to the hail of bullets from the shrapnels. The brigadier-general therefore sent orders to the battery stationed behind and to the right of the trenches to shell the houses on both sides of the street leading into Hilgard.

"Shell the houses on both sides of the street leading into Hilgard! Shell the houses on both sides of the street leading into Hilgard—Shell—Hilgard," was the command which was passed along from mouth to mouth through the trenches, until it reached the battery amid the roar of battle.

"—Shells—we have no shells—shrapnels—the battery has no shells, only shrapnels—" came back the answer after a while.

"No shells, I might have known it, only those everlasting shrapnels. How on earth can I shoot a town to pieces with shrapnel!" growled the brigadier-general, going into the protected stand where the telephone had been set up.

"Send two hundred shells immediately by automobile from Union to the 8th Battery Volunteers stationed before Hilgard," ordered the general through the telephone— "What, there aren't any shells at Union? The last have been forwarded to Longworth's Division?— But I must have at least a hundred; have them brought back at once from the right wing— No automobile, either?" It was a wonder that the telephone didn't burst with righteous indignation at the vigorous curses the brigadier-general roared into it.

But unfortunately the statement made at Union, where the field railway built from Monida for the transport service terminated, was correct. Just as in most European armies, the number of shells provided was out of all proportion to the shrapnel, and the supply of shells was consequently low at all times. Besides, most of the ammunition-motors had been put out of commission early in the game. The advantage of higher speed possessed by the automobiles was more than offset by their greater conspicuousness the moment they came within range of the enemy's guns. The clouds of dust which they threw up at once showed the enemy in which direction they were going, and as they were obliged to keep to the main road, the Japanese had only to make a target of the highway and do a little figuring to make short work of these modern vehicles. The great number of wrecked motor cars strewn along the road proved rather conclusively that the horse has not yet outlived its usefulness in modern warfare.

The officers, including the generals, had willingly dispensed with such a dangerous mode of locomotion after the first fatal experiences, for the staring fiery eyes of the motor betrayed its whereabouts by night, and the clouds of dust betrayed it by day. The moment an auto came puffing along, the enemy's shots began to fall to the right and left of it, and it was only natural, therefore, that the horse came into its own again, both because the rider was not bound to the main road and because he did not offer such a conspicuous target for the enemy's shots.

Towards noon the Japanese batteries entrenched before Hilgard began bombarding the 28th Regiment with shrapnel. Colonel Katterfeld therefore ordered half his men to seek protection under the stands.

The howling and crashing of the bursting shrapnel of course had its effect on those troops who were here under fire for the first time. But the shrapnel bullets rained on the wooden roofs without being able to penetrate them, and after half an hour this fact imbued the men in their retreats with a certain feeling of security. The enemy soon stopped this ineffective fire from his field-guns, however, and on the basis of careful observations made from a captive balloon behind Hilgard, the Japanese began using explosive shells in place of the shrapnel.

The very first shots produced terrible devastation. The long planks were tossed about like matches in the smoke of the bursting Shimose shells, and the slaughter when one of them landed right in the midst of the closely packed men in one of these subterranean mole-holes was absolutely indescribable. Back into the trenches, therefore! But the enemy had observed this change of position from his balloon, and the shots began to rain unceasingly into the trenches. And so perfect was the Japanese marksmanship that the position of the long line of trenches could easily be recognized by the parallel line of little white clouds of smoke up above them. There was nothing more to be concealed, and accordingly Colonel Katterfeld ordered his regiment to open fire on Hilgard and on the hostile artillery entrenched before the town.

Captain Lange lay with his nose pressed against the breastworks, carefully observing the effect of the fire through his field glasses. Although this was not his first campaign, he had nevertheless had some trouble in ridding himself of that miserable feeling with which every novice has to contend, the feeling that every single hostile gun and cannon is pointed straight at him. But the moment the first men of his company fell and he was obliged to arrange for the removal of the wounded to the rear, his self-possession returned at once. It was his bounden duty, moreover, to set an example of cool-headed courage to his men, so he calmly and with some fuss lighted a cigarette, yet in spite of the apparent indifference with which he puffed at it, it moved up and down rather suspiciously between his lips.

A volunteer by the name of Singley, the war-correspondent of the *New York Herald*, worked with much greater equanimity, but then he had been through five battles before he gained permission to join the 7th Company for the purpose of making pencil sketches and taking photographs of the incidents of the battle.

He now arranged a regular rest for his kodak in the breastwork of the trench and stooped down behind the apparatus, which was directed towards the six Japanese guns to the left in front of the houses at Hilgard, the position of which could only be recognized by the clouds of smoke which ascended after each shot was fired. Just then he heard the order being passed along to the 8th battery to give these guns a broadside of shrapnel, and as it would probably take a few minutes before this order could be carried out, Singley pulled out his note-book and glanced over the entries made during the last hour:

No.   843.   Japanese shell bursts through a plank covering.

"   844.   Trench manned afresh.

"   845.   Captain Lange smoking while under fire.

"   846.   Japanese shrapnels indicate the line of our trenches in the air.

Then he put his note-book down beside him and crept under his kodak again, carefully fixing the object-glass on the battery opposite. Now then! A streak of solid lightning flashed in front of the second gun, and a black funnel of smoke shot up. Click!

No.   847.   Firing at the Japanese battery before Hilgard.

Singley exchanged the film for a new one, and then looked about for another subject for his camera. He took off his cap and peeped carefully over the edge of the trench. Could he be mistaken? He saw a little black speck making straight for the spot where he was. "A shell" rushed through his thoughts like a flash, and he threw himself flat on the bottom of the trench.

With a whirring noise the heavy shell struck the back wall of the trench. "An explosive shell!" shouted Captain Lange, "everybody down!"

The air shook with a tremendous detonation; sand and stones flew all around, and the suffocating powder-gas took everybody's breath away; but gradually the soldiers began to recognize one another through the dust and smoke, thankful at finding themselves uninjured.

"Captain!" called a weak voice from the bottom of the trench, "Captain Lange, I'm wounded." The captain bent down to assist the war-correspondent, who was almost buried under a pile of earth.

"Oh, my legs," groaned Singley. Two soldiers took hold of him and placed him with his back against the wall of earth. The lower part of both his thighs had been smashed by pieces from the shell. "Will you please do me a last service?" he asked of Captain Lange.

"Of course, Singley, what is it?"

"Please take my kodak!"

Singley himself arranged the exposure and handed the camera to the captain, saying: "There, it is set at one twentieth of a second. Now please take my picture—Thank you, that's all right! And now you can have me removed to the hospital!"

Before the men came to fetch him, Singley managed to add to his list:

No. 848.   Our war-correspondent, Singley, mortally wounded by a Japanese shell. Hail Columbia!

Then he closed his book and put it in his breast pocket. Five minutes later two ambulance men carried him off to have his wounds attended to, and in the evening he was conveyed to the hospital.

A week later Captain Lange's snapshot of the war-correspondent was paraded in the *New York Herald* as the dramatic close of Singley's journalistic career. In his way he, too, had been a hero. He died in the hospital at Salubria.

He could claim the credit of having made the war plain to those at home. Or was that not the war after all? Were the black shadows on the photographic plate anything more than what is left of a flower after the botanist has pressed the faded semblance of its former self between the leaves of his collection? Certainly not much more.

No, that is not war. Just a bursting—silently bursting shell, the scattering of a company—that is not war.

Thousands of bursting shells, the howls of the whizzing bullets, the constant nerve-racking crashing and roaring overhead, the deafening cracking of splitting iron everywhere—that is war. And accompanying it all the hopeless sensation that this will never, never stop, that it will go on like this forever, until one's thoughts are dulled by some terrible, cruel, incomprehensible, demoralizing force. Those bounding puffs of smoke everywhere on the ground, rifle shots which have been aimed too short and every one of which— That abominable sharp singing as of a swarm of mosquitoes, buzz, buzz, like the buzzing of angry hornets continually knocking their heads against a window-pane. Bang! That hit a stone. Bang! two inches nearer, then—"Aim carefully, fire slowly!" calls the lieutenant in a hoarse, dry voice. You aim carefully and fire slowly and reload. Buzz— And then you fume with a fierce uncontrollable rage because you must aim carefully and fire slowly. And the whole space in front of the trenches is covered with infantry bullets glittering in the sunlight. Will it ever stop? Never! A day like that has a hundred hours—two hundred. And if you had been there all by yourself, you would never have dreamed of shooting over the edge of the trenches—you would most probably have been crouching down in the pit. But as you happen not to be alone, this can't be done. Will the enemy's ammunition never give out? It's awful the way he keeps on shooting.

And that terrible thirst! Your throat is parched and your teeth feel blunt from grinding the grains of sand which fly into your face whenever an impudent little puff of smoke jumps up directly in front of you. Sssst. The mosquitoes keep on singing, and the bees buzz perpetually. Those dogs over there, those wretches, those— Buzz, buzz, buzz—it never stops, never. Over there to the right somebody cracks a joke and several soldiers laugh. "Aim carefully, fire slowly!" sounds the warning voice of the lieutenant. And it's all done on an empty stomach—a perfectly empty stomach.

Just as the field-kitchen wagon had arrived this morning, a shell had exploded in the road and it was all over with the kitchen-wagon. How long ago that seemed! And the bees keep on humming. Bang! that hit the sergeant right in the middle of the forehead. Is this never going to stop? Never? You chew sand, you breathe sand, burning dry sand, which passes through your intestines like fire. And then that horrible, faint, sickening feeling in the stomach when you feel the ambulance men creeping up behind to take away another one of your comrades! How terrible he looks, how he screams! You are quite incensed to think that anybody can yell like that! What a fool! "Aim carefully, fire slowly," warns the lieutenant. Bouncing puffs of smoke again! And sand in your mouth and fire in your intestines. You think continually of water, beautiful, clear, ice-cold water, never-ending streams of water— A roaring, howling and crashing overhead, the clatter of splinters, a sharp pain in your brain and a horrible feeling in your stomach and all the time it goes buzz, buzz, buzz—ssst—ssst—buzz, buzz, buzz— —

That is war, not the pictures that people see at home, all those lucky people who have lots of water, who can go where they like and are not forced to stay where the bees keep up a continual buzz, buzz, buzz— —

Colonel Katterfeld was kneeling on the ground examining the map of Hilgard and marking several positions with a pencil. He could overhear the conversation of the soldiers under the board-covering next to his own.

"Do you think all this is on account of the Philippines?" asked one.

"The Philippines? Not much. It would have come sooner or later anyhow. The Japs want the whole Pacific to themselves. We wouldn't be here if it were only for the Philippines."

"We wouldn't? It's on account of imperialism, then, is it?"

"Don't talk foolish. We know very well what the Japs want, imperialism or no imperialism."

"Well, why are the papers always talking so much about imperialism?"

"They write from their own standpoint. Imperialism simply means that we wish to rule wherever the Stars and Stripes are waving."

The colonel peeped into the adjacent cover. It was Sergeant Benting who was speaking.

"Right you are, Benting," said the colonel, "imperialism is the desire for power. Imperialism means looking at the world from a great altitude. And the nation which is without it will never inherit the earth."

Then the colonel gave the order to fire at a house on the right side of the street, in which a bursting shrapnel had just effected a breach and out of which a detachment of infantry was seen to run.

Once again, just before twilight, the battle burst out on both sides with tremendous fury. The whole valley was hidden in clouds of smoke and dust, and flashes of fire and puffs of smoke flew up from the ground on all sides. Then evening came and, bit by bit, it grew more quiet as one battery after the other ceased firing. The shrill whistle of an engine came from the mountain-pass. And now, from far away, the Japanese bugle-call sounded through the silent starry night and was echoed softly by the mountain-sides, warming the hearts of all who heard it:

CHAPTER XIX
THE ASSAULT ON HILGARD

It was three o'clock in the morning. Only from the left wing of Fowler's Division was the booming of cannon occasionally heard. From the mountain-pass above came the noise of passing trains, the clash of colliding cars and the dull rumble of wheels. On the right all was still.

A low whistle went through all the trenches! And then the regiments intended for the assault on Hilgard crept slowly and carefully out of the long furrows. The front ranks carried mattresses, straw-bags, planks and sacks of earth to bridge the barbed wire barricades in case they should not succeed in chopping down the posts to which the wires were fastened. A few American batteries behind La Grande began firing. The other side continued silent.

Suddenly two red rockets rose quickly one after the other on the right near the mountain, and they were followed directly by two blue ones; they went out noiselessly high up in the air. Was it a signal of friend or foe? The regiments came to a halt for a moment, but nothing further happened, except that the two searchlights beyond Hilgard kept their eyes fixed on the spot where the rockets had ascended. A dog barked in the town, but was choked off in the middle of a howl. Then deathlike stillness reigned in front once more, but several cannon thundered in the rear and a few isolated shots rang out from the wooded valleys on the left.

The front ranks had reached the wire barricades. Suddenly a sharp cry of pain broke the silence and red flames shot forth from the ground, lighting up the posts and the network of wires. Several soldiers were seen to be caught in the wires, which were apparently charged with electricity. Now was the time! The pioneers provided with rubber gloves to protect them against the charged wires went at it with a vengeance, and were soon hacking away with their axes. Loud curses and cries of pain were heard here and there. "Shut up, you cowards!" yelled some one in a subdued voice. The black silhouettes of the men, who were tossing long boards and bags of earth on top of the wires, stood out sharply against the light of the explosives with which the Americans were attempting to loosen the supporting posts.

The light of the dancing flames fell on swaying, leaping figures. Shots rang out constantly, millions of sparks flew all around and through all the din could be distinguished the short, sharp rattatattatt—rrrrr—rattatattatt of the machine-guns, sounding more like cobble-stones being emptied out of a cart than anything else.

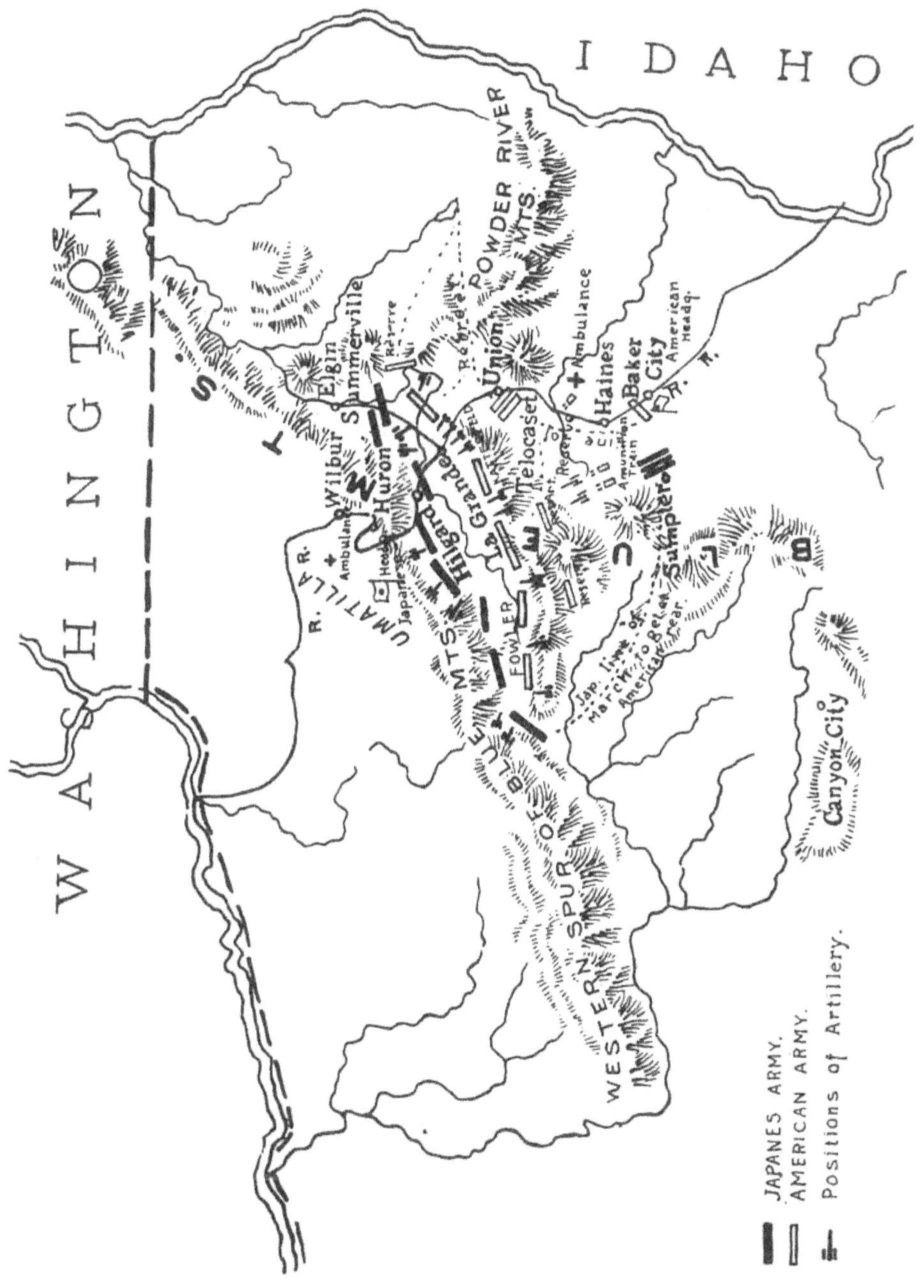

DIAGRAM OF THE BATTLE OF HILGARD

Hell had meanwhile broken loose on the other side. The attacking regiments were exposed to a perfectly terrific rifle-fire from the houses and streets of Hilgard, which was accompanied by a destructive cannonade. But on they went! Over the corpses of the slain who had breathed their last jammed in among the deadly wires, over the swaying planks and through the gaps made by the exploding bombs, the battalions swept on with loud shouts of Hurrah! What mattered it that the machine-guns, which they had brought along, were sometimes dragged through furrows of blood! On they went! The field-batteries to the right and left of the first houses and two of the enemy's machine-guns just in front of the barricade were in the hands of the 28th Regiment, and now they advanced against the houses themselves. But it was utterly impossible to get a foot further. A whole battalion was sacrificed before the high barricade at the entrance to the main street, but still they went on! There were no storming-ladders, and after all they were hardly needed, for human pyramids were speedily run up against the walls, and up these soldiers scrambled, assisted from below, until at last they were high enough to shoot into the loop-holes. Others aided in the work with axes and the butt-ends of their guns, and before long the Americans had gained possession of several houses. All of the enemy's searchlights concentrated their glare on the town, so that the fighting was done in a brilliant light. The white top of the church-tower seemed strangely near, while reddish-gold reflections played on the torn copper roof.

But no reënforcements came from the rear, and it was no wonder, for a furious fire from the enemy's artillery and machine-guns swept across the space in front of Hilgard, raining bullets and balls upon the trenches, out of which new battalions climbed again and again; the shots plowed up the land into glowing furrows and created an impassable fire-zone between the trenches and the nearest houses of Hilgard, whence shrieking bugle-calls begged for immediate assistance. If the enemy should succeed in throwing reënforcements into Hilgard, he would have no difficulty in dislodging the Americans from the positions they had won. Suddenly an attack from the wooded valley on the left at last brought relief. It was the Irish brigade under General O'Brien that came on like a whirlwind, quite unexpectedly, and joined in the fight.

This attack threw back the advancing Japanese reënforcements. The regiments could be seen retreating in the pale light of dawn, and then they were seen to form in line on the rising ground behind. Between them and the rear of the town lay the Irish sharpshooters, who went forward by leaps and bounds. But the furious artillery fire from the enemy brought the fighting temporarily to a stand-still.

Wild confusion reigned on all sides as dawn broke. The 17th Japanese Infantry Regiment was still battling with the two American regiments for the possession of the front houses of Hilgard, and the two Japanese battalions in the rear of the town directed their fire on the compact columns of the Third Irish Regiment, which had not yet been formed into line for shooting. It was a critical moment, and everything depended upon the rapidity with which the Japanese resistance in Hilgard could be overcome.

In the houses and on the illuminated streets a furious hand-to-hand encounter was going on, the men rushing at one another with bayonets and the butt-ends of their guns. No effort was made to keep the men or regiments together. Where the weapons had been destroyed or lost in the mad scramble, the soldiers fought like gorillas, tearing one another's flesh with teeth and nails. On all sides houses were on fire, and the falling beams and walls, the bursting flames, the showers of descending sparks, and the bursting shrapnels killing friend and foe alike, created an indescribable jumble.

At last reënforcements arrived in the shape of a regiment which had lost more than half its men in passing through the fire-zone in front of Hilgard.

"Where is Colonel Johnson?"

"Over there, on the other side of the street."

"A prisoner?" asked some one.

"I guess not, they're not making prisoners and we aren't either."

Slowly it grew lighter.

The Irish in the rear of Hilgard had hard work to maintain their position. To dislodge the enemy, it was absolutely necessary to turn his flank; otherwise there was no chance of advancing further. Each line of sharpshooters that leaped forward was partially mowed down by the terrible machine-guns. The enemy didn't budge an inch.

General O'Brien had already dispatched five orderlies to Fowler's division with instructions to attack the enemy from the left, but all five had been shot down the moment they left their cover. Something had to be done at once, or the entire brigade would be destroyed.

Suddenly Corporal Freeman, who had crept up along the ground, appeared beside the General.

"Here, sir," he cried, his face beaming, "here's the connection for you." And he shoved a telephone apparatus towards O'Brien. He had dragged the connecting wire behind him through the entire fire-zone.

"You must be a wizard!" cried the General, and then seizing the instrument he called: "Throw all the troops you can possibly get hold of against the right wing of the Japanese in front of us! The enemy's position is weakened, but we can't attack the ridge in the front from here."

Several minutes passed—minutes pregnant with destruction. The bursting shells thinned the ranks terribly, while the infantry fire continued to sweep along the ground, but worst of all, the ammunition of the Irish regiments was getting low. Several batteries were planted between the ruins of the houses in Hilgard, but even then the enemy did not budge.

Then came a great rush from the left: Cavalry, Indian scouts, regular cavalry, cavalry militia, volunteer regiments, and behind them all the machine-guns and the field-artillery—a perfect avalanche of human beings and horses wrapped in thick clouds of smoke from which showers of sparks descended.

That was our salvation. A wild shout of joy from the Irishmen rose above the din of battle, and after that there was no restraining them. The front ranks of the cavalry were mown down like sheaves of corn by the bullets of the enemy's machine-guns; but that made no difference, on they went, on, ever on! Whole regiments were cut to pieces. Hundreds of saddles were emptied, but the riders came on just the same, and even before they had reached the Irish sharpshooters, every man who wore the green was headed for the ridge almost without waiting for the word of command!

It was an assault the enemy could not possibly repulse. The Irish and the cavalry were right among their firing lines; a battery galloped up into the hostile ranks, crushing dead and wounded beneath its wheels. Bloody shreds of flesh were sticking to the gun-barrels, and torn limbs and even whole bodies were whirled round and round in the spokes of the wheels.

Shrill bugle-calls resounded. The horses were wheeled around and the battery unlimbered. A hostile shell suddenly struck the shaft of the gun-carriage, and in a second the horses were a bloody mass of legs wildly beating the air and of writhing, groaning bodies.

But the gun was in position. And now out with the ammunition! Bang! went the first shot, which had been in the barrel, and then everybody lent a hand; an Indian scout, bleeding at the shoulder, and an engineer helped pass the shells, while a mortally wounded gunner shoved the cartridge into the barrel.

"Aim up there to the left, near the two detached pine-trees, six hundred yards," roared a lieutenant, whose blood-covered shirt could be seen beneath his open uniform.

"The two pines to the left," answered the gunner, lying across the bracket-trail. Bang! off went the shot, and a line of Japanese sharpshooters rose like a flock of quail.

More cannon, more machine-guns, more ammunition-carts rushed up in mad haste; the batteries kept up a continual fire.

The battle moved on farther to the front. The houses of Hilgard were all in flames; only the white top of the church-tower still projected above the ruins. On the right of the town one column after another marched past to the strains of regimental music.

An orderly galloped past, and some one called out to him: "How are things in front?" "Fine, fine, we're winning!" came the answer, which was greeted with jubilant cheers. Gradually the enemy's shots became scarcer as the battle advanced up the slopes.

Engineers were hard at work getting the streets of Hilgard cleared so as to save the troops the detour round the outside of the town. The burning houses were blown up with dynamite, and a temporary hospital was established near the city, to which the wounded were brought from all parts of the battle-field.

By noon Hilgard was sufficiently cleared to allow the 36th Militia Regiment (Nebraska) to pass through. On both sides of the streets were smoking ruins filled with dead and dying and charred remains. The steps of the battalion sounded strangely hollow as the first company turned into the square where the white church still stood almost intact in the midst of the ruins. A wounded soldier was calling loudly for water.

What was that? Were the bells tolling? The soldiers involuntarily softened their step when they heard it. Yes, the bells were tolling, slowly at first and low, but then the peals rang out louder and louder until a great volume of sound burst through the little windows in the white church-spire. Ding—dong, ding—dong——

The flag-bearer of the first company lowered his flag and the soldiers marched past in silence. The captain rode over to the entrance to the tower and looked in. A little boy, about ten years old, was tugging and straining at the heavy bell-ropes. There seemed to be a number of wounded soldiers in the church, as loud groans could be heard through the half-open door.

The captain looked about him in astonishment. Near a post he saw two Japanese, presenting a fearful spectacle in the convulsions of death. Close to them lay an American foot-soldier, writhing with pain from a bayonet-wound in the abdomen; and over in the farther corner he could distinguish a woman, dressed in black, lying on a ragged mattress. Ding—dong, ding—dong, rang the bells up above, but the noise of battle did not penetrate here.

"What are you doing, sonny?" asked the captain.

"I'm ringing the bells for mother," said the little fellow.

"For mother?"

"General," called a weak voice from the corner, "please let the boy alone. I want to hear our bells just once more before I die."

"What's the matter, are you wounded?" asked the captain.

"I feel that I'm dying," was the answer; "a bullet has entered my lung; I think it's the lung."

"I'll send you a doctor," said the captain, "although we——"

"Don't bother, general; it wouldn't do any good."

"How did you get here?"

"My husband," came the answer in a weak voice, "is lying across the street in our burning home. He was the minister here in Hilgard. These last days have been fearful, general; you have no idea how fearful. First they shot my husband, and then our little Elly was killed by a piece of shell when I was running across the street to the church with her and the boy." She paused a moment, and then continued with growing agitation: "It's enough to make one lose faith in the wisdom of the Lord to see this butchery—all the heartrending sorrow that's created in the world when men begin to murder one another like this. You don't realize it in the midst of the battle, but here— And as God has seen fit to spare His church in the battle, I asked the boy to ring the bells once more, for I thought it might be a comfort to some of those dying out there to hear a voice from above proclaiming peace after these awful days. Let him keep on ringing, general, won't you?"

"Can I help you in any way?" asked the captain.

"No, only I should like some water."

The captain knelt down by the side of the poor, deserted woman and handed her his flask.

She drank greedily, and then thanked him and began to sob softly. "What will become of my boy? My poor husband——"

"My good woman," said the captain, forcing himself to speak bluntly, "it's not a question of this boy, or of a single individual who has fallen in battle, but rather of a great people which has just defeated the enemy. The widows and orphans will be taken care of by the survivors, now that the Lord has given us the victory. Those who are lying outside the town and those here have surrendered their lives for their country, and the country will not forget them."

Ding—dong, ding—dong, went the bells as the captain left the church, deeply affected. Ding—dong, ding—dong. Thousands out on the battle-field in the throes of death, and the many unfortunates lying with broken limbs in the burning houses and watching the flames creeping towards them, heard that last call from on high, like a call from God, Who seemed to have turned away from our people.

And then evening came, the evening of the sixteenth of August, which is recorded with bloody letters on the pages of our country's history. Soon all the reserves were engaged in battle. Our splendid regiments could not be checked, so eager were they to push forward, and they succeeded in storming one of the enemy's positions after the other along the mountain-side. At last the enemy began to retreat, and the thunder of the cannon was again and again drowned in the frenzied cheers. General MacArthur was continually receiving at his headquarters reports of fresh victories in the front and on both wings.

The telegraph wires had long ago spread the glad tidings over the length and breadth of the land. Great joy reigned in every town, the Stars and Stripes waved proudly from all the houses, and the people's hearts were fluttering with exultation.

General MacArthur, whose headquarters were located near Hilgard, was waiting for news of Fowler's Division, which had orders to advance on the pass through the valleys on the left wing. They were to try and outflank the enemy's right wing, but word was sent that they had met with unexpected resistance. It appeared, therefore, that the enemy had not yet begun to retreat at that point.

On the other hand, things were going better in the center. But what was the good of this reckless advance, of this bold rush, which built bridges of human bodies across the enemy's trenches and formed living ladders composed of whole companies before the enemy's earthworks—what was the good of all this heroic courage in the face of Marshal Nogi's relentless calculations? He was overjoyed to see regiment after regiment storm towards him, while from his tent he gave directions for the sharp tongs of the Japanese flanks to close in the rear of General MacArthur's army.

About seven o'clock in the evening the surprising news came from the right wing that the batteries which had begun firing on the enemy's lines retreating along the railway line were suddenly being shelled from the rear, and begged for reënforcements. But there were no reserves left; the last battalion, the last man had been pushed to the front! How did the enemy manage to outflank us?

Imploringly, eagerly, the telephone begged for reënforcements, for batteries, for machine-guns, for ammunition. The transport section of the army service corps had been exhausted long ago, and all the ammunition we had was in front, while a wide chasm yawned between the fighting troops and the depots far away in the blue distance. General MacArthur had nothing left to send.

And now from Indian Valley came the request for more machine-guns, but there wasn't one left. General MacArthur telegraphed to Union, the terminus of the field-railway, but the answer came that no assistance could be given for several hours, as the roadbed had first to be repaired. From Toll Gate, too, came stormy demands for more ammunition—all in vain.

And then, at eight o'clock, when the sun had sunk like a ball of fire in the west, and the Blue Mountains, above which hovered puffs of smoke from the bursting shrapnel, were bathed in the golden evening light and the valley became gradually veiled in darkness, the crushing news came from Baker City that large, compact bodies of Japanese troops had been seen on the stretch of broken-down railroad near Sumpter. Soon afterwards Union reported the interruption of railway communication with the rear and an attack with machine-guns by Japanese dismounted cavalry, while Wood's division in the front continued to report the capture of Japanese positions.

With relentless accuracy the arms of the gigantic tongs with which Nogi threatened to surround the entire Army of the North began to close. The American troops attacking both flanks had not noticed the Japanese reserves, which had been held concealed in the depressions and shallow valleys under cover of the woods. Two miles more to the right and left, and our cavalry would have come upon the steel teeth of the huge tongs, but there was the rub: they hadn't gone far enough.

About ten o'clock in the evening Baker City, which was in flames, was stormed by the Japanese, Indian Valley having already fallen into their hands. The attack in front, high up in the mountains, began to waver, then to stop; a few captured positions had to be abandoned, and down in the valley near La Grande, whence the field-hospitals were being removed to the rear, the ambulances and Red Cross transports encountered the troops streaming back from Baker City. One retreating force caught up with the other, and then night came—that terrible night of destruction. Again the cannon thundered across the valley, again the machine-guns joined in the tumult, while the infantry fire surged to and fro.

You may be able to urge an exhausted or famished troop on to a final assault, you may even gain the victory with their last vestige of energy, their last bit of strength, provided you can inspire them with sufficient enthusiasm; but it is impossible to save a lost cause with troops who have been hunted up and down for twenty-four hours and whose nerves are positively blunt from the strain of the prolonged battle.

The exhausted regiments went back, back into the basin of the Blue Mountains, into a flaming pit that hid death and destruction in its midst. The headquarters, too, had to be moved back. General MacArthur lost his way in the darkness, and, accompanied by a single officer, rode across the bloody battle-field right through the enemy's line of fire.

He soon ran across a cavalry brigade belonging to Longworth's division, and at once placed himself at its head and led an onslaught on a Japanese regiment. A wild *mêlée* ensued in the darkness, and, although only a few hundred riders remained in their saddles, the attack had cleared the atmosphere and the wavering battalions gained new courage.

General MacArthur ordered a retreat by way of Union, employing Wood's division, which was slowly making its way back to Hilgard, to cover the retreat. Regiment after regiment threatened to become disbanded, and only the determined action of the officers prevented a general rout. The decimated regiments of Wood's division stood like a wall before the ruins of Hilgard; they formed a rock against which the enemy's troops dashed themselves in vain. In this way Fowler's and Longworth's divisions succeeded in making a fair retreat, especially as the enemy's strength was beginning to become exhausted. The uncertainty of a night attack, when the fighting is done with bandaged eyes, as it were, and it becomes impossible to control the effect of one's own firing, contributed also towards weakening the Japanese attacks. The thin lines of hostile troops from Baker City and from the north, which had threatened to surround our army, were pierced by the determined assaults of the American regiments; and although our entire transport service and numerous guns remained in possession of the enemy, our retreat by way of Union was open.

At dawn on the seventeenth of August the remains of Wood's division began to leave Hilgard, which they had so bravely and stubbornly defended, the heroes retreating step by step in face of the enemy's artillery fire.

General MacArthur stopped just outside of Union and watched the regiments—often consisting only of a single company—pass in silence. He frowned with displeasure when he saw Colonel Smeaton riding alone in the middle of the road, followed by two foot-soldiers. The colonel was bleeding from a wound in his forehead.

General MacArthur gave spurs to his horse and rode towards the colonel, saying: "Colonel, how can you desert your regiment?"

Colonel Smeaton raised himself in his stirrups, saluted, and said: "I have the honor to report that only these two, Dan Woodlark and Abraham Bent, are left of my regiment. They are brave men, general, and I herewith recommend them for promotion."

The general's eyes grew moist, and, stifling a sigh, he held out his hand to Colonel Smeaton: "Forgive me," he said simply, "I did not intend to hurt your feelings."

"Nonsense!" cried the colonel. "We'll begin over again, general, we'll simply start all over again. As long as we don't lose faith in ourselves, nothing is lost."

Those were significant words spoken that seventeenth day of August.

CHAPTER XX
A FRIEND IN NEED

The attitude towards the war in Australia was entirely different from that of Europe. Everyone realized that this was not an ordinary war, but a war upon which the future of Australia depended. If the Japanese succeeded in conquering a foot of land in North America, if a single star was extinguished on the blue field of the American flag, it would mean that the whole continent lying in Asia's shadow would also fall a prey to the yellow race.

The early reports from the Philippines and from San Francisco, and the crushing news of the destruction of the Pacific fleet, swept like a whirlwind through the streets of Sydney, Melbourne, Adelaide, Wellington and Auckland, and gave rise to tremendous public demonstrations. Business came to a stand-still, for the Australian people had ears only for the far-off thunder of cannon, and their thoughts were occupied with the future. Huge open-air mass-meetings and innumerable demonstrations before the American consulates bore witness to Australia's honest sympathy. The time had arrived for the fifth continent to establish its political status in the council of nations.

In Sydney the mob had smashed the windows of the Japanese consulate. Satisfaction was at once categorically demanded from London, where the government trembled at the bare idea of a hostile demonstration against its ally. The apology was to take the form of a salute to the Japanese flag on the consulate by a coast battery, etc. But the Australian government refused point blank to do this, and contented itself with a simple declaration of regret; and as there was no other course open to him, the Japanese Consul had to be satisfied. But in Tokio this affair was entered on the credit side of the Anglo-Japanese ledger, offsetting the debt of gratitude for August 10, 1904, when the English fleet constituted the shifting scenery behind Togo's battleships.

A great many of the Japanese located in Australia had left the country before the outbreak of the war to join the army of invasion, and those who remained behind soon recognized that there was no work for them anywhere on the continent. When they refused to take this hint and make themselves scarce, Australian fists began to remind them that the period of Anglo-Mongolian brotherhood was a thing of the past. The last of the Japanese settlers were put aboard an English steamer at Sydney and told to shift for themselves. The Chinese, too, began to leave the country, and wherever they did not go of their own accord, they were told in pretty plain language that the yellow man's day in Australia was ended.

Australia, up to this time merely an appendage of the Old World, a colony which had received its blood from the heart of the British Empire and its ideas from the nerve-center in Downing Street, which had hitherto led a purely dependent existence, now awoke and began to develop a political life of its own. And this development, born of the outbreak of Mongolian hostilities, could not be restrained. The time had passed when the European nations could say: The world's history is created by us, other nations are of no account.

Once before Australia had taken an active part in politics. That was when the Union Jack was threatened, when British regiments were melting away before the rifles of a peasant people at Magersfontein, Colenso and Graspan, when Ladysmith was being besieged, and Downing Street trembled for the safety of the empire. Then, in the hour of dire need, a cry for help went out to all the peoples dwelling beneath the Union Jack, whose flagstaff was being shaken by sturdy peasant hands. And the colonial troops heard the call and responded nobly. Australian and Canadian heroism was ushered into being on the grassy plains and kopjes of the Transvaal. They may not have been good to look at and their manners were not those of the drawing-room, but England opened her arms to those splendid fellows from the Australian bush and was glad to use them in her hour of need—but afterwards she forgot them. But those days were not so soon forgotten in Australia; there are too many men still going around with one arm or a wooden leg. The gentlemen in Downing Street, however, have short memories, and the debt of thanks they owed the colonies quickly slipped their minds.

For the sake of her bales of cotton, her export lists, and her Indian possessions, the London government threw all the traditions of the British world empire overboard and forgot that Old England's problem of civilization was the conquest of the world for the Anglo-Saxon race. For the sake of her London merchants, Old England betrayed Greater Britain, which in the calculations of the London statesmen was only a geographical conception, while the nations without credulously accepted the decisions of English politics as the gospel of British power.

England offered the hand of fellowship to the Japanese parvenu simply because she wanted some one to hold her Russian rival in check.

What the Manchurian campaign cost England can be figured out exactly, to the pound and shilling. She simply purchased the downfall of Russia with the loan of a few hundred millions to Japan—an excellent bargain.

But Sir Charles Dilke was beginning to open the people's eyes. "Another Japanese loan," he cried, "will slip a sharp dagger into the hand of our greatest commercial rival."

England, however, would not listen, and after the war she only drew the bonds of the alliance closer for fear of the Japanese ants who were creeping secretly into India and whispering into the people's ears that the dominion of a few hundred thousand white men over three hundred million Indians was based solely on the legend of the superiority of the white race, a legend which Mukden and Tsushima had completely nullified.

After all, London was at liberty to adopt any policy it liked; but in this particular case the colonies were expected to bear the entire costs. And this was the gratitude for the aid given in South Africa for customs favors extended to English goods at Ottawa, Cape Town, and Melbourne. Deliberately disregarding the warnings of Sir Wilfred Laurier, of Seddon, and of Deakin, who clearly recognized the proximity of the danger, the gentlemen in London insisted upon unrestricted Japanese immigration into the colonies, although Hawaii furnished an eloquent example of how quickly coolie immigrants can transform an Anglo-Saxon colony into a Japanese one.

In South Africa, too, England was sowing trouble with Mongolian miners, until the Africanders took it upon themselves to rid their country of this yellow plague.

In consideration of the existing alliance with Japan, Downing Street demanded of Canada and Australia that the Japanese settlers should be granted equal privileges with the white man. New Zealand's prime minister, Seddon, a resolute man whose greatness is not appreciated in Europe, brought his fist down on the table with a vengeance at the last Colonial Conference in London and appealed to Old England's conscience in the face of the yellow danger. All in vain. Although he persisted in proclaiming New Zealand's right to adhere to her exclusive immigration laws, it was several years before Australia and Canada awoke to a realization of the dangers which the influx of Japanese coolies held in store for them, and before they began to prepare for an energetic resistance.

Then, in August, 1908, came the American fleet. Great was the rejoicing in all the Australian coast towns, and the welcome extended to the American sailors and marines proved to the world that hearts were beating in unison here in the fear of future catastrophes. Never has the feeling of the homogeneousness of the white race, of the Anglo-Saxon race, celebrated such festivals, and when the Australians and Americans shook hands at parting, the former realized that a brother was leaving with whom they would one day fight side by side—when the crisis came and the die was cast which was to decide whether the Pacific should be ruled by the Anglo-Saxon or the Mongolian race.

And now the danger that had been regarded as likely to make itself felt decades hence had become a terrible reality in less than no time. The joint Japanese foe was actually on American soil, the American dominion over the Philippines and Hawaii had been swept away at the first onset, and the great brother nation of the United States was struggling for its existence as a nation and for the future of the white race.

What had become of Great Britain's imperialism, of the All-British idea, for the sake of which Australia, Canada, and New Zealand had sent their sons to South Africa? England, whose grand mission it was to protect the palladium of Anglo-Saxon dominion, stood aloof in this conflict.

The cabinet of St. James had sent a warning to Ottawa not to permit Canadian volunteers to enter the United States, and similar instructions had been forwarded to Melbourne and Wellington.

But when England, at Japan's instigation, tried to persuade the European powers to compel Mexico to prevent American volunteer regiments from crossing the frontier by concentrating her army opposite El Paso, Germany frustrated this plan by declaring that the acknowledgment of the Monroe Doctrine as a political principle in 1903 rendered it impossible for her to meddle in America's political affairs. In spite of this failure, the cabinet of St. James continued to play the rôle of international watchman, and employed the influence secured by *ententes* in previous years to carefully prevent other European governments from violating the laws of neutrality towards Japan. It was, of course, the worry over India which made the English government, generally very elastic in its views regarding neutrality, all at once so extremely virtuous.

London felt very uncomfortable when, in July, a Canadian paper published an alleged conversation between a Japanese and an English diplomatist. "What will Great Britain do in case of war?" the Japanese is said to have asked, whereupon he received the ambiguous answer: "Her duty." Then, with the daring candor assumed by these people when they feel that they are masters of the situation, the Japanese had declared: "The London government must bear in mind that the continuation of British rule in India depends absolutely on the wishes of Japan; that England, in other words, can support the United States only at the price of an Indian insurrection."

This conversation, which was published by a curious act of indiscretion, and of course at once denied in London, nevertheless threw a flood of light on England's political situation. Japan did not directly ask for military aid, which, as a matter of fact, she had no right to expect under the terms of the second Anglo-Japanese agreement, but she did demand favorable neutrality on the part of Great Britain as the guardian of the mobile forces of the Anglo-Saxon world-empire; in other words, Japan insisted that England should betray her own race for the sake of India.

This political trick of the Japanese government was the yellow man's revenge for the half promises with which England had driven Japan into the conflict with Russia, and then, after the outbreak of the war, had offered only meager messages of sympathy instead of furnishing the expected military assistance.

England's destiny now hung in the balance; the threads reaching from Ottawa, Cape Town, Melbourne, and Wellington to Downing Street were becoming severed, not by a sword-cut, but by England's own policy.

If imperialism should leave no room for a "white" policy, then Australia and Canada must throw off the burdensome fetters which threatened to hand over the white man under the Union Jack, bound hand and foot, to the Mongolians.

It was not easy to come to such a decision, and it was months before it was finally reached. But one day, towards the end of August, the entire Australian press advertised for volunteers for the American army. Thousands responded, and no one asked where the large sums of money came from with which these men were provided with arms and uniforms.

A vehement Japanese protest, sent by way of London, only elicited the reply that the Australian government had received no official notification of the enlistment of volunteers for the United States, and was therefore not in a position to interfere in any such movement.

A feeling of joyous confidence reigned among the volunteers; they were going to take the field and fight for their big brother. The racial feeling, so strong in every white man, had been aroused and could withstand any Mongolian attack. By October the first steamers of volunteers left for America. As there were no Japanese or Chinese spies left, and as the government kept a strict watch on the entire news and telegraph service, the departure of the steamers remained concealed from the enemy. As Japanese ships were cruising in the Straits of Magellan, the route via Suez was chosen, and in due course the steamers arrived safely at Hampton Roads.

Wherever the conscience of the Anglo-Saxon race was not wrapped in bales of cotton and in stock quotations, wherever the feeling of Anglo-Saxon solidarity still inspired the people, there was a stir. And so the objections of the London government were not heeded in the colonies.

Why should the citizen of Canada, of British Columbia, care for Downing Street's consideration for India, when he was suffering commercially from the yellow invasion just as much as the citizen of the United States, and when he realized that he would surely be the next victim if the Japanese should be victorious this time?

In this epoch-making hour of the world's history, England had neglected her bounden duty, because she was indissolubly bound to Japan. By the same right with which George Washington had once raised the flag, crowds of men streamed across the frontier from Canada and British Columbia, and by that same right Ottawa now categorically demanded the removal of the Japanese ships from the harbor of Esquimault. "They must either lower their flag and disarm, or they must leave the harbor!" wrote the Canadian papers, and the Canadian Secretary of State, William Mackenzie, couched the protest which he sent to London in similar terms. It was recognized in London that threats were no longer of avail in the face of this spontaneous enthusiasm. England had staked much and lost.

Canadian and Australian regiments were soon found fighting side by side with their American brothers. And now at last, with the united good-will of two continents behind us, there was a fair prospect of the early realization of the boastful words uttered by the American press at the beginning of the war: "We'll drive the yellow monkeys into the Pacific."

CHAPTER XXI

DARK SHADOWS

Autumn had come, and all was serene at the seat of war, except for a few insignificant skirmishes. Slowly, far more slowly than the impatience of our people could stand, the new bodies of troops were prepared for action, and before we could possibly think of again assuming the offensive, winter was at the door.

In the middle of November, three Japanese orderlies, bearing a white flag of truce, rode up to our outposts, and a few days later it was learned from Washington that the enemy had offered to make peace, the terms of which, however, remained a mystery for a short time, until they were ultimately published in the capital.

The States of Washington, Oregon, Nevada, and California were to become Japanese possessions, but at the same time continue as members of the Union. They were to have Japanese garrisons and to permit Japanese immigration; the strength of the garrisons was to be regulated later. In the various State legislatures and in the municipal administration half the members were to be Americans and half Japanese. If these terms were accepted, Japan would relinquish all claim to further immigration of Japanese to the other States of the Union. The United States was to pay Japan a war-indemnity of two billion dollars, in installments, exclusive of the sums previously levied in the Pacific States. San Francisco was to be Japan's naval port on the Pacific coast, and the navy-yard and arsenals located there were to pass into the hands of the Japanese. The Philippines, Hawaii and Guam were to be ceded to Japan.

A universal cry of indignation resounded from the Atlantic to the Rockies in answer to these humiliating terms of peace. To acknowledge defeat and keep the enemy in the country, would be sealing the doom of American honor with a stroke of the pen. No! anything but that! Let us fight on at any price! At thousands of mass meetings the same cry was heard: Let us fight on until the last enemy has been driven out of the country.

But what is public opinion? Nothing more than the naïve feeling of the masses of yesterday, to-day and perhaps the day after to-morrow. The terrible sacrifices claimed by the war had not been without effect. Of course there was no hesitation on the part of the old American citizens nor of the German, Scandinavian and Irish settlers—they would all remain faithful to the Star Spangled Banner. But the others, the thousands and hundreds of thousands of Romanic and Slavonic descent, the Italian and Russian proletariat, and the scum of the peoples of Asia Minor, all these elements, who regarded the United States merely as a promising market for employment and not as a home, were of a different opinion.

And these elements of the population now demanded the reëstablishment of opportunities for profitable employment, insisting upon their rights as naturalized citizens, which had been so readily accorded them. Scarcely had the first storm of indignation passed, when other public meetings began to be held—loud, stormy demonstrations, which usually ended in a grand street row—and to this were added passionate appeals from the Socialist leaders to accept Japan's terms and conclude peace, in order that the idle laborer might once more return to work.

And this feeling spread more and more and gradually became a force in public life and in the press, and unfortunately the agitation was not entirely without effect on those elements of the population whose American citizenship was not yet deeply rooted. However indignant the better elements may have felt at first over this cowardly desertion of the flag, the continual repetition of such arguments evoked faint-hearted considerations of the desirability of peace in ever widening circles.

The fighting of our troops on the plateaus of the Rocky Mountains no longer formed the chief topic of conversation, but rather the proffered terms of peace, which were discussed before the bars, on the street, at meetings, and in the family-circle.

Scarcely a fortnight after the presentation of the Japanese offer of peace, two bitterly hostile parties confronted each other in the Union: the one gathered round the country's flag full of determination and enthusiasm, the other was willing to sacrifice the dollar on the altar of Buddha.

And other forces were also at work. Enthusiastic preachers arose in numerous sects and religious denominations, applying the mysterious revelations of the prophet of Patmos—revelations employed in all ages for the forging of mystic weapons—to the events of the time. In the dim light of evening meetings they spoke of the "beast with the seven heads" to whom was given power "over all kindreds, tongues and nations," and fanatical men and women came after months of infinite misery and hopeless woe to look upon the occupant of the White House as the Antichrist. They conceived it their bounden duty to oppose his will, and quite gradually these evening prayer-meetings began to influence our people to such a degree that the Japanese terms were no longer regarded as insulting, and peace without honor was preferred to a continuance of the fight to the bitter end. Had God really turned the light of his countenance from us?

While the enemy was waiting for an answer to his message, the voices at home became louder and louder in their demands for the conclusion of peace and the acceptance of the enemy's terms. The sound common-sense and the buoyant patriotism of those who had their country's interests close at heart struggled in vain against the selfish doctrine of those who preferred to vegetate peacefully without one brave effort for freedom. Our whole past history, replete with acts of bravery and self-sacrifice, seemed to be disappearing in the horrors of night.

And while the socialist agitators were goading on the starving workmen everywhere to oppose the continuation of the war, while innumerable forces were apparently uniting to retire the God of War, who determines the fate of nations on bloody fields, there remained at least one possibility of clearing the sultry atmosphere: a battle. But how dared we continue the fight before our armies were absolutely prepared to begin the attack, how dared we attempt what would no doubt prove the decisive battle before we were certain of success? The battle of Hilgard furnished an eloquent reply. The War Department said no, it said no with a heavy heart; weeks must pass, weeks must be borne and overcome, before we could assume the offensive once more.

The Japanese terms of peace were therefore declined. At the seat of war skirmishes continued to take place, the soldiers freezing in their thin coats, while restless activity was shown in all the encampments.

Extras were being sold on the streets of Washington, telling of a naval engagement off the Argentine coast. They were eagerly bought and read, but no one believed the news, for we had lost hope and faith. Excited crowds had collected in front of the Army and Navy building in the hope of obtaining more detailed news; but no one could give any information. An automobile suddenly drew up in front of the south side of the long building, before the entrance to the offices of the Committee on Foreign Affairs.

The Secretary of State, who had not been able to get the President by 'phone at the White House but learned that he was somewhere in the naval barracks, had decided to look him up. Scarcely had he entered his car, before he was surrounded by hundreds of people clamoring for verification of the news from Buenos Ayres. He declared again and again that he knew nothing more than what he had just read in the extras, but no one believed him. Several policemen cleared the way in front of the puffing machine, which at last managed to get clear of the crowd, but a few blocks further on the chauffeur was again compelled to stop.

An immense mob was pouring out of a side street, where they had just smashed the windows of the offices of a socialist newspaper, which had supplemented the Argentine dispatch with spiteful comments under the headlines: "Another Patriotic Swindle."

The Secretary of State told the chauffeur to take a different route to the naval barracks, and this order saved his life, for as he bent forward to speak to the chauffeur, the force of an explosion threw him against the front seat. Behind him, on the upper edge of the rear seat, a bomb had exploded with a burst of blinding white light. The secretary, whose coat was torn by some splinters of glass, stood up and showed himself to the multitude.

"Murder, murder," yelled the mob, "down with the assassin." And the secretary saw them seize a degenerate-looking wretch and begin pounding him with their fists. After a little while he was thrown to the ground, but was dragged up again and at last, as the chauffeur was guiding his car backwards through the crowd, the secretary heard a man say:

"Thank God, they've strung him up on a lamp-post!"

The mob had administered quick justice.

Utterly exhausted by this experience, the Secretary of State returned to his home, where he gave orders that the President should be informed at once of what had occurred.

The servant had scarcely left the secretary's study when his wife entered. She threw her arms passionately around his neck and refused to be quieted. "It's all right, Edith, I haven't been scratched."

"But you'll be killed the next time," she sobbed.

"It makes but little difference, Edith, whether I die here on the pavement or out yonder on the battle-field: we must all die at our posts if need be. Death may come to us any day here as well as there, but," and freeing himself from his wife's embrace, he walked to his desk and pointed to a picture of Abraham Lincoln hanging over it, saying, "if I fall as that man fell, there are hundreds who are ready to step into my shoes without the slightest fuss and with the same solemn sense of duty."

A servant entered and announced that the British Ambassador asked to be received by the secretary. "One minute," was the answer, "ask His Excellency to wait one minute."

The sound of many voices could be heard outside. The secretary walked to the window and looked out.

"Look," he said to his wife, "there are some people at least who are glad that the bomb failed to accomplish its purpose." His appearance at the window was a signal for loud cheers from the people on the street. Holding the hand of his faithful wife in his own, he said: "Edith, I know we are on the right road. We can read our destiny only in the stars on our banner. There is only one future for the United States, only one, that beneath the Stars and Stripes, and not a single star must be missing—neither that of Washington, nor that of Oregon, nor that of California. We had a hard fight to establish our independence, and the inheritance of our fathers we must ever cherish as sacred and inviolable. The yellow men have won their place in the world by an inexorable sense of national duty, and we can conquer them only if we employ the same weapons. I know what we have at stake in this war, and I am quite ready to answer to myself and to our people for each life lost on the field of battle. I am only one of many, and if I fall, it will be in the knowledge that I have done my duty. Let the cowardly mob step over my corpse, it won't matter to me nor to my successor if he will only hold our drooping flag with a firm hand. The favor of the people is here to-day and gone to-morrow, and we must not be led astray by it. The blind creatures who inspired that miserable wretch to hurl the bomb regard us, the bearers of responsible posts, with the same feelings as the lions do their tamer when he enters the cage. If he comes out alive, well and good; if he is torn to pieces it makes no difference, for there'll be some one else to take his place the next day. It is my duty to fight against desertion in our own ranks and to shield American citizenship against the foreign elements gathered here who have no fatherland, and to whom the Stars and Stripes have no deeper meaning than a piece of cloth; that is the duty, in the performance of which

I shall live or die."

Mad cheers from below induced the secretary to open the window, and immediately the sounds of the "Star Spangled Banner" came floating up from thousands of throats. Suddenly his wife touched his arm saying: "James, here's a telegram."

The secretary turned around and literally tore the telegram out of the servant's hand. He ran his eye over it hurriedly and then drew a deep breath. And with tears in his eyes at the almost incredible news, he said softly to his wife:

"This will deliver us from the dark slough of despair."

Then he returned to the window, but his emotion made it impossible for him to speak; he made a sign with his hand and gradually the noise of the crowd ceased and all became still.

"Fellow Citizens," began the secretary, "I have just this moment received—" Loud cheers interrupted him, but quiet was soon restored, and then in a clear voice he read the following dispatch:

"Bahia Blanca, December 8:

The torpedo-destroyer *Paul Jones* arrived here this morning with the following message from Admiral Dayton: 'On the 4th of December I found the Japanese cruisers *Adzuma* and *Asama* and three destroyers coaling in the harbor of Port Stanley (Falkland Islands). I demanded of the British authorities that the Japanese ships be forced to leave the harbor at once, as I should otherwise be obliged to attack them in the harbor on the morning of the following day. On the afternoon of the 4th I opened fire on the Japanese ships four miles outside of Port Stanley. After an hour's fighting all five Japanese ships were sunk. On our side the destroyer *Dale* was sunk. Total loss, 180 men. Damaged cruiser *Maryland* sent to Buenos Ayres. Sighted the Japanese cruisers *Idzumo*, *Tokiwa*, *Jakumo* and four destroyers at the entrance to the Straits of Magellan on the morning of December 6th. Pursued them with entire fleet. Battle with the *Idzumo* and *Tokiwa* at noon, in which former was sunk. Battle temporarily suspended on account of appearance of two hostile battleships. Destroyers keeping in touch with the Japanese squadron.'

DAYTON."

Perfect silence greeted these words; no one seemed able to believe the news of this American victory: the first joyful tidings after almost nine months of constant adversity. But then the enthusiasm of the people broke loose in a perfect hurricane that swept everything before it. In the rear the crowd began to thin out rapidly, for everybody was anxious to spread the glad tidings of victory, but their places were soon taken by others pouring in from all sides to hear the telegram read once more.

And now on the opposite side of 17th Street the American flag suddenly ran up the bare flagstaff on the roof of the Winders Building, unfurling with a rustle in the fresh breeze. The secretary pointed up to it, and at once the jubilant crowd joined once more in the air of the "Star Spangled Banner."

"This is a day," said the secretary, taking his wife's hand, "which our country will never forget. But now I must get to work and then I'm off to the President."

As his wife left the room, he rang the bell and asked the servant who appeared in answer to his summons to show in the British Ambassador.

The man disappeared noiselessly, and the next moment the ambassador entered.

"I must ask Your Excellency's pardon for having kept you waiting," said the secretary, advancing a few steps to meet him. "To what do I owe the honor of this visit— —"

"I have come to reply to the protest lodged against us by the United States government for permitting the Japanese to use the harbor of Esquimault as a station for their ships. The British government fully recognizes the justice of the protest, and will see to it that in future only damages that affect a ship's seaworthiness are repaired at Esquimault, and that no other ships are allowed to enter the harbor. The British government is desirous of observing the strictest neutrality and is determined to employ every means in its power to maintain it."

"I thank Your Excellency and thoroughly appreciate the efforts of your government, but regret exceedingly that they are made somewhat late in the day. I am convinced the English government would not consider it within the bounds of strict neutrality for a Japanese squadron to employ an English port as its base of operations— —"

"Certainly not," said the ambassador emphatically, "and I am certain such a thing has never happened."

"Indeed?" answered the secretary seriously, "our latest dispatches tell a different story. May I ask Your Excellency to glance over this telegram?"

He handed the telegram from Bahia Blanca to the ambassador, who read it and handed it back.

The two men regarded each other in silence for a few moments. Then the ambassador lowered his eyes, saying, "I have no instructions with regard to this case. It really comes as a great surprise to me," he added, "a very great surprise," and then seizing the secretary's hand he shook it heartily, saying: "Allow me to extend my private but most sincere congratulations on this success of your arms."

"Thank you, Your Excellency. The United States have learned during the past few months to distinguish between correct and friendly relations with other powers. The English government has taken a warm interest in the military successes of its Japanese ally, as is apparently stipulated in their agreement. We are sorry to have been obliged to upset some of England's calculations by turning Japanese ships out of an English harbor. If we succeed in gaining the upper hand, we may perhaps look forward to similar favors being shown us by the English government as have thus far been extended to victorious Japan?"

"That would depend," said the ambassador rather dubiously, "on the extent to which such friendly relations would interfere with our conceptions of neutrality."

At this moment the President was announced and the ambassador took his leave.

CHAPTER XXII
REMEMBER HILGARD!

Just as in the war between Russia and Japan, the paper strategists found comfort in the thought that the Japanese successes on American soil were only temporary and that their victorious career would soon come to an end. The supposition that Japan had no money to carry on the war was soon seen to lack all real foundation. Thus far the war had cost Japan not even two hundred millions, for it was not Japan, but the Pacific States that had borne the brunt of the expense. Japan had already levied in the States occupied by her troops a sum larger by far than the total amount of the indemnity which they had hoped to collect at Portsmouth several years before.

The overwhelming defeat of the Army of the North at Hilgard had taken the wind out of a great many sails. The terrible catastrophe even succeeded in stirring up the nations of the Old World, who had been watching developments at a safe distance, to a proper realization of the seriousness and proximity of the yellow peril.

Even England began to edge quietly away from Japan, this change in British policy being at once recognized in Tokio when, at Canada's request, England refused to allow Japanese ships to continue to use the docks and coal depots at Esquimault. Later, when after the victories of the American fleet off Port Stanley and near the Straits of Magellan, the governor of the Falkland Islands was made the scape-goat and banished—he had at first intended exposing the cabinet of St. James by publishing the instructions received from them in July, but finally thought better of it—and when the governors of all the British colonies were ordered to observe strict neutrality, Japan interpreted this action correctly. But she was prepared for this emergency, and now came the retribution for having fooled the Japanese nation with hopes of a permanent alliance. Japan pressed a button, and Great Britain was made to realize the danger of playing with the destiny of a nation.

Apparently without the slightest connection with the war in America, an insurrection suddenly broke out in Bengal, at the foot of the Himalayas and on the plateaus of Deccan, which threatened to shake the very foundations of British sovereignty. It was as much as England could do to dispatch enough troops to India in time to stop the flood from bursting all the dams. At the same time an insurrection broke out in French Indo-China, and while England and France were sending transport-ships, escorted by cruisers, to the Far East, great upheavals took place in all parts of Africa. The Europeans had their hands full in dozens of different directions: garrisons and naval stations required reënforcements, and all had to be on guard constantly in order to avoid a surprise.

These were Japan's last resources for preventing the white races from coming to the aid of the United States.

Remember Hilgard! This was the shibboleth with which Congress passed the bill providing for the creation of a standing militia-army and making the military training of every American citizen a national duty. And how willingly they all responded to their country's call—every one realized that the final decision was approaching.

Remember Hilgard! That was the war-cry, and that was the thought which trembled in every heart and proved to the world that when the American nation once comes to its senses, it is utterly irresistible.

What did we care for the theories of diplomats about international law and neutrality; they were swept away like cobwebs. Just as Japan during the Russian war had been provided with arms and equipment from the East, because the crippling of the Russian fleet had left the road to the Japanese harbors open and complaints were consequently not to be feared, so German steamers especially now brought to our Atlantic ports war-materials and weapons that had been manufactured in Germany for the new American armies, since the American factories could not possibly supply the enormous demand within such a short period.

Remember Hilgard! were the words which accompanied every command at drill and in the encampments where our new army was being trained. The regiments waited impatiently for the moment when they would be led against the enemy, but we dared not again make the mistake of leading an unprepared army against such an experienced foe. Week after week, month after month passed, before we could begin our march in the winter snow.

The Pacific Army, which advanced in January to attack the Japanese position on the high plateaus of the Rocky Mountains towards Granger, numbered more than a third of a million. After three days of severe fighting, this important stronghold of the Japanese center was captured and the enemy forced to retreat.

Great rejoicing rang through the whole land. A complete victory at last! Fourteen Japanese guns were captured by the two Missouri regiments after four assaults and with the loss of half their men. The guns were dragged in triumph through the States, and the slightly wounded soldiers on the ammunition-carts declared, after the triumphal entry into St. Louis, that the tumultuous embraces and thousands of handclasps from the enthusiastic crowds had used them up more than the three days' battle.

The capture of Granger had interrupted the communication between the Union Pacific Railroad and the Oregon Short Line branching off to the northwest; but this didn't bother the enemy much, for he simply sent his transports over the line from Pocatello to the South via Ogden, so that when the commander-in-chief of the Pacific Army renewed the attack on the Japanese positions, he found them stronger than he had anticipated.

The attack on Fort Bridger began on the second of February, but the enemy's position on the mountain heights remained unshaken. Several captive balloons and two motor air-ships (one of which was destroyed, shortly after its ascent, by hostile shots) brought the information that the Japanese artillery and entrenchments on the face of the mountain formed an almost impregnable position. Thus while the people were still rejoicing over the latest victory, the Pacific Army was in a position where each step forward was sure to be accompanied by a severe loss of life.

Six fresh divisions from different encampments arrived on the field of battle on the fourth and fifth of February. They received orders to attack the seemingly weak positions of the enemy near Bell's Pass, and then to cross the snow-covered pass and fall upon the left flank of the Japanese center. All manner of obstacles interfered with the advance, which was at last begun. Whole companies had to be harnessed to the guns; but they pressed forward somehow. The small detachments of Japanese cavalry defending the pass were compelled to retreat, and the pass itself was taken by a night assault. Frost now set in, and the guns and baggage wagons were drawn up the mountain paths by means of ropes. The men suffered terribly from the cold, but the knowledge that they were making progress prevented them from grumbling.

On the seventh of February, just as Fisher's division, the first of General Elliott's army to pass Bell's Pass, had reached the valley of the Bear River preparatory to marching southward, via Almy and Evanston, in the rear of the Japanese positions, cavalry scouts, who had been patrolling downstream as far as Georgetown, reported that large bodies of hostile troops were approaching from the North. General Elliott ordered Fisher's division to continue its advance on Almy, and also dispatched Hardy's and Livingstone's divisions to the South, while Wilson's division remained behind to guard the pass, and the divisions of Milton and Stranger were sent to the North to stop the advance of the enemy's reënforcements. Milton's division was to advance along the left bank of the Bear River and to occupy the passes in the Bear River Range, in order to prevent the enemy from making a diversion via Logan. Mounted engineers destroyed the tracks at several spots in front of and behind Logan.

It will be seen, therefore, that General Elliott's six divisions were all stationed in the narrow Bear River Valley between the two hostile armies: Fisher's, Hardy's and Livingstone's divisions were headed South to fall upon the left wing of the enemy's main army, commanded by Marshal Oyama; while Milton's and Stranger's divisions were marching to the North, and came upon the enemy, who was on his way from Pocatello, at Georgetown. General Elliott therefore had to conduct a battle in two directions: In the South he had to assume the offensive against Oyama's wing as quickly and energetically as possible, whereas at Georgetown he would be on the defensive. Bell's Pass lay almost exactly between the two lines, and there General Elliott had posted only the reserves, consisting of the three weak brigades belonging to Wilson's division. If the Japanese succeeded in gaining a decisive victory at Georgetown, General Elliott's whole army would be in a position of the utmost danger.

CHAPTER XXIII

IN THE WHITE HOUSE

On the streets of Washington there was a wild scramble for the extras containing the latest news from the front. The people stood for hours in front of the newspaper offices, but definite news was so long in coming, that despair once more seized their hearts and they again became sceptical of ultimate victory.

Seven long anxious days of waiting! Were we fighting against supernatural forces, which no human heroism could overcome?

A telegraph instrument had been set up next to the President's study in the White House so that all news from the front might reach him without delay. On a table lay a large map of the battle-field where the fighting was now going on, and his private secretary had marked the positions of the American troops with little wooden blocks and colored flags.

Suddenly the instrument began to click, a fresh report from the general staff of the Pacific Army appeared on the tape:

> "Fort Bridger, Feb. 8, 6 p.m. Our captive balloon reports that the enemy seems to be shifting his troops on the left flank. Two Japanese battalions have abandoned their positions, which were at once occupied by a line of skirmishers from the 86th Regiment supported by two machine-guns. An assault of the second battalion of the 64th Regiment on the Japanese infantry position was repulsed, as the enemy quite unexpectedly brought several masked machine-guns into action. The firing continues, and General Elliott reports that the battle with the hostile forces advancing along the Bear River Valley began at 3 p.m. south of Georgetown. As the enemy has appeared in unexpectedly large numbers, two brigades of Wood's division have been sent from Bell's Pass to the North.
>
> MAJOR GENERAL ILLING."

The private secretary changed the position of several blocks on the map, moving the flags at Bell's Pass and pushing two little blue flags in the direction of Georgetown. Then he took the report to the President.

At midnight the report came that the stubborn resistance of the enemy at Georgetown had made it advisable to send Wilson's last brigade from Bell's Pass to the North.

"Our last reserves," said the President, looking at the map; "we're playing a venturesome game." Then he glanced at his secretary and saw that the latter was utterly exhausted. And no wonder, for he hadn't slept a wink in three nights. "Go and take a nap, Johnson," said the President; "I'll stay up, as I have some work to finish. Take a nap, Johnson, I don't need you just now."

"What about the instrument, sir?" asked the secretary.

"I can hear everything in the next room. I'll have no peace anyhow till it is all over. Besides, the Secretary of War is coming over, so I'll get along all right."

The President sat down at his desk and affixed his signature to a number of documents. Half an hour later the Secretary of War was announced.

"Sit down, Harry," said the President, pointing to a chair, "I'll be ready in five minutes." And while the President was finishing his work, the Secretary of War settled down in his chair and took up a book. But the next moment he laid it down again and took up a paper instead; then he took up another one and read a few lines mechanically, stopping every now and then to stare vacantly over the edge of the paper into space. At last he jumped up and began pacing slowly up and down. Then he went into the telegraph-room, and glanced over the report, a copy of which he had received half an hour ago. Then he examined the various positions on the map, placing some of the blocks more accurately.

Then a bell rang and steps could be heard in the hall. The door of the adjacent room opened and shut, and he heard the President fold up the documents and say: "Take these with you, they are all signed. Tomorrow morning—oh, I forgot, it's morning now—the ninth of February."

Then some one went out and closed the door and the President was alone again. The next moment he joined the Secretary of War in the telegraph-room.

"Harry," he said in a low voice, "our destiny will be decided within the next few hours. I sent Johnson off to bed; he needed some sleep. Besides, we want to be alone when the fate of our country is decided."

The Secretary of War walked up and down the room with his hands in his pockets, puffing away at a cigar. Both men avoided looking at each other; neither wished the other to see how nervous he was. Both were listening intently for the sound of the telegraph-bell.

"A message arrived from Fort Bridger about ten o'clock," said the President after a long pause, "to the effect that our captive balloons reported a change in the positions of the enemy's left wing. This may mean——"

"Yes, it may mean—" repeated the Secretary of War mechanically.

Then they both became silent once more, puffing vigorously at their cigars.

"Suppose it's all in vain again, suppose the enemy—" began the Secretary of War, when he was interrupted by the ringing of the bell in the next room.

The message ran:

"Bell's Pass, Feb. 9, 12.15 a.m. Milton's division has succeeded in wresting several important positions from the enemy after a night of severe fighting. Unimportant reverses suffered by Stranger's division more than offset with the aid of reënforcements from Bell's Pass.

Colonel Tarditt."

"If they can only hold Georgetown," said the Secretary of War, "our last reserves have gone there now."

"God grant they may."

Then they both went back to the study. The President remained standing in front of the portrait of Lincoln hanging on the wall.

"He went through just such hours as these," he said quietly, "just such hours, and perhaps in this very room, when the battle between the *Monitor* and the *Merrimac* was being fought at Hampton Roads, and news was being sent to him hour by hour. Oh, Abraham Lincoln, if you were only here to-day to deliver your message over the length and breadth of our land."

The Secretary of War looked hard at the President as he answered: "Yes, we have need of men, but we have men, too, some perhaps who are even greater than Lincoln."

The President shook his head sadly, saying: "I don't know, we've done everything we could, we've done our duty, yet perhaps we might have made even greater efforts. I'm so nervous over the outcome of this battle; it seems to me we are facing the enemy without weapons, or at best with very blunt ones."

Again the bell rang and the President moved towards the door, but stopped halfway and said: "You better go and see what it is, Harry."

"Fort Bridger, Feb. 8, 11.50 p.m. From Fisher's division the report comes via Bell's Pass that two of his regiments have driven the enemy from their positions with the aid of searchlights, and that they are now in hot pursuit.

Major General Illing."

Without saying a word the Secretary of War moved the blocks representing Fisher's division further South. Then he remarked quietly: "It doesn't make much difference what happens at Georgetown, the decision rests right here now and the next hour may decide it all," and he put his finger on the spot in the mountains occupied by the enemy's left wing. "If an attack on the enemy's front should make a gap— —"

He didn't complete the sentence, for the President's hand rested heavily on his shoulder. "Yes, Harry," he said, "if—that's what we've been saying for nine months. If—and our If has always been followed by a But—the enemy's But."

He threw himself into a chair and shaded his tired eyes with his hand, while the Secretary of War walked incessantly up and down, puffing on a fresh cigar.—

The night was almost over.—The shrill little bell rang again, causing the President to start violently. Slowly, inch by inch, the white strip of paper was rolled off, and stooping together over the ticking instrument, the two men watched one letter, one word, one sentence after another appear, until at last it was all there:

> "Fort Bridger, Feb. 9, 1.15 a.m. A returning motor air-ship reports a furious artillery fight in the rear of the enemy's left wing. Have just issued orders for a general attack on the hostile positions on the heights. Cannonade raging all along the line. Reports from Bell's Pass state that enemy is retreating from Georgetown. Twelve of the enemy's guns captured.
>
> "Major General Illing."

"Harry!" cried the President, seizing his friend's hand, "suppose this means victory!"

"It does, it must," was the answer. "Look here," he said, as he rearranged the blocks on the map, "the whole pressure of General Elliott's three divisions is concentrated on the enemy's left wing. All that's necessary is a determined attack— —"

"On the entrenchments in the dark?" broke in the President, "when the men are so apt to lose touch with their leaders, when they're shooting at random, when a mere chance may wrest away the victory and give it to the enemy?"

The Secretary of War shook his head, saying: "The fate of battles rests in the hands of God; we must have faith in our troops."

He walked around the table with long strides, while the President compared the positions of the armies on the map with the contents of the last telegram.

"Harry," he said, looking up, "do you remember the speech I made at Harvard years ago on the unity of nations? That was my first speech, and who would have thought that we should now be sitting together in this room? It's strange how it all comes back to me now. Even then, as a young man, I was deeply interested in the development of the idea of German national unity as expressed in German poetry; and much that I read then has become full of meaning for us, too, especially in these latter days. One of those German songs is ringing in my ears to-night. Oh, if it could only come true, if our brave men over there storming the rocky heights could only make it come true—" At this moment the telegraph-bell again rang sharply:

> "Fort Bridger, Feb. 9, 2.36 a.m. With enormous losses the brigades of Lennox and Malmberg have stormed the positions occupied by the artillery on the enemy's left wing, and have captured numerous guns. The thunder of cannon coming from the valley can be distinctly heard here on the heights. Fisher's division has signaled that they have successfully driven back the enemy. The Japanese are beginning to retreat all along the line. Our troops— —"

The President could read no further, for the words were dancing before his eyes. This stern man, whom nothing could bend or break, now had tears in his eyes as he folded his hands over the telegraph instrument, from which the tape continued to come forth, and said in a deeply moved voice: "Harry, this hour is greater than the Fourth of July. And now, Harry, I remember it, that song of the German poet; may it become our prayer of thanksgiving:"

> "From tower to tower let the bells be rung,
> Throughout our land let our joy be sung!
> Light every beacon far and near,
> To show that God hath helped us here!
> Praise be to God on High!"

Then the President stepped over to the window and pushing aside the curtains, opened it and looked out into the cold winter morning for a long time.

"Harry," he called presently, "doesn't it seem as though the bells were ringing? Thus far no one knows the glad tidings but you and I; but very soon they'll awake to pæans of victory and then our flag will wave proudly once more and we'll have no trouble in winning back the missing stars."

It was a moment of the highest national exaltation, such as a nation experiences only once in a hundred years.

A solitary policeman was patrolling up and down before the White House, and he started violently as he heard a voice above him calling out:

"Run as hard as you can and call out on all the streets: The enemy is defeated, our troops have conquered, the Japanese army is in full retreat! Knock at the doors and windows and shout into every home: we have won, the enemy is retreating."

The policeman hurried off, leaving big black footprints in the white snow, and he could be heard yelling out: "Victory, victory, we've beaten the Japs!" as he ran.

People began to collect in the streets and a coachman jumped down from his box and ran towards the White House, looking up at its lighted windows.

"Leave your carriage here," shouted the President, "and run as hard as you can and tell everybody you meet that we have won and that the Japanese are in full retreat! Our country will be free once more!"

Shouts were heard in the distance, and the noise of loud knocking. And then the President closed the window and came back into the room. But when the Secretary of War wanted to read the balance of the message, he said: "Don't, Harry; I couldn't listen to another word now, but please rouse everybody in the house."

Then bells rang in the halls and people were heard to stir in the rooms. There was a joyous awakening in the quiet capital that ninth day of February, the day that dispelled the darkness and the gloom.

That day marked the beginning of the end. *The yellow peril had been averted!*

Lector House believes that a society develops through a two-fold approach of continuous learning and adaptation, which is derived from the study of classic literary works spread across the historic timeline of literature records. Therefore, we aim at reviving, repairing and redeveloping all those inaccessible or damaged but historically as well as culturally important literature across subjects so that the future generations may have an opportunity to study and learn from past works to embark upon a journey of creating a better future.

This book is a result of an effort made by Lector House towards making a contribution to the preservation and repair of original ancient works which might hold historical significance to the approach of continuous learning across subjects.

HAPPY READING & LEARNING!

LECTOR HOUSE LLP
E-MAIL: lectorpublishing@gmail.com

Lightning Source UK Ltd.
Milton Keynes UK
UKHW010646090820
367908UK00002B/436